MW01225000

THE CRUSADER'S HEART

A Medieval Romance

Claire Delacroix

ISBN-13: 978-1-989367-76-6

Books by Claire Delacroix

Time Travel Romances
ONCE UPON A KISS
THE LAST HIGHLANDER
THE MOONSTONE
LOVE POTION #9

Medieval Romances
ROMANCE OF THE ROSE
HONEYED LIES
UNICORN BRIDE
THE SORCERESS
ROARKE'S FOLLY
PEARL BEYOND PRICE
THE MAGICIAN'S QUEST
UNICORN VENGEANCE
MY LADY'S CHAMPION
ENCHANTED
MY LADY'S DESIRE

The Bride Quest
THE PRINCESS
THE DAMSEL
THE HEIRESS
THE COUNTESS
THE BEAUTY
THE TEMPTRESS

The Rogues of Ravensmuir
THE ROGUE
THE SCOUNDREL
THE WARRIOR

The Jewels of Kinfairlie
THE BEAUTY BRIDE
THE ROSE RED BRIDE
THE SNOW WHITE BRIDE
The Ballad of Rosamunde

The True Love Brides
THE RENEGADE'S HEART
THE HIGHLANDER'S CURSE
THE FROST MAIDEN'S KISS

THE WARRIOR'S PRIZE

The Brides of Inverfyre
THE MERCENARY'S BRIDE
THE RUNAWAY BRIDE

The Champions of St. Euphemia
THE CRUSADER'S BRIDE
THE CRUSADER'S HEART
THE CRUSADER'S KISS
THE CRUSADER'S VOW
THE CRUSADER'S HANDFAST

Rogues & Angels
ONE KNIGHT ENCHANTED
ONE KNIGHT'S RETURN

The Brides of North Barrows
SOMETHING WICKED THIS WAY COMES
A DUKE BY ANY OTHER NAME

Short Stories and Novellas
An Elegy for Melusine
BEGUILED

Dear Reader;

With **The Crusader's Heart**, the quest of our company of knights, started in **The Crusader's Bride**, continues. This is Wulfe and Christina's story, and it begins in Venice, when this pair meets. At first, they seem to be complete opposites—a knight upholding justice and a courtesan who is paid for pleasure—but it quickly becomes apparent that these two have a great deal in common. They are both alone in the world and have learned to make the most of what few opportunities come their way. They're both pretty stubborn, but only a determined woman could change Wulfe's thinking about anything—and only a man who will not be diverted from his course could win Christina's reluctant heart. Neither of them is particularly optimistic, but love, as we'll see, will change that.

We met Wulfe and Christina in Gaston and Ysmaine's book, but we didn't see their thoughts behind their reactions in that story. It's been wonderful for me to explore their characters, convictions, and history more thoroughly.

I always enjoy characters who tell stories, especially if their choices illuminate something of their own truth: Christina certainly does that with her tales of the saints' lives. There is a small discrepancy to acknowledge here, though. The closest written source I could find for Christina's stories is Jacobus de Voragine's **The Golden Legend**, a medieval bestseller but one that was not compiled until the thirteenth century. Jacobus was born around 1230 and died in 1298, which means his volume was not available to Christina in 1187. Jacobus wrote down stories that were well known, however, so I'm assuming that Christina heard the same or similar oral versions of these tales. I've also taken a small liberty with the assignment of saints' days in the calendar—although the story of the Seven Sleepers was well known in the west (recounted in the sixth century by Gregory of Tours and included in the **History of the Lombards** by Paul the Deacon in the eighth century), it is not clear that these saints were assigned a feast day before the **Roman**

Martyrology was compiled in 1582. I think they're worth an exception, though, especially as their assigned feast day falls within the chronology of the story. This is a story that originated in the Muslim world: it is known as 'the companions of the cave' and is recounted in the Qu'ran. The story of the men escaping religious persecution and sleeping for centuries was adopted by Christians, and was very popular during the Crusades. You can see that there are few differences between Leila's and Christina's versions. I like how this exemplifies the exchanges and influences between the two cultures in this era, and also that it makes a nice metaphor for Christina and Wulfe's new beginnings. The relics of the Seven Sleepers were moved to Marseilles during the Crusades and became part of the treasury of the Abbey of Saint Victor.

With **The Crusader's Heart**, the story of the knights' journey becomes more dimensional, as we see scenes and situations from the perspective of other characters. This continues in book #3, **The Crusader's Kiss**, as Bartholomew returns home to avenge his family and regain his rightful legacy. It won't be a simple task, and he'll need the help of a most unexpected ally. Meanwhile, Fergus will continue his journey north to Scotland, a tale to be recounted in book #4, **The Crusader's Vow**. What will happen to the Templar treasure? You'll have to read on to find out!

I've enjoyed the challenge of writing this series and hope you are enjoying it as well. I've created Pinterest boards for these books, primarily for my own inspiration, although you might also enjoy checking them out—there's one for the series overall, then individual boards for each book. You can find the links on my website.

Until next time, I hope you are well and have plenty of good books to read.

All my best
Claire
http://delacroix.net

The Crusader's Heart

WEDNESDAY, JULY 22, 1187

Feast Day of Saint Mary Magdalene and Saint Agnes

CHAPTER ONE

Venice

ulfe could not believe his ill fortune. The list of his woes was long indeed, and he ground his teeth as he marched through the twisted streets of Venice in search of relief.

First, he had been compelled to leave Jerusalem just when that city faced a challenge to its survival as a crusader holding. As a knight and a Templar, he knew his blade should be raised in defense of the Temple, not undertaking some errand that could have been managed by a clerk or lay brother. He had joined the order to fight for justice, and there could be no greater cause than the defense of the Holy City.

Worse, this duty demanded that he ride all the way to Paris to deliver said missive, which meant that by the time Wulfe returned to Outremer, any battle might be completed. He might miss the opportunity to defend what he loved best, which was an abomination by any accounting.

Thirdly, he had only the appearance of leadership of the party that traveled with him. In fact, he had to cede to the dictate of

Gaston, a former brother of the Temple who secretly was in command of this quest. That a knight who had left the order was more trusted by the preceptor in the Jerusalem Temple than Wulfe was salt in the wound.

That Gaston made choices Wulfe would never have made, and Wulfe had to present them as his own notions, was galling. It was Gaston's fault that the mission had so nearly failed at Acre, for Gaston had insisted upon riding for that port instead of departing more quickly from the closer port of Jaffa. Wulfe snarled that he should be blamed for such a close call.

Though it was somewhat mollifying that Gaston had defended the party alone when they had been attacked and might have paid for his error with his own life.

Still, had the choice been Wulfe's, no one would have been compelled to render *any* price at Acre.

It was sufficient to make his blood boil.

The final straw was that Wulfe had been saddled with the most vexing company imaginable for the journey to Paris. A fortnight trapped on a ship with them all had left him nigh murderous.

There was Gaston, so calm and deliberate, so unshakeable in his confidence, that Wulfe was tempted to challenge him to a fight. He wanted to see Gaston riled over some matter or another. There was Gaston's wife, Ysmaine, a beauty who, like all women, should neither be trusted nor riding with knights on an errand. Indeed, she evidently had knowledge of dangerous herbs, had acquired a poisonous root and brought it along. They were entrusted with a prize beyond price and had no need of such temptation to a villain so close at hand.

There was Gaston's squire, Bartholomew, a man of such an age that he should long ago have been knighted himself. Wulfe had no patience for men with little ambition. Although the younger man did not appear to be lazy, Wulfe could not understand why he did not aspire to more. It was unnatural to be content with one's lot.

Another former Templar, Fergus, had completed his military service in Outremer and journeyed with the party on his return to Scotland to wed his betrothed. Wulfe could not comprehend why Fergus would stick to the date of his planned departure when the

Holy City was likely to be besieged. Indeed, he could make no sense in the decision of any of these men to abandon Jerusalem in its moment of need.

That the secret treasure they carried in trust for the Temple in Jerusalem was entrusted to the care of Fergus, another brother who had left the order, and not himself, vexed Wulfe beyond belief. He did not even know what the prize was!

At the dictate of the preceptor, the party had swollen to include pilgrims needing the order's defense. While this disguised the mission, it also slowed their progress. Large companies were ungainly, in Wulfe's opinion.

The merchant, Joscelin de Provins, as soft as a grub and rightly fearful of his survival in any trouble. It was perfectly reasonable that such a plump man, so concerned with the value of his goods, would wish to be away from war. Wulfe neither liked nor respected Joscelin, but it was the sworn task of the order to defend pilgrims and he would do as much.

There was the knight, Everard, who apparently left a holding in the Latin Kingdoms to visit the deathbed of his father in France. Wulfe was incredulous that any man would abandon his hard-won wealth over sentimentality. Who would squander such a gift entrusted to him as the county of Blanche Garde? Wulfe would have defended the holding to his dying breath. It seemed to him that Everard made a poor choice in leaving Outremer and his holding.

Perhaps Everard was a coward.

Perhaps he thought to gain more from his dying father, although Wulfe would never have cast aside one prize before the second was firmly in his grasp. Matters in this world had a way of changing, so that expectation was thwarted.

He had only to look at this quest to see the truth of that.

As a man who had been given few gifts in this life, and who had labored hard for all he had won to his own hand, Wulfe knew he was a harsh judge of others. He found much of mankind wanting, but was protective of those for whom he took responsibility. He would have laid down his own life in defense of either of his squires, for example, and had taken blows intended for his destrier.

In return, the loyalty of those beings—Stephen, Simon, and Teufel—was complete.

Wulfe also was a man who had learned to manage his own passions. By the time the party reached Venice, disembarked, saw to the care of the injured squire, and found accommodation, he knew his temper was incendiary. How could such simple feats consume so much time? Contrary to his expectation that they would take a single night to fortify themselves before riding out, Gaston was resolved to wait the three days decreed by the apothecary as being necessary rest for the injured squire.

For a squire, who was sufficiently clumsy to have inflicted his own injury. For a squire who appeared to be hale enough. Wulfe could not understand why the boy could not ride with another and be watched with care as they continued.

But Gaston had spoken.

Wulfe could bear their company no longer. He had left the rented house, knowing that he had need of a war or a whore. The only way to control his escalating frustration was to expend passion in one feat or the other. Venice was at peace, its laws against violence and its courts known to be harsh.

Its courtesans were also highly reputed.

The choice was an easy one.

Stephen and Simon hastened behind him, undoubtedly understanding his intent. They would ensure that he was neither robbed nor injured on this quest, though more than once a whore had found their presence unsettling. Wulfe did not care what such women thought. They were paid and paid well, and he knew himself to be a considerate lover, as well as a passionate one.

He was as demanding in the pursuit of pleasure as in all others.

He would choose a young and vigorous woman on this night.

Perhaps she would remember him well. The prospect made Wulfe smile.

Another day.

And worse, another night.

Christina turned from her prayers to survey the large room where the women slept together. The draughty chamber took up most of the top floor of the house and was roughly finished. The roof leaked and the wind was always cold, just as the blankets were always too thin. The door was locked each night from the outside and in all of Christina's time at the house, only one woman had been brave enough to try to escape from the window. She had slipped and her cries had awakened the entire house as she fell.

The silence after she had struck the stone road below had been chilling.

It was yet more troubling that Christina sometimes found appeal in that woman's choice, though she knew it had been wrong. Living under Costanzia's thumb had a way of breeding desperation within Christina.

The attic's sole redeeming feature was the view. Christina knelt each morning at the window that faced east, praying toward distant Jerusalem. Though the Holy City had been her destination years before, Venice was as far as she had journeyed before tragedy struck.

Every morning she recalled Gunther's routine jest that she prayed like a heathen and mourned his loss all the more.

Christina surreptitiously kissed the ring that Gunther had put upon her finger one fine day that might have been an eternity before, then secreted it once again from view. On some days, it was impossible to believe that she had ever been young, filled with hope, affluent, and treasured. Had she truly believed that good would triumph, or that ill fortune could be overcome? She had believed in divine intervention, but had seen little of it since passing through the gates of this city.

The ring with its square blue stone slid into the hiding place she had created for it in the hem of her chemise, perfectly disguised from view. She had sewn a tiny pocket into the hem of every garment she owned to ensure that Gunther's ring was never separated from her. Losing the sole token that remained of her previous life would ensure that she lost hope of ever escaping this place.

She rose from her prayers and stretched, looking down into the city. The wind was crisp and there were new ships in the harbor. The rain at least had ceased. There were a few people abroad in the cobbled streets below, and several small craft plied the canals. Vendors making deliveries, to be sure. More than one would halt at Costanzia's abode.

The house was on a corner, the main entrance on a broad canal where guests disembarked each night. Once inside the building, there was a pretty stone courtyard with a fountain and gardens that could be used by the guests in afternoons or evenings. A guest would see only the lavish luxury of the public rooms where music played and appetites were encouraged, perhaps the fine bedrooms above the mezzanine if they opened their purses.

The attic was part of the hidden side of the house. From this vantage point, Christina could see small courtyard behind the kitchens, a meaner, simpler space than the garden courtyard. Here chickens were kept and herbs grew. A door in the rear wall led to the dock on that smaller canal. Deliveries were made there, and vendors sometimes tried to peer into the windows above, seeking a glimpse of Costanzia's beauties.

Costanzia was already arguing with someone, her voice rising shrilly from below. Christina couldn't distinguish the words of her patroness, though she guessed that the older woman was swearing at a vendor in the local Venetian dialect. Though Christina could make a fair job of sounding Venetian, when Costanzia spoke quickly and with vulgarity, Christina often could not follow the words.

The meaning, however, was always clear.

Next, Costanzia would be swearing at the resident women. No matter how much coin had been earned the night before, it would not have been sufficient.

Christina sighed. Costanzia's routine was as relentless as her will. It was yet another day when the girdle of orange stones fastened around her waist seemed so much more weighty than it was in truth.

A large tub had been set in the smaller courtyard and maids were pouring hot water into it. Christina heard footfalls on the stairs and knew there would soon be a pounding upon the door. Then the key would turn in the lock, and the women would all be marched down to the courtyard to bathe, in order of Costanzia's preference.

Christina had not entertained a man the night before, which suited her well but had not pleased her patroness. She would be one of the last to bathe, no doubt. She did not care. She had not liked the look of the one man who had approached her, a gleam in his eye that hinted at violence. She had lied—again—about her courses.

There was a delicate balance to be managed between her ethics and her safety, and not for the first time, Christina wished she had other options. For years, she had had two: stay in this bordello or flee. To run meant starving in the streets or being hunted by Costanzia's enforcers. They were brutal and quick with their knives. Any escaped woman caught by them would be so scarred that she could never work as a whore again.

Then she would starve.

She supposed leaping from the window offered a third choice, but it was no more appealing.

Christina shivered and wrapped her arms around herself as she turned from the window. The current favorite, Flavia, was snoring softly on her pallet when Christina returned to hers. She watched the other woman sleep, admiring her beauty. Flavia's ebony hair cast over the pillow and her lips were parted, as if in invitation even while she slumbered. The woman was luscious and bold, nigh irresistible to the patrons of the house.

Flavia deserved her slumber. She had an audacity about her that Christina tried to emulate. It was a kind of armor to laugh at disapproval, to flaunt one's charms, to even cultivate a lustful reputation.

Christina and Flavia were of an age and often displayed together for contrast. Flavia, dark-haired and dark-eyed, with her red lips and lush curves, drew the attention of many men. Christina, auburn-haired and green-eyed, more slender but of a similar height, attracted others. Flavia was bold and daring, challenging men outright, while Christina was more demure, perhaps appearing to have a dozen secrets. When they stood together, it seemed no man could keep himself from staring. Costanzia profited mightily from the view.

At least she did as much when Christina did not lie.

The two women were different in more than coloring, though. Christina was a reluctant member of this household, and one who would never reconcile herself to her duties. Whoring was better than starving to death in the street, but only by a narrow margin. There had been nights when she would have argued the other choice. Flavia, in contrast, had sought out this life, determined as she was to make her own decisions without marrying. She swore she would never be beholden to man and intended to establish her own house. Her ambition had already intrigued Costanzia, who without a daughter of her own, might well be seeking an heir.

Christina, in contrast, sought an escape.

The lock was turned, a fist hammered upon the door as it was opened, and Costanzia herself strode into the chamber. "Arise, all of you!" she cried and the sleeping women were awakened with a jolt. "Flavia, you are first to the bath, my beauty," Costanzia continued in a coo, tickling that woman under the chin. She rapped a younger girl on the shoulder. "Teresa, if you do not yet have your courses, you will see Raoul for a potion."

Christina prayed that she would not be singled out. Costanzia strode up and down between the pallets, dispatching directions, praising the profitable, scolding the old and the unchosen. Christina's heart beat loudly as the older woman approached.

It sank to her toes when Costanzia paused directly before her. "And you," the patroness said softly. Her tone sounded threatening, and Christina dared to peek at her face, only to find those dark eyes narrowed. "You have forgotten your very good fortune, my dear," Costanzia said, her voice as hard as her gaze. "I do not need mouths to feed who do not bring in coin."

"I cannot help that he chose another..."

"Can you not?" Costanzia mused, and Christina wondered what she had heard. "On this night, you will ensure that you are chosen. I do not care what you have to do to see it done."

Christina knotted her hands together. "Of course."

"In fact, you will be occupied the entire night, or in the morning, you will be on the streets. There are nights for which you have not yet earned your keep."

Christina's lips parted in dismay. The entire night?

"Are we understood?"

Christina nodded and bowed her head in agreement, as much to disguise her anger as to feign compliance. By all that was holy, there had to be a way out of this hell.

She had but one day and night to find it.

The best house of courtesans was located with relative ease, for Wulfe asked in the marketplace by the port. Sailors always knew where to find whores. The boys, too, sought information, and by the time they conferred in the mid-afternoon, one answer was clear.

He should seek the establishment of one Costanzia.

The canals and bridges were confounding, and the directions less clear than might have been ideal. Wulfe became convinced that Venice was a burg designed to aid the trade of thieves, for it seemed a warren of crooked streets with a hundred places for a villain to hide and await his prey. Worse, many of those alleys ended abruptly with a wall or a canal. The houses were shuttered tightly on the street level, and he glimpsed that the lowest floor of the richest ones sheltered docks on the bigger canals. They all had at least two stories overhead, often with high arching windows, and he imagined that people preferred to be away from the water.

It did have a foul smell when the breeze stilled.

They finally located the house in question and were questioned before the heavy door was unbolted. The patroness came halfway down the flight of stairs on the far side of the foyer, her garb appearing as rich as the men in her employ looked dangerous. She was shrewd-eyed but well-mannered, and what he could see of the house was in good repair. Wulfe noted that once she must have been a beauty and wondered whether she had labored upon her back in her youth. She certainly was direct. A short conversation ensured his preferences were made clear and his coin was good, then the patroness gestured graciously that he should follow her up the stairs.

The door was locked audibly behind them.

Wulfe was astounded by the generous proportions and richness of the room that nigh filled the second floor of the house. Sunlight shone through high, arched windows and there was a view of the harbor, the sea sparkling blue. Velvet draperies hung alongside those windows, their dark hue unmistakably costly. A long table was laid with fine cloths and rich fare, and young boys poured generous goblets of wine. The women were both numerous and beautiful. Some stood and chatted with each other, several played lutes, more than one lounged and granted him encouraging smiles. They did not look to be starved or bruised, and he decided that, in this case, rumor had provided the truth. They all wore girdles of stones that were clearly not gems, their hues revealing that they must be wrought of glass. Was this jeweled belt a mark of the house?

In truth, Wulfe did not care.

Indeed, his mood improved by the moment. It must be that the company was amiable, for he had no taste for luxury.

"A maiden?" the patroness suggested, gesturing to a pair of young girls. They flushed and dropped their gazes as if shy, but Wulfe did not doubt that their maidenheads had already been sold repeatedly.

"I have little fondness for innocence," he said, for it was true. He liked to be with a woman who knew her body and her desires, as well as one who could anticipate his own. "Teaching is not a pastime I care to pursue abed," he clarified, and the patroness gave a throaty chuckle.

"Ah! A tigress, then," this Costanzia countered, gesturing to a woman who might have seen thirty summers. "Flavia will make you roar!" There was a slyness in this Flavia's expression that Wulfe did not find alluring. She might take more than he wished to surrender. Her hair was dark and her smile was knowing, and truly she had curves enough to tempt any man.

But not Wulfe.

The patroness noted how his gaze slid past her suggestion and snapped her fingers for other women to come forward. "You are early this day, sir, which gives you the finest choice. Of course, given the time, I must assume that you desire companionship only for the afternoon." She clapped her hands when the women did not move quickly enough for her taste, and Wulfe caught a glimpse of one at the far end of the room.

She was exquisitely beautiful, her hair like red-gold silk. She wore it loose and the length of it gleamed, falling as it did to her hips. The color of her hair was rare in this city, where most of the other women had tresses of dark brown or black. She was taller than most of the other women, as well, slender and elegant in the way that Wulfe preferred. She was dressed in gold and green, the richness of her garb not unlike that of a noblewoman. Wulfe knew that the neckline was more revealing than would have been the choice of any aristocrat, but as she walked toward him at her mistress' summons, he could imagine that a queen approached him.

There was a reluctance in her manner that he admired as well. Not for him the harlot who threw herself at his feet, willing and eager for his touch and his coin. Perhaps this one merely took her time. Perhaps she had the confidence that once a man looked upon her, he would wait. Wulfe did not care. He was entranced by her grace, by his own impression that she did not belong in this place.

Or by the way her smile hinted at mysteries that would not be confessed.

He supposed the rich garb revealed that she earned well for her patroness, but preferred not to consider that. Her full lips tightened slightly, as she followed the other women. He thought he spied both defiance and resignation in her expression, but then she lifted her head and smiled at him.

And there was the key. Hers was not a genuine smile, for its light did not reach her eyes. Her lips curved in sensuous welcome, but her gaze remained wary, another hint of that reluctance.

Wulfe understood immediately that this life was not her choice, and with that realization, his own decision was made. Indeed, he felt a strange affinity with this woman, though he did not know even her name as yet. He knew what it was to put aside one's own desires to serve those of another. He knew what it was to feel trapped, and to have few options. He knew what it was to make the best of one's circumstance, regardless of the price. Indeed, he did that hourly on this quest.

Wulfe also knew what it was to await a better choice, with as much patience as could be mustered.

"This one," he said, gesturing to the beauty who had claimed his attention. He did not care that he was interrupting the patroness as she listed the charms of her women.

"Ah, Christina is a popular choice," she acknowledged, even as the woman's gaze rose to meet Wulfe's own. Her eyes were a bewitching shade of green, thickly lashed and not without intelligence. Was she surprised? She halted before Wulfe, more gracious and lovely than any woman he had ever seen. He liked that he could not discern her thoughts, that she kept some part of herself in reserve.

He understood that habit, as well.

Costanzia looked between them. "You may find her price high," she warned, more than a little gleeful.

Wulfe cared only for the lady he had chosen. Christina held his gaze, as if knowing her own worth and perhaps not expecting him to pay it. Aye, there were shadows in those wondrous eyes, shadows that told of disappointment.

Perhaps from men.

Perhaps from a man.

Wulfe felt an unexpected valor rise within him and heighten his need.

"Name it," he said, unable to imagine what Christina had seen of the world. He doubted it had all been good and wished to surprise her.

The patroness did as much, clearly expecting Wulfe to haggle. He did not, though, for he never tainted the acquisition of any desire with such mean bargaining. His purse was not so light as that. He exercised restraint and saved his coin, so when he indulged, he could acquire the woman he desired most. It was better to savor pleasure seldom and have one's true desire, than to indulge frequently and compromise.

"That, of course, is only for the afternoon," the patroness added slyly.

"And for the night as well?"

A flicker of interest shone in her eyes as Christina considered him anew.

"Triple," the older woman said crisply. "For there are ships in the harbor."

Christina lowered her lashes, evidently anticipating his refusal.

"Triple," Wulfe agreed so readily that he was certain the patroness regretted not asking for more. He cared only for the way Christina's gaze flew to his face again. She was surprised, and he was glad. He was more glad that she seemed to be pleased. He smiled outright at her, paid the patroness, then offered his hand to the lady he so desired.

He kissed her hand and saw her eyes narrow slightly. "I assume you have a private chamber where our pleasure might be pursued?"

"Of course, sir," she said, and he liked that her voice was both rich and husky. She spoke in the same Venetian dialect as her patroness, but not so fluidly as one born in this city of cities.

"Wulfe," he corrected, and she nodded acquiescence.

"Wulfe," she said, smiling ever so slightly as she gripped his fingers, turned and led him toward the display of food and drink. The patroness stood back, smiling with satisfaction as she counted the coins again, but Wulfe was interested only in the alluring Christina.

Where was she from? What had brought her to this house? Wulfe was surprised by how much he wished to know.

Indeed, his frustrations faded already, and the pursuit of pleasure had not yet begun.

Christina did not believe for a moment that the Templar was truly different from any of the other men who visited Costanzia's house, but it was harmless to hope otherwise. She had not yet bedded a Templar, after all, and there was something intriguing about his determination to have her for both day and night.

The order was pledged to defend pilgrims, which was almost sufficient to make her smile. Would this knight defend her, if he learned that she was a pilgrim who had lost her way?

Though she teased herself, the prospect was worthy of

consideration.

Might he help her?

How could she convince him to do so?

This Wulfe had no shortage of coin—at least, he had not before his arrival in this place—and there was a resolve about him that she admired. He was easy to look upon, a man who clearly earned his way with hard labor. He was broad and tall, fair of hair and resolute in every way. His face was tanned, which only made his hair look more golden and his eyes more pale. There was a scar on his cheek, the mark of an old and deep wound, but otherwise, he appeared to be hale. His manner was crisp and he did not linger over his choices. Christina admired decisive men.

Indeed, if her father had been more decisive, she might not have found herself in her current circumstance.

But there was naught to be gained by regret, or by bitterness. What she needed was change.

Was Wulfe the solution she sought? If naught else, it appeared she would not be cast out to starve with morning's light. She found herself greedy for more. Christina preferred not to talk overmuch with her patrons, choosing instead to render the debt and be rid of them. It might be wise to adapt her strategy on this night.

"Have you journeyed far this day?" she asked, slipping her hand into his elbow as if they strolled at some fine celebration.

Wulfe slanted a glance her way. Their silvery hue was not quite blue and not quite grey. She imagined that they might change based upon his mood, shifting from the hue of ice to that of the sky. "Of what import is that? I am not tired, if that is your concern."

Christina smiled with a serenity she did not quite feel. "I merely make conversation."

Some of her vexation must have shown, or else he was particularly perceptive, for Wulfe almost smiled. His eyes did twinkle, and the sight tempted Christina to smile in truth. "I knew there was aught different about you," he said, humor in his tone.

"Indeed?"

"Indeed." He surveyed the room, and she sensed that he took an inventory of its occupants and contents. "I have journeyed only from the harbor on this day, for our ship arrived on the morning tide." He met her gaze and his eyes were more blue than they had been. "We sailed from Acre, before you ask, upon the last ship to depart before the Saracens attacked."

"It is true then," Christina said. She realized that her grip had tightened upon his arm only when Wulfe put his other hand over hers. His skin was warm, but it was the protectiveness of his gesture that made her heart leap. "We had heard that the Latin Kingdoms were besieged."

"And many of my order lost, as well as those sworn to the Hospitaliers," he said, a frown drawing his brows together. He must have lost comrades.

"What of the Holy City?"

Wulfe took a breath, delaying his response, and she feared for his words. "Strong when we left, but expecting an assault."

"Surely it can be defended?"

"With so many knights slaughtered and the King of Jerusalem himself captured?" His expression turned grim. "I fear there will be bad tidings before there are better ones."

"Yet you left Outremer," she said before she caught herself. "Why?"

"Because I was so ordered, and the rule forbids that a Templar should disobey an order." He turned a steely gaze upon her and his expression made her shiver. It was easy to believe that he had slaughtered infidels when he looked like this. "It would be better for me to die."

How could he cite the rule of the order when he stood in a brothel? Surely the rule forbade his custom here.

Perhaps this Templar was no better than a mercenary. Christina had been obliged to service some of those men and did not relish the prospect of entertaining another.

Perhaps she could see him drunken in the passing of a day and a night, then slip out of the house with his fat purse. Two boys followed behind them, and she guessed they were his squires. They were small enough of stature that she thought she could best them both, if necessary.

Still, she did not like that there were three of them. Her heart fluttered and she exchanged a glance with one of the men who stood by the door. Clients were told that these men defended the house and its coin, but Christina knew that a sharp cry would bring at least one of them running to the defense of one of the women.

She supposed that was also a defense of the possessions of the house.

Christina nodded, aware that Wulfe waited for her reply. "Do you intend to return to the Latin Kingdoms?"

"As soon as may be. I am charged with a task, and once it is completed, I will return immediately to Outremer. Every knight's blade will be needed to defend all that is holy. I can only pray I do not arrive too late to do my part."

"Might I ask after your task?"

"Nay." He fell silent then, such tension in his body that Christina knew she had done little to put him at ease. She was well aware of Costanzia's watchful gaze and smiled up at the knight as if naught were amiss.

"Would you not partake of a meal?" she asked, guiding Wulfe to the table as she had been instructed. It seemed a safer subject than his recent history. She would think about the prospect of Jerusalem being lost later. "Some wine? Or ale? Meat and bread?"

He exhaled mightily and turned to face her. "I have only the appetite for one feast in this moment," he said. "I apologize if my commitment to my order offended you."

Christina forced herself to smile. "Not at all. Fighting men are always so resolute."

"Fighting men?" Wulfe arched a brow and she sensed that he teased her. "Is that what you call knights in this city? It was no small task to earn my spurs."

"And many mercenaries have labored hard to buy theirs," Christina retorted before she caught herself. "I am not certain the distinction of rank in the trade of war is of as much import as many knights would insist."

Wulfe laughed at that, surprising her. "Fair enough," he acknowledged. "I suppose men are much the same when naked. A prick and some coin."

Christina itched to slap him, so confident was his smile, but she guessed he tried to provoke her. It was only reasonable to provoke him in return.

"You might be surprised," she countered mildly. "The very fact that you are a warrior monk makes you appear to be different from others thus far."

His eyes glinted but she saw the color rise on the back of his neck. "Indeed?"

"Surely your rule precludes the frequenting of brothels?"

"Surely it does," he acknowledged. "But I cannot be that uncommon. This is Venice, the city of such repute that all of Christendom speaks of its sins. I am certain there are bishops and priests aplenty who visit this abode."

"You would be right in that," Christina admitted. "But I had believed that knights sworn to your order held to higher ideals."

"Disappointed?" There was a challenge in his expression that made her heart skip a beat, but Christina disguised her reaction.

"We shall see." She looked him up and down. "Wulfe."

He grinned outright at that. "I should have visited a brothel in this city sooner," he said, his gaze locked with hers. "The company is most enticing." He lifted her hand and kissed her fingers, managing to look both wicked and alluring.

"No more enticing than others."

Wulfe shook his head. "Infinitely more enticing," he corrected. "For never have I had a whore converse with me as you do, much less match wits with me."

Christina winced at the name she had earned. "Courtesan," she corrected.

"If you so prefer." He turned her hand over and planted a warm kiss in her palm, his gaze never leaving hers. "I cannot wait for the delights of this night to reveal themselves."

His desire for her was so evident that Christina's mouth went dry. It was different, though, for he responded to her words, not her face or her breasts. Her heart was racing with an anticipation she rarely felt, and one she feared would be disappointed.

She wanted this moment of flirtation to endure.

"At least savor one cup of wine," she urged, drawing him to her side again and trailing her fingers over his arm. "My patroness is most proud of the vintages she acquires." Christina reminded herself that it was impossible to know what to expect from a man before the chamber door was closed. Wulfe's charm might be fleeting indeed. It was easier if the patron had at least one cup of wine, for it evened the odds should she have to fight for her survival.

Wulfe accepted a cup and let her fill it, but barely let the wine touch his lips when he sipped. Curse him for being temperate!

"The room?" he asked, evidently determined to have his one desire fulfilled sooner rather than later.

All night. How many times would it be?

She hoped she was not expected to welcome the boys as well.

Christina beckoned to a servant, but one of the knight's squires stepped forward to take the chalice and pitcher instead. "The boys can remain here in the hall..." she began to suggest.

He shook his head with such resolve that she fell silent. "They will accompany me. You need not fear their intervention. They merely protect me and my purse." Wulfe smiled but she knew from his eyes that he would not be swayed. "They will practice their chess."

Christina glanced toward the boys, not particularly reassured.

Costanzia gave her a hard look from the far side of the chamber, and Christina bit back any argument she might have made. In this moment, the streets seemed meaner than the knight before her.

The bed chamber it would be.

CHAPTER TWO

ave you been long sworn to the order, then?" Christina asked, turning her steps toward the stairs. She drew Wulfe fast against her side, ensuring that her breast was pressed against his arm, hoping that her perfume teased his nostrils.

The boys followed.

She saw the knight's fleeting frown. "Of what import is that?"

"I thought perhaps your appetite was whetted by a hunger unsatisfied." She fell silent for a moment, then continued, wanting to know his measure. "I thought perhaps you were devoted to the rule of the order until this day."

Wulfe laughed then, and it was not forced. Indeed, his eyes twinkled. "When I heard of the beauty of Christina and cast aside my vows in search of the truth."

"Do not mock me."

"It is not my intent to do so," he said, sobering. "But you speak aright in naming my shortcoming. It is my personal challenge to uphold the pledge of chastity."

Christina did not like the sound of that, but she smiled. "Then you often pay for satisfaction?"

"Not often," he acknowledged. "But there are times when a man has need of a woman's caress."

"And you find yourself in such a time." It was easier if men talked about themselves, if she learned more of their needs and desires before reaching the bed. "Are such times predictable?"

"Only in their link with frustration in other arenas." Wulfe grimaced when she glanced his way. "I endeavor to be temperate. You need not fear you will be granted a pox by me. I am not so lusty as to have earned that doom." Christina was relieved by his attempt to reassure her and only hoped he told the truth. "But there are moments when I know myself to be vexed."

"Vexed?" Christina echoed, amused by his choice of words despite herself.

"Vexed," Wulfe agreed. "If I cannot change my situation, I must endeavor to find release in other ways, lest my fighting abilities be compromised by my mood." He flicked her an intent glance. "An irked man will strike too soon and err in his choices. It is my sworn pledge to defend those weaker than myself, and I will not permit vexation to compromise that vow."

Christina could understand that well enough. "You choose for the greater good."

He nodded. "It is a weakness and I know it well. Until I conquer it, though, my ability to do my duty must be protected, at whatever price."

With another man, Christina might have thought he constructed an excuse for his dalliance, but Wulfe was so serious that she believed him. "What situation could cause such a state?" They reached the next floor, and she guided him toward the far end of the corridor where the best chamber was located. There could be no greater contrast between this wide corridor, with its parquet floor and elaborately painted ceiling, and the attic above. The difference was greater again in the chambers.

"An assignment that proves annoying to fulfill." Wulfe heaved a sigh. "Indeed, I fear this one may not be completed with anything like timeliness, and that vexes me beyond all."

"Why? Surely the Temple ensures your comfort regardless of your task?"

Consideration and perhaps humor lit his eyes. "As this place ensures yours?"

Christina found herself flushing. "There is food and a roof."

"Aye, there is food and a roof. Do you not ever aspire to more?"

It was curious to see any commonality in their situations, particularly since he had noted it first. He, after all, was a Templar knight. She preferred to call herself a courtesan, but the truth was that she was a whore. Either way, the sexual expectations of their respective roles could not have been more different. "Do you?"

"Of course." Wulfe shook his head. "But aspirations do not ensure food and a roof, so choices must be made. Perhaps compromises must be made."

Christina was surprised to find his reasoning so close to her own. "In service to the greater good?" she asked lightly as they reached the end of the corridor. The sound of the music below was faint, and she could hear the cries of the sea birds.

Wulfe looked around with undisguised curiosity, and she knew he noticed the door at the end of the corridor with its doughty lock. "In service of one's own survival. One's life, after all, is what one makes of it."

What had brought him to the Templars? She halted at the end of the corridor, outside the room she would choose, her bravery faltering in this moment. How much more of him could she learn before meeting him abed?

Wulfe caught her looking at him, and their gazes locked. "How came you to this place?"

"Does it matter?"

"Only that I would wager that you made a similar choice to mine." Wulfe leaned closer and she caught the scent of his skin. It was beguiling, more beguiling than anticipated. There was much to be said for a man who was clean. "To ensure your own survival, despite a high price."

"You would win that wager," she admitted, then wished she had not. He watched her more closely, curious, but Christina dared not confide any more. She changed the subject. "I had thought your coin was held in common by the order. Is the acquisition of coin another weakness of yours?" She earned a sidelong glance for that.

"You know so much of Templars, then?"

"Nay, but all monastic orders forbid the holding of personal wealth."

"But leave the matter to the discretion of the master of the priory. In Outremer, it is not uncommon for coin gained by a knight and surrendered to the master to be returned, at least in part, to the knight himself."

"Is discipline so lax then?"

His expression became guarded. "The life is hard and fraught with peril. It is a wise master who understands how to ensure his men are sustained."

"How is coin won?"

"Ransoms, primarily," he acknowledged readily. "At least that is the source of mine. The capture of an important individual from the opposite side oft ensures that a ransom is paid."

Christina could believe that Wulfe might be successful in such an endeavor and found herself relieved that he had not earned his coin at dice or other gambling. "But secular knights in Outremer oft win their fortunes there."

"True enough."

"We hear of younger sons returned with titles and fortunes. Surely you could have ridden east without joining the Templars."

He shook his head. "I should have starved far west of here." He gestured to his garb and his squires. "All that comes to my hand has been earned by my own labor, but there will never be sufficient for a holding."

"You might sell your blade."

"Never," Wulfe replied with a finality that indicated he had considered the matter. "A man who sells his blade is a mercenary or no better than one, condemned to follow the dictate of whichever man will pay, be his cause right or nay."

"You could swear to the service of a lord you knew to be moral."

He eyed her, his eyes still twinkling but his expression more sober. "With no noble lineage? It will not happen, Christina. The

Templars will be my life, that much is certain."

She did not know what to say to that. She respected that he had considered his choices thoroughly and found herself wishing he had had better ones.

Wulfe surprised her again with a sudden glance. "And you? Will this be your life?"

It was a horrifying notion. Christina dropped her gaze to hide her revulsion. "We have more interesting matters to accomplish this day than making such conversation," she murmured, ensuring her voice was low and seductive.

His responding smile was quick. Was he relieved that she brought discussion back to the matter at hand? "You speak the truth in that." His gaze swept over her, his appreciation clear. "Lead on, fair Christina. I find myself challenged to prove to you that not all men are the same."

Christina hid her reaction to that pledge. She took Wulfe's hand and opened the door to the very best room. The first to take a client, and one who paid for the entire night, gave her the right of choice. Christina would make the option count.

It was strange how a few words of conversation with a man she actually found alluring could change her view. This Templar *was* different from the men she usually had to satisfy, and it was more than his handsome visage. Wulfe truly looked at her. He asked about her own life. He spoke to her as if she were his equal, even if only for a day and a night. Tricking him was out of the question, for she felt that this knight was an honorable man.

Would Wulfe help her to escape this place if she asked him to do so? Nay, he could not have sufficient coin to see her freed—and why should he? Wulfe might have saved his coin for a bit of pleasure, but it would not be enough. Costanzia would empty his purse and demand yet more. Plus he was a knight sworn to the service of a monastic order, not a man who could wed—or even keep a mistress. He said himself that he would always be a Templar.

Nay, she would have to find another way to escape this place.

The silence between herself and Wulfe seemed fraught to

Christina as they entered the richest of the rooms reserved for clients. He halted in the midst of the chamber and turned in place, surveying his surroundings. His expression was impossible to read and she hoped he was not displeased.

The boys, in contrast, were clearly awed. The mouth of one hung open and the other's eyes were round. Christina might have laughed if she had not been impressed herself.

This corner room boasted a pillared bed draped in red silk, the dark wood lavishly gilded. The pillows were stacked high and the mattress thick, of finest down. It was a bed fit for an emperor. This was the largest room, with the finest view over the Adriatic through the arched windows alongside the bed. Also, the bed was curtained and the door could be locked. In the corner was a fireplace, and at the far end, a pair of low divans faced an even lower table. She had never been granted this chamber, had only glimpsed it, but this night it would be hers.

In that moment, Christina resolved that this would be her last night in Costanzia's house. She would win Wulfe's assistance.

Somehow.

"Does it displease you?" she asked him when he remained silent.

He shrugged. "It is more lavish than my usual accommodations." He surveyed the chamber again, and she realized he was no less impressed than his squires. "I wonder how a man's view of the world would be changed if he slept thus every night."

"I doubt he would fight Saracens."

Wulfe snorted. "Likely not. If he could afford such a chamber, he would pay others to fight for him."

"Did you fight Saracens?"

"Of course." He turned away with a frown and she knew she had sent his thoughts in a direction that was unwelcome. It was her task to kindle his desire anew, to put her curiosity aside for the moment.

Christina strolled to the bed, knowing Wulfe's gaze followed her. She let her hips sway in the way she had been taught was seductive. Indeed, she would recall every lesson granted in this house and put it to use on this night. She trailed a hand along the velvet that covered the mattress, then loosed the lacings on the sides of her kirtle.

She took an age over the task, drawing out the moment to encourage Wulfe's interest. She rolled her shoulders to encourage her garment to drop to the floor and heard his breath catch at the sight of her long white chemise. Doubtless he could discern the shadows of her curves through the fine cloth. She bent to pick up the kirtle, laid it across a bench, then turned to face him. She perched on the edge of the mattress and began to loosen her hair, before looking at him again.

Wulfe's gaze was locked upon her. Indeed, she was not certain he breathed.

Christina smiled in satisfaction. "I suppose the Knights Templar do not sleep in luxury."

He stood before the window, arms folded across his chest. His features were shadowed thus, but she heard humor in his tone. "One straw mattress, one bolster, and one blanket is supplied, according to the rule, and every brother must wear his chemise, belt, chausses, and shoes to bed." He gestured to the lantern on the table before the window then spared her a glance. "And no brother shall ever sleep in darkness, lest he be tempted by wickedness."

"Wickedness?" Christina's lips twitched. "Given where you stand, it might be too late for that."

Wulfe chuckled, then bade the boys light the fire on the hearth. Christina watched him, aware that the uncertainty she usually felt in this moment was much diminished. He spoke to the boys in a firm tone, giving instruction but not speaking harshly to them. Christina was reminded of Gunther with his brother's young sons and had to blink back unbidden tears of recollection.

How absurd to trust a man, knowing so little about him. She went to the window and looked out over the city, noting that the shadows were already lengthening.

"If you object, I can extinguish it." Wulfe had moved to stand behind her and the weight of his hands fell on her shoulders. Christina jumped a little, since she had not heard him move, and he swept her hair aside with a leisurely fingertip.

"I have no objection to the light," she said, her voice husky.

Desire. She actually felt desire. Christina was amazed. It had been years since this deed had aroused her.

"You only say as much because it is too late," Wulfe countered quietly. He touched his lips to her nape, sending a thrill through her, and continued in a whisper. "As you noted, I have already succumbed to temptation."

Christina caught her breath at the vigor of her own reaction, and took refuge in teasing him anew. "This exchange will be complicated, though, should you insist upon remaining garbed until morning." She glanced over her shoulder at him.

Wulfe nodded, apparently serious, but his eyes were sparkling so brightly that she was tempted to smile. "I believe an exception will have to be made," he said, clearly endeavoring to sound rueful. His gaze dropped to the front of her chemise and she saw his eyes gleam. His desire for her fed her confidence and made her want to tease him.

"And so you break the rule again," Christina chided and clicked her tongue in mock disapproval. "Brother Wulfe, are you always so wayward?"

Again, his grin flashed. "Nay, but on this day I am enchanted and know not what I do." Wulfe spun her in his embrace, then brushed his lips across hers, his touch sending fire through her. His quick kiss was both gentle and confident, a good sign for the night ahead. He considered her for a moment that was long enough for her mouth to go dry, then strode to the door.

"Enchanted?" Christina echoed, guessing what he would do and feeling that cursed trepidation rise anew.

"Surely." He turned the key in the lock, just as she had expected.

Christina stood as if struck to stone, unable to forget past nights and experiences, though she knew she should hide her reaction. To her amazement, Wulfe sauntered back across the floor. He halted before her, then offered the key to her with a gallant bow.

"You have no cause to fear me, and I will not give you one," he said, to Christina's astonishment.

He had noticed.

His protectiveness was not an illusion.

Wulfe closed Christina's fingers over the weight of the key, his warm hand locked briefly around her own, and her mouth went dry.

She had not expected gallantry.

Perhaps she was enchanted as well.

Perhaps he *could* be convinced to help her escape.

Wulfe must have interpreted her silence as concern. He went to the boys, checking the fire they had kindled and instructing them to lay out their chess board on the low table between the divans. One unfastened Wulfe's belt and took custody of his sword, showing much care for that weapon. The other helped Wulfe to shed his tabard, his aketon, and then his mail shirt and coif.

"Tend the fire well," Wulfe instructed. "Even while you play chess."

"Aye, sir," the boys agreed in unison. Christina took note of their manner, obedient but not cringing, and knew they were fairly treated by this knight.

Wulfe returned to her then, in his boots, chausses, and chemise. His hair was tousled and he looked less formidable without his armor. He pulled the curtains on the bed on the side of the door, then across the foot. His choice would ensure that the boys could not see them coupling, and that they two would have a view only of the sea. He came to her side, unfastening the tie at the neck of his chemise.

His gaze was assessing. "And so they call you Christina?"

"And so they call you Wulfe." Christina's mouth was dry with a certainty that he had discerned one of her secrets.

He arched a fair brow. "Sometimes even Wulfe Stürmer."

"Fighting wolf," she translated easily, believing he likely was a fearsome foe.

"Just so." He leaned closer and lowered his voice, amusement lifting the corner of his lips. "But neither is really my name." He surveyed her, as if he sought the answer to some riddle in her eyes. "Do we have something else in common, Christina?" He placed a slight emphasis on her name.

Christina fought the urge to admit the truth. Instead she held his gaze and lied. "I am Christina."

She was Christina, now, and in this place.

She might be Juliana again, one day, but she could only reclaim that name when her life was her own again—if ever it was.

"I do not believe you were always Christina," Wulfe said, his hands dropping to her girdle. "Just as I do not believe that Venetian is your mother tongue."

Christina dropped her gaze to his hands, fighting the urge to step away. "Why ever not?" she asked, trying to keep her tone light. He had fine, strong hands, and though he could have overwhelmed her readily, he unfastened the jeweled girdle slowly.

He considered it for such a long moment she wondered whether he knew its import. "You understood my nickname, which is not Venetian."

"Many women in my trade understand more than one language."

"And many in your trade in this city were not born here." He glanced up suddenly, surprising her with his intent look. "Where did your journey begin, Christina?"

This would not do. She owed Wulfe no tales of her past and no confessions. Her body might have been sold, but her thoughts and her history were her own.

The door was locked. She had to deliver the service for which he had paid.

And that eliminated any possibility of confiding in him.

"Of what import is that?" Christina smiled, seeing how he watched her mouth. She parted her lips, letting him see her tongue, then leaned closer to whisper. "I am here now, as are you." She had been taught a thousand arts to seduce a man, and she deliberately recalled her training. She ran a hand across his chest, hoping that a caress would distract him from his queries. "Even names are not of import in this moment."

"Then what is?"

"Only pleasure." Christina touched her lips to this throat. He had shaved, which she liked well. He smelled clean, and as a man should. Not perfumed or touched with the scent of another woman. She heard him catch his breath as she let her lips linger against his skin and felt him swallow. When she might have drawn back, he bent and pressed a kiss to the spot below her ear. His lips were warm and Christina was startled that he should be so gentle.

Tender, even.

Wulfe pulled back slightly and considered her, his eyes glinting. "Not always Christina and not always a whore," he said with a conviction she might have found irksome had she not been so enthralled with him.

She could not confess her secrets so readily, though.

"No woman is always a whore."

"Most women do not hold their secrets so closely as you," he countered. "Fear not, for I admire your discretion." Wulfe smiled and kissed her earlobe, his hands locking around her waist. When he murmured in her ear, Christina shivered, both at his touch and his pledge. "But I find myself challenged. Let us see if I can convince you to confide the truth in me," he said, his words no more than a breath. "I have all the day and all the night to persuade you. I assure you that I shall make the surrender worth your while."

He kissed her fully then, before she could reply, and Christina found herself melting against him. His embrace was persuasive indeed, both tender and potent, so seductive that Christina might have forgotten she was the one charged to provide pleasure.

But she could never forget that.

Christina pulled back to regard him, then guided him closer to the bed. "It is not my place to confide in you," she warned with a playful smile. She tugged the lace of his chemise free, so that the neckline of the garment opened. His skin was tanned and he was as muscled as she had anticipated. She felt a rare thrill of anticipation. "It is *your* secrets that must be revealed, to guarantee your pleasure this night."

She reached and caressed him, then began to unlace his chausses. He caught his breath as he watched her. His eyes were more blue now, his smile more readily won. Whatever vexation had plagued him was already diminished, and she felt glad of that.

A satisfied man was a safer companion, to be sure.

Christina could not afford to surrender to pleasure herself. She had a service to deliver and had to ensure his pleasure at any price. She touched him, knowing full well how to conjure his reaction, but he closed one hand over hers and she glanced up.

"I know what you do in this," he charged quietly.

"I would not expect you to be innocent," she replied, softening her words with a kiss.

Wulfe smiled beneath her embrace. "You mean to distract me from this challenge. But be warned, Christina, I am not easily dissuaded as that. I will be your champion this night and unravel all of your secrets before dawn."

Before she could argue, Wulfe cupped her nape in one hand, pulled her to her toes, and kissed her with new demand. It was a kiss that she could not deny, one intended to make her lose her reservations and her restraint, and it came very close to succeeding.

And it was only the beginning of Wulfe's amorous assault.

Wulfe had chosen aright. Of that, he could have no doubt.

Christina was a rare prize, a woman both confident of her allure and protective of her privacy. She was not quick to confess any detail of her life, which only fed his curiosity about her. He liked the glimpse he had had of her quick wits, too.

She was different from the women he usually found in brothels. She was neither so hardened nor so vulnerable. He guessed that she had not come willingly to this trade. She had chosen it, doing what she had to do to survive, and given the tilt of her chin, he would have wagered that her previous life had been such that she might have expected better.

His sense that she had conquered adversity fed his dawning admiration. He found himself interested in learning more of her than in embarking upon the deed for which they were together.

Once she had led him to the bed, though, Christina's manner changed. She moved with greater purpose yet at the same time, was more elusive. Wulfe could tell by her eyes that she followed a routine, that he might have been any man at all. It was galling to be the next prick who offered coin.

He yearned for the lady he had escorted up the stairs. Wulfe wanted to seduce the woman he had glimpsed, not be coaxed to his pleasure as if he were any man at all.

To be sure, there was no evading her intent. Christina had been well instructed in the arts of the chamber, and he was already aroused. She touched him with a surety of his response that took Wulfe's breath away—and conjured his desire as surely as a flint touched to a tinder. Her timing was exquisite, her mastery of the amorous skills complete. She undressed him and washed him, caressing him all the while. When he might have protested, she kissed him to silence. He was weak enough to surrender. She pleasured him and beguiled him, her seduction so perfect that Wulfe could not have denied her any thing he had to offer.

The first time was quicker than he might have preferred, but truly, given his vexation with the quest, it could not have been otherwise.

The second time was more leisurely, as he was determined to see to her pleasure as well. He wanted Christina to be aware of him, not hidden in her own thoughts. He felt triumph when her eyes widened and her gaze flew to his, when her lips parted and her skin flushed in release. She mouthed his name, which made his heart thunder with pride. Though he knew that many in her trade feigned such a response, the surprise in her expression—and the fact that she truly looked at him again—told him of his own success.

That was sufficient to take him over the brink for the second time.

In the aftermath, he was exhausted. He was not a man who trusted luxury or reveled in it, but on this day, he could not resist its allure. Wulfe liked to think it was because he lay with Christina.

The true woman he had glimpsed, not the practiced courtesan.

Although it was not his habit, Wulfe slumbered against the perfumed softness of her skin, the musk of her pleasure giving him tremendous satisfaction. Did he truly trust her? It seemed he did. Wulfe felt her fingers in his hair, and her breasts pressed against his chest, and felt an unfamiliar satisfaction fill him.

"Do not leave," he whispered and heard only her assent before he dozed.

He liked to think that he would have noticed if Christina had left him there, but in truth, Wulfe slept hard and longer than he might have preferred.

The journey from Outremer had been arduous and he had been vigilant each night since the baggage had been investigated by some soul in Samaria. His dreams were restless, his uncertainties about the quest taking the guise of phantoms and peril. Even as he battled mysterious foes, Wulfe was aware that Christina remained beside him, her fingertips stroking his brow.

She granted him sanctuary and a welcome haven he was already reluctant to abandon.

Wulfe was startled when he awakened to find that the room was growing darker. There were great bands of color streaking the sky outside the windows and the air had turned cool. He could hear loud music and laughter, undoubtedly from the common room below, and smell roasted meat. His squires bickered quietly over their game at the far end of the chamber—Wulfe discerned that Simon was winning, a rare occurrence that Stephen did not always accept with grace. The fire crackled on the hearth, casting a warm glow over the room.

Christina was nestled against his side, her gaze fixed on the sky over the sea. Unless he erred completely in his understanding of women, the woman he had glimpsed on the stairs was yet in his company.

Wulfe rolled to his side, the better to draw her against him, and braced himself on his elbow to look down at her. He pulled up the velvet to cover her breasts, earning a surprised glance from her.

"Recalling other times?" he asked, then bent to kiss her shoulder. She was soft and sweetly scented, her skin silken against him. The feel of his arousal seemed to encourage the return of the paid seductress, for she dropped her gaze to hide her thoughts.

She smiled and made to rise. "Would you like some wine?"

Wulfe tightened his arm briefly around her waist, not so much to restrain her as to show his preference. How could he encourage her to trust him? "Nay. Not before we make a wager."

Christina eyed him warily. "Our wager is made." Her voice was sultry and he heard the seductress in her tone. She leaned back and reached to twine her arms around his neck, but Wulfe caught her hands in his.

He was intrigued by the real woman. He was not sated and would not be so until she shared the moment with him.

Wulfe realized then that Christina had donned a mask to deliver the service he had paid for, hiding her true self as she did what had to be done. Wulfe knew that he did much the same when he rode to war, for killing was not his instinct.

In war, it was his sworn duty, though, and he fought better than most. He disguised his thoughts when he did as much, though, just as Christina hid her own.

"I think we have much in common," he said and her gaze flew to his.

"Because you are sworn to chastity and I am in the trade of promiscuity?" she said, arching a brow.

Wulfe smiled at her quick response. He liked how clever she was. "We both do what must be done and make our peace with it. You provide pleasure and I mete out death. Neither of us comes to the task with enthusiasm."

"Perhaps so." She turned away then, once more hiding her thoughts.

"Tell me how you came to be in this place," he invited.

Christina abruptly left the bed at that. She donned her chemise, and he recognized that she put a barrier between them with the thin cloth. Instead of returning to the bed, she went to the window, standing there to stare out at the dusk. She might have been alone, but Wulfe was not fooled. He could see that she breathed quickly yet.

He waited a moment, then rose from the bed in his turn. He donned his own chemise before joining her. She spared him a glance when he placed a hand on her shoulder, but her expression was not discouraging. Wulfe made to pull her into his embrace. "You will become cold," he murmured when she resisted him, and to his relief, she leaned back against him.

She *was* cold, and he drew her closer. His arms were around her waist, and she folded her own on top of his. He stood behind her, her curves pressed against him, and felt a curious contentment. They fit together well, to his thinking, her height such that he could tuck her beneath his chin. He felt that he sheltered her and liked the sensation well.

"We are both stubborn," she said softly, and Wulfe could not help but chuckle at that observation.

"Perhaps not such an admirable trait to have in common."

"But a useful one, to be sure."

"Indeed." He watched a shooting star trace its path across the sky, even as the last light danced on the waves of the sea. What an unlikely place for him to find tranquility.

Wulfe guessed that his mood could be attributed more to the company than the location. The boys bickered good naturedly over Simon's win, then commenced another game. They fell silent in their concentration.

"Do you know that today is the feast day of Mary Magdalene?" Christina asked.

"I did not realize as much," Wulfe admitted, wondering at the point of this confession.

"Do you know her tale?"

Wulfe shrugged. "A prostitute who followed Jesus."

"More than that," Christina murmured, then sighed. "So much more than that."

"Tell me," he urged, wanting to know why she had mentioned the story.

"Mary was the daughter of a noble family and born to wealth. She is called Magdalene because she held the town of Magdalum in her own right."

"Truly?" Wulfe said, because he was surprised by this detail.

Christina twisted in his arms to grant him a small smile. "Are you surprised by the notion of a woman holding title to property?"

"Not in our times, for I have seen women rule holdings in the absence of their husbands and fathers, but in those days, aye, I am."

"It must have been more common, for no one in the tale seems surprised by her responsibilities. Indeed, her father divided his holdings between his three children, two daughters and a son."

"That would be unusual in our times."

She eyed him. "Do you find it offensive?"

"That the one who rules a holding is fair and just is of greater import than whether the responsibility is held by man or woman."

This reply, which was honest, seemed to please his companion. Christina nodded, then continued with her tale. "Mary was a great beauty as well as wealthy. She chose to surrender the management of her holding to her sister, Martha, so that she could indulge herself in savoring the pleasures of the flesh. Her brother, Lazarus, made the same allocation, though he chose as much so that he could concentrate upon his military career."

Wulfe could understand that choice well enough. He was intrigued that her tale featured both a warrior and a whore.

"And so it was that Mary heard of Jesus and his teachings, and she wanted to see him. She went to the house of Simon the leper, where Jesus was a guest. She knew her reputation well and had often been shunned by others for her sinful choices. She dared not mingle with the company, lest she be rejected. She also knew herself to be lost, and hoped that hearing Jesus teach would give her guidance. She was with the servants when it came time to wash the guests' feet and so it was that she took it upon herself to wash the feet of Jesus. She dried his feet with her hair and anointed them. Mary was recognized by the others, of course, including the host, Simon, who was certain that Jesus would not allow such a woman to touch him. He did, though, and then he took her hands and raised her to her feet, forgiving all her sins and rebuking those who would condemn her. For this precious gift, she granted him her love and her service for all the days and nights of her life."

"She followed him," Wulfe recalled.

"She followed him and she served him, with more love than all his other disciples combined. She did penance for her sins as he instructed in order to fill her heart with God's love once more, and she sat at his feet to listen best to his sermons. He defended her from those who said she was unclean, lazy, and wasteful. He wept when she wept, more touched by her sorrow than that any other person. He raised her brother, Lazarus, from the grave when he had been four days dead and, she remained by his side while he hung on the cross. It was Mary who prepared the spices to anoint the body of Jesus, and she who did not abandon the vigil even when the other disciples left the tomb where he had been laid."

Christina lifted her chin and met Wulfe's gaze. "He did not judge her. He did not find her unworthy because of her past choices, and in this, he won her devotion and her love."

Wulfe understood her implication well. But he knew the limits of what he could offer, and a place by his side, however devoted Christina might be, was not a possibility.

"I am no savior," he whispered into her hair. "Though you make me wish I could be."

She spun then to face him, and her smile sent heat through his veins. "Perhaps your desire is not sufficiently strong," she whispered, then pulled his head down. He felt her stretch to her toes, then her fingers slid into his hair. Her eyes shone with full awareness of her effect upon him, and he might have cursed her skills if he had not felt so very good.

"You do not fight fairly," he charged and liked how she chuckled.

"Do you, when all is at stake?"

Wulfe might have asked for more detail, but Christina kissed him, deepening her kiss with a slow deliberation that dismissed any thought of protest. She was so soft and enticing, and more, so artful that he could not resist her siren's call. He groaned and caught her closer, slanting his mouth over hers and glad to be beguiled anew.

CHAPTER THREE

She made progress in winning Wulfe to her side, Christina was certain of it.

And he made progress in convincing her of his merit. Her champion indeed. If she could only persuade him to help her to not only leave Costanzia's house but Venice itself, she might be able to return home. Hope flickered in Christina's heart for the first time in years. She had been certain that it would be impossible to leave the city.

With a champion, it could happen.

She had to take care to not ask too much of him too soon.

When Wulfe awakened next, night had fallen. Christina heard the change in his breathing and felt the weight of his gaze before he spoke.

"Are you lonely in this place?" he asked, so surprising her that she looked at him.

"Lonely? There is no solitude to be had in this house."

"And none in a garrison, either. But the loneliness I speak of comes from being able to confide in another."

"I have no need of such a luxury," Christina protested, but her voice caught.

"I do, though I never thought I would."

Christina was intrigued. Who had Wulfe confided in before? And what would he confide?

He watched her with a smile that hinted he had anticipated her reaction. "I would suggest that we share confidences."

"Nay." Christina shook her head, fearful of what he would ask of her. She would surrender truths to him at her own discretion and her own pace, the better to ensure she kept this tentative alliance.

Wulfe smoothed the coverlet, and she followed the gesture, noting how golden his skin looked against the cloth. His tone was idle but she was not fooled: he was intent upon this goal. Already she considered what truth she might offer to ensure she did not lose his good will. Such was the power of this man. "But as you have noted, I have paid."

"Some things cannot be bought."

Wulfe softened his voice. "Consider this, Christina. Once morning comes, we will never see each other again."

There was a prospect she did not like.

"I will continue upon my journey and you will remain here," Wulfe continued easily, mistaking the reason for her reticence. "What harm could there be in sharing a tale of our past with each other? Indeed, I see only a gain."

Which truth of her past would sway him to her side? He was not lacking in compassion. Did she dare to confess all of it? "How so?"

He shrugged. "Solitude can wear upon the heart and mind."

She was watching him, unable to hide her interest.

"Tell me how you came to be in this place," he invited, then smiled. "Think of it as a respite for a tired warrior before we resume the night's entertainment."

Christina smiled then. "I am not so convinced that you have need of such respite," she teased and slid her toe up his calf. "I had no notion that a Templar would be so vigorous abed." She reached for him, aware that he was aroused again, but Wulfe closed his hand over hers, halting her move.

"Not the courtesan," he said softly. "Not this time."

"What do you mean?" she asked, although she knew.

"I would be with *you.* I would know more of you." His gaze was intent. "I would know what compelled you to join this household."

"And the boys?"

"Cannot hear us." He dropped his voice to a whisper. "Especially if we speak like this." He beckoned to her with one finger but Christina did not move toward him. They would negotiate this without his seductive touch muddling her thoughts.

"Do you always interview your whores?"

"Nay. I never have before."

"Why me?"

"Because you are different, and I would know why."

She smiled at that and eyed him. "And what will you tell me?"

He blinked, his reaction so close to her own that Christina almost smiled. "I beg your pardon?"

"This must be an exchange. A tale for a tale. Two equal tales, one for the other."

Wulfe was clearly discomfited by this. He rolled to his back and appeared to be fascinated by the canopy. Christina knew he evaded her gaze and was heartened that their need for privacy was so similar. "I do not know how to tell a tale."

"Everyone knows how to tell the tale he has lived," she insisted. "Tell me how you became a Templar. All your reassurances to me apply equally to you."

He considered her, eyes narrowed. "Then you will tell me your tale?"

"If yours is honest enough."

"And will you judge as much?"

"I will." Christina rose to her feet. She took the few steps to the low table, knowing that she granted Wulfe a view of her nudity and that it might convince him as her words had not. She poured a goblet of wine with leisure then brought it back to him, aware that he watched her keenly. She sat on the side of the bed and offered him the goblet. "You first," she said, hoping he did as much.

Their gazes locked and held for a potent moment.

Then Wulfe sat up, letting the velvet fall to his waist, bracing his back against the headboard before accepting the chalice of wine.

He sipped deeply of it, nodding approval at the quality, then beckoned to her. She returned to the bed but sat opposite him, at the foot, wanting to watch his expression. He lifted the velvet coverlet and she slid beneath it, her legs stretched out alongside his. She was well aware of the points their flesh touched and of the heat emanating from his body. He dropped his hand so that it rested on the cloth, its weight upon her ankles. It was a strangely convivial moment and she had the sense the great bed offered a haven from the world beyond.

A place where they could speak the truth, without a price.

Wulfe glanced toward the window before he spoke. "I was raised by a gamekeeper in the woods. He was old by the time I have memories of my youth, ancient even, and he compelled me to work hard. He taught me that a man must earn what he would call his own."

"Your mother was his wife?"

Wulfe shook his head. "Nay. He said she abandoned me in the forest when I was an infant. He took me in, though he had no desire for a babe in his hut, because he said he could not leave me to die of exposure." He lifted his brows. "It was winter."

Christina was appalled by his mother's choice, although Wulfe had either made his peace with it or he disguised his thoughts well. "How could she do such a deed?"

"He told me that women were untrustworthy."

"In this, her sex is of less import than her nature!"

Wulfe said nothing but sipped of the wine, savoring it.

Christina wondered whether he meant to continue, so prompted him. "Was he your father?"

"Nay, not that. He bade me call him the old man, no more and no less."

It seemed a heartless way for a boy to grow up.

Wulfe considered the view of the harbor, his voice dropping low as he continued. "The old man died when I was ten summers of age or so. As I said, he was very old, and he granted himself little kindness. He took a cough that winter and suffered long into the spring with the illness. By the time he took to his bed, he told me that he would die. He spoke more to me in those few weeks than he had in years. He told me how to bury him once he died, told me where to dig the grave, made me describe it once it was done so he knew it was done right." Wulfe met her gaze. "In fact, he sent me back to dig it deeper. He told me that I had to leave the hut, which was the only place I had ever known, after his death. He made me promise to do all of this, and then, just as he had predicted, he died."

He swirled the wine in his cup, staring down at it. "It was precisely as he had forecast. I do not think I believed him until it happened, until there was no beat of his heart." His smile was wry. "I do not know how long I sat there, waiting for him to take another breath."

Christina had the urge to console him. She reached down the length of the bed and touched Wulfe's hand. He did not look at her, but he locked their fingers together.

Then he shrugged. "I did all as he had instructed, then left the hut behind with reluctance. I might not have left at all if I had not feared he might yet round a corner to chastise me. It was spring and the forest was turning green with new growth. I remember how beautiful it was, and how uncertain I felt. I had no destination or goal, and for the first time, there was no one to give me one."

"You could have sought your mother."

"She who had abandoned me of her own choice? I think not. And how would I have known her, even if I had been so foolish as that? Nay, I knew I had to find myself some other abode, somewhere. Another old man, perhaps. I did not know where to turn, but in the end, the choice was made for me."

His brow darkened. "I heard the horses before I saw them. There was a lord of the manor, of course, who called these woods his own, and he rode regularly to hunt. I had always stayed out of the way of his party, as the old man had bidden me, but on this day, the dogs were fast behind me. I ran, thinking to outdistance them, but they bayed and lent chase." Wulfe looked at her, his expression outraged. "They hunted *me*. I could scarce believe it, not until I was cornered in a clearing, hounds snapping at my heels. I was hauling myself into a tree when the lord himself called for me to halt." He shook his head at his own folly. "I thought he meant to save me from his dogs."

"He did not?"

Wulfe cupped the chalice in his hands. "You must realize that no man of his ilk had ever spoken to me. His horse was fine and enormous, his armor gleamed, and his cloak fluttered behind him. His hair was as white as fresh snow and his eyes as cold as ice. I had the thought that he might be a snow king or one of the Fae, stepped from the tales the old man had told me on winter nights." He pursed his lips. "When he fixed his attention upon me with that fierce gaze, I feared him more than his pack of hounds."

Christina had the sense that Wulfe's trepidation might have been justified.

"There had to be twenty men with him, nigh a dozen on horseback, riding finer steeds than I had ever seen, and dressed in finery. There were men in rougher dress, too, beaters and those who managed the dogs, although I did not know their roles then. I had never seen so many men at once. I certainly had never had so many people intent upon me, or been cornered by hunting dogs who snarled and snapped. I am surprised I managed to speak at all."

"He asked you questions then?"

"He wanted to know about the gamekeeper and his whereabouts. It seemed he had sought out the old man, only to find the hut empty. I told him that the old man had died and where he was buried. There was no guile in me, and I had no ability to lie. Indeed, I was so astonished that I could not have summoned any untruth."

"Surely he believed you?"

"I am not certain." Wulfe pursed his lips and shook his head. "He dismounted and strode toward me, as fearsome a man as I had ever seen. He caught me by the chin and lifted me fairly off my feet, then stared at me. It was clear enough that the sight of me offended him, though there was little I might do about it. 'You should be dead,' he growled, then flung me to the ground. Before I could move, he had drawn his dagger and cut my cheek. Quick and deep, so that the blood flowed warmly down my face."

Wulfe's hand rose to the scar on his face, and Christina knew he touched it unwittingly. His lips set. "Then he whistled for the dogs. He ran his gloved finger across my cheek, then let the lead hound taste it."

Christina gasped.

"I ran."

"Indeed!"

"The hounds hunted me with a fervor they had not shown before. It was the blood, the scent of it and the taste of it. It made them frantic. I ran as I had never run before. I dropped the pack of the gamekeeper's prizes, I tore my garments, I lost my cloak. I ran through undergrowth, thorns tearing at me, the pack of barking dogs fast on my heels. I crossed a stream, the water filling my boots and slowing my pace dangerously. The lead one caught me then, sinking his teeth into my thigh as I struggled to climb up the bank. I can see him yet, a reddish hound with a short coat, green eyes, and fierce white teeth. The others bayed on the far shore, then lunged into the water. I knew I had but a moment to ensure my own survival."

"What about the men?"

"They rode after the dogs, laughing and encouraging them. I saw the baron halt on the opposite bank. I saw him smile and knew it would be worse if I was captured. I kicked his hound hard in the face, kicked it again so it fell into the stream with a howl. I saw the baron's disapproval, but then I ran anew."

"But why would he do such a foul deed?"

"Because he could, I suppose. As I ran, I recalled that the old man had taught me the boundary of the lord's lands. "

"So you might leave?"

"So we might aid another to leave. We had found a doe who had given birth uncommonly late in the summer. The gamekeeper encouraged her to leave the baron's lands, with her fawn, before that man rode to his fall hunt."

Christina bit her lip, recognizing that the old man had understood his overlord's lack of concern for any but himself.

"Once my wits returned to me, I realized where I was and I ran for that border. The party pursued me well beyond it, but there was a town and they did not dare to chase me as far as its walls."

"And you found sanctuary there?"

Wulfe scoffed. "I did not dare to seek any, given my sole experience of the kindness of strangers. I ran for the better part of a month, determined to put as much distance between myself and that forest as possible. And in the end, I reached another forest, different from the one I had known all my life but familiar in its tranquility. I found another gamekeeper there, one who grew older, and I offered to help him. He was suspicious, just as the man who had raised me had been, but I knew his kind and I knew the work that had to be done, and I showed him with my deeds that I was unafraid of hard labor."

"He must have been glad of your help."

"He might have been. But when the lord who governed that forest rode to hunt that fall, he came to the gamekeeper to share a cup of ale. It seemed this was his custom. It also seemed that this baron was a kindly one. I might have fled at the sight of his approaching party, but the gamekeeper bade me stay. This baron had a son and a daughter, so the gamekeeper told me, and I saw that the son was of an age with me when their party halted before the gamekeeper's hut. The baron immediately took an interest in me, and the gamekeeper, to my surprise, suggested that I might be the solution he sought."

"To what problem?"

Wulfe smiled. "The son was earning his spurs and had need of an opponent to train for battle. His cousins were older and knighted already, and his father sought another boy of similar age. I suspect he sought a boy who his own son might defeat, at least on occasion. By the time the hunting party rode on, gamekeeper and baron had agreed that the boy in question should be me—and such was the goodness of both men that it had also been agreed that my reward in performing this service would be the chance to earn my own spurs."

"That is no small expense."

"They were good men, honorable and true." Wulfe's brows drew together. "It was not easy, but it was a good life, and I was accustomed to hard work. Five years later, I was dubbed a knight, given a sword and a steed, then shown to the gate of their abode. I had earned my due, my fighting companion would continue to train as his father's heir, and there was no place in that household for me any longer. I had no coin and refused to sell what I had earned. I could have become a mercenary, but I chose to join the Templars. I wanted to serve justice, not whosoever paid the price."

Christina frowned at this hasty and unexpected conclusion. "But that cannot be all of the tale," she protested. "Why would they cast you out? How could there not have been a place in their household for you? All barons hire men-at-arms to defend their walls. There must be more to the tale than this!"

Wulfe was resolute. "That is the tale of how I became a Templar. I became a knight but had no holding, prospects, patron, or fortune. I am not nobly born and could never have expected a good marriage. I have been sworn to the order ever since." He leaned forward, his eyes glinting, offering the cup to Christina. "And now, fair lady, my part of the wager is fulfilled. It is time for your tale." He arched a brow when she straightened. "Surely you do not mean to break your word?"

Christina saw the challenge in his eyes and knew he anticipated that she would do that very deed. She wanted to surprise him, this man who thought he understood her so well. She smiled and took the chalice, drinking deeply of the wine. "Of course not," she said, noting his satisfaction even as she began.

She was sorely tempted to do as he had done and to surrender only part of her truth. But this, Christina knew, was her opportunity to win Wulfe's sympathy and his support.

She dared not sacrifice this chance, even if it meant confessing more than she would have preferred. She had to leave this place on the morrow, which meant she had to leave with Wulfe.

"I was wedded at twelve summers," Christina confessed quietly. "And to a man many years my senior." She handed the chalice of wine back to Wulfe.

"How many years?"

Christina shrugged. "Forty? He was a friend of my father and a kindly man. Though I feared the union at first, our match was a happy one. I did not know it at the time, but his inclinations abed were modest and his desires easily met, even for one so innocent as myself. He was good to me." She frowned. "He had a modest abode, for he was a younger son, but it was not too far from my parents' holding. We visited often and I was not so lonely as my mother had feared I might be."

When she fell silent, Wulfe squeezed her hand. "But?" he prompted.

Christina straightened. "But there was a shadow upon our match. He had wed me because he desired a son. His first wife had been barren, but he had not been one to put a match aside to suit his own convenience. It was only upon her death, and her urging before that for him to do as much, that he chose to wed again." She met Wulfe's gaze. "He said she chose me for him."

"Indeed?"

"Indeed. He said she noted that I was young enough to bear him many children, clever enough to converse with him, and pretty enough to tempt him."

"And he took such counsel?" Wulfe was clearly surprised, perhaps that a man would not choose his own bed partner.

Christina smiled. "He was not a decisive man. He was patient and tolerant, and though I appreciated these qualities upon our nuptials, I have since wondered if all might have ended differently if he had been resolute or determined." She swallowed. "The shadow upon our match was a predictable one."

"You did not conceive a son."

"Nary a one. Soon my husband became convinced there was a deeper cause."

"Which was?"

"Sin. Either his or mine, it did not matter. The one choice he made in our time together was that we should go upon a pilgrimage, to atone for our sins, and that, given the magnitude of the issue, that we should journey to Jerusalem. He believed that this alone would see me bear a healthy son."

"But you are neither in Jerusalem nor wed."

"And I am far more of a sinner than I was nine years ago," Christina said with a thin smile, then sobered. She could not look at Wulfe, but watched her restless fingers instead. "He had gone to secure our passage to Outremer. I was tired and perhaps he hoped that I had conceived again, for he insisted that I remain behind. When the hour grew late and he did not return, several of those who had traveled with us helped me to seek him out." She bit her lip. "He was dead when I found him. I shall never forget the sight of him, curled up in his cloak, the blood pooling beneath him. He deserved far better a fate." She blinked back her tears. "Perhaps he fought his assailants. Perhaps he did not give up his coin readily enough. Perhaps they were simply vindictive. Either way, he was killed for seven silver pennies." She could not keep the bitterness from her voice.

"And you had naught," Wulfe said gently.

"No coin, no husband, no hope." She omitted some details, not wanting to sound as if she blamed others for her fate and her choices. "The party continued on to Jerusalem without me and I remained in the basilica to pray. It was days before I realized my hunger. The priest recalled me to my senses and sent me to a convent." She lifted her gaze to Wulfe's. "They would not shelter me without a donation. I begged in this heartless city, and when I gained a coin, I bought a morsel of food. I walked endlessly, fearful of being molested if I fell asleep. I prayed. I believed I saw my husband, my father, my mother, in the busy streets, and shouted after them, to no avail."

She frowned, disliking this part of her tale. "I do not know how long I lived on the streets of Venice. I do know that one morn, I watched from the shadows as a merchant unloaded a boat laden with fruits and vegetables at the gate of a house surrounded by high walls. I watched another bring meat, cured hams and sausages, and great rinds of cheese to that same abode. Another brought live peacocks and chickens, another fresh fish, yet another great casks of wine. It was clear that all within the walls of this house ate well. I could not tear myself away. I salivated when I smelled the fresh bread being delivered and it was then that I revealed myself, unable to resist the temptation."

"It was the gate of this house," Wulfe guessed.

Christina nodded. "The back portal, where foodstuffs are delivered. Costanzia took one look at me, and despite my filthy ragged state, she smiled. She took a fresh piece of bread, smearing it with butter so creamy it nearly made me weep. Then she offered it to me. 'How much would you give for this?' she asked me then. I smelled the bread and there was only one answer I could give."

"Everything," Wulfe guessed.

"Everything," Christina agreed, and she averted her face as a single tear fell. How she wished her price could have been higher than a crust of fresh bread. "You need not fear, Wulfe, that you will leave a child behind. My womb bears no fruit."

Wulfe set the wine aside and reached for her, framing her face in his hands. To her relief, Christina saw compassion in his eyes. "You did what was necessary to survive," he murmured, brushing his lips once across her own. "Just as I have done. Did I not tell you that we had much in common, Christina?"

He kissed her again, not leaving her a chance to reply. Christina moved into his embrace as if there was no other place she would rather be.

And truly there was not. When he deepened his kiss, she played no courtesan's game, but opened herself to him, giving more than she had before, inviting him to partake of her all.

She could only hope it would be sufficient to persuade him to truly take her cause.

THURSDAY, JULY 23, 1187

Feast Day of Saint Apollinaris
and of the martyrs
Saint Nabor and Saint Felix

CHAPTER FOUR

Wulfe dreamed of cold streams, barking dogs, and men with hatred in their eyes.

He awakened abruptly and was momentarily disoriented. He smelled Christina's perfume and felt the luxurious velvet beneath his fingers, but his dream rekindled his distrust of luxury and women. Had he confessed too much to her? Had he been seduced too readily?

Why had he told her the story of his youth? He had only ever shared the tale once before, with markedly poor results.

Had he failed to learn from his mistakes? There was the mark of a fool, and Wulfe had never desired to be in that company.

Beyond the shadowed haven of the pillared bed, he could see the night sky and the glitter of stars. The music and laughter from the chamber below had fallen silent and the city slept in darkness.

Christina, Wulfe suspected, did not sleep. She was still but not at ease. She feigned slumber, which was all the reminder he needed that she might be as unworthy of trust as other women he had known. Did she mean to fool him? Why did she remain awake?

Wulfe forced himself to exhale slowly and steadily. He might have believed the nightmare to have been only that, but it was more. Christina's pretense prompted him to realize it had been a warning.

A reminder.

For Wulfe knew better than most that women should never be trusted. He had believed as much before he had pledged his blade to the Templars, and certainly had learned little to challenge his conviction since. He had been enchanted by this woman, so beguiled that he had nigh forgotten what he knew to be true.

The dream recalled him to his own convictions.

He would not feel compassion for her.

He would not believe her to be different from her fellow whores or even from other women. She tried to manipulate him to some purpose of her own. Was the tale she had told him even true? He told himself to be skeptical.

What could she desire of him? That he remove her from this house? That he take her as his mistress? That he provide her with a house of her own, to continue her trade and keep the coin for herself? Wulfe knew no such transition would be easily won. Aiding Christina would bring the vengeance of the house upon him. He would be hunted, as he had been once before, and he might well pay a very high price for his deed.

One heard of those who cheated the brothels in Venice being pursued or killed. At the very least, they were robbed.

Wulfe would not put himself in such peril. He had a responsibility to the order, after all, to fulfill his quest and deliver the treasure to Paris.

It did not matter how well the lovely Christina cast her spell. Nay, he had paid for what he had desired and he had possessed her four times. He could not afford more.

All between them was done.

Wulfe wished to leave immediately, but only fools and thieves frequented the streets of Venice at night. He had to linger for a few more hours, but he would feign sleep as well as she.

As soon as the sky lightened, Wulfe would be gone, never to return.

Christina only slept when she was locked into the attic with the other women. She might have remained awake even then, disliking the powerlessness of her situation, but exhaustion always took its toll. It was comparatively safe in the attic.

There was no similar guarantee of safety in the company of a client. To sleep beside a man was to be vulnerable, and Christina had no aspiration to be so again. The time that her patrons slept was the time she had to herself, to think, to hope, to dream. She knew the pattern of many ceilings in this house and the canopies over many a bed. She knew where the wood was chipped on the pillars or a thread caught in the hanging tapestry, where the plaster was in need of repair, where the spiders preferred to spin their webs. She knew the sound of the house at night, after the patrons were sleeping, the creak of the boards, the lap of the water of the canal, the sigh of the house settling a little deeper onto its foundations.

She had lain beside men who snored, men who moaned, men who confessed their secrets, and men who thrashed in the grip of their nightmares. She had been rolled upon, embraced, seized, and even pummeled. She had been taken again, both in ardor and in desperation. She had consoled men who could not take her again and fled those turned violent by their own failures.

Yet on this night, she lay beside a man who was no more asleep than she. She and Wulfe were both upon their backs, mere inches between them. This was novel.

Christina knew Wulfe had dozed after their last bout of lovemaking. They had eaten of the morsels provided by the house before he slept deeply. She believed he had had some dream that troubled him, for he had started and caught his breath. But when she had expected him to reach for her, he had pretended to fall asleep again.

It could have been that he was unaware that she was awake, but Christina doubted that. Most patrons had no issue with awakening the whore they had paid. It could have been that Wulfe was sated, but she doubted that just as much. She could only conclude that Wulfe distrusted her.

And that was most curious, after the intimacy of their last mating.

Why had his mood changed?

Or did she see peril where there was none? For truly, if Wulfe had turned against her, he would not aid her to escape, and that possibility made Christina's hands clench. Was this simply fear on her part? She thought not. Though she did not know for certain, she had the sense that he was steeling himself against her.

And that could only mean that he would *not* assist her.

Should she appeal to him? Or would that only worsen the situation?

Christina heard to the soft snores of the boys at the far end of the room and had no doubt of their state. Wulfe had bidden them to take turns so that at least one was awake, but it was clear they had been unable to follow his command. Would he beat them? Chastise them? Given the way he had pleasured her, she guessed he would be stern but not strike them. She listened to his breathing, so deliberate and measured. Had she not been right beside him, she might have believed him to be sleeping, but there was a tension in his body that she could not ignore with such proximity.

Did he know that she was awake? Christina guessed as much, for she had already noted how observant he was.

Her champion. The pledge had been made in jest, but still Christina hoped there might be truth buried within it. She nibbled at her lip, aware that time was slipping away and that opportunity might be lost.

Still, it was not within her to beg.

Even for something as important as her freedom.

Perhaps she should find it within herself to beg.

There was a creak from outside the door of the room then, a whisper of a sole on the wood. Christina did not catch her breath, but she listened more intently. She heard the minute sound of a key turning in the lock, a scrape of metal upon metal so quiet that she would not have discerned it had she not expected it.

Who came to the chamber? It was not done in this house. The client's pleasure was never interrupted.

Was Wulfe awake because he had anticipated that he would be assaulted?

But how would any attacker pass the guards at the portals?

With coin, of course. That was no mystery, at least.

There was a tiny click as the lock released, then a sigh as the door was eased open. Christina felt rather than heard it, sensing the change in the air. She could smell the roasted meat that had been served that evening more vehemently, for it wafted through the open portal. She bit her lip, doubting that any assailant came for her. She slid her hand across the linens and touched a fingertip to the back of Wulfe's hand.

He returned the gesture immediately, accepting her warning and granting one of his own. He had known she was awake, then, just as she had suspected. He stirred and rolled over to face her with a mumble, as if deeply asleep.

His eyes, however, shone briefly in the darkness. Christina felt the knife between them on the bed, and knew he had either drawn it or seized it when he moved. She was reminded of a falcon at hunt and knew he would not be surprised, no matter what the intruder did.

Nor would he be merciful.

Strangely enough, she was confident of her own safety in his presence. Christina believed that a man's true nature was revealed abed, for it was difficult to feign any matter when naked. Wulfe had been considerate of her, and she trusted him.

He gave her a hard look, then the pressure of his hand against hers increased slightly. Christina understood that he gave an instruction. His knife was in his right hand and he lay on his left side. He wanted her clear of his strike, she wagered. She emitted a sleepy purr and rolled to her belly, flattening herself against the bed. She heard satisfaction in the way he exhaled.

She felt the coldness of the blade against her skin, hidden between them, and narrowed her eyes to mere slits. Her heart thumped.

Another floor board creaked, but she knew she no longer needed to warn her companion.

It seemed an eternity passed before Christina saw the silhouette of the intruder against the window. There were three windows in this room and they were large on this, the third floor of the house, for there was little threat of thieves at such height. All arched high in graceful curves, framing views of the night sky. From this angle, Christina could not even see the rooftops of the city, just the stars above. From the deep hue of the sky and the silence of the city, she knew it was very late, after midnight. She watched the intruder's silhouette through her lashes, ensuring she breathed deeply and evenly.

He or she wore a cloak with a hood, disguising both features and shape. She thought the intruder might be taller than herself, but it was hard to be sure from this angle. The intent was clearly theft, for the intruder sifted quickly through Wulfe's belongings. The squires had taken the knight's weapons and tabard, but the remainder of his garb was on a low broad table between the bed and window.

As was his purse.

What riches could a Templar carry? Christina knew Wulfe's purse was not light—though lighter than it had been—but the thief did not appear to touch it. There was no jingle of coin as Wulfe's garments were searched.

How strange. It was as if the villain sought something specific, other than coin, something the Templar carried himself.

Wulfe had confessed to being upon a quest. Did he carry some token or treasure? Had he been entrusted with a valuable, or a secret message?

She hoped the boys were not injured by this intruder, in some effort to compel them to confess Wulfe's secrets.

Her heart stopped cold when the intruder pivoted to stare at the bed. She could see the villain's hands and could not see that any item had been claimed from Wulfe's belongings. Did this person know they were awake? Was there more than thievery in the plan? The shadowed silhouette loomed closer, and Christina closed her eyes tightly, lest her wakefulness be revealed. It was horrible to not be able to see what transpired, but she was terrified. Surely the villain would hear the thunder of her heart?

Christina felt a rush of air and dared to peek through her lashes again.

There was no shadow before her. Where had the intruder gone?

She strained to hear the sound of the thief's breath, had time to fear that the boys were in peril, then Wulfe moved with lightning speed.

The knight rolled out of bed in one fluid gesture and slashed his blade into the curtain on the back side of the bed. Christina saw the glint of a second knife blade and realized that the intruder had tried to stab Wulfe. The drapery was cut so that she saw the intruder's shadow again, then Wulfe leapt toward his attacker.

There was a grunt, then some weight was slammed into the wall. A scuffle ensued. The boys cried out and Christina heard them stumble to their feet. She slipped out of the bed in search of a lantern, not wanting any of them to mistake an ally for a foe.

By the time she had struck the flint and lit the lantern, the battling pair were by the window. Wulfe grappled with the thief, and it seemed they were evenly matched. Wulfe wore nothing at all, while the thief was swathed in black.

Suddenly, the assailant struck Wulfe across the face with a gloved hand, the full cloak having disguised the blow. Wulfe staggered backward, dropping his blade. His attacker lunged for it, but Christina saw it had been a feint: Wulfe tripped his opponent so the thief fell hard to the floor. The knight seized the thief from behind, locking one arm around that individual's throat and reaching for his hood. Christina saw the flash of teeth in the shadow framed by the hood, then the thief bit Wulfe's arm hard. The thief spun and jabbed an elbow into the knight's ribs, kicking up a heel in the same moment. Wulfe blanched and his grip must have loosened, for the thief tore free. The boys shouted and made to attack, but the thief seized the oil lantern from Christina's grasp and flung it at the boys.

"No!" she cried but it was too late. Though the boys ducked, the glass reservoir shattered against the wall, and the oil ran over the draperies. The flames leapt in hungry pursuit. The smaller boy tried to extinguish the flames, but his clothes also caught fire. Some of the oil must have fallen from the airborne vessel to his garb.

Christina seized Wulfe's cloak and hastened to the squire. She wrapped him in the garment and Wulfe helped to roll him on the ground until the flames were extinguished.

"We must leave!" Wulfe said, reaching for his boots.

She glanced back and saw that the intruder lurked in the shadows. That villain had not fled the chamber, as she had expected. Why?

She cried out and pointed, and Wulfe gave chase. The intruder darted across the chamber then; Wulfe fast behind. There were always a trio of lanterns left alight in the corridor, for the convenience of those guests who departed during the night. The intruder seized the closest one and flung it at the knight.

Wulfe jumped out of its path and the lantern landed in the middle of the great bed, spilling oil onto the linens. The pillared bed was a conflagration in a trio of heartbeats. Christina heard the fleeing footfalls of the attacker.

Wulfe swore with a vigor that might have made Christina blink under other circumstance. As it was, she wanted to add some foul words of her own. He dressed with haste, drawing on his chemise, chausses, and tabard, shoving on his boots as the taller boy belted his scabbard around his waist. Christina, too, donned her kirtle and shoes, pushing her stockings into her belt. She glared at the jeweled girdle, then donned it as well, recalling how she had seen women beaten for daring to remove it.

One day she would cast it aside as well as all it represented, but not yet.

"Leave naught behind," Wulfe bade the boys. "We will not return. Quickly now!" The boys scurried, quick to pick up his remaining garments and possessions, even as the fire spread. Wulfe saw all of them out of the chamber, then shut the door. "It will not hold the flames back for long," he said grimly. "You must rouse the others," he said to her, then raced to the summit of the stairs.

"I would go with you!" Christina cried.

But Wulfe paused on the lip of the stairs to glance back, then shook his head. "It cannot be so," he said and there might have been regret in his tone. "Be well, Christina," he added, then pivoted to leap down the stairs, his cloak flaring behind him.

It was clear he meant to abandon her and pursue the villain. He took the stairs two or three at a time, ushering the boys out of the house ahead of him.

Christina would not be abandoned here, not now.

"Fire!" she shouted as she raced after the knight and his squires, matching his pace on the stairs. "The house burns!" she cried in the local dialect, making as much noise as she could. By the time she reached the second floor, Wulfe was already disappearing down the staircase at the far end of the house. Christina swore under her breath and ran faster.

She reached the ground floor and could see that Wulfe had emerged into the street, framed by the open portal as he looked to the left and to the right. The boys were with him. She ran to the door, but the porter moved to close the door anew.

"Fire!" Christina cried, seizing his meaty hand.

"You cannot leave."

"He has paid for the entire night. I merely keep the wager that was made."

"It is not common..."

"Nor is it common for to have a client who pays so well," Christina snapped. "Would it not be wise to ensure his return?"

The porter's eyes narrowed. "Let us ask the signora what she says."

"Aye," Christina agreed, seeing opportunity slip away. She heard chaos erupting above her and Costanzia's shouts and knew that once that woman arrived, there would be no chance of passing through this portal. "Let us ask what she says about you admitting that thief to the house."

"What thief?" the porter demanded, but Christina saw that he knew.

"The one who tried to stab my client. The one who set the house afire. How much did he pay you? Enough to sate the signora, too?" Christina lowered her voice. "Enough to repair the damage being done by this fire? Perhaps she will take it from your wages."

"You would not tell her!"

"Rely upon it: I would." Christina smiled with resolve. "Unless you let me pass."

Their gazes held for a long moment.

"Tell her I tricked you," Christina invited.

The porter's eyes narrowed for a moment, then he raised a hand as if he would summon Costanzia. But Christina seized the heavy wooden portal and hauled it open. She ducked beneath his arm and ran into the night, knowing she was doomed unless she found a defender in this unholy city.

"You will be back!" he roared after her. "And you will pay!"

But Christina had been doomed before, just as she had been threatened. She had yearned for an opportunity to change her circumstance. Now that it had come—in the unlikely guise of a Templar knight—she would not be left behind.

No matter what the price.

Gone!

Wulfe spun in the small square where he had last glimpsed his assailant. He could still feel the cold touch of that blade against his back, a sure sign that he had waited a beat too long to respond to the threat.

That error might have cost him dearly.

Enchantment was the root.

Christina's enchantment. He might have paid dearly for the pleasure she had granted, and with more than coin.

Wulfe stared into the dark alleys on the far side of the square, uncertain which one the wretch had chosen. There were too many shadows in this cursed city—even the space behind the well in the middle of the square looked ominous. He closed his eyes, listening, and heard the faint sound of boots on stone.

There! Wulfe crossed the plaza in haste, the boys fast on his heels. He reached the far side where two alleys wound crookedly into darkness just as the bells of the church that faced this square rang out, pealing the hour.

To his dismay, he could hear only the bells, their resonant peals obscuring all other sound.

Wulfe exhaled. Though the sky was yet dark, it was time for *matins*.

The sun would rise soon, but not soon enough to spot his prey.

By the time the bells had ceased, there was no sound but his own breathing.

The cur had escaped.

Wulfe pivoted, vexed, and slapped his gloves upon his own palm. He seethed at his own failure. He had not been sufficiently quick. He had not wanted to injure the attacker beyond any ability to confess his intent, and he certainly had seen no point in killing the assailant. Wulfe had been foiled because he had wanted to know the thief's identity and his scheme.

Alone in the streets of Venice but for the boys, he regretted his own mercy.

And what had the villain wanted from him? Not his coin. Not his weapons. The missive that Gaston carried for the Master of the Paris Temple, the one that officially Wulfe carried? The treasure, secretly entrusted to Fergus? Wulfe recalled how Hamish, the squire of Fergus, had been injured on the ship and wondered whether the boy truly had been pushed.

Though he did not have possession of the treasure, Wulfe still was responsible for its delivery. He would have to verify that Fergus still carried it.

Why had the thief lingered?

To see what Wulfe would save when the room was afire, of course.

In this moment, he must choose one alley or the other and hope he picked aright. How would he know the villain? He had glimpsed no more than a dark cloak and had only a rough notion of the attacker's size. He had not wounded the fiend sufficiently for the injury to be evidence of his deed. Indeed, he was not entirely certain it had been a man who assailed him in the dark.

What if it had been a woman? What if it had been some woman in the employ of Costanzia's house? Was that why Christina had been awake? Because she had anticipated the assault, or known of it in advance? It was common enough for patrons to be robbed and even killed in brothels, and the boys, his usual source of security, had been asleep. He could not suppress the sense that he had survived by luck alone.

Even as he debated his course, the people of this wretched city rose from their slumber. He could hear a bustling on all sides as fires were stoked and days begun.

Wulfe ground his teeth in annoyance. He had known in the Holy Land that someone pursued their party, and even Gaston had agreed. Gaston had been certain that no one could have pursued them over the seas, for they had taken the last ship from Acre.

But their party *had* been followed across the Adriatic. Gaston had been wrong, again, but Wulfe had been the one to nearly pay the price. He marched down the right alley, his mood nigh as sour as when he had gone to the brothel.

Good coin he had spent for no good result. Wulfe's temper simmered anew. He feared that the sole way any villain could have pursued them from Acre was to have taken passage on the same ship.

Did the fiend travel in their own party? It was a horrifying prospect.

"Wulfe! Wait!" a woman cried from behind him.

He turned to find that the alluring Christina had followed him. Even though he had savored her wares thoroughly, his body still responded to the sight of her.

Clearly he had not sated himself.

Perhaps it was the return of his annoyance that fed his desire anew.

Or the lady's spell.

Either way, even knowing he should do as much, Wulfe could not turn his back upon her twice in short order. He stood, like a man struck to stone, and watched her run toward him. Zounds, but the woman was a beauty. He remembered the way her voice had broken with the confession of what she had done to survive and felt again the urge to assist her. He was snared as surely as a rabbit in a trap and did not like the realization in the least.

In fact, that was as good a reminder of his dream and his own convictions as he needed. Women were deceitful. Women beguiled men and used them for their own purposes, not caring about the fate of their victims. And Wulfe knew well enough that Christina had enchanted him. She was but half a dozen steps away, when he regained control of his unruly desires. He pivoted on his heel and began to stride after the villain.

Who surely was long gone.

Was that why she called him to a halt? To ensure that the villain escaped fully?

"Wulfe!" Christina cried again. "Wait!"

He kept walking.

Doubtless she wanted his aid.

Doubtless some barbarians in the employ of her mistress were fast behind. He had seen the pair at the gates upon his admission into the house and did not doubt that there were more.

"Wulfe!"

He spun to face her then, intent upon seeing the end of this matter, his own inclination to assist her to the contrary. "What is this you do?" he demanded, ensuring his tone was rough. "Our wager is done, madame, and you had best return to the house."

Christina did not falter, but lifted her chin with a determination he found admirable. "You paid for the night," she said. "And it is not yet dawn."

A shutter opened above them, the minute creak and catch of breath revealing that their conversation had an audience.

"I have had my fill," Wulfe insisted.

"Yet you have not had what you paid to possess." Christina's lips had a stubborn set and her eyes gleamed with resolve. She loosed the neckline of her dress, holding his gaze all the while. The woman's skin was as creamy as he recalled, and he knew its softness. He was certain she saw him swallow before he averted his gaze. "Do you not wish to complete our business?" she asked in a sultry voice and strolled closer. He could smell her perfume. He could recall the feel of her beneath his hand. He could taste the sweet ardor of her kiss, and the combination was sufficient to make him forget the intruder.

Almost.

He met her gaze, knowing his own was icy. "Do you imagine that I wish to be hunted down and slaughtered by your mistress for stealing a treasure from her hoard?"

The observers above whispered to each other and fairly leaned out the window, the better to listen to such salacious detail.

Christina scoffed. "How can you be stealing what you have

bought?" She unfastened her chemise slowly, a siren determined to claim him fully. She smiled, sultry and tempting. "I but ensure that you have what you deserve."

Wulfe inhaled sharply, then closed the distance between them. He caught her wrist in his hand, needing to halt her before she exposed herself fully. Stephen and Simon stood back and watched with round eyes. "Perhaps you ensure that the villain escapes," he charged and her outrage was clear.

"I warned you!" she reminded him, her eyes flashing fire.

"When it was too late to save myself."

Christina enraged was even more alluring than Christina bent on seduction, for in this, he spied the real woman. "How dare you suggest as much," she demanded, her voice falling low. "I believed you were a man of honor, one who would aid me..."

"You cannot come with me," Wulfe said, interrupting her with quiet force before she convinced him to ignore what he knew to be true. "You know this. There is no future after the dawn, and I would end matters now."

"I will not be left behind." Christina arched a brow when he might have argued. "It would not be right."

"Nor would it be right for me to earn the ire of your mistress."

She grimaced. "I will not return there, and I do not care what I must do to ensure as much." Her gaze locked with his. "Name your price."

Wulfe looked left and right, enticed more than he knew was wise. "You should go back to the house. A roof and regular meals, as we said. You will be defended there..."

"Not again," she said, her tone hard. "That price is too high."

He felt exasperation, caught between his desire to do what was right and the awareness of his own vulnerability. It was never good to be in the thrall of another—which only meant that he understood her desperation. "And what am I to do with you?" he demanded in a whisper that had the two old hens leaning farther out the window, lest they miss a morsel.

Christina smiled. "Anything you desire," she purred and slid her fingertip up his arm.

She played the courtesan again, using her arts against him, but this time, Wulfe could not halt his reaction. His body responded to her touch as if she commanded him. "Nay! I am a Templar, a knight sworn to chastity..."

"That vow seems somewhat elusive to you."

"That is as may be, but I cannot take a companion, or a female servant, much less a wife. You cannot journey with me! It is too public."

Christina tilted her head to regard him. "But surely, it is your sworn pledge to defend pilgrims? I was a pilgrim..."

"But no longer."

"Who is to say as much? I would go home, and embarking on such a perilous journey requires a defender." Her gaze darkened. "If not a champion." She gave weight to that last word and he felt a cur for ever having uttered it.

Wulfe exhaled again, shoving a hand through his hair. He felt a stab of envy that this was one thing he did not have in common with Christina—she had a home to which she might return, while he did not. He could understand well enough her desire to go there, but not how he would manage it.

"But I am granted a quest, granted by my superior..."

"To sample the brothels of Venice?" she asked so archly that he felt the back of his neck heat.

"To deliver a missive to Paris," he snapped. "And once it is fulfilled, I return to the east..."

"Paris?" Christina interrupted him with satisfaction. "That destination will suit me well. It is close enough to home and far enough from here to make a good beginning."

Wulfe flung out a hand. "But you cannot travel with me!"

"Whyever not? Because you would not have others realize how you flaunt your vows?"

"Because it is not fitting," he huffed, that reason sounding thin even to his own ears. "Because you have no coin to pay for your way."

"I shall pay in kind," she insisted and trailed that hand up his arm again. The women above tittered. "From here to Paris, sir, I shall offer myself to you as often as you desire."

Wulfe knew he should not be tempted but he was.

"Impossible," he said, but heard the lack of conviction in his voice. He was watching her lips, so soft and full, so close—and he well knew how luscious her kisses were.

Christina clearly discerned the war within him, for she used her touch to tip the balance in her own favor. The press of her lips against his throat sent pleasure surging through him, and Wulfe found himself closing his eyes against his own will. "I shall make it worth your while, sir," she whispered before touching her lips to his.

Wulfe should have protested, but he was lost, in thrall to this courtesan's seductive kiss.

And that was worrisome indeed.

Christina knew that Wulfe was not convinced of the merit of her plan, but having no other option, she was determined to make it come to be. From Paris, she could find her way home readily enough. It was the escape from Venice that was the challenge, for Costanzia would pay any gatekeeper to return women she considered her property. Christina had need of a man unafraid to fight, at least until they were a good week away from this place. She needed a disguise as well, and thought that traveling with a Knight Templar would offer a good one.

Wulfe pulled back, forcibly breaking her kiss, and Christina knew this would be her last chance to secure her desire. If he left her now, she would never find him again.

Costanzia, though, would.

If she could not convince him with her touch, she would show herself useful to him in other ways. Aye, he had said that he preferred to talk to her, rather than savor the skills of the courtesan. Too late, she realized she would not win his full agreement with her caress.

She had to change tactics.

Before Wulfe could protest again, Christina placed her fingertips over his mouth, and glanced upward to the women who listened so avidly. She tucked her hand into his elbow, turned him in the direction he had been walking, and they proceeded down the alley together. There was laundry hanging overhead.

"Hastily now," she said in an undertone. "Before the pails of slops are emptied upon us." She spoke in German and chose a northern dialect apurpose. She had discerned that accent in his own speech and hoped to establish a stronger bond between them.

He chuckled at her comment, then started that she had changed languages. "I was right," he murmured. "Venetian is not your mother tongue."

"And was I right in guessing yours?"

"More right than I should have preferred. You cannot come with me."

"We but walk together. There is no harm in that."

He slanted a glance her way and she doubted that he was fooled. "You will not change my thinking. It cannot be done."

Christina changed the subject, endeavoring to show herself to be useful. "That thief came in search of some specific item. The intruder searched your garb and only your garb, then tried to kill you. What manner of missive do you carry to Paris?"

Wulfe stiffened. "You need not know of it."

"But I already know some. And if you tell me more, I may be able to help you more. There is much of this city I have learned."

He slanted a glance her way, intrigued against his will. "Like what?"

"Like where a thief will hide. Is yours from Venice? Or were you followed?"

Wulfe's eyes narrowed. "Perhaps the villain came from within Costanzia's house. Perhaps you knew of it."

Christina shook her head. "I warned you when I heard the step on the floor. If I had been complicit, that would have ensured a beating."

"Which perhaps is why you desire to leave the house."

"You think it a risk to confide in me," Christina insisted. "But I think it folly not to do so. Who else is in your company? Where have the boys been? Have they made acquisitions for you? Bought food? Had your armor repaired and your blades honed? Where do you sleep, when you are not at a brothel? Where is your horse stabled? There are a thousand places where details of you and your habits might have been shared, and you will be vulnerable in each one of them." She knew she had Wulfe's attention. "There are not that many Templars in Venice with hair of gold and eyes of silver."

She felt his body tighten and knew he had not considered himself to be so readily identified. He considered her, his eyes that icy hue that made her think of the predator for which he was named.

He arched a brow. "While one such Templar with a beautiful whore on his arm will be less readily noted?"

Christina smiled. She could not halt herself. It was true that having her accompany him would make him more remarkable. She leaned closer and dropped her voice to a whisper. "Which is why I suggest that we remain secluded until your departure, the better for me to compensate you for your assistance. There are few would see you in your bed, save me, I should think."

She could not read his thoughts, which might have troubled her more if she had not felt the skip of his heart.

"We must depart this very day," he said crisply. "There will be no time..."

"There is *always* time," Christina interrupted him, speeding her steps. "But we had best secret ourselves soon. If you ride out this day, it will be after the dawn, and the sky grows rosy even now."

"You mean to distract me from chasing the villain."

"You had already lost the trail by the time I caught up to you."

Wulfe walked beside her, the boys trailing behind, and seemed for a moment to be uncertain what to say. "Are you always so stubborn as this?" he asked finally.

"Only when a matter is of dire import," she replied, doubting there was much to be lost in honesty. "Though it could be said that in this matter, we are both equally resolute."

Wulfe pursed his lips, evidently deciding, and she knew she would not have to wait long. "Will they beat you?" he asked and she nodded, not needing to lie.

"Of course."

His lips tightened and she knew his choice was made. He turned down a street and strode with greater purpose. His path was not in the direction of Costanzia's house, and Christina dared to hope.

"You may stay with me until the dawn," Wulfe ceded. "But only because there is no place for you to take refuge so early as this."

Christina was thrilled that he made any concession to her at all and was determined to ensure he did not regret it.

CHAPTER FIVE

ulfe was a fool and he knew it.

He knew he had little to offer Christina and this was at best a reprieve. Still, what manner of man would send her to be beaten and abused? He could not bear the thought. There had to be another solution. He strode quickly back to the rented house, not wanting to give her another chance to win his sympathy. Perhaps Christina could remain at the house, after their departure. Perhaps they would give her work in the kitchens there. Perhaps he could find another solution that would see her free of the brothel.

It was madness for him to take such an interest, but he could do naught else. He feared he would not be free of Christina soon.

A part of him did not want to be.

Did he dare to believe that she had not known of the assault? If he did, then either the owner of the brothel was at root, or the villain had followed Wulfe to that place and awaited his moment. It seemed suddenly critical to get back to the rented house.

Wulfe turned down the street, taking Christina to the portal of the house, only to discover that the entry had been locked against him.

He pounded upon the wooden doors of the rented house with his fist, knowing it was good sense for their small party to have secured themselves thus but disliking the indignity of being required to demand admission.

He was well aware of the mingled curiosity and surprise in Christina's regard.

He was also aware that Venice was too shadowed and quiet behind him.

"I demand admission!" he shouted and pounded yet more. To his relief, the portal was unlocked, though not as quickly as he might have hoped. The door was opened so abruptly that he fairly stumbled into the courtyard. He ushered Christina and the boys into the space and Bartholomew secured the doors behind them. It was clear the others had heard him sooner, for Gaston was by the well, awaiting him.

That knight's disapproval was clear, but Wulfe was not so enamored of his fellow knight this morn either. He had, after all, been attacked because of Gaston's mistaken confidence that they had not been pursued, let alone his choice of the more distant port.

Wulfe was not yet prepared to concede that it was good he had not carried the missive, given the night's events.

Gaston arched a dark brow, fairly inviting a confession. It was this attitude of Gaston's that irked Wulfe beyond all, this calm conviction that seemed to measure Wulfe and constantly find him lacking. Aye, he was passionate, and aye, he was headstrong, and aye, he was a bastard. He was well aware of his shortcomings when Gaston gave him that look.

"We are in peril and must ride out at once," he declared. "I have been attacked!"

Gaston, curse him, leaned against the pillar that supported the stable roof, looking disinclined to go anywhere anytime soon. But Wulfe was supposed to be the one leading this party! Gaston could at least make a show of heeding his words to preserve the illusion.

"We ride out this morn!" Wulfe roared. "If not this very *moment.*"

The other former Templar, Fergus, appeared in the portal of

the common room. He yawned and shoved his hand through his hair, before he spoke. "What a ruckus you make for so early in the day." His man-at-arms, Duncan, stood behind him, rubbing his chin as he openly surveyed Christina.

Aye, they all looked at Christina. Wulfe glanced back at his companion and felt an unwelcome stab of desire. Her hair was yet unbound and it shone. She ignored the staring men in what had to be a deliberate choice, and one intended to feed their curiosity.

Indeed, she took the opportunity to arrange her garb. She might have been at leisure in her chamber, for she laced the sides of her kirtle with care. The courtesan was back. The languid way she moved, the way she tossed her hair over her shoulder, the secretive smile upon her lips, all combined to make her occupation abundantly clear to all. Her kirtle looked uncommonly rich in the shadows, and that mysterious girdle glinted as if more valuable than Wulfe knew it had to be.

Duncan's eyes were alight with interest, and Wulfe wondered whether she would turn to another man in this company to defend her, when he declined to aid her.

That thought did naught to dispel his rising temper.

He spun to face the others. "It is yet night and I was attacked while I lay abed," he snapped. "It is sufficient to weary me of this city. I order our immediate departure."

Fergus shook his head with infuriating defiance. "Hamish needs more rest before he rides," he said, referring to his injured squire. "So the apothecary says and so it shall be." He nodded amiably at Everard and Joscelin who had followed him from the common room. Beyond it were stairs to the chambers above, and Wulfe could only conclude that they had been roused by his knocking. "I would not answer to his mother for the boy's health." The men chuckled together, but Wulfe bristled.

This was no jest. Truly, he tired of this attitude that they could linger over this journey, as if they visited sites of interest at their leisure. He would complete the quest in haste and return to aid his brethren in Outremer.

Why did no other soul in the party share his sense of urgency?

"I will *not* be delayed because of a squire, let alone one so witless that he falls into the hold of the ship when unsupervised," he said, heat in his words. He hoped Christina concluded that he was without compassion.

"I was pushed," Hamish declared from the shadows of the stable.

"You tripped," scoffed Kerr.

Fergus shook his head, ignoring the dispute between his two squires. "It matters little how the injury was inflicted. I will stay in Venice two more days."

"This party must remain together," Wulfe insisted. "And I am in command! I say we leave this very day. It is not safe for us to linger."

"Because you were attacked by this woman?" Duncan asked, his tone jovial. "I wager few men would resent that assault." Fergus chuckled with him. Wulfe thought about inflicting injury upon the Scotsman, but Gaston finally roused himself to speak.

"What has happened?" that knight asked, his tone temperate. "It was only last eve that you were glad to have a night away from all of us." Gaston looked pointedly at Christina, who ignored him as well as Duncan.

"Surely you wish to remain in Venice and entertain your guest," Fergus teased.

Wulfe glared at him. "She is not my *guest*. She is a whore..."

"Courtesan," Christina interrupted crisply. "And my name is Christina, as I told you."

Fergus inclined his head and might have spoken to her, but Wulfe interrupted before he could. Perhaps if he spoke harshly, Christina would be dissuaded of his merit as a protector. "Her name is of no import. Her trade can be called whatever you desire to call it. No matter how honeyed the choice of word, it is what it is."

He was aware of Christina's disapproval and told himself that he welcomed it. The truth was that he felt a cur, but there was little point in pretending that matters could be other than they were. He continued. "I have paid her in full, but she follows me..."

"He declared himself my champion last night," Christina said, her tone both sweet and commanding. Wulfe was not surprised by how readily she summoned his desire to be of aid to her. He truly was beguiled.

Every man turned to look at her, even Wulfe, who would have preferred to have done otherwise. Christina smiled with a confidence in her own allure, and he knew that every man in the courtyard was sworn to her cause.

"And indeed, I owe my life to this knight," she continued. She flicked him a look hard enough to make him flinch, although her tone remained sweet. "Of course, I must follow him that the debt might be repaid in kind."

"You would surrender your life for *him*?" Kerr asked, clearly incredulous. The others snickered, though Wulfe seethed at the boy's impertinence.

And the failure of any knight to correct that attitude. Some soul had blackened Kerr's eye on the ship, and Wulfe thought the boy should have learned something from the experience.

"You should not be deceived by appearances," Christina chided the squire. "Or judge a man by your first impression of him." Her eyes glowed as she smiled at Wulfe and Wulfe's heart thundered. "The lion with a thorn in his paw is yet a noble creature, though his pain may make him terrifying."

Heat flooded through Wulfe that she could think so well of him, feeding that urge to assist her.

Perhaps that was her intent.

That Christina could provoke such a reaction in him when he was determined to separate their paths was a sign of weakness that Wulfe did not welcome. "You owe me no debt," he said to Christina, keeping his tone cool. "I paid for the pleasure you granted and our agreement is fully satisfied."

She replied mildly. "I say it is not satisfied, and if it is an *agreement*, then the consensus of both parties is required to call it fulfilled." She smiled at Wulfe, as if untroubled by his annoyance, but again, he saw that glint of resolve in her eyes.

"I did *not* pay to have my life threatened, to need to defend myself in a moment of leisure or to have to flee from certain destruction."

"As bad as that?" Fergus drawled, then winked at Christina. "I would not have expected a mating with you to be so dire."

"There was an attack upon the house," she informed the other knight, and Wulfe was surprised she could speak of it so calmly. "As can happen, when there are wealthy patrons in residence." She cleared her throat. "And brigands looted both house and patrons after setting fire to the establishment. The other women..." Her words faded and she straightened, casting a smile at Wulfe.

Wulfe marveled that she concocted a tale with such ease. Was she hiding the truth to defend his secrets, or did she protect the brothel? Where did her alliances lie?

Christina stepped toward him, that alluring smile curving her lips. "My fate would certainly have been worse, had I not been abed with a *champion* who defended me."

Wulfe felt his neck burn. "I defended myself," he corrected. "I was attacked and I ensured my own survival."

"And mine as well, to my eternal gratitude." Christina bowed deeply to him.

"Your gratitude need not last so long as that. I will give you another coin, even two, that you might continue on your way as we continue on our own." His party had to leave for Paris this very day. He would talk to the owners before they rode out, in the hope that Christina could find honest labor here.

But Christina lifted her chin. "And I say you shall be repaid, in kind or in trade, for saving my life. Wherever you go, sir, I will follow." Her manner was, if anything, more resolute than it had been in the streets. "Rely upon it."

Wulfe could well understand a desire to abandon the past and begin anew, never mind the urge to return home.

But she was not his responsibility. His duty to the order had to come first.

"There are worse fates," Duncan murmured.

The man-at-arms smiled at Christina, hoping to ease her mood. She did not avert her gaze from Wulfe, her expectation clear.

"Were you injured?" Gaston asked, recalling Wulfe to the matter at hand.

He indicated his own back. "It is naught, but it is naught because I was awake. Had I been asleep, the blade would have slid between my very ribs." Consideration dawned in Gaston's eyes, and Wulfe knew they would speak of it in more detail later.

"I suppose such peril is a hazard of visiting such establishments," Everard mused, his tone prim. Wulfe could have done without that man's moral commentary.

"It is of no matter what you believe you owe to me," he said to Christina, his tone less vehement than it had been. "We ride out with all haste. You have no steed, therefore you will not depart with us."

"Just because you have been routed in the midst of your pleasure by some unfortunate incident, I see no reason to hasten away," Fergus drawled. "And still Hamish requires those days of rest."

Wulfe raised his fist. "A squire will not..."

"I say we break our fast," Gaston said flatly. "And review the situation after that."

Wulfe fell silent reluctantly, but Gaston continued as if unaware of his annoyance.

Again, Gaston took command of the company.

Again, the illusion of Wulfe's authority was compromised. He was well aware of Christina, watching them and no doubt seeing more than he would have preferred.

"No good decisions are made when the belly is empty," Gaston said. "And my wife has purchases to collect on this day. Perhaps we will compromise and depart on the morrow."

"We need to reach our destination sooner rather than later, that I might return to Jerusalem to aid in its defense," Wulfe protested, though he guessed it to be futile.

"And a delay of a day will make little difference," Gaston replied, his tone revealing that his thinking would not be changed.

It was appalling.

It was wrong.

But Wulfe knew what he had to do.

He exhaled slowly, tempering his reaction. "Perhaps there is good sense in your advice," he acknowledged, though it nigh pained him to do as much. "I will break my fast before making my decision."

"Perhaps your guest would join us," Fergus said, bowing to Christina. "Since I gather that her previous abode is no longer hospitable."

"It is not, and I should be delighted to accept your invitation," she said and put her hand on his elbow. Fergus escorted her into the common room, followed by Joscelin and Duncan. Everard marched up the stairs to his chamber, sweeping his cloak around himself in a gesture of disapproval. At a pointed glance from Bartholomew, the squires returned to their duties in the stables, leaving the two knights alone in the courtyard.

Wulfe did not know where to begin. He glared at Gaston, certain the man had to understand the source of his vexation. Gaston returned his gaze with that infuriating calm, though, and Wulfe knew that once again, his will and supposed command would be overruled.

It was Gaston's fault that their departure from the Holy Land had been so late, that they had been followed and not caught the culprit, that they would linger in Venice so that his very life was in peril.

Perhaps that was Gaston's plan. Perhaps he intended to see Wulfe sacrificed in a hope to draw the villain into the open. There were a hundred questions he could have asked, a hundred answers he could have demanded, but in this place, they were too likely to be overheard. He hoped Gaston could discern all of those concerns in his expression.

The knight nodded, as if he did.

"This afternoon," Gaston murmured as he passed Wulfe, heading toward the common room and the others.

Wulfe stared at his boots, knowing that discussion could not come too soon. He glanced toward the company breaking their fast, watched Christina charm the other men with remarkable ease, then her attention flicked to him. Their gazes locked for a charged moment, sending a fearsome jolt of desire through him.

He was ten times more frustrated than he had been the night before, when he had sought relief so that would ensure his skills were not compromised.

And Christina was more than willing.

But he would not be tempted because it would only encourage her expectations. He crossed the courtyard with quick steps, and passed through the common room. He dispatched Stephen with a gesture to bring him a meal, then climbed the stairs alone.

He had to leave Christina behind, though he knew it would not be readily done. He was well aware of the irony of his situation—he was the one who had charged Gaston with adding his whore to their party in Jerusalem. He would not add his own to the party now. Christina had to remain in Venice, and the longer she remained in his company, the more he would fall beneath her spell.

At dawn, their ways must part, one way or the other.

It could not be *him*.

Christina caught only a glimpse of the nobleman in Wulfe's party, but it was enough to turn her blood to ice. She reminded herself that nine years had passed, that people changed and that her memory might not be reliable.

Still, she could not shake a conviction that a familiar serpent was part of Wulfe's party.

She wanted to speak with Wulfe, but he was clearly irked. She knew better than to pursue a man when he was vexed.

At least he did not leave the house. He climbed the stairs, undoubtedly to a chamber he had claimed for his own. The younger squire hastened after him, while the other gathered bread, honey, fruit, and a pitcher of ale for his knight before following on fleet feet.

Christina would grant Wulfe time to compose himself before lending chase. She would take the opportunity to learn as much as she could, so that she could prove her usefulness to him. Indeed, she found it nigh as vexing as Wulfe that he was treated with such indignity, but she believed she hid her response better. If he led the party, his command should be respected, not challenged. Christina thought it outrageous that he was nigh ignored.

She ensured no hint of her churning thoughts was revealed to her companions. She accepted a seat at the board at the urging of the man-at-arms, feigning delight in the conversation and the company. For once in her days, Christina was grateful to Costanzia for the lessons learned in that house. It was easy to laugh with the three men who sat with her in the common room, to pretend they had her undivided attention, even as her thoughts returned to that unnamed nobleman.

Could it be Helmut? Here? After all these years, it defied belief. But perhaps not—she had met him en route to Jerusalem and Wulfe's party came from that very city.

If she was right, what was Helmut's scheme? She recalled enough of him to know that he always had a scheme, and it was assuredly one that saw to his own advantage, if not the detriment of everyone else. Why was he in this party at all? Was it coincidence or a plan? She had heard about Saladin attacking the Latin Kingdoms and Wulfe had confirmed their precarious state. She knew that a man like Helmut would not remain behind to fight, if there was any chance he might have broken a fingernail.

But where was he going?

And why?

She heard a door slam overhead, then no more.

Surely Wulfe had not gone to consult with Helmut? Surely they were not in league with each other? Nay, it could not be. They two were as different as men could be. Wulfe could not know Helmut's true nature.

Christina was tempted to warn Wulfe, but what would she say? She had no proof of any foul deed committed by Helmut, simply her own suspicions and memories. It was too easy to recall Gunther's warning that she not leap to conclusions and soil a man's reputation without proof.

Even if her instincts were invariably right.

Wulfe might not believe her, even if she did speak out, or worse, he might consult his fellow travelers—and in that, Helmut would be warned. Nay, the wisest course would be to keep silent while discovering as much as possible about this party and its members.

Christina smiled at the knight who sat across from her, the one with the easy manner and the sparkle in his eyes. His hair was dark and wavy, falling to his shoulders, and he spoke in a rollicking brogue. "I hear Scotland in your voice," she said. "What brings you so far from home?"

He smiled readily. "An instruction from my father. He decreed that I should serve the Templars before wedding my betrothed."

"Then you are to be wed?"

The knight nodded with the satisfaction of a man well content with his fate and Christina could not help but like him for that. "The day cannot come soon enough, to my view."

"Then you know your betrothed already."

"All my life. She is a neighbor's daughter and our fathers schemed over her cradle that our match would be made." He grinned. "From first glimpse, I found myself in vehement agreement."

"You must have been young, if your families are neighbors."

"I was but seven years of age, and she a sleeping babe. Even then, I saw that she was an angel come to earth." He grinned. "I confess I became only more convinced of that in the years since."

The mercenary cleared his throat. "No woman is an angel in truth," he corrected gruffly, but with similar good humor. His accent was heavier than that of the knight he accompanied, but it was clear they shared the same homeland. "I hope you do not spurn your bride when you realize she is a mere mortal."

"Or that her feet do tread the earth," Christina teased.

The knight laughed. "Not my Isobel. I will cherish her all my days and nights."

His conviction was such that Christina believed his affection would not be readily swayed. It was good to meet a man so content with his life and destiny.

"And whose heart is it that fair Isobel has won?" she asked lightly.

"I beg your pardon," the knight said, as gracious if she were a noblewoman. "I am Fergus of Killairic." He gestured to the mercenary, a man a good twenty years older than him. "And this is Duncan MacDonald, my kinsman and escort."

"His nanny," Duncan said with wry humor and they laughed together. "Charged to bring him home hale and whole." Christina imagined there was some truth in it, but that neither man was offended by it. Indeed, they seemed to be good friends.

"At the behest of Isobel or your father?" Christina teased.

"Both!" Duncan acknowledged and inclined his head to her. "But what man of merit would not put the request of a lady above all else?"

His manner indicated that he would put her request high on his list, but Christina only smiled.

The plump merchant seated beside her then cleared his throat, and she suspected he had felt overlooked. "And I am Joscelin de Provins."

"How delightful to make your acquaintance," Christina said, noting how that man flushed and became discomfited when she turned her gaze upon him. Not wanting to encourage any man in this party to think she courted any affections beyond those of Wulfe, she spoke to Fergus, the man besotted with his betrothed.

"And so you all travel together," she said lightly, ensuring she did not sound overly curious. She might have been idly passing the time, polite but not truly interested. "Did you create your party in Jerusalem?"

Fergus nodded, his manner turning sober. "You may have heard that Saladin musters in opposition to the Latin Kingdoms." Christina nodded. "But perhaps not that the King of Jerusalem was routed at the Horns of Hattin a few weeks ago."

"Routed?" Christina echoed, as if Wulfe had not already told her some of these tidings. "As bad as that?"

Fergus leaned closer. "I suppose there is no peril in acknowledging that the military orders have paid dearly in this loss. By our departure, there was already fear that Jerusalem itself would fall."

"We barely escaped Acre," Joscelin contributed in an obvious effort to sound important. "We departed on the very last ship to sail from the port."

"Indeed? Such a near escape as that?"

"It was terrifying," the merchant confided. He eyed her, perhaps thinking she might offer a certain kind of solace.

Christina pretended to have not noticed and spoke to Fergus. "There was word of the loss of Acre, for many Venetians have warehouses there."

"Doubtless they sailed hastily in defense of their goods," Duncan said with a shake of his head. "More hastily than in defense of any pilgrims or holy sanctuary."

Fergus chuckled at the truth in that, but the merchant took umbrage.

"There was tremendous value to reclaim," Joscelin protested. "I have friends in this city, and they were most intent upon defending their possessions, as they should be. Investments lost in war are not readily regained or rebuilt. Praise be that Tyre has not fallen, for I have a goodly quantity of spice yet to be shipped from there."

"It is all about silk, spices, and gems," Duncan noted.

The merchant bristled. "I do not care solely about goods," he huffed, then smiled at Christina. "But certainly a trade in fine goods has given me an appreciation for beauty."

"You are too kind," she said smoothly, trying to ease the tension between the men. "So, you return home to wed your beloved, having completed your service, and your faithful companion rides at your side," she said to Fergus who nodded acknowledgment. "And you, sir, journey home after making your acquisitions for the coming winter," she said to Joscelin who agreed with that. "Who else joins your party? There seemed to be quite a number of people in the courtyard."

"There is safety in numbers," Joscelin informed her.

"The knight Wulfe leads us, of course," Fergus said, with a conviction that rang false to Christina's ears. Both Duncan and Joscelin averted their gazes, as if knowing just the opposite to be true.

Indeed, it seemed almost that the dark-haired knight in the courtyard led the party, though Christina could make no sense of that. She had called Wulfe a lion with a thorn in his paw on impulse, but there was no doubting that his manner was more forthright in this place than she had seen previously. Was this the root of his annoyance?

"And he is a Templar," she said with undisguised admiration. "How fortunate you are to have such vigorous defense. Are there pilgrims in your party?"

"The lady Ysmaine and her maid," Duncan said. "They have a

chamber above."

"Though she is a pilgrim no longer," Joscelin added, clearly trying to regain Christina's attention. "For the knight Gaston wed her in Jerusalem, taking her as his bride nigh the moment he left the order." He leaned closer. "He is to be the Baron of Châmont-sur-Maine and his lady will have much to manage in that fine household."

It was clear that Joscelin had identified a potential customer.

It was less clear to Christina how or why a secular knight could command a Templar.

"Was that the other knight in the courtyard?" she asked and Fergus nodded. If his wife slept upstairs, why had he not been with her there? She chose her words and her tone with care. "He seems most resolute."

"Eighteen years in service to the Templars can do that to a man," Fergus noted with a smile.

"What else might it do to him?" she asked in a teasing tone.

Duncan laughed aloud. "I see your thinking," he noted with a wag of his finger. "Though he visits his lady, he does not slumber in her chamber."

Fergus lifted a brow. "Perhaps he thinks our party better defended when he is in the stables."

Christina eyed the bolted gate that opened to the street. "Surely you are safe in this abode?"

Fergus smiled a little, though there was little humor in the expression. "Perhaps eighteen years in service to the Templars teaches a man to be vigilant in guarding what he holds of value."

His wife? But Lady Ysmaine was not in the stables, by their report.

What was? His destrier, for certain.

Or did he guard something else?

How did Helmut fit into these arrangements? "Your party *is* considerable," she said. "And you must have servants as well."

Duncan nodded. "Six boys, one injured, in addition to Lady Ysmaine's maid."

"Which reminds me of a task left undone," Fergus said, pushing to his feet. He gave Duncan a nod. "We should check upon

Hamish this morn, perhaps summon the apothecary for another look at him."

"The boy's head is hard enough," Duncan said, showing no intention of moving. "I doubt he will sustain a lingering injury."

"He is under my custody, though," Fergus said. "And I would see him hale upon his return home."

Duncan winked at Christina. "You see how protective we are of all our chicks. You must think us like old women."

She laughed. "Hardly that. I think it most admirable when men defend those weaker than themselves." Duncan eyed her for a moment and she thought he might say more, but Fergus cleared his throat from the portal and the pair strode to the stables together. The dark-haired knight joined them there, and she supposed he had been with the horses. They conferred before disappearing into the shadowed stables.

"I too am inclined to be protective of those under my care," Joscelin said. "Why, just last year, a neighbor's boy took employ in my storehouse..."

Christina smiled and nodded, but did not heed Joscelin's words. She recalled the exchange between Wulfe and the knight who must be Gaston. It was clear the dark-haired knight irked Wulfe mightily, or perhaps his true role in this expedition did that. Was it simply a matter of personality, a question of past encounters, or was there more at root?

What was the true quest of this party? What did Wulfe deliver to Paris? Why did he travel with so many others? If Christina could discover that, she might discover why Wulfe had been attacked in Costanzia's house. She might also determine why Helmut was part of the group.

If it was him in truth. Only after the Scotsmen had departed and Joscelin strove to interest her in his own eligibility did she realize the other nobleman had never been identified by them.

Why not? Was he not with them? Or did they dislike him?

Christina should speak with Wulfe.

She interrupted Joscelin sweetly and asked for the location of Wulfe's chamber. The little man was flustered but told her the Templar had taken the room immediately above the common room. Christina excused herself politely and went in search of her champion.

She was climbing the stairs when a notion struck her, an intuitive conclusion that explained Wulfe's manner with such elegance that she hoped it were true.

There was but one way to find out.

Christina hurried up the stairs with new purpose.

Wulfe knew Christina would come to him.

Who else could she appeal to? She was alone and he was the sole one who had shown her kindness—such as it was. He wished he could offer more, but to promise what he could not deliver would be worse than no promise at all. Wulfe understood her predicament all too well. Though he was resolved not to let her remain with him, he guessed she would not abandon this opportunity quickly. She had a determination about her, that was for certain.

He admired that mightily.

Wulfe, however, had only the order. In the absence of the temptation offered by Christina, he could review his own choices more clearly. He knew there were no other good prospects for him and he still had no desire to become a mercenary. He had yet to meet a baron who might employ him whose aims he could be certain would always be just.

It was forbidden by the order to consort with women, but Wulfe had been blessed in Palestine to report to men who understood earthy truths. The Master of the Gaza Priory had been inclined to overlook transgressions of that part of the rule, so long as the occurrences were neither frequent nor disruptive. Their garrison had been under constant assault at Gaza, and the community they defended had been small. Much had been conceded in ensuring the survival of both knights and settlers there.

It was not reasonable, though, to assume that the Master at the Paris Temple would be so lenient. Indeed, his brethren faced no similar peril in that city, so the enforcement of the rule would be strict. Wulfe would have been disappointed if it had been otherwise. He could not arrive there with a whore as a companion and expect to remain a Templar.

Save if she were a pilgrim he defended.

Save if he did not enjoy her pleasures.

Save if she left their party before they reached the Temple. Would his fellow travelers report such activities to the Master? Wulfe knew he did not win alliances readily, particularly when he could not do so in battle, and suspected they might. Gaston was righteous, to be sure.

The only responsible choice was to deny Christina here and now, though the prospects for her fate were less than encouraging. He was not responsible for her, not truly, but he *felt* responsible.

Wulfe broke his fast, not really tasting the bread, forcing himself to consider other issues. He reviewed the assault as he did so, seeking a clue to the villain's identity. What if it had not been an assault arranged by the brothel? The villain then would have pursued him and had to bribe his way into the brothel, which indicated a serious intent.

Was the perpetrator in their party? Who had been out of the house the night before? He should ask. The boys brought him hot water then and Stephen unpacked a clean chemise as Wulfe bathed. He had donned his aketon and mail once again when there was a rap at the door.

Christina.

He would not lie to himself, though he would disguise his reaction from the lady.

Wulfe was glad she had come.

And that was the most worrisome detail of all.

CHAPTER SIX

ulfe dismissed the boys, following them to the portal. He ensured his expression was stern when he faced Christina, hoping she did not guess how his chest tightened at the sight of her. She was fingering that belt, an apparently idle gesture, but one that drew his gaze to it.

"It is dawn," he noted. "You had best return."

Instead, she stepped into his room, as he had guessed she would. Her gaze flitted over the simple furnishings and she almost smiled. "A little more austere than last night's accommodations."

"Yet my custom all the same."

She nodded, undeterred by this evidence that his life held few luxuries. The door closed audibly behind Stephen and Simon, and it seemed Christina had waited for that. Her gaze immediately lifted to his. "He was your father," she said with conviction and Wulfe was too startled to hide his surprise.

"Who?" he asked, endeavoring to hide his reaction all the same. He knew precisely who she meant and he knew she was right. But how had she discerned the truth?

"A knight with hair as white as snow and eyes as pale as ice. You will look like that in twenty years." She watched him, doubtless seeing more of his reaction than he preferred. "He recognized you by the same means. Likely your eyes, for they are uncommonly pale." Her tone hardened. "Perhaps he recognized all his bastards thus."

Wulfe took a step back. "You cannot know this..."

"No, I cannot." Christina interrupted him with conviction. "But I see the pattern. He was outraged at the sight of you, because he knew you were his son and he had believed you to be dead." She strolled around the room, her fingers sliding across a bare table then the stone sill. Wulfe could not tear his gaze away from her. "He could only have believed as much because your mother had told him of you, but had lied to him about your survival." She spun to face Wulfe. "Which means that your mother brought you to the old man in the woods. Perhaps the truth was what convinced a man who had no need for the responsibility of a child to take you in. He was your lone chance of survival and he must have known it."

"You speculate with enthusiasm," Wulfe said gruffly.

"I speculate because it is useful."

"Useful?" He flung out a hand. "Of what use is this tale you have spun?"

"It explains your fury, on this morn, in this courtyard."

A chill settled in Wulfe's gut. "I do not know what you mean."

Christina was only too prepared to explain. "You are irked by this knight Gaston, because he truly has leadership of your party, although you are given the appearance of leadership."

Wulfe frowned. How did this woman understand him so readily? "Nonsense," he retorted, knowing his protest would make no difference.

"It is not nonsense. You proved as much this morning in your reactions to his counsel. You could have made it look as if you conferred with him and chose to take his advice. Instead, you protested his interference, which had the result of proving to all who had not known before that Gaston is the true leader of your quest."

"But I..."

"It was a witless choice on your part, one I would not have

expected, save that Gaston must somehow remind you of your father. This injustice recalls the other, which is why it prompts your fury and why you spoke without due consideration."

Wulfe's heart clenched that he had revealed matters so clearly. "You speculate overmuch."

"Do I?" Christina was resolute. "If the villain is in your party, he knows that Gaston is the true leader. The villain attacked you last night. By your reaction, you have made Gaston his prey."

Wulfe spun on his heel to pace the room, dismayed that he might be responsible for such a thing. Why had he not been more temperate? He had managed to be so in Outremer, when Gaston had insisting upon riding to Acre instead of Jaffa.

Why had he been so furious this morn?

Was Christina right, that injustice had sparked his anger?

She spoke softly behind him. "Your father, a baron and a landholder, ensured you gained no birthright from him. He cheated you of what should have been yours. Gaston leads this party, unabashedly, and could be said to be cheating you of the authority that should be yours."

All the same, making Gaston the target of the villain was no good reward.

"You do not know that the villain is in our party."

"Nay, I do not," Christina conceded, but her lips tightened as if she suspected as much.

Of course, she did. Otherwise, the villain would have been part of the house where she worked and the responsibility might have been laid there.

"You do not know that admittance could be gained to the brothel at night," he argued. "Surely its portals are secured?"

"And surely in a house such as that one, coin can buy any thing at all." There was a weariness in her voice and Wulfe could not argue the point.

He turned to face her. "Still, you do not know that all in the party heard our argument."

Christina spared a glance to the window. "I will wager that nigh every chamber has a window that overlooks the courtyard, and if not, the corridor outside that chamber's portal does. No one could have slept through your demand for admission, save one drunk beyond belief. The one who attacked you has had no time to become so besotted." She shrugged. "Any soul with a speck of sense would have been curious about the uproar."

She was right.

Wulfe fought the urge to curse. He was a fool seven times over. He paced the chamber again, aware that she watched him. "What does it mean?" he demanded with impatience.

She shook her head, not understanding.

"The girdle you wear." He pointed to the jeweled belt. "What does it mean? Every woman in the house wore one."

Christina grimaced. "It is Costanzia's mark of ownership."

"It is not locked. You could remove it."

Her smile was sad. "We are quickly taught the price of so doing."

"But what is its purpose?"

"Any soul who sees me will know where I belong, whether that person recognizes my face or not. Any gatekeeper will deny me passage, once he glimpses it, for he will have been paid to do so."

Wulfe understood. "So you cannot leave the city, not while wearing it."

She shook her head.

"You should take it off, then."

"If I am ever destined to return there, the price of having removed it will be high." She frowned. "You must recognize that this city is not so populous as one might think. Those who abide here recognize each other and ignore the flow of pilgrims, crusaders, and merchants who come and go with the tides." She toyed with the belt and smiled a little. "There is another trait we have in common, Wulfe."

They would both be readily identified in this city, by virtue of their coloring alone.

Wulfe knew what Christina was asking him, but could not give her the answer she desired. "It is dawn," he repeated. "You should return before your situation becomes worse."

"I would argue that scheme."

"I cannot help you leave the city!" he protested, even as he considered how it might be done.

That fire flashed in Christina's eyes. "You will remain in this house two more days, by what I understand. I ask you for those two days, here, sheltered in this house, as a reprieve. After that, I shall do whatever is necessary, I vow it to you." Her voice softened. "Grant me this, I beg of you. I will ensure you do not regret it."

Wulfe could not find it within himself to send her back to that place. He guessed that she would try to convince him to take her to Paris and wondered already if she would succeed. It was inappropriate for him to keep a whore, but not to defend a pilgrim. The very tumult of his feelings was no good sign, for he knew that emotion was an unruly master.

He had only to look at how he had revealed Gaston's role this morn to see the truth of that.

Wulfe shrugged, making light of the concession he was about to make, and turned his back upon Christina. "I suppose it will harm little. Take your leisure here, for I have errands to complete. I will have the boys bring you hot water and tell the mistress of this house that you are my guest."

He heard Christina exhale and could not resist the impulse to glance back. To his surprise, her eyes were filled with tears. "I thank you, Wulfe," she said softly, her gratitude so evident that he felt a cur for granting her so little. "I will ensure you find the concession a profitable one."

Wulfe could not think about that, not when she looked both vulnerable and radiant, not when she was in his chamber and would soon be nude, not when he had tasks to perform. He nodded once and curtly in her direction, then took his leave. "There will be no exchange of favors between us," he said more sternly than he felt. "You request a reprieve from your labor, after all."

Wulfe left the chamber then before Christina could argue—or worse, tempt him—for he feared she would do as much. He was a hundred times a fool in this, but the true peril was that he could not regret it.

He was enchanted and snared, to be sure.

Worse, he wished to remain so with an ardor that shook him.

Contrary to Wulfe's expectation, there were other favors Christina could render than those delivered upon her back.

If he did not know as much, she would prove it to him.

She could not guess how long he would be gone, so she had best make the moments count. The taller of the two squires brought her a bucket of hot water, a sponge and some soap. Christina welcomed the simplicity of it all. The boy set the bucket upon the floor with sufficient care that the water did not spill and kept his gaze lowered.

"Did you win at chess last night?" Christina asked and he looked up in surprise.

"Twice but not the third time," he admitted. "Simon was fortunate in that match."

"Or perhaps you were sleepy."

He smiled a little. "Maybe. He does not win often."

"But you do not like it when he does."

"I am three years older, and have been a squire two years more. I should win."

"Age does not always determine victory, nor even practice."

He considered this, then recalled his manners and bowed. "I am Stephen, my lady."

"And I am Christina, though perhaps it would be better if you did not call me by name." She watched as he nodded and flushed a little. He bowed again, clearly intending to retreat, but Christina tried to put him at ease. "Have you always been squire to Wulfe?"

He nodded.

"And how did that come about?" She washed her hands, glad that the water was so warm.

"My parents were settlers in Gaza, my lady. I was born there. The village is in the shadow of the Temple, and the knights garrisoned there guard our boundaries. My parents grew grapes for wine. They had come to Outremer because my mother could no longer bear the cold." He recited this like a lesson learned and she guessed that his parents had died tragically.

Christina smiled. "I will guess that you liked to watch the

knights, from the time you were very young. I know I did, when I was home."

"There were knights at your home?"

"Aye, my father always employed several. When I was a little girl, I thought them wondrous."

Stephen's face lit then, his shyness banished by enthusiasm. "Aye! Such horses! Bigger than any others and stepping so proudly. Such armor! It shone in the sunlight like it was made of silver. They fought so bravely on our behalf, like angels come to defend us." His expression changed then and he looked away, biting his lip.

Christina crouched down beside the boy. "But one time, they did not do as much," she suggested softly.

"It was not their fault." Stephen scrubbed at his eyes before any tears could fall. "The village was attacked by Saracens, just before the dawn. I was asleep until I heard..." His voice caught, but he frowned and continued with a persistence that reminded Christina of Wulfe. "My mother had already gone to tend the grapes. It was the harvest and a good one. There was much to be done before the grapes spoiled."

"And so she was alone, thinking herself safe when she was not."

He nodded. "As soon as the hue was raised, my father ran to her, but he was too late. The knights rode from the Temple and won the day." Stephen straightened. "By evening, I was an orphan, and the master took me under his care." He met Christina's gaze. "They fed all the orphans at the priory, by command of the master, until homes could be found for us. No one chose me, though, so after a year, the master said I should learn to be Wulfe's squire that I might earn my way."

"And is he good to you?"

Stephen stood tall. "There is no better knight, my lady."

"And Simon?"

"He was an oblate, my lady, left on the porch of the Temple after his birth. It is against the rule for the order to take infants and children into their care, but the master said he refused to watch a child starve."

"He sounds like a good man." This master sounded like a man who understood the challenges of his area and the need for concessions. She supposed he was the same man who had ignored Wulfe's relief of his carnal needs and respected that he had not enforced a rule that would only lead to hardship. Knights with compassion in their hearts were the most admirable of all, in her view.

"Aye, my lady. Simon sorted beans in the kitchens, to ensure there were no stones, then helped in the stables, too. After I had been squire for a year, the master decreed that my knight had need of a second squire."

Christina could imagine how Wulfe might have responded to that, though he had no choice but to follow an order. "And was Wulfe pleased by this?"

Stephen considered this. "He does not talk much, my lady, but he is a good teacher, and he is fair. I know that more than once, we two ate meat when he did not."

"For there was not sufficient?"

Stephen nodded. "He said it was his fast day but I fear that might have been untrue."

"So, he must like having two squires."

"I think in the beginning, he had doubts, my lady, but Simon and I try our best to show our merit."

"I am certain that you do." Christina smiled and the boy beamed at her, then bowed again.

"Your water will become cold, my lady," he counseled.

"Indeed, and that will make a waste of your effort to bring it hot. I thank you for sharing your tale, Stephen," she said and meant it, for she had seen yet more kindness in Wulfe's history with these boys. It seemed he had learned more from the old man than from his father, and she was glad of it. "I would wager that the master of the Gaza priory chose well for you both."

"I, too, my lady." He bowed again then left the chamber, closing the door quietly behind himself. Christina followed him and locked the portal, savoring the weight of the key in her hand, then went to the window.

Stephen conferred with Simon in the courtyard below, then the pair of them went into the stables, presumably to tend Wulfe's steed. She considered the room, feeling blessed by its simple solitude and this precious privacy. She had not jested to Wulfe about the merit of a reprieve, although now that it was her own, she found herself appreciating it more than anticipated. She shed her garb and washed, even while thinking what she could do for Wulfe in return. There was one obvious feat, but she would give him more than pleasure.

Clad only in her shift, Christina removed Gunther's ring from her hem, deduced which direction was east by the sun, and prayed with fervor.

She had good reason to give thanks.

And much guidance to seek.

Christina was aware of the return of some party during her prayers and heard the laughter of the knight's lady wife and her maid as they mounted the stairs. The door slammed overhead and there were many footsteps back and forth across the floor. Christina recalled the dark-haired knight's comment that his wife's purchases had to be collected and could well imagine the scene in the chamber above.

It made her smile to remember returns from similar expeditions with her mother and sisters, and for the first time in years, Christina dared to hope she might see them all again. Were they well? Her situation had been hopeless for so long, but now her future held new promise.

Thanks to Wulfe.

By the time she concluded her prayers and kissed the ring, Christina knew what to do. She dressed quickly, intent upon gathering as much information for her reluctant champion as possible. The stables might be the best place to learn of the house's guests, for the boys would know much of their knights and lords.

She eyed the wretched girdle for a long moment, wanting to discard it.

But she was not safely out of Venice yet and did not even know who owned this house or labored in its kitchens. There might be those employed in the stables who lived here, or others might make deliveries to the house and catch a glimpse of her. That would be bad enough but without the girdle, she would pay a higher price.

After all, every soul in the house would have heard her earlier declaration of her status, for all would have listened to the argument in the courtyard. If she shed the girdle or hid it now, her plan to abandon her trade might be perceived. Who knew whether word had already been dispatched to Costanzia of her location. Christina locked the girdle around her waist with a grimace, then turned at the sound of activity in the courtyard.

Wulfe, she knew, had already departed. She saw now that any scheme to speak with the squires would have to wait, for Fergus called to the boys. "Stephen and Simon! Duncan and I have need of your assistance. Laurent is still too weakened from the voyage to aid with provisions, and Hamish must rest. Come with me. Wulfe will be glad that you can be of use."

"Aye, sir," the boys agreed in unison and followed a taller fair-haired boy. Fergus ushered them out to the street and shut the wooden portal behind them, leaving the courtyard to fill with silence.

Christina stared out the window. Who remained in the house? She had not seen the dark-haired knight leave or his squire, but they might have done as much. Where had the man she feared to be Helmut gone? And what of the plump little merchant who sought to ingratiate himself? She heard a whisper overhead and recalled that the knight's lady had the chamber above. Surely her maid was yet with her?

She drew nearer to the window, wondering why the women whispered. Though she could hear the sibilants, she could not discern their words. Was that the sound of footsteps overhead? Christina had no doubt that she heard the door on the floor above open, then stealthily close.

She moved silently across the room and bent to peer through the keyhole. The maid descended, and even a brief glimpse of her gave Christina the impression that the girl was agitated. She carried a bundle of a size that would fit into a saddlebag.

Perhaps these were the lady's old garments. Did she mean to

discard them after gathering her purchases? If she meant to give alms to beggars, Christina would not have minded a kirtle that did not look like the garb for a whore. She watched with interest as the maid disappeared down the stairs. She might have followed, to ask the girl after a dress, but her impulse was to remain hidden.

It made no sense to be covert about giving alms.

Aye, she had a sense that something was afoot. Christina returned to the window, ensuring she remained out of sight when she saw the maid appear in the courtyard.

The maid paused on the threshold of the roofed area used as a stable and called a greeting. The roof cast shadows over the space, although there was no wall on the courtyard side. The first few feet of the stables could be seen, then there were shadows behind.

"Hoy there! Is anyone about?"

"I am left to watch Hamish," a small voice replied and Christina saw movement to one side. There was a boy there, huddled in the hay, hugging a saddlebag.

The maid chatted with such animation and made such a fuss over the steeds that Christina knew she meant to hide some truth. But what?

Then Christina heard the door on the floor above open again. A quick peek through the keyhole revealed that the lady herself descended, her manner furtive.

The maid cried out suddenly. "Hamish! Mother of God, what is amiss?"

Christina returned to the window in time to see the maid disappear into the shadows. She had dropped that bundle in her dismay and it sat in the sunlight, abandoned. "Laurent! Quickly! You must aid me!" the maid declared. "Oh, *Hamish*!"

Christina saw the boy start, then disappear into the shadows in pursuit of the maid.

To her astonishment, the noblewoman from the chamber above then hastened across the courtyard. This must be Lady Ysmaine. She seized the bundle dropped by her maid, then moved to the spot the boy had vacated. She wore a long cloak, despite the warmth of the day, a fact that Christina only now found curious.

It was also vexing, for Christina could not discern what she did.

"He had a convulsion before my very eyes!" the maid cried. "Mother of God, what shall we do?"

The boy mumbled a reply that Christina could not discern.

What did Lady Ysmaine do?

"But this manner of illness is deceptive," the maid insisted. "I saw it once in a man brought to my mother. He twitched in his sleep, shook and thrashed, then choked on his own bile."

"Nay!" protested the boy.

"Aye. Hamish must not be left alone, not for a moment."

"But what shall we do?" Now the boy's voice was rising in fear.

In that moment, Lady Ysmaine departed hastily from the stables, leaving the saddlebag where the boy had been and replacing the maid's dropped bundle.

Christina bit her lip, guessing neither bundle was as it had been. The noblewoman raced across the courtyard, moving silently but with speed, and flung herself into the common room. But a moment later, Christina heard her quiet footfalls on the stairs.

"You must watch him closely," the maid instructed. "I will fetch my lady, for she knows something of these matters."

"But what will I do if it happens again?"

"Hold fast to his hand and speak to him."

"But I have to fetch the baggage of my lord knight. I cannot leave it unprotected."

"Fetch it now, then, and I will hold his hand. Be quick!"

The boy retrieved the saddlebag he had been guarding, then retreated into the shadows anew. The maid marched out of the stables with purpose, calling for her mistress. She swept up her abandoned bundle as she passed, then carried it toward the house.

Overhead, the door slammed and was audibly locked. Lady Ysmaine hummed as she descended the stairs more noisily, acting as if this was the first time she left the chamber. The two women's paths met below.

"My lady! Hamish has had a fit!" declared the maid, and the noblewoman responded with horror. "He has need of your assistance in this very moment."

"Truly!" A key flashed in Ysmaine's hand as she passed it to the maid. "I bought some lavender this very day to soothe my own sleep. Fetch it for me, if you please, for it may be of aid to him."

"Of course, my lady." The maid hastened to do her lady's bidding, her feet pounding on the stairs.

When she descended, she carried no bundle.

Christina considered the key that Wulfe had left her. Did she dare to hope that all locks within the house were opened by the same key?

She wanted to know what was in the bundle Ysmaine had locked in her chamber, that much was certain. Indeed, she had no doubt that Wulfe would be interested, as well.

Wulfe felt exposed.

How had Christina perceived the part of his tale he had never confided in anyone? The sole person who knew the truth was his father, and Wulfe knew that man would never acknowledge him. The old man was dead and could tell no one, even if he knew the truth. Wulfe assumed his mother was dead, but truly, did not care about her fate, given that she had abandoned him.

Yet, Christina had spied the truth. Had he given some hint or inadvertently revealed himself? Who else would hear of his history? She had pledged to keep his confidence, but to have his secret revealed was troubling.

He told himself that it made no difference. Christina could not guess his father's name, and she could not compel him to return to the place he had sworn to never go again. In merely two days, their paths would part forever, and no one would have interest in her tale of his origins.

Still. Wulfe shuddered and tried to shake off a sense of foreboding.

He had lied to the order upon joining its ranks, and if that falsehood were revealed, he might be cast from their gates. On the other hand, he might be dispatched to his father to plead for a donation. Nay, it was far better that the baron believed him dead.

Far better that he was fatherless himself.

The old man had been a better parent to him, to be sure.

As he gave direction to the boys, Wulfe wondered for the first time in years about his mother. Had she been mistress or whore?

Had she been a courtesan? Had she, like Christina, been left with few choices?

Had she, like Wulfe himself, done what was necessary to survive? If so, perhaps she had chosen herself over her infant son. Perhaps he had judged her too harshly. What of the baron's wife? Had she been dead? Or had she known of her husband's infidelity?

In truth, such matters had naught to do with him any longer and were best forgotten. Wulfe felt the need for action, though, to push such notions from his thought, so he left the house. The boys were instructed to continue with their labor, and he walked out alone.

He would explore this city until the time he met Gaston. It was said to be full of marvels, after all, and when he passed through Venice again on his way back to Outremer, he certainly would not linger. He would ride hard in an effort to make up the time lost with this company.

Determined to ensure the delay had some merit, he visited the basilica, reputed far and wide for its beauty. It was elaborately decorated to be sure, and the mosaics were a marvel, but Wulfe noticed the number of ragged urchins begging in the streets. He could not readily tell whether they were boys or girls, but they were painfully thin, their eyes too large for their faces. He found himself wanting to make a difference to these children.

"Where do you find shelter and food?" he asked of one who followed him with dogged persistence. He spoke in the local dialect, though his speech was halting for its unfamiliarity. The child shook his head, though Wulfe knew he had been understood. He held up a penny. "Where?"

The child snatched for the coin but Wulfe stood up, holding it out of reach. "You may have it when you show me."

The child ran then, moving so quickly that Wulfe might have lost sight of him, had the child not doubled back repeatedly to ensure that the coin was not lost. He led Wulfe to a poor part of the city, where the streets were narrower and the smell of the canals was stronger. The child knocked on a heavy portal then ducked behind Wulfe. Wulfe felt him fingering the hem of his mail tabard.

A tonsured monk opened the door, his surprise at the sight of Wulfe more than clear. His gaze dropped to the boy and he smiled in welcome, an indication that the child was familiar. He eyed the insignia on Wulfe's tabard, then inclined his head. "May I be of assistance, brother?" To Wulfe's relief, the monk spoke the French dialect he knew best from Paris.

"He says you give them food and shelter," Wulfe said and the monk ran a hand over his brow.

"As much as we can, brother," he said, his voice weary. "Though it seems each day, there are more children in this city. I am Brother Franco." A cat the color of soot wound around his ankles, mewling, her eyes a clear green. Wulfe noted that neither she nor the monk were plump.

Wulfe opened the purse containing his own funds and gave his remaining coins, save three pennies, to the monk. He had several commitments yet to pay or he would have surrendered it all. He still had the funds provided by Brother Terricus in Jerusalem for the costs of this journey to Paris, but that coin was not his to distribute as he chose. "Perhaps this will enable you to do more." The monk blinked in surprise, but Wulfe turned to give one of the remaining pennies to the boy. "As promised," he said. "I thank you for being such a good guide."

The boy clutched the penny, his delight no less than that of the monk with his donation. His gaze danced between the two men.

"I thank you greatly for this," the monk said. "Might I ask your name, that you might be included in our prayers this night?"

"Brother Wulfe."

"And so we shall sing a mass for you, Brother Wulfe."

"I thank you for that."

The monk made to reply, but the child stepped between them. He offered the coin to the monk. "I do as the knight does and give alms," the boy said.

"For you would be a knight one day, as well," the monk said with an affectionate smile. "May you be so blessed for your generosity, Pedro." He ruffled the boy's hair. "Go and tell them in the kitchen that you are to have one of the buns fresh from the oven."

Pedro hooted as he ducked around the monk and the cat trotted after him. The monk gestured to the room behind him and Wulfe glimpsed a courtyard beyond. "Will you come in and see all we do?"

It was Wulfe's nature to remain aloof from such intimacy and to decline similar invitations. He was curious, though, and accepted on impulse. "I should be honored to witness such good work. Have you fellow brethren here?"

"Aye, it is a small house, with only five of us. We live simply and allow as many children as possible to sleep under our roof each night. Brother Xavier has a talent with herbs, so he tends injuries as well as he can with the herbs he grows here..."

Wulfe followed the monk, listening to his explanations, intrigued by the peaceful nature of the monk's abode. The garden was lush with herbs and there was a small well in the midst of the courtyard. He could smell fresh bread and was surprised by the number of cats. He glimpsed a chapel to one side, a beeswax candle burning steadily on the altar, then was welcomed into the kitchen.

The brothers were amiable and visibly impressed that he had traveled from Outremer. Pedro sat beside him, eating warm bread and cuddling a cat, as Wulfe told them of the losses at Hattin. He sensed that several of the brothers had been fighting men before joining the order, for they listened avidly.

"And you ride to Paris to inform the order of the need for men to save Jerusalem?" asked Brother Franco.

"I ride to Paris to tell the Grand Master of what transpires," Wulfe said. "There is great fear that by the time of my return, Jerusalem will be lost."

"But that cannot be!"

"Surely that is not God's will!"

"There are not enough knights to defend it," Wulfe said, his tone pragmatic. "Saladin would be a fool not to attempt to gain the Holy City."

"And he is no fool," murmured one of the monks.

"Not in matters of war," Wulfe acknowledged. "He knows the land and he has a considerable army sworn to him. They were poised to take Acre as we departed, which happened the next day, by the reports we hear here."

"These are bad tidings," Brother Xavier said. "Do you travel alone?"

"Nay, the Grand Master assembled a party, including some pilgrims desiring to return home while they could." Wulfe frowned, seeing a potential solution to Christina's situation. "Among them is a woman, widowed and left destitute while on pilgrimage," he said, editing the tale. "I fear she has few prospects at home, either. Is there a religious house in this city, perhaps like this one, that might welcome her?"

The monks shook their heads as one. "There are nigh as many impoverished women as children, Brother Wulfe," Brother Franco confided. "The religious houses here are overwhelmed. They take novices only from affluent families, those who can bring a large donation to see them sustained or connections with the local nobility that can do the same."

"It is the brothels who take the other women," contributed an older brother. Wulfe thought his name was Matteo. "And God save their souls once they enter such places."

"How so?"

"They are confined if they earn coin for the house and cast out if they do not," Brother Franco said. "There is no escape, save by death or injury so foul that they can provide such services no longer."

"Take this woman away from this city," urged Brother Xavier. "It is your duty to see her safely away from its perils."

Wulfe bowed his head, thinking of this.

"You fear to break your vows," Brother Franco murmured with understanding. "But the greater good must be served, Brother Wulfe, sometimes by endangering ourselves." He laid a lined hand over Wulfe's own. "God only grants a test to show us the fullness of our strength."

Wulfe wanted to believe the older monk. He wanted to ensure Christina's safety. He glanced around himself and saw that these monks gave all of themselves to assist their young charges.

Surely he could do the same?

Surely he could resist temptation for the sake of the greater good?

CHAPTER SEVEN

ady Ysmaine had stolen a reliquary.

Indeed, it was a treasure of such magnificence that Christina could only stare at it, stunned. She had thought that the bundle must contain some token of value, but when she pushed back the cloth and saw the gold studded with gems, she was astonished.

Christina did not dare to unwrap the treasure fully, for she knew the lady and her maid would not linger in the stables and she dared not be caught. The area revealed, about the size of her palm, was more than sufficient to make her heart race. The amethysts and sapphires were each as large as her thumbnail and she could feel that the surface was covered with gems of similar size. It was large then, large and richly adorned. She could see the end of the inscription.

Euphemia.

That told her all. Christina held a reliquary containing the holy relics of Saint Euphemia. Her heart beat so hard that she was almost dizzy. This had to be the prize sought by the villain! She could not even guess the price that such a treasure would command.

Of course, it should not be sold.

Her hands trembled as she ensured the prize was wrapped as it had been. She left the noblewoman's room with haste, locking the door behind herself, then scurrying down the stairs with a pounding heart. Once she reached the door of Wulfe's room, she repeated the lady's feint, slamming the door and locking it audibly, then descending to the common room more noisily.

She even hummed, as the lady had done.

There was no one in that room to witness her arrival, though Gaston's wife was crossing the courtyard with purpose in her step.

"Is something amiss?" Christina asked, expecting to be ignored.

To her surprise, the lady did not ignore or disdain her. Indeed, she forced a smile. Her gaze did flick to the stairs, and Christina guessed that she wanted to check on her secreted prize. She lingered for a moment, though, doubtless in an attempt to disguise her impulse.

And protect her secret.

"One of the boys fell and struck his head the other night. My maid just saw him have a convulsion."

"The poor boy! Can I be of aid?"

The noblewoman hesitated as if uncertain what to ask. "I have awakened him, and he seems to be improved, but he must rest to heal fully."

"Then I shall tell him a tale to entertain him."

"Indeed? Do you know tales fit for young boys?"

Christina fought a smile at the woman's skeptical expression. "I will tell him only the tales of saints' lives, my lady. They sufficed for me when I was young."

Ysmaine's relief was visible. "And so they will be good for him. I thank you for the offer." Once again, her gaze flicked to the stairs and back, but she compelled herself to hold her ground. "I fear we have not been introduced. I am Lady Ysmaine, the new wife of Gaston, Baron of Châmont-sur-Maine."

"I am Christina." She curtseyed, impressed that Ysmaine had acknowledged her. It was a fine change not to be judged so harshly for her choices. "I am delighted to make your acquaintance, my lady."

"I thank you for the offer to entertain Hamish. It is so difficult to convince boys to remain abed when their condition improves." Ysmaine's words fairly fell over themselves, and she did not await a reply before she continued past Christina.

Christina appreciated that the lady made no comment about her skills in keeping men abed. She smiled at the sound of Ysmaine running up the stairs. She would find her prize untouched, though.

Did the lady steal the treasure for herself?

Or did she try to ensure its protection? Christina had no doubt that this was the prize entrusted to Wulfe's party, and perhaps the entire reason for the party's departure from Jerusalem. She had heard plenty of the riches of the Templar treasury, and this was no small prize. She knew the tale of Euphemia well enough.

Could it be that the Templars had retained the lost relic of that saint's head? Many miracles had been attributed to Euphemia's relics before all had been cast into the sea five hundred years before. Although some of the relics had been regained and were held in Constantinople, the head was said to be lost. If the Templars held it, this treasure might well be the prize of their reputedly large collection.

It would make sense to them to send it to Paris to ensure its safety if they feared Jerusalem would be taken by the Saracens.

Did the knights in the party know what they defended?

Fergus returned with the boys then, all of them carrying goods and chattering. The small boy told him of Hamish's fit, and he hastened toward the stables with concern. The mercenary Duncan noted her in the doorway of the common room and bowed, but Christina followed Fergus with purpose. Fergus was demanding the fullness of what had transpired. It was clear that the small dirty boy did not realize the prize in his custody had been claimed, for he held fast to it still.

Or was the story other than she assumed? It had been Fergus' squire who defended the prize. Had Fergus acquired the relic in the Holy Land, by means legitimate or otherwise? Did he take it home as a souvenir? She had a difficult time attributing such a theft to that charming knight, but appearances could be deceiving.

After all, if its delivery to Paris was a Templar quest, then the relic should have been in Wulfe's possession.

Or had Wulfe entrusted it to Fergus, knowing that knight's baggage to be so much more fulsome that it would be readily disguised?

Why had the lady Ysmaine claimed it?

Who else knew of its presence?

Christina had more questions than answers, to be sure. If the unnamed nobleman was truly Helmut, his presence in the party suddenly made more sense. Aye, there was a man who would do any deed to serve his own avarice. If he knew of the reliquary, she had little doubt he would endeavor to make it his own.

She needed to know more before telling Wulfe of her suspicions. The knights were unlikely to confide much in her, and Wulfe would not be readily convinced to surrender any secret he was charged to defend. The lady Ysmaine would never confide in a whore. Her maid might share her views, if Christina befriended her.

But she would take this opportunity first to find out what the boys knew.

She smiled at Duncan, who had sauntered across the courtyard behind her. Now he lingered on the threshold of the stables, watching. "The lady Ysmaine told me of Hamish's state and thought he might like to hear a story," she said.

Duncan's eyes twinkled, but he merely inclined his head in agreement. "A fine notion."

How much did he know of matters? He was perceptive, to be sure, and Christina might have spoken more to Duncan, if she had not guessed that he would desire some token in exchange.

Without doubt, he would request the very thing she preferred to surrender to Wulfe.

Wulfe walked back toward the basilica, considering the counsel of the monks. The streets were thronged with people and he made slow progress. Of course, he had not told them all of Christina's story, but what they had confided in him made him believe he should do as she asked and escort her from the city. If their party remained together, she would be but another pilgrim in their ranks.

Surely, he could travel with her and not be seduced by her charms?

He returned to the stall of an armorer, who had been entrusted with the repair of the hilt of his dagger. The man recognized him immediately—recalling Christina's words to Wulfe of how distinctive he was in this city—and presented the blade with a flourish. Wulfe examined the work and complimented the armorer on his skill. He felt someone's gaze upon him but paid the artisan before he glanced up.

Gaston watched him from a distance.

Had he truly put that knight in danger?

Gaston indicated that he would enter the square in front of the basilica and Wulfe gave a minute nod of understanding. He completed his transaction, sheathed the repaired blade, then made his way in that direction. He spied Gaston immediately, looking out over the sea at the far end. He meandered as Gaston did, covertly watching his companion.

When Gaston turned down a street, Wulfe strolled in the same direction. He caught a glimpse of Gaston ahead and pursued him, noting how the other knight increased his pace. Long moments later, he entered a plaza that was apparently abandoned.

Save for Gaston leaning against a wall in its shadow. There were few windows facing this square, perhaps because the wind from the sea was crisp, and those windows that did exist were high in the walls and shuttered against wind and sun.

"Followed?" Gaston murmured when Wulfe stood beside him.

Wulfe shook his head, but they waited a few moments just to be sure. No other soul appeared.

"It defies belief," he said quietly, beginning with the last conclusion they had shared. He was not certain that Gaston would welcome any accusation against members of their own group. "Our party is yet followed, even though no ship departed Acre after ours."

"I am not convinced that we were followed from Acre," Gaston said. "The baggage was searched on the ship, after all."

Wulfe recalled that detail well. "Do you think someone seeks the treasure entrusted to us?"

"I think someone in our own party is curious, if not more." Gaston drummed his fingers. "Did you catch any glimpse of your assailant?"

Wulfe shook his head and summarized events of the night before. "I thought the establishment meant to rob me, as can occur, but the floor creaked as the intruder entered."

"One unfamiliar with the room, then."

Wulfe agreed. "I waited, feigning sleep, and finally saw the intruder, silhouetted against the window."

"Man? Woman?"

"Tall enough to be a man, but otherwise impossible to be sure. He or she wore a voluminous cloak."

"A thief, then."

"A thief who went through my purse and garments, yet left the coin." Wulfe thought of the heavy purse granted by Brother Terricus. Though he kept it hidden, it would have been readily found during the villain's search of his garb.

Yet it had not been touched.

"And then?" Gaston prompted.

"And then, the flames. The oil from the lantern was spilled and set alight, the entire room quickly engulfed in fire."

"The intruder fled?"

Wulfe shook his head. "The intruder *lingered*, drawing back into the shadows of one corner."

"He or she wanted to see what you saved."

That had been Wulfe's conclusion as well. He continued his tale even as Gaston frowned.

"You saved the woman's life," that knight noted. "She speaks aright that this leaves her in your debt."

"I did what any man would have done."

"I think we both know that is not true," Gaston corrected. "More importantly, she knows it is not true."

"She should remain here." Wulfe felt obliged to insist. "There is no future for her with me."

"And what makes you imagine there is a future for her in Venice?"

Wulfe faced the other knight, surprised by the resignation in his tone.

"Women are not born whores any more than men are born knights," Gaston continued.

That was true enough.

"You smell of smoke," Gaston noted. "We must be alert to that scent on any of the others, or take note of any injury."

"You think the intruder is in our party." Wulfe was relieved that they had come to the same conclusion. "You believe that whoever pursued us in Outremer sought the missing girl mentioned in Acre by your ally, and not the root of our errand."

"I fear that is the only possibility that addresses all details." Gaston's expression turned somber. "And truly, what do we know of any in our party?"

"We were assembled by Brother Terricus..."

"On the basis of timing and convenience, as well as some urgency. The fact remains that we know precious little of our fellow travelers."

"I suppose this is true, but it is not unusual." Wulfe might be frustrated with his fellow knights, even if they had left the order, but he was disinclined to suspect them, given their military service. Let the perpetrator be the merchant Joscelin, Fergus' companion Duncan, Gaston's new wife, or one of the other men's squires.

"Even you and I know little of each other," Gaston noted with that annoying calm. "To be sure, I have heard of Brother Wulfe at the Gaza Priory and his black destrier, but we have never met."

Wulfe leaned back and considered that. "I could be a brigand who had assaulted him on the road and replaced him."

"Though the squires would have been difficult to find," the other man admitted with a smile. "And truly, I have heard sufficient of the Gaza brethren to doubt that you would have survived such a battle unscathed were you not the true Brother Wulfe." He raised a hand to gesture as he continued. "You can follow the same logic throughout our party. I first encountered Fergus a mere two years ago and have never served closely with him. The sole person in this company I can vouch for is Bartholomew, for I have known him since he was a boy."

Wulfe nodded. "And we know yet less of the merchant Joscelin de Provins."

"Save his repute."

"And of your lady wife."

Gaston winced and Wulfe knew his companion knight had considered that already. "At least we know Everard de Montmorency to be who he claims to be."

"Do we?" Wulfe asked, for he did not share that conviction. To be sure, he had heard of the man, but had never met or even seen him. He too might have been replaced by a brigand.

But Gaston shook his head. "He has been part of the royal court at Jerusalem for at least eight years as Count of Blanche Garde. I have seen him many a time at court."

So, Gaston could vouch for Everard. The list of suspects grew smaller. "Why did he leave Outremer, just as it faces its greatest challenge?"

"His father lies ill. He returns home as a dutiful son to say his farewell."

"But as Count of Blanche Garde, he has a holding, or did before he abandoned it."

"Perhaps he did not wish to witness its loss to Saladin. Perhaps, like many others, he yearns for the familiarity of home, despite his gains in Outremer."

Wulfe was skeptical. No man of sense abandoned a holding so readily as that, not without a fight. He could not imagine surrendering his fortune to sit at his own father's deathbed. "Perhaps there is something amiss that he did not remain to defend it, or ride out with King Guy."

"Perhaps he has not your taste for warfare."

"A man of wealth and privilege, who rides alone. I am reminded of a thief in the night, attempting to flee detection."

"If that were so, then he would have ridden north from Blanche Garde to Jaffa, and not troubled with Jerusalem or seek the defense of the Templars."

Wulfe was not convinced, but he doubted Gaston could be swayed. "I shall keep him on my list of suspects, even if you do not. Along with your lady wife."

"My wife is above reproach..." Gaston retorted, his voice rising.

Wulfe interrupted him with a reminder. "She acquired poison and confers often with the merchant Joscelin..."

"Who tries to gain a guarantee from her that she will buy spices from him once home in France."

"And who is always missing when matters go awry."

Gaston scowled, so Wulfe insisted upon his point. "They could be in league together and disguising their plotting as discussions over spice."

The other knight shook his head. "I shall not keep a list of suspects, for I believe no one can be put upon it with surety, save perhaps your lady courtesan."

"She is not my lady courtesan..."

"She argues otherwise."

"To have a courtesan or mistress would be defy my vows!"

Gaston's knowing smile did not ease Wulfe's annoyance. "While visiting a brothel did not?'

Wulfe straightened. "I would be gone from this place with all haste," he insisted. "Tell me that we need not await the welfare of a squire."

"We must, lest *we* appear to be thieves fleeing in the night." Gaston lowered his voice. "But that does not mean that our time in this city shall be wasted. Let us try to lure your assailant into making another attempt."

"Upon my life?" It was a better choice, to Wulfe's thinking, than to leave Gaston prey to assault because of his own comments that morning.

"Of course. You are the one who leads this party, after all."

Wulfe chose not to comment upon that. "You have a scheme?"

"A feeble one, but it might be effective. The villain believes you to be the leader of our party and thus the one charged with possession of the item he seeks. Your baggage was searched at Samaria, that of all the others in our party searched on the ship. Last night, I suspect you were followed and your more intimate belongings searched, again in a quest for some hint of the location of the prize. It may be clear to the villain that you do not carry it."

"And so?"

"What if you acted as a man bent on collecting it?" Gaston

dropped his voice and Wulfe leaned closer. "There are those in Venice oft used by the order for the safekeeping or sale of gems and precious goods. I would not threaten the security of any of them, but this practice is well known. After all retire this night, you might leave the house, as if keeping an assignation in secret. I will follow you, leaving sufficient space that the villain may lend chase."

"And that fiend will find his reckoning in the streets of Venice." Wulfe nodded. "I like it well, for this city is known to be violent at night."

"I will watch for your departure."

The two knights shook hands, then Wulfe left the square with new purpose. Aye, their journey would be much simpler if the villain could be revealed before they left Venice. That would give value to their lingering in this city.

Christina was aware of the way that conversation halted as soon as she stepped into the stables. Simon and Stephen were away from the portal, tending a massive black destrier that had to belong to Wulfe. A pair of palfreys were stabled near the warhorse, indicating that they also belonged to the Templar. She could see a dappled destrier and another of a deep chestnut hue with a star on its brow and white socks. Still another warhorse was so dark a brown as to be almost black.

She had a closer look at that small boy seated to one side, still clinging to a saddlebag like a barnacle. This squire of Fergus' was fairly lost in the shadows and looked even more thin and dirty at close proximity. He also smelled vehemently of dung. It was remarkable that she could tell as much while standing in a stable, but it was clear the boy had been filthy for a long time. He dropped his gaze when he noted her curiosity and hugged the baggage more closely.

He did not know its contents had been exchanged, then.

In the back and out of sight, some discussion fell silent. Hay crackled as someone crept closer to look at her, and she spied the blond hair of a squire as he peeked around the end of the last stall. It was the one with the blackened eye who had mocked her earlier.

Before she could speak, he disappeared.

Baggage was piled at the back left corner of the stable, and the trap for the horses was hung there, as well. There were buckets of water and of oats for the steeds, and the familiar smell of hay, manure, and leather that she remembered very well from home.

A dark-haired young man appeared a moment later from the same point where the blond boy had disappeared, moving with purpose until he saw her. He froze in place then and stared, though his disapproval was clear. Christina refused to be deterred and did not leave the stables, however much this man might have desired her to do so.

There were palfreys aplenty, in various shades of brown and grey, and Christina wondered whether they all traveled with Wulfe's party. She could not help but notice that they were more openly curious than either destriers or squires.

It seemed that the female of any kind was the one most likely to establish rapport.

"Well, good morning," Christina said to the first palfrey that stretched to sniff her outstretched hand. "You are a lovely creature. Have you a name?" She stroked the horse's nose, admiring the palfrey's white socks, aware that the boys and men watched her. She let them take a good look.

If they thought silence or disapproval would compel her to run away, they could think again. She had faced worse in her days.

"No name?" she mused. "What an oversight. Perhaps I should give you one."

"That is Bella," Stephen supplied, raising his voice a bit.

"And she is *bella*." Christina proceeded to the next horse, which was more curious given her attention to the first. This second mare sniffed Christina's palm, then closed her eyes with satisfaction when Christina scratched her ears. "Oh, and you like that. How long since your ears have been rubbed just so?"

The horse nickered with satisfaction, and Duncan chuckled. He remained in the doorway behind her, watching and listening. "You have a touch, lass, but then, who would be surprised by that?"

She smiled despite herself.

He nodded at the horse before her. "That is Vera, for she

knows the truth of any situation."

"Indeed?"

"Indeed. When she will not leave the stable, you can count on a storm breaking. When she breaks to a run, you had best let her flee for there is trouble fast behind."

"Then you are a clever horse, Vera," Christina informed the palfrey, who nickered and nodded in apparent agreement. "Whosoever rides you is fortunate indeed. I hope your warnings are heeded." The mare nibbled at her fingertips.

Stephen came to Christina's side and bowed. "Please meet Teufel, my lady," he said, indicating the black destrier with a gesture. She could not help thinking that he might have been introducing nobility at court for all the solemnity of his manner.

"Your master calls his horse a devil?"

"Teufel is most opinionated, my lady, and I understand was not in a hurry to be tamed to the saddle."

It was clear the creature did not lack confidence, and rightly so, for he was magnificent. His proportions were perfect though he was very large, and his coat shone like silk of a midnight hue. His mane and tail were long and brushed to a gloss. There was a gleam in his dark eye that spoke of determination and he stamped his foot with impatience even as she stood before him.

"Do you not like your name, sir?" Christina asked the horse playfully and the stallion exhaled. He surveyed her and his nostrils flared before he deigned to let her stroke his nose.

"He is willful, my lady, but loyal."

"Ah, so your master recognized a kindred spirit," Christina teased, but only Duncan chuckled. The other young man sniffed and made to leave the stables. "We have not been introduced," Christina said, stepping into his path.

He looked her up and down, his brow dark. "I am Bartholomew, the squire of Gaston."

Squire? And so old as this? Christina hid her surprise. "And I am—"

"I know what you are," Bartholomew said brusquely and stepped past her, leaving the stables with quick strides.

The small boy, the dirty one with the bag, inhaled sharply in disapproval, and Stephen dropped his gaze as if ashamed of his fellow. Bartholomew glanced only at the dirty squire before leaving. Were they friends? If so, it seemed an unlikely alliance. Perhaps the young man defended the smallest boy in the party.

If so, Christina would think better of him.

Christina smiled at Stephen to ease his discomfiture. "Do the other horses have names?"

The boy showed her the other horses and also introduced the squires. The one she had glimpsed at the back was Kerr, who served Fergus, though Christina did not like how quickly his gaze slid away. This one was not to be trusted, in her view. That blackened eye hinted that there was one other who took issue with him.

A second squire pledged to Fergus slept in the back of the stables, the freckles on his cheeks seeming unnaturally dark against his pallor. His hair was red and tousled.

"This then would be the injured boy," she said quietly to Stephen, who nodded.

Fergus was beside Hamish, his hand upon the boy's brow. "It is most strange," he said. "I would have thought you better, but for this report."

"I do not remember it, sir," Hamish said.

"You do not remember striking your head on the ship, either," Kerr noted, derision in his tone.

Perhaps Hamish *had* been pushed, just as he had not had a convulsion.

Stephen straightened beside her. "The apothecary decreed that he must rest through tomorrow, for he was struck upon the head just before we left the ship."

Duncan had followed them and looked down on the boy, bending to feel the heat of his brow in his turn. He exchanged a glance with Fergus, and Christina could only admire how protective they were of the boys entrusted to their service.

"Hamish will be hale in no time at all," Duncan said gruffly and the men straightened. "The blood of champions runs in his veins, after all, mingling with the spirit of the Highlands."

"Doubtless you speak the truth," Fergus said with a cheer that seemed forced. "Let me see if some soup can be found for you."

"Aye, my mother always insisted a good soup was the best," Duncan agreed, and Fergus departed with purpose.

Evidently encouraged, Hamish sat up and eyed Christina after bobbing his head in greeting.

"I was struck," he insisted again.

"Of course you were," Duncan agreed, though Christina was not certain he believed as much. When Hamish would have argued, Duncan raised a finger. "What is done is done, lad. You have only to recover."

Alarm flashed in the squire's eyes, and Christina wondered whether the boy feared to be left behind.

She could not help but notice that neither the squires nor Fergus paid much attention to the small boy tucked in the far corner with his bag. Of course, the stench of him was sufficient to bring a tear to one's eye. Perhaps that was the sole reason they shunned him.

Perhaps his dirt was not an accident. Christina felt a bit sorry for the boy.

She brushed off a bale of hay and took a seat, ensuring that Hamish could see her, then looked at the watchful boys. All she had to do was encourage them to confide in her. It looked like a difficult feat in this moment, but Christina smiled.

"When I was a girl, I went to the stables whenever I wanted to hear a tale," she admitted in a cheerful tone. "The ostler was a fine storyteller, and I knew he would always have one to share that I had never heard before."

"Always?" Kerr scoffed. "How many times did you go?"

"Hundreds," Christina said, holding the boy's challenging stare until he looked away. She would not be daunted by his impertinence, that was certain. "And doubtless he knew hundreds more. Whenever I am in a stable like this one, I think of that ostler, and remember how I loved his tales. That is why I suggested to Lady Ysmaine that I tell Hamish a tale, though you are all welcome to listen."

"Why should we?" Kerr asked, his manner insolent.

Christina smiled with deliberation. "Because I have invited you to do so."

"We are not supposed to speak with you, though," Hamish countered. The boys exchanged glances of reluctant agreement.

Christina nodded as if considering this. "I see. And you always do what you are bidden to do?"

Duncan bit back a smile at that, although the boys nodded.

"Aye, my lady," Stephen said. "We are charged to do our knights' will."

Christina shook her head. "Yet you are boys, and truly if you all are utterly obedient boys, then this must be the most remarkable gathering in all of Christendom." She lowered her voice to confide in Stephen, though the others surely could hear. "What makes boys endearing is their capacity for mischief and their frequent inability to do as they have been instructed to do."

Stephen colored and dropped his gaze as if she had caught him out. Hamish feigned sleep again, and Kerr busied himself with the hay. Simon checked the water for Teufel, which was both clear and plentiful. The small dirty boy appeared to be asleep. Duncan seated himself on a bale of hay, obviously entertained.

"I thought to tell you the tale of the saint you were named for, Hamish, but that is one tale I do not know. Instead, I will tell you of the saint I am named for. Saint Christina."

She was well aware of Duncan's amusement that she should tell the story of a saint, and of Kerr's smirk, but she told the tale to Stephen, perhaps her greatest ally in the stables. That boy continued to brush Teufel—who surely needed no more grooming, but the task ensured that the boy was close enough to both watch and listen to her. Christina did not think it an accident.

"Christina was born in Outremer, in Tyre, to a noble family."

"I have been to Tyre," Stephen said. "We rode there once with a missive from the master."

"How fortunate you are. I have not visited that place."

"The harbor was wondrous. It was the largest city that I had ever visited." Stephen glanced around himself. "Before this one."

Christina nodded. "This happened in the days of the Roman Empire, when most people believed in the pagan gods. Christina was extremely beautiful but her father wished for her to be a virgin in service to the gods. Since many men desired her and he refused to let her wed, he had her shut up in a tower with twelve of her waiting women to protect her chastity until that fate could be arranged. But Christina had heard the word of God, and had become Christian. She refused to sacrifice to the pagan gods and even hid the incense she was supposed to burn in their honor, rather than light it on the altar in the tower."

"She disobeyed her father," Stephen said, clearly uncertain whether to be horrified by her defiance or admiring of her faith.

"Indeed, she did." Christina noted that the small dirty boy had drawn closer, with his saddlebag, to listen. The boy hugged it close as he heeded her tale. "And the serving women were quick to report her transgression to her father."

"As more than one serving woman is apt to do," Duncan noted wryly.

"Her father was enraged by these tidings and came to challenge Christina himself. He feared that her decision would bring the wrath of the gods upon her and argued with her, insisting that she sacrifice to all of the gods lest any be offended. Christina vowed she would pray only to the Father, the Son, and the Holy Spirit. Her father could not understand why she would pray to three gods but not the rest, but Christina told him that these three were one, the Trinity and the godhead. He insisted upon his course, then left his daughter, certain she would be obedient."

"But she was not," the dirty boy guessed with some gusto.

Christina smiled at him, pleased that he both understood her and chose to reply. "She was not, for she believed her father to be in error. Indeed, she destroyed the idols of his gods that were upon the altar in her tower prison, ensuring that no one could worship them."

"And the maids told her father," Simon guessed.

"And he returned in fury. Perhaps he had doubted Christina's defiance, but when he saw the broken idols, he could not deny her deeds. He was resolved to correct her thinking, no matter what the price. He ordered her to be stripped naked by her maids, then summoned twelve men to beat her with all their might. When the men dropped from exhaustion, Christina challenged her father, saying that his gods should give his men new strength as God had given endurance to her. Instead, he had her bound with chains and thrown into a prison."

"He could do this to his own daughter?" Stephen asked, and Christina was pleased that he had so little experience of wickedness.

"No doubt he did worse," the small boy said grimly, his tone revealing that his history had been quite different.

"He did that," Christina admitted, then shrugged. "And yet more."

"He feared for her future," Duncan said. "As many a father does."

"But he was wrong," Simon protested. "He was pagan!"

"And yet convinced of his beliefs all the same," Duncan said gently. "I do not excuse his wickedness, merely note that it is natural for a man to wish for the best for his children."

He sounded weary, and Christina wondered whether Duncan had family himself.

"His motivation could be argued in this case," Christina noted. "For it was scarce good for Christina to be beaten and imprisoned." Duncan bowed his head in acknowledgment. "Her mother came to the prison and entreated Christina to do whatever was necessary to win her father's favor, but Christina knew that only one deed would do. She was adamant that she would not sacrifice to false gods. And so it was that her father ordered more punishment for her, thinking that pain would change her mind. Her flesh was torn from her body with hooks, but Christina threw the fallen pieces at him, challenging him to eat the flesh he had begotten."

The small dirty boy grinned at this.

"Her father then had her stretched on a wheel of iron and commanded a fire be lit beneath her so she might be burned to death. The fire, though, fanned out from beneath the wheel and killed hundreds of men who had gathered to watch, leaving Christina unscathed."

"I would like to have seen that," Kerr murmured, and Christina wondered which part of the tale intrigued him.

"Her father resolved that Christina must be a witch, then, for he could see no other reason for her survival than magic. He had her bound and a rock tied around her neck, then she was cast into the sea. All were certain she would drown, but angels came to her aid, lifting her from the sea in their arms. Christina saw Jesus Christ himself and was baptized by him in the waters of the sea. She was given then to the custody of the archangel Michael who bore her back to the shore with care."

Stephen sat down hard, his awe clear and his tasks forgotten.

"Christina's father was only more convinced of his daughter's evil magic. He called her a witch and she laughed at him, telling him that it was no sorcery that saved her but the blessing of Jesus himself. He sent her to prison, then, commanding that she be beheaded in the morning."

Christina smoothed her skirt, uncertain that all the details of her namesake's torture were relevant. The boys clearly enjoyed the violent details, but she would hasten to the point of her tale. "Christina's father died that night, but since she had been committed to the prison, a judge assumed responsibility for her punishment. He was as determined as her father to convince her to sacrifice to the pagan gods and to drive the sorcery out of her. He had her confined to a cradle of iron filled with burning pitch, but Christina praised God for her rebirth through baptism and said she was rocked like a new babe. The judge had her head shorn and insisted she be led naked through the streets to the temple of Apollo, where she would be forced to acknowledge that god. Instead, Christina called to God and the great statue of Apollo crumbled to dust before the eyes of all. The judge was so stricken by this sight that he died on the spot."

"I would like to see *that*," Hamish whispered.

"It might have been a trick," Kerr said, obviously trying to appear more worldly than the injured boy. Christina could not help but note he was listening to her tale as intently as the others.

"The next judge had Christina thrown into a large furnace built for the very task, where a massive fire burned hot. She walked around in this prison for five days, singing the praises of God with the angels, until the fire was mere coals beneath her bare feet. The judge was certain then that she was a witch and had adders, cobras, and vipers cast into the prison with her. The deadly serpents did not attack her but cleaned the sweat from her skin and licked her feet. The conjuror commanded to rouse the snakes was instead attacked and killed by them himself. Christina ordered the vipers to the desert, then raised the conjuror from the dead, upon which he asked to be baptized in Christ as well."

"I would like to see *that*!" Simon said. "A man raised from the dead."

Stephen frowned.

"But he was a conjuror," Kerr noted. "Maybe he was not really dead."

"I wish God would raise everybody from the dead," Stephen said softly.

"He does," Christina said to the boy, knowing he thought of his parents. "For he takes the believers into heaven for all eternity. That is where we will see our loved ones again, if our faith is true."

He nodded, encouraged.

Christina continued. "The judge was intent upon silencing this woman who won the support of more than his conjuror. He had her breasts sliced off, but milk flowed from the wounds instead of blood. He had her tongue cut out, but Christina flung it at him. It struck him in the face and made him even more angry. The judge shot two arrows into her heart and one into her side, piercing Christina through, and this maiden surrendered her spirit to God, true to the last. The year was 287, *anno Domini*." Christina paused before she continued. "And so it is that I bear the name of a woman whose faith could not be shaken, no matter what torment was inflicted upon her, and what indignity she was compelled to endure. Her faith sustained her through all."

Christina looked up in time to catch Duncan's thoughtful consideration of her, then the man-at-arms turned away. She wondered at what conclusions he had made about her.

She surveyed the boys, letting her expectation show. "Now, who has a tale for me?" She shook a finger at them. "It is only fair that each of you tell me one. You have just come from Outremer and surely have heard many fine tales there. Who will be first?"

CHAPTER EIGHT

ontrary to Wulfe's hope, it was not the villain who was revealed that afternoon.

Soon after parting from Gaston, Wulfe suspected he was being followed.

He hastened his steps, ducking down one alley and then another, losing track of his location in the blink of an eye. By the time he realized he was lost, he knew for certain that someone stalked his steps.

Wulfe also knew that he had made a mistake. The path he had most recently chosen bent hard to the right, only to reveal that it terminated in a canal.

It was but a heartbeat later that a large man strolled leisurely around the corner after him. Wulfe recognized one of the men who had guarded the portal of Costanzia's establishment the night before.

The look on his face revealed that he recognized Wulfe as well.

He was joined by a second man. His companion, if anything, was both larger and looked meaner. Wulfe retreated, only to hear a throat cleared behind him. He spun to see a third man of similar size step from a small boat into the far end of the alley. There was a fourth in the boat, but that man rowed the vessel out of sight. The man who had disembarked smiled at Wulfe.

It was not a friendly smile.

Wulfe glanced back to find the other two close behind them. Evidently they had moved more quickly than he might have expected to be possible. His hand dropped to the hilt of his knife, but they pulled their daggers in unison.

"We want only to speak with you," said the one Wulfe recalled. He let the blade of his knife catch the sunlight, a gesture which belied his words.

"There is no need to complicate matters," said the third one, compelling Wulfe to spin and glance back at him. He, too, had moved closer, and also toyed with his knife.

"We merely seek Christina," continued the first. "Do you know where she is?

Wulfe looked around and realized that he was in an alley with no windows. He could see no one but his assailants and he doubted any would hear him cry for aid.

Much less come to his assistance.

"Or maybe," suggested the second man in a low voice. "You need some encouragement to prompt your memory."

"Christina is so deeply missed," murmured the first, his tone making a mockery of his words. "We are charged not to return without her."

Wulfe heard the third man's footfall behind him just before that man dropped his hand on Wulfe's shoulder. "Perhaps you might be so kind as to assist us," he said with quiet threat, and Wulfe felt the point of a knife on his throat.

He had two knives, the one he always carried and the one the armorer had repaired, although he did not wear his sword. He could fight with both hands, although he would disguise that fact for as long as possible.

If God sent tests to reveal a man's strengths, Wulfe must have more hidden power than he realized.

More importantly, he had the funds granted by the Temple. He would not offer those coins readily, but if the choice was between his life and the Temple's coin, Wulfe knew he would decide in favor of his own survival.

But these men would not gain that prize readily, to be sure.

Christina waited an eternity for a response from the others in the stables. Just when she thought she might have misjudged her audience, a voice came from the far corner.

"I know a tale," said the small dark boy with the bag. "And like yours, it is of people who refused to be told what to believe."

Christina laughed. "Perfect! Come and share it with us, if you please."

Kerr winced. "No closer," he said and pinched his nose with a grimace.

"Laurent stinks," Stephen confided in a whisper.

"I assure you, the stable does not smell like roses," Christina noted.

"But Laurent..." Stephen fell silent then shook his head.

Meanwhile, the boy Laurent came a little closer, that bag yet in his grip. The scent of him doubled and redoubled, so the boy might have been a walking dung heap. Christina doubted that he saw much kindness, though, so she hid her reaction. Laurent sat down beside her and leaned against the saddlebag protectively. Christina had already noted that he was both small and slight. His skin was golden and he was finely boned. His eyes were dark and thickly lashed, giving him an exotic air.

Nay, a feminine air. She glanced at his face and his hands, peered at his proportions and was certain of the truth.

Laurent was a girl.

Who else knew?

"Surely you could loose your grip on your baggage?" Christina suggested but Laurent held it only tighter.

"My lord Fergus entrusted it to me as a test, my lady, and I will not fail him in this."

What would transpire when the boy discovered that the relic had been exchanged?

"Do you know what is in it?" she asked lightly.

"I suspect it is naught at all," Laurent confided. "For who would grant a token of any worth to my care, before I had proven myself?"

Certainly Laurent was not from Scotland. "But if you are Fergus' squire..."

"Only recently," Duncan interjected. "The boy joined us only upon our flight from Jerusalem, though he was familiar to us from the stables of the Templars."

"He knows much of horses," Stephen contributed.

"And more than that," Kerr whispered, earning dark glances from the other boys. "It is why he stinks," he said. "He sleeps in their dung."

Christina thought that was a good strategy to keep others from looking too closely. "I see," she said mildly. "I would hear your tale, Laurent, if you would share it."

Laurent's smile was elfin and charming. "Once upon a time, there was a group of good friends, all of whom believed in the true God. Like Saint Christina, they were chastised for not making offerings to false idols. Unlike Saint Christina, they chose to flee the city, in order to worship as they knew to be right."

Christina was intrigued by the tale. Had Laurent joined the party to flee Jerusalem? If so, why?

"And so they hid in the hills, taking refuge in a cave they discovered. Some say there were three of them, while others say they were five or even seven. All agree that a loyal dog accompanied them. They prayed in this place and God sent a blessing to them: He ensured that they all fell into a sound sleep. The dog slept, too, although it slept at the door to the cave, as if guarding them. They awakened later, believing they had slept but a day or so, and were hungry. One of them chose to go into the city and buy bread for them, and this was when they discovered the truth."

"What truth?" Stephen asked.

Laurent smiled. "The city had changed so much that this one of the companions scarcely recognized it. He thought his wits addled by hunger and tried to buy bread, but the baker would not take his coin. A hue and cry was raised, and a crowd gathered, for the coin was ancient and valuable. The baker thought this man must have stolen it, while others thought he had found a treasure and should share its location. As you might imagine, he was most confused by all of this."

Christina glanced around the stable, intrigued that Laurent held the attention of the others so easily, given their reactions to his presence.

"The crowd demanded that the man they believed to be a stranger prove his origins. The man gave his name and that of his parents, but no one knew of any of them. He cried out in vexation, for still they called him a liar, and demanded to be taken to a magistrate of the emperor. When he named the emperor who he knew ruled the territory containing the city, the crowd fell back in awe. He could make no sense of their reaction and asked what was amiss." Laurent dropped his voice. "The baker told him that emperor had been dead for centuries."

The boys caught their breath as one and leaned forward as one to hear how this marvel could be.

"The companions of the cave had slept for three hundred and nine years, by the will of God."

Christina frowned, for she knew a variant of this tale. It was told as that of the Seven Sleepers of Ephesus, but she had heard that the story had originated amongst the Saracens.

Was Laurent a Saracen, as well as a girl?

Wulfe stepped through the portal of the rented house, endeavoring to look composed but more shaken than he preferred. He paused for a moment, wanting to bar the door, but knowing that would only arouse the suspicions of the others given the hour. They did not need to know what had transpired.

Save Gaston.

It irked him mightily that he had been relieved of his favored dagger, particularly as he had just paid for its repair. The blade had been of fine Toledo steel, and he would miss it. It burned yet more that he would have to admit his failure to Gaston, but Wulfe knew it had to be done. He was not one to shirk an unpleasant task, although he would not savor the doing, to be sure. The fact was that Gaston had accumulated some wealth and could fund the journey. The Grand Master in Paris would repay him, for he would trust Gaston's accounting, and the others need not know the difference.

Wulfe ached from the blows inflicted upon him. Costanzia's men had broken no bones, for they had found the coin in time. They had not marred his face, either. To all appearances, he was but slightly disheveled.

In truth, he was more agitated than that, and not just from his injuries. The moment they had left him, he had doubted his choice. Should he have pursued them? Could he have secured the coin again?

What had halted Wulfe was the conviction that if he succeeded in regaining the coin, their retribution would be taken next upon Christina. He could not bear to think of her being injured. He also was skeptical that he could best his opponents, so quickly after having lost to them.

And so, it appeared he had bought himself a courtesan with the funds of the Temple.

Another man might have found the notion amusing, but Wulfe was appalled.

There was but one way to make this wrong right—he must not so much as touch Christina again. Only then could he argue that he had been robbed in defense of a pilgrim. Only if there was no personal advantage to be gained by himself could he hold up his head and confess to the Grand Master in Paris.

It was also the only way he could keep his position in the order.

Even that was more precarious a future than Wulfe might have liked. He would be reliant upon the good will of the Grand Master in Paris, a man he did not know, and also upon the testimony offered by Gaston.

How foolish that he had put himself in such a position of weakness.

Wulfe squared his shoulders and stepped into the courtyard, seeing that most of his fellow travelers were gathered there, in the common room, or in the stables. Gaston had returned before him and that man's eyes narrowed after he surveyed Wulfe.

Wulfe went to the other knight, contriving to appear as impatient as had been his custom. "And so?" he demanded. "Did you collect your wife's purchases?"

"Indeed." Gaston glanced upward. "She folds and packs them now."

"And how fares the boy? Do we ride out on the morrow?"

"The apothecary visited, for Hamish had a fit." Gaston rubbed his chin. "Yet it seems that if the boy's recovery continues, we might depart on the morrow."

"That is excellent news." Wulfe raised his voice. "I suggest all make preparations to depart in the morning, assuming, of course, that Hamish improves yet more." Everard retreated to the common room from the position he had taken on the threshold. Joscelin departed, destined for a friend's board for the evening. Still there were too many ears close by, and he would have to await a more private moment to confide in Gaston.

Christina came from the stables, granting Wulfe a smile of welcome that warmed him to his toes.

He had bought her.

Yet he could never touch her again, if he was to have a future.

If Wulfe had been determined to complete this journey to Paris with all speed, that desire for haste had just redoubled. A swift passage was the sole chance he had of keeping his resolve.

And that was a terrifying realization indeed.

Christina knew with a single glance at Wulfe that something had gone awry. He avoided both her gaze and her company. She had anticipated he might do as much, since he had only allowed her to remain with reluctance. The difference was that he seemed taut and alert, as if he had faced a threat since his departure this morn.

What had happened?

It was equally clear that he did not intend to speak to the others about whatever had occurred. He appeared to exchange no confidence with Gaston upon his return, although he did better at disguising that knight's true role. He was polite but aloof at their evening meal, not joining in the camaraderie of the company. Christina wished she knew whether this was unusual or not. She forced herself to appear at ease, but it was difficult given how much she wished to speak with Wulfe.

Instead, she endeavored to collect information and impressions.

She supposed she should not have been surprised that the meal was served as if they sat in some feudal lord's hall. They were seated by rank, both above the salt and below. Christina was relieved by this, for she was below the salt, and the man she feared to be Helmut sat at the very opposite end of the table. No man sat at either head or foot, but only along the sides. Gaston was opposite the nobleman, that knight's lady wife by his side. Wulfe sat beside the nobleman and opposite the lady, Duncan beside him and Fergus beside the lady Ysmaine.

Christina chose the last seat on the same side as Wulfe, which would keep her out of view of the nobleman, and allow her to covertly study Gaston's bride. The boys served at the table, with Bartholomew dispensing the fish stew, Stephen pouring wine, and Simon offering the bread that Kerr cut. It must be an austere meal for some in the company, but a lavish one for others. It certainly was a less sumptuous feast than Costanzia served to her patrons, but it was far better than the meals Christina had been granted with the other women resident in that house.

One of the boys had told the tale of Gaston's nuptials in the stables this afternoon, evidently relishing how that knight had saved the lady from her misfortunes. It seemed that Ysmaine and her maid Radegunde had been robbed but continued on their pilgrimage, only to find themselves destitute in Jerusalem when that city might anticipate an attack by Saracens.

The tale was too close to Christina's own for her to hear it with indifference. She suspected that none in the company realized the fullness of what Ysmaine's life might have become, if she had been compelled to make the same choice as Christina, and Christina could only be glad to know that this woman had escaped that fate.

Ysmaine herself was a beauty. She was at least five years younger than Christina, though said to have been widowed twice before wedding Gaston. Doubtless her beauty had driven that situation. She was petite and finely wrought, such a perfect contrast to Gaston that they might have been made for each other. Her manners were elegant and she was soft-spoken at the board, thanking her maid and deferring to her husband. There was something about her posture, though, that made Christina conclude that Ysmaine was not so fragile as she might appear.

Indeed, that woman had survived a considerable challenge.

Why had she taken the reliquary?

Christina had a difficult time believing ill of someone who had spoken to her with kindness. It seemed a small thing, to be polite, but she knew it was more than could be expected from most. She was inclined to think well of Ysmaine.

Once the boys had served the meal, they took their seats below the salt and ate with gusto. The fish stew was not so delicious that any other than the larger boys requested more. It was decent fare, but not the concoction of a skilled cook. The sauce could have had more spice, to Christina's thinking, but the ingredients were fresh and that was no small thing. The bread was plentiful, and the wine was much more thin than that served to patrons at Costanzia's abode. It was a more robust wine than what she had shared with the other women, though, and Christina sipped it with pleasure.

A mediocre meal was a small price to pay for another night of freedom.

But what about the morrow, when the party departed from Venice? Christina feared that Wulfe's changed manner could only be an indication of her own prospects. He meant to leave her behind. It was only a matter of time before she was found by Costanzia and forced back to that house. She did not want to imagine the beating she would be given, or how much less desirable her life would become. She had heard fearsome tales of how the defiant were reminded of their place.

She yearned to speak with Wulfe, but knew such a discussion must be held in private.

Christina endeavored to engage the others in conversation at the board, which was no small feat. The mercenary Duncan and his knight Fergus were cordial enough, but Gaston's wife spoke to her husband and her maid only. Gaston's squire was similarly unresponsive and Joscelin had left to dine with friends. She had not anticipated that she would miss the merchant's company but at least he spoke to her. The nobleman who so resembled Helmut did not so much as glance at her and she had yet to hear him called by name. He was the Count of Blanche Garde, which she gathered was a holding in Outremer.

Was she wrong about his true identity?

More importantly, where did Wulfe intend that she should sleep this night? With him, or not? Bartholomew was the first to rise from the board, and Christina watched as he filled two more bowls with stew. He nodded at Kerr as he picked up two crockery cups. That boy's lips tightened before he fetched a goodly quantity of bread and a pitcher of wine. They went to the stables together, such a silence and a space between them that Christina sensed they were not friends.

At least someone fed Laurent and Hamish.

When Wulfe rose from the board, Christina remained in place. To her surprise, he went through the courtyard to the kitchens and she heard his voice as he spoke to the women there. She could not quite make out his words, but there was some debate.

Did he settle the bill? Make arrangements for the morning? Christina could not imagine what errand he performed that could not be done by another.

He returned moments later, his brow dark, and strode up the stairs to his chamber without another word. Simon and Stephen finished their meals quickly, Stephen eating a final piece of bread so quickly that Christina feared the boy would choke. They followed their knight with water for bathing and another pitcher of wine. She knotted her hands together in her lap, waiting until Wulfe was alone.

As soon as she heard the boys in the corridor above, Christina excused herself and pursued Wulfe.

She had to know the worst of it.

Puttana.

Mona.

Wulfe knew the first word and he could guess what that the second one also meant 'whore' but in a less flattering way. Truly, even if he had not understood any word the two women in the kitchen had uttered, their expressions had made their meaning clear.

Not to mention the way the second had spit into the fireplace.

There would be no labor for Christina in this house.

Indeed, without his protection, she might have been chased into the streets this very day, for her occupation was clearly not in doubt. He recalled her conviction that she would be recognized and returned to Costanzia and understood only now how true that was.

He retreated to his chamber, considering his course. He could not abandon Christina in Venice, but could he escort her all the way to Paris? He should be able to do so, treating her as a pilgrim, but he feared his own weakness. He could not risk any scandal linked to his name, especially now that the coin of the Temple was lost.

He could not dismiss the thought that he had paid for her and should savor her.

The woman was temptation itself.

Was there some half measure that would see her saved but removed from his company sooner? Perhaps, once she left Venice, her past could be disguised and she could join a different company of travelers.

But how? She had no coin to pay her way and he had none to grant her.

So intently did he consider the issue that Wulfe barely spoke to the boys as they completed their duties. Stephen removed his belt and frowned that his scabbards were both empty. Wulfe ignored the boy's reaction and was glad he had not carried his sword on this day. That was a loss he would have sorely regretted.

Simon helped to remove his chain mail hauberk, then Stephen unlaced his aketon. Wulfe kept his features impassive, hiding any evidence of the aches he was beginning to feel. He declined further assistance, in case there were already visible bruises. He reminded the boys that they would likely depart in the morning, so they had best be prepared to ride out.

Wulfe was not truly surprised when Stephen opened the portal to reveal Christina outside it. He knew this discussion was inevitable and reminded himself of his resolve even as it faltered. She was not just beautiful, but strong and vulnerable. The sight of her awakened a chivalry Wulfe had not known he possessed and made him yearn for what he had always known could not be his own.

He was a Templar knight. A warrior and a monk. The order was his past, his present, and his future.

The boys ducked past Christina as she studied him with obvious expectation.

"They will not let you remain here to labor honestly in the kitchens," he said by way of greeting. "I asked."

"I would not stay if they did," she countered, stepping into the chamber as Stephen reached the summit of the stairs. She smiled at the boy, then closed the door and leaned back against it. Wulfe was certain he could smell her perfume.

Though it might simply have been the scent of her skin. Either way, it sent fire through him. He averted his gaze, his mouth dry.

He frowned. "Do you not wish to leave your trade?"

"Of course, but I must leave Venice to do as much." She gestured. "They will find me and drag me back, upon that you may rely, and there will be no second chance of escape." She stifled a shudder and Wulfe could well understand her reaction.

"You do not have to go back," he said, without having intended to do as much.

She fixed him with a look, curiosity bright in her eyes. "Have you changed your thinking?"

Wulfe grimaced. "It was changed for me."

Christina watched him, waiting.

He grimaced and admitted the worst of it. "I will have to tell Gaston that I was robbed this day."

"Nay!" She fairly flew across the chamber, her concern evident. Her hands danced over him, moving as quickly and lightly as butterflies. "Are you injured? Were you wounded? Was it the villain from last night? How could that fiend still target you..."

"It was not the villain from last night." Wulfe held her gaze deliberately.

"But if you know who it is..." Christina fumed, then abruptly fell silent. The color left her cheeks, making her look fragile, and she took a step back. "Costanzia," she whispered.

"Not exactly. It was the guardian from the portal and two of his friends. The fourth kept a boat at the ready for their escape." Wulfe sighed and went to the window, where he tapped his fingers on the sill. He was simmering, keenly aware of Christina's presence and proximity. He reminded himself that he should be her defender, not her patron.

"They relieved you of all your coin." Christina was close behind him, for he could feel the heat of her presence.

He closed his eyes and wished for strength. "I chose and I am not proud of it." Wulfe closed his eyes when she gripped his arms and leaned her cheek against his back. He could turn around and have her in his arms. He could take one step and claim a kiss that would heat him for the entire night...

"You were wise," she whispered. "They have killed others without remorse."

"But I must lie about it as well." He winced at the truth of that. "The coin was not mine. It was granted to me for expenses that would be incurred on the journey west. I should have defended it to my last."

"Then you would have been dead and they still would have had the coin," she said with a pragmatism he appreciated.

When he did not reply, Christina ran her hands over him in a gentle but thrilling caress. She knew her trade, to be sure. Wulfe kept his back to her and fought his yearning for more.

"You judge yourself more harshly than any other soul would do, Wulfe," she whispered. Her hand slid down his side and he stiffened slightly. "Did they injure you?"

"A good beating, no more than that." He tried to be brusque. "I fared well enough, given that they were three."

"And they struck only where the bruises would not show. Some tendencies are never forgotten." Christina reached beneath his chemise before he could stop her, then her attentions were so welcome that he did not want her to stop. Her hands were so soft that he knew he would soon be seduced by such pleasure. He tried to step back when she pulled up his chemise, but Christina scolded him.

"Do not fuss so," she chided. "Simply stand still. I will not hurt you."

"That is not what I fear," he murmured. Their gazes locked and held, even as his heart pounded with greater vigor. A sparkle lit in Christina's eyes as she understood, and a flush touched her cheeks.

"Have you bought me, Wulfe?" she asked in a playful tone. "How should I reward such valor?" Her hand slid downward and Wulfe caught his breath as she caressed him.

"Nay, Christina. Do not do as much." Wulfe stepped back again, denying them both the pleasure he wanted. "What does *mona* mean?"

Her gaze became steely. "It is not polite."

"Tell me."

She stretched and whispered a word in his ear that he never thought to hear from a lady's lips. It was a crude reference to a woman's genitals, and Wulfe found himself shocked—not that the word existed, but that the women in the kitchen had used it so readily in reference to Christina.

She smiled at his outrage and quickly kissed his cheek, as if aware that she had to steal such a touch. His cheek burned at the point, the imprint of her lips making him clench his fists. "I have heard worse," she said lightly.

"As have I, but not from women."

Christina shrugged, her manner turning practical. "We are the most harsh judges of each other. Let me see your injuries. Costanzia's men are good at breaking ribs, and ribs should be tended sooner rather than later."

Wulfe found himself divested of his chemise, and Christina traced each rib in succession. Her touch was not seductive, yet he found himself enticed by her all the same. He liked that she was concerned for him. He liked that they could talk as if they were allied in this quest, though truly he had never spoken so openly to a woman before as he did with her.

He looked down at her, his chest tight with the reality of what she had endured. She knew how these men gave beatings. How many times had she watched them? How many such beatings had she endured herself? He both wanted to know and could not bear to ask.

The marvel was that, despite all Christina had seen and been compelled to do, there was an elegance about her. He could never have called her by either of those names. He found it hard to even call her by the more familiar ones. She had the manners of a noblewoman and he could not think of her otherwise.

Christina was so close before him, her hair falling over her shoulder in a gleaming braid, that Wulfe could not keep himself from lifting one hand and resting it upon her shoulder. His fingers curved around her and he acknowledged a desire to protect her, though he could do little about it.

What if he had been born to advantage? What if he had been a man with choices? Wulfe had never yearned for a different life before, but now he did with vehemence.

Christina spared him a smile then checked his other side, her fingers sliding over his skin in a way that made him wish she would never stop.

When she looked up at him, she was close enough to kiss. "You seem to be most resilient," she said. "I cannot find a break, though you will be bruised to be sure."

"A mail hauberk has its advantages."

"I suppose so. Your bones may have cracks, though so you should take care." Her gaze dropped to his lips and she smiled just a little, a secretive smile that made her eyes dance. "Perhaps it is just as well that you are so hale."

"How so?" Wulfe found his voice husky.

Christina's smile broadened as she turned, somehow ensuring that in one smooth gesture she was in his arms when she stood before him. There was but a finger's span between them but he could feel her heat and smell her arousal. Naught could have fed his own desire more than that beguiling scent.

She was the most alluring woman he had ever met.

Christina touched her lips to his throat and Wulfe closed his eyes as his resolve melted. He was alive and he wanted to celebrate that fact. He wanted to celebrate his survival, and her freedom, with Christina.

One kiss, Wulfe resolved. He would allow himself one kiss. Surely there could be no harm in that.

"You will have need of your strength," Christina whispered against his skin. "As I mean to reward you this night for your deed."

"What deed?" Wulfe murmured as her kisses burned a path toward his lips.

"You bought me," she replied, her breath making him shiver. Her hand slid down the length of him, then made quick work of the laces on his chausses. "And such an investment must be rewarded."

There it was: the unwelcome acknowledgment that this was a transaction, just like every other transaction she had made in this city. Wulfe found himself wanting far more.

Indeed, Christina's summary of the situation restored his lost resolve.

Wulfe stepped back, putting distance between them, and forced his tone to be resolute. Officious, even. "There is no reward due. You are a pilgrim who will be escorted from this city, and I will perform my duty in this." He expected her to be insulted that she was so rebuffed, but should have anticipated by now that Christina would surprise him anew.

"Truly?" she demanded, her expression alight with pleasure. "You will allow me to remain in your party? You will escort me out of Venice?"

Her excitement made her, if anything, more enticing than she had been when bent on seduction. Wulfe shook a finger at her, sensing that he would lose this battle. "I escort you as a pilgrim and naught else. There will be no relations between us, for I cannot risk the loss of my place in the order..."

He managed to protest no more before Christina flung herself at him with a laugh of delight. "You truly are my champion!" she declared. "I knew it would be so!" Wulfe lost his balance and they fell back together on the pallet, the lady atop him. He could not protest his state, not when her eyes shone with such delight.

Not when she kissed him so soundly.

Not when it was Christina herself who finally embraced him. She was astride him and framed his face in hands, but her eyes had been clear. There was a new hunger in her kiss, an enthusiasm for the deed that she had not shown the night before. He knew it was the true woman who would seduce him. She wore no courtesan's mask, or performed an intimacy as she had been taught. Christina herself was with him.

His resistance crumbled to naught even before her lips closed over his own.

Then Wulfe was lost in her kiss.

For this one night, he had no wish to be found.

Wulfe would help her!

Christina wanted to ensure that the knight had no chance to regret his choice. There might be no other opportunity for intimacy after they left this house, so in this moment, on this night, she had to show her appreciation fully.

She straddled him, holding him captive to the kiss she was determined to give. She framed his face in her hands and kissed him with sweet ardor, endeavoring to show the magnitude of her relief with her touch. Wulfe was aroused, but he was tense, his hands balled into fists at his sides. She knew he intended to resist her, but Christina would not accept that response. She slanted her mouth over his and slipped her tongue between his lips, threading her fingers through his hair.

She knew the moment he surrendered to her. He shivered then sighed, his hands locking around her waist. His fingers fanned across her back and he pulled her closer. Then he rolled her to her back, his weight between her thighs, and kissed her with a potency that made her dizzy. She laughed when he lifted his head, glad to see his lips curved in a sensuous smile and his eyes dark with desire.

"You are indeed hale," she whispered, rubbing herself against his arousal.

"And you appear to be most ardent," he murmured. He looked a different man in this moment, at his ease and filled with humor, and her heart clenched at the sight. Wulfe unfastened her jeweled girdle and flung it across the room with satisfying force. It hit the far wall and clattered to the floor. Christine hoped it was broken beyond repair.

Her laces were unfastened with satisfying speed and her kirtle cast aside. She arched her back with pleasure at the feel of Wulfe's hands upon her. He was strong but gentle, firm but seductive. She had but a mere glimpse of a surprisingly mischievous smile, then he pushed up the hem of her chemise. His hands were on her thighs, and she thought he would caress her with his fingers. Indeed, she was so aroused that she did not know how she would bear such a touch.

When he closed his mouth over her, she gasped in surprise. "Wulfe," she whispered, knowing only the routine of granting pleasure and not that of accepting it. He was undeterred by her protest. Indeed, he spread his hands across her thighs and held her open to his wicked tongue.

Christina could only surrender to the pleasure he was determined to give. She fell back against the pallet and closed her eyes, her fingers still locked in his hair. He showed uncommon persistence in his chosen task, teasing her with his teeth and his tongue, coaxing her passion to new heights. Christina burned as she never had burned before. She felt savored and even indulged to be the focus of his attention.

Even as she moaned in pleasure, she noted the similarities in his technique to what she had been taught. He took her to the threshold of release then halted, the better to increase her ultimate satisfaction. He alternated between firm caresses and gentle ones, even grazing her with his teeth before he blew on that most sensitive part of her. Christina found her hips twitching on the pallet. Indeed, she writhed beneath his touch, parting her thighs wide like a wanton as she burned for the release that only Wulfe could give.

She was breathing quickly when he summoned the fever again, and she felt the flush heat her skin from head to toe. She was achingly sensitive to his touch, her blood simmering and her hands locked in his hair. She felt the passion rise, her heart thunder, her ardor increase...

Then Wulfe pulled back.

Christina cried out that he cheated her again. "God's blood, but you are a vexing man!" she muttered and he grinned. He braced himself on his elbows, his eyes dancing with merriment as he regarded her.

"Shall I halt?"

"Nay!" Christina declared. "You should finish what you have begun."

He laughed, his breath fanning the inside of her thighs. He closed his mouth over her again and she moaned his name at the glory of his intimate kiss.

"By Saint Felicity," she whispered, invoking the patron saint of barren women. If ever a coupling should create a son, it should be this one.

If Gunther had taken her like this, perhaps she would have given him a son.

Wulfe became more demanding at her words, so Christina thought he must like her response.

"By Saint Rupert of Bingen," she cried, invoking the patron saint of pilgrims.

Wulfe laughed then grazed her with his teeth, a most delicious sensation.

"By Saint Christopher!" Christina cried and was rewarded with a more vehement touch. She was feverish again, thrashing beneath him, yearning and burning for more. "Saint Felicity and the Archangel Raphael!" she cried. "Saint Rupert again!"

She appealed to a long list of saints, some of which might have been appalled to have been invoked in this moment, but Christina did not care. Wulfe ate her with vigor, clutching her buttocks in his hands. His fingers dug into her and he lifted her from the pallet, feasting upon her as Christina writhed in his embrace. She began to whisper to him of what she wanted him to do to her, and Wulfe made a sudden move that flung her over the edge.

She moaned his name as the release claimed her, shaking in its vigor and completely in his power. It took her some moments to catch her breath, by which time, Wulfe had shed his boots and chausses. He stood, sipping from a cup of wine, watching her with undisguised satisfaction.

His own arousal was more than evident.

Christina stretched, savoring the weight of his gaze upon her. "I would have helped you disrobe," she whispered.

"There was no need." Wulfe put down the chalice and flung his chemise aside with purpose. She liked the gleam in his eyes well and removed her own chemise, baring herself to his view. She unfastened her braid and shook out her hair as she approached him, then locked her arms around his neck.

"All of you," she whispered as she held his gaze. "Fast and hard this time."

"You like that?"

"I like you."

Her reply seemed to please him. Wulfe closed his hands around her waist then picked her up. Christina braced her feet upon his thighs as he lowered her over himself. She liked different poses and liked that he had the strength to hold her so easily. She knew he would not drop her.

He smiled, then kissed her. She tasted the red wine mingled with her own pleasure and loved the combination. She cupped his head in her hands and slanted her mouth over his, claiming his mouth and deepening their kiss even as he eased inside her. She wriggled her hips a little, ensuring that he was deeply inside her and Wulfe caught his breath. He gripped her buttocks and she began to move, riding him and loving how he moaned.

"Too fast," he whispered, breaking their kiss to protest.

Christina chuckled. "Fear not. I will make it last." She rolled her hips and rose high above him, tormenting him just as he had tormented her. Wulfe moaned and she loved that she could grant him this pleasure. She saw him inhale sharply and noted how his eyes glittered, then he withdrew and rubbed himself over her, teasing her anew.

"By Saint Felicity," she cried as the tumult rose within her again. Wulfe grinned, so she summoned every saint she could think of. At the same time, she rode him with resolve, drawing him deeply inside her with every stroke. She found his rhythm and though she endeavored to make the union last, the heat that drove them on would not be slowed this time.

When she could bear it no longer, she seized a fistful of Wulfe's hair and kissed him anew. She fairly devoured him, demanding satisfaction, and he dropped to the pallet again. He rolled as he fell, ensuring that she landed atop him, and Christina writhed against him even as she drove him to the brink.

Wulfe cast her a bright glance, then moved abruptly. He slid a hand between them and pinched her clitoris so sweetly and thoroughly that Christina could not hold back. She cried his name as pleasure seized her, pounding the floor with her fist to punctuate the moment. To her delight, Wulfe gained his release with a roar of satisfaction in nigh the same moment. His grip tight upon her as he surrendered to the fire she had kindled.

She collapsed atop him and smiled, knowing that he had waited for her.

"God's blood, woman, you would wake the dead," Wulfe murmured, pressing a kiss to her temple.

Christina recalled only then that she was in a house filled with people who knew little of her trade and realized they must have been shocked by the sounds emanating from Wulfe's chamber. At the brothel, in contrast, the robust sounds of lovemaking were considered to be good for business. She could not find it within herself in this moment to fret over what was done, though.

Indeed, she began to laugh. "Are you not charged with ensuring the education of Stephen and Simon?" she teased, bracing her elbows on Wulfe's chest.

Wulfe took a deep breath, then shoved his hand through the disarray of her hair with affection as he smiled. "I was thinking of the women in the kitchen," he admitted, then began to laugh as well.

Once they had started to laugh, it seemed impossible to stop. Christina tumbled down beside Wulfe, well content to have his warmth against her and his arm around her shoulders.

Having this knight as her champion suited Christina well indeed.

"Saint Felicity?" he asked, his voice a rumble beneath her fingertips.

"Patron saint of barren women."

She earned a quick sidelong glance for that, but Wulfe did not comment. "Saint Rupert of Bingen?"

"Patron saint of pilgrims."

"I know Saint Christopher is the patron saint of travelers."

"And of those seeking what is lost."

Wulfe frowned. "Did you truly desire the intercession of an archangel?"

"Nay, but I always liked Raphael."

"Indeed?"

"Indeed. He alone dared to take flesh and walk amongst us. I admire any man, angelic or mortal, bold enough to challenge his own assumptions." She eased her hand down his chest, granting him a coy smile. "I fear that I failed in my quest to make your pleasure last," she whispered when her exploring fingers found evidence of his mood.

Wulfe arched a brow. "And what remedy would you propose?" He leaned on one elbow, his other hand easing between her thighs.

"Not again!" she said, although she granted him access anew.

He smiled. "It is but a quest for knowledge," he admitted. "For it is said that women can find their pleasure with twice the frequency as men. I would know for certain."

Christina could not argue with that intent, particularly when he pursued the matter with such resolve that she found herself moaning anew.

Christina was intoxicating. No matter how many times he claimed her, Wulfe only desired more. His desire for her was curiously persistent, and in that, unlike any he had felt before.

Worse, it was dangerous.

Wulfe held her against his side as she slept hours later, knowing he had to step away from her. He could lose all he held dear by pursuing such intimacy with her. Yet, even knowing as much, even as a practical man, he did not want to put her aside.

He had heard of men finding themselves in thrall to desire, or even love, but had never expected he might join such company.

But there was so much in the balance. Not only did the entire house know Christina's trade, but all had to know he had partaken of her charms on this night.

It could not happen again.

No matter the cost to himself.

At least he had the scheme to pursue with Gaston this night. Wulfe recognized that he could not have remained upon this pallet for the night and restrained his desire. The need to depart was a blessing in disguise.

And after this night, they would depart from Venice. He could ensure that he and Christina never shared a chamber or had the opportunity for intimacy.

He would have to be stern with Christina and keep her at a distance. Even as Wulfe resolved as much, he realized his fingertips were moving against her back in a caress. He treated himself to one last look. Christina had buried her face against him and was deeply asleep. Her hair was loose over her shoulders, its hue making her skin look like ivory. Her hands were curled together and between them, as if she protected some treasure within her grasp. The pose made her look young and vulnerable, so sweet that his breath caught.

There was no point in regrets. His life would never be other than it was. Wulfe hoped that Christina's life, though, would change for the better when this city's walls were behind them. He pressed a kiss to her brow and closed his eyes at the sweet perfume of her skin.

He would never forget this moment.

He would never forget her.

But she needed to believe that he spurned her. He would only succeed in his goal if she ceased to tempt him. It was a cruel choice, but letting her believe in what could not be would have been more cruel.

Wulfe rose from the pallet, ensuring he did not disturb her sleep. Indeed, he had never seen her sleep so deeply. Was it because she no longer believed she had to be vigilant in the night? He covered her with his sole blanket, then dressed, his gaze fixed upon her the entire time. Wulfe carried his aketon and hauberk when he departed, intending to seek the assistance of Stephen before leaving the house. He should have been thinking of the ploy he and Gaston would follow this night, but instead, he could think only of Christina.

Her past, her strength, and her future.

Wulfe paused by the portal, drank in one last sight of Christina, then placed the key to the chamber on the table beside the lantern. He knew she would want to have it, so that she could lock the portal herself. Wulfe then extinguished the lantern and left her to sleep in peace.

He knew he would feel no such tranquility any time soon.

Perhaps he should appeal to a saint or two for strength.

Friday, July 24, 1187

Feast Day of Saint Lupus, Saint Wulfhade, and Saint Ruffinus of Mercia

CHAPTER NINE

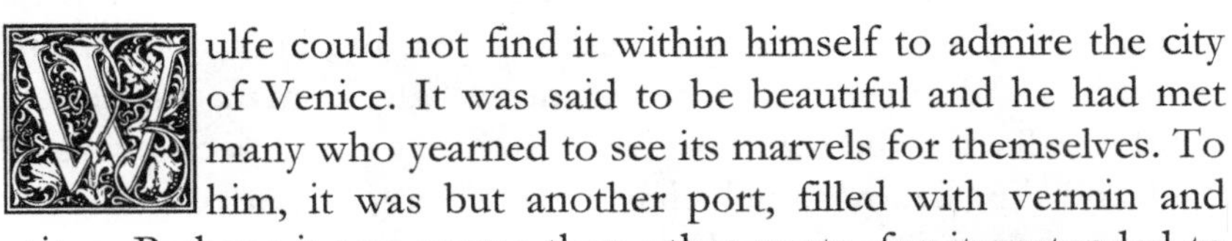

Wulfe could not find it within himself to admire the city of Venice. It was said to be beautiful and he had met many who yearned to see its marvels for themselves. To him, it was but another port, filled with vermin and crime. Perhaps it was worse than other ports, for it pretended to be elegant and fine, while its underworld seethed with activity.

It seemed that the finely garbed noblemen who governed this city did not care about vice.

But then, that might be the city's lure to many.

The streets were quiet when Wulfe left the house. He knew that Gaston followed him at a distance. He was well aware that Bartholomew followed Gaston, as well, and doubted he was the sole one who was filled with trepidation. If Gaston was right about the villain's intent, Wulfe would be soon attacked.

If Christina was right, it would be Gaston who paid the price.

Wulfe hoped Gaston's plan led to the anticipated results. He hoped he remained the target, though he did not relish the prospect of another fight. He carried naught of value, at Gaston's suggestion, and walked with purpose. If he was to gather a prize from a merchant used by the Templars, he would need only a word to prove his identity, for that could not be stolen from his hand.

He walked as if he had a firm destination, though in truth, he simply endeavored to draw out the thief. He worked his way steadily toward the Arsenale, which was quiet this time of night. The men who built ships there were either asleep after their long day of labor or drinking heartily. He could hear distant laughter and rough singing but kept away from the taverns.

Footsteps echoed suddenly behind him, the sound making him jump. The stone surfaces played with the sound so its origin was not readily discerned, and then all was silent again. Was Gaston so far behind him as that? The attack upon him earlier in the day was at the fore of his thoughts, though he knew Costanzia's men had other labor at this hour. Wulfe peered into the shadowed way behind him and imagined he caught a glimpse of Gaston's silhouette.

He exhaled then walked onward, his hand on the hilt of his sword. The moonlight was particularly bright on this night and thousands of stars shone overhead. Despite the light, the streets were filled with mystery. Wulfe was not a fanciful man, but he felt as if he walked in the realm of the dead. Not a living person was in sight and the shadows might have hidden untold horrors. The air was damp and still, as if might have been in a crypt, or as if the city itself held its breath.

And watched his progress. Wulfe had never had such a strong sense that he was observed, though he could not see anyone else. Indeed, the shutters were locked over the windows, the streets were empty and the portals were barred against the night. The city might have been abandoned, at least when he was out of earshot of the taverns.

Yet there was that persistent sense of being observed. It was strange to have the hair prickle on the back of his neck, even as he felt so alone. His boots echoed loudly on the stone and even his breath seemed loud. He could smell the moisture that invaded every detail of this city and began to fear that their ploy would fail completely.

Wulfe shivered with the cold and decided it was time to force any man who pursued him to show his intent. He peered at addresses, as if seeking a specific door in the street, then looked left and right before ducking into the alcove before a portal. He raised a hand as if to knock, wondering what he would say to any soul who answered, then he heard a cry of pain. It was not so loud as that, but he guessed it had been Gaston.

Wulfe lunged out of the archway and retraced his path. The sound of a splash made him break into a run. He could hear a struggle ahead and rounded a corner to find two figures locked in battle. They were of a size with each other, and though one was Bartholomew, the other was cloaked.

"Halt!" Wulfe roared and drew his sword. He leapt at the villain. That man spun and flung Bartholomew toward Wulfe before he fled. Bartholomew stumbled into Wulfe and the pair felt backward. Once they separated, Wulfe might have given chase, but Bartholomew swore at him.

"That is not the task of greater import!"

Wulfe looked at the dark water of the canal in horror. The splash! Gaston had been cast into the water. But there was no sign of the other knight, just the dark surface of the canal. It might have been a dark mirror.

Wulfe stared in horror at the water. He could not swim.

Bartholomew swore again. "Of course, you would not wish to mire your tabard," he spat. He unbuckled his belt and dropped his weapons, then dove into the canal with grace.

It took the younger man three dives to bring Gaston to the surface. Wulfe bent over the lip of the canal and helped to haul Gaston out of the water. The older knight was as pale as a fish's belly and unconscious. He must have sunk due to the weight of his mail.

"We must get him back to the inn," Bartholomew said when he climbed out to stand beside them.

"Not yet." Wulfe had locked his hands together. He pushed on Gaston's chest, doing as he had seen a sailor treat a pilgrim who had been swept overboard.

"What is this you do? He has need of warmth..."

"He will not survive unless the water is expelled." Wulfe flicked a glance at the younger man. "I may not be able to swim, but I have seen people saved from drowning."

"You cannot swim?" Bartholomew echoed.

Wulfe shook his head and pumped. He hoped he did aright for there had been no effect, but suddenly Gaston vomited dark water. If Wulfe had truly been concerned for his tabard's cleanliness, this exercise would have left him appalled. Instead, he repeated the exercise so that the other knight spewed water twice more. Then Gaston coughed and rolled to his side weakly. He did not open his eyes, but his color had improved.

"Have you any *eau-de-vie*?" Wulfe asked the squire.

Bartholomew shook his head. "I am sorry..."

"It is no matter," Wulfe said, his tone more gentle than his words. "We shall have to hope that some soul at the inn has a warming draught."

"The lady Ysmaine has some skill with healing," the squire contributed.

"Indeed. Now we take him to the inn with haste," Wulfe said, pushing to his feet with purpose. "We shall carry him together."

"I am sorry..." Bartholomew began, and Wulfe acknowledged his words with a nod.

"And I am glad you followed us this night." He smiled a little, knowing the other man felt badly for his comment. "Head or feet?"

"Head, sir."

They hefted Gaston, who was not a small man, and set off at as brisk a pace as they could manage. Wulfe could only hope they did not become lost in the maze of this city's streets, for now Gaston needed to be warm.

Some slight sound awakened Christina.

She blinked in the darkness, amazed that she had slept so deeply. Wulfe was gone and it was clearly very late. She remained still, straining her ears.

There it was again. The scrape of a footstep against stone. She narrowed her eyes, certain she heard a minute thump.

There was no one in the chamber with her. She told herself not to be disappointed, though in truth, she was. Why had Wulfe not spoken to her before he left? Where had he gone in the midst of the night?

Christina could not dismiss the notion that she had been abandoned, deliberately so. But why? Did Wulfe blame himself for the theft of the order's funds? She knew well enough that the sole other option for ending that exchange would have been his demise.

Where was he? She rose silently and eased toward the window, then looked down into the courtyard below. The space was empty, save for a beam of moonlight. The moon was just past full and the skies were clear on this night, the rooftops lit nigh as brightly as they were in the midday sun.

Christina could discern no movement at all. What had she heard? She was certain it had been within the house, near her chamber.

She went to the door, listening at it for a moment. There was no sound from the corridor beyond. Even in the shadows, she could discern the small table beside the door and the glass vessel for the oil of the lantern there gleamed. Christina touched the glass, discovering that it was cold. The lantern had been lit when she fell asleep, so a goodly measure of time had passed.

How long had Wulfe been gone? Christina realized that his boots were missing, as well as his armor and sword.

That only increased her conviction that he had left her for good. That she could not explain his choice did not make it impossible.

Her fingertips brushed inadvertently across hard metal and she realized that the key to the room had been left beside the lantern. She doubted this was an accident and swallowed, guessing it had been Wulfe who had left her the means to bar the door.

It also meant he did not intend to return.

Christina tried the door, discovered that it was unlocked, and peeked into the dark corridor.

Not so much as a mouse.

She closed the door silently and leaned back against it, then turned the key quietly in the lock. She felt a portent of trouble, though she could not name the reason why. Perhaps it was because she had thought a new accord had dawned between herself and Wulfe. That he had left without a word meant she was mistaken.

That troubled her. Christina washed in the water that the boys had brought for Wulfe, though it was now cold, and dressed. Her instinct prompted her to be prepared for some event she could not name.

When she was fully garbed, she removed Gunther's ring from her hem and said her prayers. When she murmured her final "amen," the sky was still as dark as indigo. Her sense that some event was imminent could not be dismissed, and there was no possibility of further sleep this night.

Christina sat then, hands folded in her lap, and waited, though she could not have said for what.

She knew it when she heard it. Indeed, she could not have missed Wulfe's bellow for assistance.

No one in that abode could have done.

She ran to the window but could not see Wulfe. He had already disappeared into the common room below, and she could hear boots on the stairs. Another man was with him from the sound. Christina raced to the door and unlocked it, catching Wulfe's eye as he marched past.

He and Fergus carried an oblivious Gaston, who left a dripping trail of mingled water and blood. Fergus looked to have been roused from sleep and wore only his chemise and boots, but Wulfe was fully garbed. Bartholomew raced ahead of them, also fully garbed.

Where had they been?

"Open the portal, my lady, if you please," Wulfe cried, as one of the men hammered on the door of the chamber on the top floor that had been claimed by the other knight for his bride.

Christina heard the maid protest. The squires were roused from the stables and she heard their whispering in the courtyard.

"I beg leave to bring my lord knight to the lady's chamber," Bartholomew said, his voice high with agitation. "For he has been attacked."

Christina joined the rest of the company as they assembled on the stairs in their curiosity and concern. She saw the lady Ysmaine, her hair bound in a long, fair plait, take in the sight of her fallen spouse. The lady paled, her dismay clear.

If there was not affection between these two, Christina would have been greatly surprised. The lady then straightened with resolve. She seemed larger in that moment, and Christina admired how she took command of the situation.

Ysmaine spoke briskly. "Radegunde, please put every blanket upon the pallet and fetch water for my husband. If he is injured, the wounds will need to be cleaned."

"I can do as much, my lady," Bartholomew protested.

"You may aid me in removing his armor." Ysmaine pointed at Wulfe, her gaze steely. "And you will tell me how this transpired." She surveyed the remainder of the party. "The rest of you may retire again. We shall confer in the morning, when there is less to be done."

The maid raced down the steps with a bucket, brushing past Christina. Gaston was carried into the chamber and doubtless laid on a pallet. The lady clicked her tongue, her displeasure most clear.

"He was in one of these filthy canals," she said with disgust, and Christina thought she was probably correct. The boys returned to the stables, taking direction from Duncan, but Christina lingered to listen.

"I will send for an apothecary," Bartholomew said but his knight's wife spun to face him.

"I would see the extent of his injuries first," she said curtly. "There might be no need to expend extra coin to summon an apothecary at this hour of the night."

The lady would deny her husband an apothecary? Christina was surprised by this and saw that the other knights were shocked.

Then Christina realized the truth. Ysmaine wanted only those she trusted in the chamber with that reliquary.

Wulfe hid his disapproval by bending to remove the other knight's tabard.

Ysmaine would have none of it. "Sir, that is not a fitting task for you," she declared, positioning herself between the Templar and her spouse when Wulfe did not halt. "You are neither squire nor servant." Indeed, she ushered Wulfe from the room with undeserved haste. Christina considered the import of this. Ysmaine trusted only her husband and her maid. Had the women stolen the relic at Gaston's command? As a former knight of the Temple, he would know of the order's prizes, and perhaps the truth of Wulfe's quest. Did he seek a souvenir to fund his new life?

She recalled her certainty that he truly led the party and wondered whether he feared simply for the security of the relic. The assault upon him this night would imply that such concern was deserved.

Without knowing the character of the man, it was impossible to guess his motives. That Ysmaine trusted him was the only conclusion Christina could make.

"Your service is better needed in telling us what transpired," Ysmaine declared to Wulfe. "How was he so injured in the stables?"

There was a pause, only the sound of Bartholomew unbuckling Gaston's belt in the chamber. Neither man replied, which intrigued Christina. Had Bartholomew attacked his knight? Did Wulfe suspect as much? Or had the pair of them tried to wrest control from the former Templar?

"He was not in the stables," Ysmaine concluded, quite reasonably, the lack of dispute or correction proving that she was right. Her voice rose. "Indeed, you were abroad in this perilous town, long after the hour when all sensible men are locked into their homes, and so my husband paid the price."

"It was his idea," Wulfe muttered.

Christina narrowed her eyes. Why would Gaston suggest that they three go abroad in Venice at night? Had they been seeking the villain who had attacked Wulfe?

Or trying to lure that assailant into the open?

If so, their scheme had failed. It was clear to Christina that the villain had realized that Gaston was the true leader of the party—or perhaps the one who carried whatever item of value had been entrusted to the knights.

It was no consolation to find her suspicions proven correct.

Christina wondered whether the relic was still in the lady Ysmaine's possession. "I do not believe it," that woman retorted.

"My lord husband has more sense than that."

Meanwhile, Bartholomew had continued to disrobe his knight. The lady gave a small cry and Christina guessed she could see the extent of her husband's injury. She eased forward, wanting to see herself.

"He must have sunk."

"Indeed, my lady," Bartholomew admitted. "He was struck from behind and pushed into the canal. He is not small and the weight of his armor is considerable."

"Fiends and thieves," Ysmaine fumed. "They wished to ensure that he could not stand witness to their crime."

"Undoubtedly so, my lady," Wulfe agreed.

"You pulled him out?" Ysmaine said and Christina was not certain which man she addressed.

"I had to dive in after him, my lady," Bartholomew admitted, his consternation most clear. "I thought...I feared..."

"My lord husband is fortunate indeed to have such a loyal man in his service. I thank you, Bartholomew."

Christina leaned back against the wall. She had too many questions. If Gaston and Wulfe had embarked upon this scheme together, why had Wulfe not saved his fellow knight? She knew he did not lack valor.

Perhaps he had not wanted Gaston to survive.

He could not have attacked the other knight, though.

Unless Wulfe knew that Gaston intended to steal the relic.

Why had he not confided in her?

The maid returned with bucket of water, panting slightly with the effort of hauling it up the stairs. She spared Christina a look that spoke volumes, then hastened into the chamber.

"Now, let us see him dry and warm. I think that will aid him as much as any other cure. Feel the strength of his pulse," Ysmaine said.

"What shall I do, my lady?" demanded the maid.

"Squeeze the water from his tabard and hang it to dry," her mistress instructed. "Then I would ask you to attempt to draw the blood out of his aketon." Her voice hardened and Christina guessed that one of the men looked likely to protest. "Radegunde is very skilled with textiles, and I would ensure that all meets Gaston's approval. Could you ensure that his mail and weapons are undamaged by this drenching?"

"Indeed, my lady," Bartholomew said.

"I will wash the wounds," Gaston's wife continued, her manner brisk. "Is there a brazier to be had in this establishment? A warm beverage would serve him well. Perhaps a cup of mulled wine."

"I will see to that," Christina offered.

The noblewoman spun to face her and held her gaze for a moment. Christina feared the other woman had discerned that she knew of the relic, then Ysmaine nodded in gratitude. Well aware that Wulfe watched her, Christina turned her back and descended the stairs to fetch the wine.

She had to unravel this mystery.

Indeed, she had a growing sense that Wulfe would pay the price if she did not.

Wulfe had failed.

And Gaston had nigh paid the price of his folly.

He had cursed himself all the way back to the house for not telling Gaston that the villain might realize he led the party, not Wulfe. He had doubted Christina's notion and dismissed his own intuition, and in so doing, had nearly lost Gaston.

He had betrayed his fellow knight.

He had betrayed the order and his vows.

He had been a fool.

If he meant to remain a Templar, Wulfe had to repent of his transgressions and ensure the success of this quest.

His awareness of Christina had not been a welcome feeling. The moment she had arrived on the stairs, he had sensed her presence keenly. It was troubling that she did not need to speak to him or touch him for him to know she stood there.

Wulfe did not acknowledge her, but his thoughts churned. Christina had been right about the villain changing his target to Gaston, which meant she was right about the fiend being in their party. He slept in a house with one intent upon killing whoever held the treasure, and worse, they would soon leave Venice behind.

They would be more at risk on the open road.

He could not suspect Christina, though. He had told her naught of their plan for this night. Wulfe was surprised by the depth of his relief that she could not be in league with the true villain. He had hoped as much, but now he knew for certain.

Though not awakening her before his departure had been borne of another choice, the result was welcome. He was glad to know Christina was trustworthy, even if he was resolved to have no further intimacy with her.

What of the treasure? Wulfe fought to keep from looking at Fergus, but he would have to confer with that man about the prize. What was it? He had already guessed that it was within the saddlebag guarded by Laurent, but now, Wulfe had to see it. They were sworn to secrecy and to carrying the parcel in trust, but when one's life was at risk, the rules changed.

Gaston could have died for this quest on this night. Wulfe did not mind dying in pursuit of a noble goal, but he would know what it was. To die in ignorance was not an ambition of merit in his view.

Ysmaine, shook her head as she washed Gaston's shoulder. "I do not blame her for being distressed," she said, clearly referring to Christina. She spared him a hard look. "Given where you have been."

Wulfe was startled to be chided by this woman after he had helped to save her husband's life. "Do you address me?" he asked.

"Indeed. What other man's actions would concern Christina, at least of the company in this chamber?"

Wulfe straightened. "My affairs are not your concern."

"My husband's situation is. Will you grant me an explanation for this?"

"I need not do so."

"Then I will make a guess." Ysmaine considered her husband and spoke quickly. "She is dismayed because you had need of a second whore," she declared, and Wulfe had a difficult time hiding his astonishment at that ridiculous charge. "Yet you could not indulge in such vice without leaving my husband to sleep as he desired. You had to draw him into your scheme and doubtless lured him to some part of the city of ill repute where you were assaulted. Were you both robbed? Or only my lord husband?" The lady fairly curled her lip in her disdain. "Praise be that you did not leave him to rot in the streets. Praise be that his squire saw fit to follow you both, that he might defend my lord husband in such peril as you invited with your sinful urges."

Wulfe was outraged by this assault upon his character, but before he responded with force in his own defense, he realized the usefulness of the lady's explanation. He could not tell her truly what they had been doing, and he had no inkling of what Gaston had confided in his wife. This tale would serve as well as any other.

Indeed, it might put the distance between himself and Christina that he knew was required. He hung his head, as if guilty, and sighed.

To his relief, Bartholomew held his tongue and did not reveal the lie.

The lady Ysmaine bristled with righteous indignation.

"Leave this chamber, sir," she commanded him. "I have no more to say to you, although your courtesan may no longer believe you to be her champion." She bent over Gaston, then spared Wulfe a look of loathing. "But then, perhaps that was the root of your scheme this night."

"My lady," Wulfe began before he could halt himself.

The lady protested quickly, silencing him before he could say too much. "Leave us, sir. I will bar my door against men of such base desires as yours."

Christina returned in that moment, directing Stephen to place the brazier he carried in the corner of the chamber. She must have summoned the boy to help. Stephen lit the coal within it, fighting to hide his reaction to the sight of Gaston. He was a valiant boy, but did not fare well in the face of injury. Wulfe supposed it reminded him of his parents' loss. Christina gave the wine to Radegunde, then departed. Wulfe deliberately ignored her.

He did not want Ysmaine to repeat her accusations when Christina might hear them.

Gaston was so pale and still that Wulfe could not leave the chamber without some reassurance. His guilt redoubled as he surveyed the other knight. They did not always agree, but he did not wish Gaston ill.

Surely, his lady wife could better assess his state. Even though their marriage was a recent one, they had been intimate. She would be a better judge.

"He is not so badly injured, is he?" Wulfe watched Ysmaine closely, for he suspected the truth as more likely to be revealed in her expression than her words. To his relief, she appeared to be concerned but not fearful as she surveyed her spouse.

"I suspect not," she acknowledged, her tone gentler. Perhaps she liked that he showed a care for Gaston. "But if so, I will send Radegunde to tell you of it."

Wulfe bowed then and departed, striding past Christina who yet lingered outside the door to the chamber. He wanted a cup of mulled wine himself though it would take more than that to drive the chill from inside him.

What if Gaston had been killed? There would have been a hearing in Paris, to be sure, and he doubted any in this company would defend his choices. His chest was tight with the reality that he was making solid progress in losing all he treasured on this journey. Stephen came galloping after him, passing him before he reached the ground floor. He carried Gaston's boots for Bartholomew and took them directly to the stables.

The door at the summit of the stairs was slammed and a key turned audibly in the lock. Wulfe looked up because he knew Christina had not moved. Even though he had anticipated that she would be watching him, his heart leapt to find her doing so.

He was yet enchanted, and perhaps a fool, but he could not be churlish. Wulfe had no regrets. "The chamber is yours from this moment forth," he said quietly.

She remained impassive. "Will you not return and confer with me?"

Wulfe shook his head. "Never again," he said with finality.

"But..."

Wulfe interrupted Christina, knowing he would not be immune to any appeal she might make. "Consider, if you will, whether you need join our party for the duration, or if you can make your own course sooner than Paris. Without knowing your destination, I cannot make such a choice."

She descended the stairs to his side, moving with a quiet grace. Her steps were almost fluid and he found himself watching the sway of her hips, savoring the brief glimpses of her feet beneath her hem. When she halted beside him, it was all he could do to keep from looking into her eyes or inhaling deeply of her scent.

That way lay temptation.

"Without knowing all of the truth, you cannot make a choice at all," Christina said, her words so quietly uttered that only he would hear.

Wulfe's gaze flew to hers at that. "I do not understand."

"I suspected as much." She nodded, her manner curiously efficient. "What do you know of the treasure?"

He blinked. "What treasure?"

"The one you carry to Paris at the command of the order," Christina replied with such surety that he was shocked anew. "Do you know what it is? Where it is? Who wants it? Because I know two of those three, and I would wager that if we conferred we might resolve the third."

Wulfe was stunned, but there was no doubting her own conviction in her words. He spared a glance up the stairs and another down to the common room, then raised his voice. "Aye, a cup of mulled wine would be most welcome." He held Christina's gaze. "I shall see if there is another brazier to be found, if you would fetch some wine."

"I am at your service, as ever, sir," she replied so demurely that Wulfe might have smiled under other circumstance.

As it was, he wanted only to know the fullness of what she had learned.

And how she had discovered it.

Was it possible that he might have an ally? It was a strange notion for Wulfe, who always carved his path alone, but he could not deny that it was an enticing one.

Desperate times called for bold choices.

One glimpse of Wulfe's set expression had told Christina that she had been right about his plan to abandon her.

Did he mean to leave her in Venice? Just outside the gates? Christine knew she needed yet more aid from him, yet also understood he would not take pleasure as his compensation. She had to assist him to succeed in his mission.

She did not doubt he would argue with her about that. Wulfe was accustomed to solitude to be sure, and to keeping his secrets. His trust thus far had been hard won and it was far from complete.

The secrets of the order would be the last he surrendered, to be sure.

Christina knew she would have little chance to convince Wulfe to share his observations with her. She composed her argument as she gathered a pitcher of wine from the common room, a pair of crockery cups, and a small pot. By the time she returned to Wulfe's chamber, he had set a brazier before the window and lit a small blaze within it. It cast a welcome glow into the chamber, which seemed more chilly to Christina than it had before. She could not deny her sense that he had set the brazier particularly close to the large arched window. She guessed that he wanted those in the stables to see that no intimacy was exchanged by them.

Fair enough, but the most important intimacy was not physical. Christina took a seat and poured wine into the pan. She was keenly aware of the man near her side, his vitality and power. She could not imagine the world without him.

What if Wulfe had been attacked instead of Gaston?

What if the assailant had succeeded?

Christina shivered at the notion. Wulfe noted her gesture and offered his cloak to her. "Let me help you with your hauberk first," she suggested. To her relief, he did not argue with her. In moments, his sword, tabard and hauberk were set aside, his aketon following soon after. He offered his cloak to her then, wincing as he sat down, and turned his attention to heating the wine. The task appeared to require undue concentration.

"Tell me what you know," he invited quietly.

"Tell me first what happened this night. Where did you go and why?"

He flicked her a look so stern that she thought he might

decline. "I do not need to tell you as much."

"You do, if you mean to solve the puzzle with my aid."

Wulfe frowned and spoke softly. "It was Gaston's scheme, to draw out the villain. He thought that if I departed with purpose, the villain would follow me. His plan was to surprise the villain from behind."

"But the fiend already knew that you do not lead the party."

"It seems as much." His eyes seemed very blue. "You were right."

"And of greater import, the villain knew that you did not carry whatever he seeks."

Wulfe's expression became strained. "What is it?"

Christina was astonished. "Do you not even know?"

He shrugged, swirling the wine. "It was not believed we had a need to know. We had to pledge to secrecy and to refraining from satisfying our curiosity."

"You were simply to deliver a package," she guessed. Wulfe nodded. "And if necessary, die in its defense."

His gaze clung to hers. "That detail might have been implied but it was not uttered aloud." He pursed his lips, hesitating, then continued. "There is a missive, as well. Gaston carries it."

Christina was delighted that he had chosen to trust her, but also insulted on his behalf. "Why not you?"

His frown deepened though his tone was mild. "Because Gaston was better known and thus better trusted by the preceptor, Brother Terricus. He has negotiated treaties these years and has been much relied upon in matters of some sensitivity, by my understanding."

"While you?"

"Fight. And usually win." Wulfe poured the wine into the crockery cups, a swirl of steam rising as he did so. "I suppose it could be said that Terricus delegated responsibility as he saw fit."

"But neither of you carries the treasure. Whose choice was that?"

He granted her a look, inviting her speculation.

"Terricus." She felt her lips tighten. "And a brother of the order cannot defy an order."

Wulfe saluted her with his cup for that conclusion, then took a sip. "He can, however, voice a protest, as I have done repeatedly. I might as well have saved my breath."

"I think it a grievous insult to you."

"I assure you that I have felt it more keenly, but given the situation, the feint may be what has protected the prize from the thief. That surely is of greatest import." He stared down into the contents of his cup, then impaled her with a sudden glance. "Have you seen it?"

Christina nodded.

"Do you know where it is?"

She nodded again. "I believe it is safe in its current place."

"Current?" Wulfe arched a brow.

"It was moved."

"Ah." He thought about this. "But you are not positive of its safety."

"It is impossible for me to be certain, without knowing the motives of all those in your party."

He nodded, bracing his elbows on his knees and evidently fascinated by the wine. "It is of great value then?"

"Beyond price."

He looked up at that, surprised. Christina nodded.

Wulfe rose to his feet and paced the width of the room, his wine apparently forgotten. "It is true that we are a company of strangers," he said. "I could be intent upon claiming such a prize, whatever it is, to buy myself a better future than one serving the order. Fergus could be in need of funds for the estate he returns to claim, as could Gaston. I do not know Bartholomew's history, although Gaston vouches for him. The lady Ysmaine could have any scheme, even without her husband knowing of it." He pivoted to face her. "And you, of course, will be suspected, too."

"But not by you?"

Wulfe smiled.

Christina forced herself to continue their line of discussion, though she was delighted by his endorsement of her character. "A mercenary, a merchant, and a nobleman are in your party, too. Any of them could desire it."

"As could any of the boys, or the women laboring in the kitchens here, or a thief who caught a glimpse of it." Wulfe lifted a hand.

"I think that unlikely," Christina said. "It was too closely secured for a casual glimpse. Someone knows it is carried by this party."

He nodded. "And it might be desired in its own right, to blackmail any of us to pay for its safe return, or sold."

"Coin solves any number of woes," Christina agreed. "Although this item will not be readily sold. One would have need of connections in high places to gain a suitable price for it."

"If it is that fine, even connections in low places might confer a price worth the having," he noted.

"I do not understand."

"A valuable prize sold for even a tenth of its true value can yield an impressive sum."

Christina nodded reluctant agreement. His gaze searched hers, his curiosity clear, then he spun away to pace anew. She had a definite sense of his frustration.

"Do you not care what it is?"

"Of course. But as I was sworn not to investigate the burden granted to us, I suspect there may be a test as to whether I have done so. I have failed the order already on this journey and I dare not do as much again."

"How can you say as much?"

"I did not warn Gaston of my suspicions." Wulfe's tone was hard. "I did not tell him that the villain might already suspect that he led the party in truth. If I had done as much, he might have suggested another plan. He might not have been assailed."

Christina appreciated his doubts, but she was dismissive of his conclusions. "From my experience, Gaston does not heed your counsel, no matter how wise it might be."

"But I did not even try. I chose to believe that he was right, and now he lies injured. If he dies because of this incident, it will be forgotten that the scheme was his. All that will be recalled is that I did not leap into the water to save him." Wulfe threw back the rest of his wine and put the cup down hard.

"Why did you not?" Christina dared to ask.

He granted her a sidelong glance. "Can you not guess?"

"I know you are not a coward."

"I cannot swim," he admitted with quiet heat.

"And so one of you would have drowned for certain, because Bartholomew could not have saved you both. I doubt he would have leapt back into the water for you."

"I know he would not have done so." Wulfe shrugged, and she wondered whether he was as untroubled by this as he would clearly like her to believe. She saw in that moment that his distrust of others and aloof manner had been learned by experience. "And why should he have been expected to risk his life twice? Nay, better that I stood back, he saved Gaston, even if both despise me for my cowardice."

That last word was uttered with a measure of bitterness that revealed his true feelings.

Wulfe had need of solace. He had need of an ally. And Christina would give him as much of both as he would accept from her.

Maybe it would be enough to change the futures of both of them.

Either way, she would regret naught at all.

CHAPTER TEN

hristina picked up the pot and went to Wulfe's side, steadying his cup before she poured the rest of the warmed wine into it. "It is not cowardice to choose to live," she said quietly. "Indeed, that is often the most bold choice of all."

Wulfe exhaled, his expression solemn. "Understand, Christina, that my entire future rides upon the goodwill of the Grand Master in Paris. I have failed. I have betrayed Gaston's trust and I have neglected my vows. That must change. I must reform my ways to ensure that I can remain with the order." He eyed her. "Otherwise, I will starve."

"For you will not become a mercenary, even to survive."

"Never," he said with quiet heat. "To live without principle is no life at all."

"And you will not pledge to a nobleman's service because you cannot be assured that his cause will always be just."

He nodded again, no less grim than before. "The sole righteous path is with an order like the Templars."

Christina granted him a smile, lifted the cup out of his hand, and sipped from it. "Yet where is it writ that I cannot help you?"

Wulfe reached for the wine but she held it out of his reach. "Surely the rule requires that a knight sworn to the order be temperate?" she teased and was gratified to see his reluctant smile.

"You know my concern. We cannot lie together again."

"But that does not mean that we cannot speak to each other, or that I cannot ride from Venice with your company," she said, keeping her voice calm even though she feared he would spurn her suggestion. "I will be a pilgrim again, Wulfe, one returning home escorted by a noble knight. In truth, I would like the next man I welcome to my bed to be my lord husband, whoever that might prove to be."

She saw his eyes flash then he pivoted to stride to the window. He looked down on the courtyard, and she had the definite sense that she had offended him.

"Am I not to spurn your touch then?" she asked. "I thought it would be better to facilitate your choice, then to cast myself at you and attempt to change your thinking on this matter with earthy persuasion."

He snorted. "Wiser, certainly." Wulfe lifted his gaze and surveyed her, his admiration clear. His voice dropped low. "But not better, not by any accounting."

Their gazes locked, the intensity of his expression setting Christina's desire alight all over again. He was right—their union had been a marvel, far beyond anything she had experienced before.

And she, for one, was not prepared to relinquish all hope of a future.

Indeed, she dared to believe that she might have found what she sought above all else. A champion, to be sure, but also a man who appreciated her for herself.

Not for her appearance.

Not for the skills she had learned in Costanzia's house.

Not even for the legacy that she might claim with a man's aid, the one Gunther had so desired. But she, like Wulfe, had learned to be cautious and would not promise what she doubted she could offer in the end.

Still, she would have a taste of him to keep her warm.

"One kiss," she whispered and his eyes flared.

Christina crossed the floor in haste then, confident that she could claim the kiss she so desired. Wulfe spun her out of view of the window, then gathered her into his arms. She loved how he caught her close and kissed her deeply, as if he could do naught else. The heat rose between them, conjured by the merest touch. His passion filled her with pleasure and anticipation. She twined her arms around his neck and slid her fingers into his hair, welcoming him, wanting all he had to give.

Whatever it might be.

This kiss might be their last one, certainly the last before Paris, and she never wanted it to end. Wulfe seemed to share her view, for he slanted his mouth over hers, cradling her against his chest as he kissed her deeply. Christina felt cherished as she never had before.

Long moments later, Wulfe lifted his head, his fingers running down her cheeks. "You have seen it?" he whispered, his gaze searching hers. Christina nodded, but he put a fingertip over her lips, halting her confession of its truth. "Is it worth a man surrendering his life?"

She nodded immediately, and he brushed his lips across hers.

"Watch it with vigilance then, as we journey, and tell me if its location changes. You must swear to tell me if it is in peril."

"I will, Wulfe. You can rely upon me."

Wulfe smiled down at her, his fingers speared into her hair. "I will not be able to resist you all the way to Paris."

"Aye, you will," Christina said, stepping out of his embrace while she could summon the strength to do so. They had to join forces and aid each other to see the greater good served. If she tempted him to her bed and that cost him his place in the order, he would despise her for it. Christina could not risk that.

She moved to the window, so she would be in view of whoever watched. "I will leave the party at the Saint Bernard Pass," she said softly but with conviction.

It was for the best.

Wulfe was visibly startled. "That is but a little more than halfway."

"But close to home. When we part, I will tell you where the prize is, and you shall guard it from there." She stepped back at his nod, offering him the last of the wine again. "The lesser of two evils," she invited softly, but could not smile.

Wulfe did not smile either. He considered her then accepted the cup, the warmth of his fingers brushing hers in the transaction. His gaze clung to hers as he drained the cup, then he handed it back to her.

He strode to the door, pausing on the threshold. "Sleep well, Christina," he said, without looking back.

"And you as well."

Wulfe was out the door then, halting in the corridor with the key in his hand. He cast it to her and Christina caught it, smiling at him for understanding her so well. Then the door closed and she was alone, cold despite the heat emanating from the brazier. She went to the window and watched Wulfe cross the courtyard to the stables, marveling that for the first time in years, she wanted a man's hands upon her.

Not just any man.

Wulfe.

But his favor had to be earned. Christina dared to believe that it could be done—and that if she succeeded, Fortune might smile upon them both.

Had either of her sisters claimed their family legacy as yet? Christina had not been able to bear to think of home, or the legacy that had been the cause of their pilgrimage, all these years, but in this moment she did. Gunther had not just desired a son for his own price, after all. Had her sisters born sons?

It had been nine years. Miriam had been betrothed just before Gunther had insisted upon the pilgrimage. Surely her husband's seed had taken root in all this time?

And if not, Anna might well be wedded and mother to a son.

Aye, Christina had to think that one of them had claimed the legacy. And there was little chance of her ever doing so, given her years of being barren. Nay, the best she could hope was that whichever of her sisters reigned at their family holding offered her a haven.

A home and a haven were both more than she had known these many years, after all.

She watched Wulfe disappear into the stables and realized the fullness of that blessing.

Indeed, there were many who were not so fortunate as she.

Wulfe did not miss the irony. In Jerusalem, he had angrily accused Gaston of slowing the progress of their party by that man's apparent insistence upon collecting his whores, insisting that women would not be able to ride as long or as hard each day. Lady Ysmaine had challenged his assumptions, not just by her position as Gaston's wife, but by her determination to ride as long as necessary each day.

And now, he would add his whore to the party.

Even though Christina was no longer a whore nor his. She was a pilgrim, destined for the pass and no farther. Already he was dreading the day they would part.

But there were practical matters to resolve. She had need of a horse to ride with the party, and he had not a penny to his name. He had been relieved of his best dagger, so he could not sell that—though in truth, even it would not have gained sufficient coin to buy a palfrey unless he deceived the buyer.

What else did he have to sell of value?

Wulfe knew that although Costanzia's men had taken all of the Templar's coin that he had carried, Christina's escape from that house would only be complete if she left the city forever. One could not expect such villains to be above deceit. He understood her conviction that there could be no honest labor for her here, given the reaction of the women in the kitchens, and trusted her assessment that she would only be drawn back to the life she yearned to leave.

He had to find a way for her to ride out with them.

Which meant he needed to find another horse.

Wulfe went to the stables intent upon reviewing the meager contents of his saddlebags. The boys were asleep and though Stephen stirred, Wulfe gestured him back to sleep. It was peaceful in the stables, with little sound other than the soft snores of sleep and horses swishing their tails.

Wulfe crouched down in the makeshift stall where Teufel was saddled and the horse nuzzled him with affection. The destrier was in need of exercise, and Wulfe wished again that they would depart. With Gaston injured, though, it could not be soon.

Only when he was alone could Wulfe acknowledge the fullness of his sense of responsibility, and the magnitude of his failure. If Gaston died, he could not imagine that there would be no repercussion for him.

The greater concern, however, was Gaston's welfare. As much as Wulfe had resented being commanded to be subordinate to the other knight, he had come to admire him. They still might not always agree, but Wulfe could see why Gaston was so trusted and respected. That man's steady manner and quiet persistence would oft yield good results.

And Gaston had friends. His wife already admired him, and his nature kept the company together. Wulfe could not have rallied their consensus so readily as Gaston had. He had not gift with diplomacy, save that variety delivered at the point of a sword.

Wulfe sat in the straw, enduring Teufel's assault upon his collar and hair, and opened his bags. He was not optimistic and suspected he might fail again. The truth was that he owned precious little, as was reasonable given his vows. His armor was key to his occupation. His sword could not be surrendered. His harness was not lavish, and he had neither lavish caparisons for his destrier nor a cloak of fine wool that he might live without. His boots had been repaired too many times to fetch a good price, and his belt was merely serviceable.

Teufel gave him a little nip, discontent to be ignored, and Wulfe stood up to rub the beast's ears. He had shared more experience with this horse than with any soul since his days with the old man. He certainly had never trusted another so much. Perhaps it was because they had much in common. Not only was the black destrier proud and powerful, confident in his abilities, but he remained apart from other steeds, even at pasture. Perhaps it was because they defended each other and survived battles together. Wulfe fetched the brush and groomed the steed, finding that the exercise soothed him as well as Teufel.

He had brushed one flank when the truth struck him like a bolt of lightning. His most valuable possession was the destrier. He could sell Teufel and buy two horses, perhaps even a palfrey and a destrier less fine. The notion was galling, for he had thought he would ride Teufel always.

The alternative of leaving Christina behind, nigh ensuring her return to that brothel, was even more wrenching.

He sought another solution, even as he guessed this was what must be done. Two adults could not share a mount, not at speed and for a long distance. Independent of how it would fatigue the horse, it would compromise his own need to appear to be holding to his vows. Christina could not walk, and she could not be left behind.

It was true that he had been betrayed twice by women. Christina was different from either of those women, though.

Christina had need of the protection only he could give. Had she not labored here for years, without any intercession from a kindly stranger? Her fate was little different from that of the lady Ysmaine, save there had been no honorable man to offer his hand in marriage.

He could ensure she left this city. It was not as much as Wulfe would have liked to have granted to her, but it was all he had to offer.

Even if it would demand nigh all he had to give.

It was time for him to show compassion as well as mete justice.

Wulfe stepped back and looked the steed in the eye. He could ensure the buyer was a kind one, perhaps. He owed Teufel that much, and more. He imagined that the destrier held his regard out of understanding.

Perhaps even agreement.

Wulfe began to groom the horse with greater vigor, telling himself that he needed to ensure Teufel looked his best. The truth was that he wanted to spend every possible moment with the destrier before their ways parted.

He had to do this quickly, at first light, for even if he had to defend his choice to Stephen and Simon, his will might be compromised.

And Christina would be lost.

The Templar's defenses were crumbling.

Fergus had seen it before, and he recognized the signs. He had fought with many a knight in this order who had naught but the order, naught but his might and his blade and his valor. He had recognized Wulfe as one of that company immediately. They were merciless in battle, these warriors, and their will might have been wrought of iron. It was good to have several of them in any sortie, for they invariably ignored their injuries and ensured the majority—if not all—of the company returned. When not in battle, they kept to themselves, never compromising their motives with emotion, and their choices were utterly predictable.

Honorable, no matter what the price.

Fergus thought of them as fortresses, men who had built doughty towers to shelter their hearts, then added to such formidable defenses over their years of solitude. Their brusque manners might have been high curtain walls, and their apparent disinterest in their fellow men could have been wide, deep moats that kept all from their portals. It seemed they cared only for themselves.

The truth was that such men could not have fought with such resolve if they had not been driven by a deeper motive. Each and every one of them in the acquaintance of Fergus had been committed to the ideal of justice for his fellow men.

Wulfe was the same. He argued with Gaston because he felt responsibility to his fellows and was driven to ensure that the quest succeeded. He might be perceived as cold by others, but the devotion of his two squires—not to mention the affection of his destrier—revealed that his stern demeanor was part of that protective facade. Fergus did not doubt that squires and steed survived due to some intervention by the knight.

Perhaps multiple interventions, none of which the Templar would discuss.

And now, Fergus watched Wulfe make a choice of some kind, that knight believing himself unobserved, and Fergus knew the

Templar's curtain wall had been breached. It was because of the woman, the whore Wulfe had brought back to the house against all expectation, and the one who continued to remain. Christina had cracked the mortar somehow, and Wulfe's defensive walls had begun to crumble.

Fergus had known the truth when he had unlocked the portal the night before and seen Wulfe's stricken expression as he and Bartholomew carried Gaston. Bartholomew's reaction had been consistent with expectation, but for Wulfe to be so visibly shaken, this man who hid his emotions so well, could only mean one thing.

The fact was that they could not support the loss of two knights. Gaston had been injured and might not be able to lead the party, even in secret. Where was the missive that Brother Terricus had entrusted to Gaston? What had it said? Fergus could repeat what Terricus had told him to the Paris master, but that might be only part of the tale.

Worse, if Wulfe faltered, the treasure might be lost and the quest could fail. He had seen these men compromised before. Their defenses were formidable, but once the chink of weakness was found, their walls were undermined and the gates inevitably fell.

Against all expectation, he had to offer assistance to Wulfe, and do so in a way that did not offer insult. He saw that Duncan was awake beside him, that man's eyes glinting as he, too, watched Wulfe's thorough grooming of the destrier. They exchanged a look, needing no words to communicate their concern, and Fergus gave a quick nod.

Duncan rose, stretched, and sauntered toward the other knight, amiable and unthreatening.

Fergus listened, the better to discern what he might do to help. The curtain wall might be compromised, but he would see Wulfe hold the tower against all assault.

The prospect of surrendering the horse shook Wulfe.

It was startling to feel so much emotion over the decision to part with a steed. Indeed, he might have sat down and wept, which was most unlike him and would achieve naught at all. He knew the task had to be done, but he refused to dwell upon it. Instead of considering his regrets, he recalled the times he had shared with this destrier, the battles they had fought together, the patrols they had ridden and the company they had kept.

"Do you mean to leave the creature with any hide at all?" demanded a friendly voice from behind him, startling Wulfe from his thoughts.

He turned to find the mercenary Duncan behind him. The older man was grinning, but there was a gleam in his eye.

He was perceptive this one, and Wulfe suspected he was often underestimated. That might have been a warning to hide his thoughts.

"There is naught amiss with a good grooming," Wulfe said, turning back to his labor. He bent to buff Teufel's hooves. They were black and looked most remarkable when polished to a shine. He hoped the Scotsman would leave him alone, but his wish was not to be fulfilled.

Indeed, Duncan seemed to settle in to chat. "It seems to me that either you have missed riding this steed, or you mean to sell him."

Wulfe glanced back at the other man, alarmed that his choice might be so readily discerned. To his regret, he realized Duncan had been watching for just such a reaction. What had happened to his impassivity? He strove to keep his tone mild. "Why would you say as much?"

Duncan shrugged. "I merely make a guess. Which is it?"

"I do not need to confide in you."

"Nay, you do not, but I am curious to be sure. Most knights I have known would part with their lives before their destriers, swords, or hauberks." Duncan grimaced as he considered his own words. "In that order, as well."

"Perhaps I am not like other knights you have known."

Duncan chuckled. "That is the truth and then some. I might also think you a vexed man, had I not had ears last eve."

Wulfe halted his brushing. "When we returned with Gaston?"

Duncan chuckled. "Before that, lad, when the lady expressed her delight with your skills."

It was a reminder Wulfe did not need. He took a breath and turned to confront Duncan. "What is it that you desire of me this morn?" he asked, not troubling to hide his impatience at being so interrupted.

"To understand you better," Duncan replied easily. "You are not an easy one, lad, that is certain." He moved into the booth, running a hand over the horse with admiration. "A Templar sworn to chastity who knows how to please a woman better than any man I have ever known." He winked. "At least from the sound of it."

Wulfe bristled.

Duncan continued, undeterred. "An aloof man who understands human nature so well as to pluck the pearl from the dung heap." Wulfe might have argued but the older man raised a finger. "She is a pearl, who has been cast before swine, and you noticed it, whether you realize as much or not."

Wulfe clamped his lips together, feeling exposed that this man had observed so much about him.

Duncan rubbed Teufel's ears. "A cold warrior whose squires, orphans both, serve him with a loyalty rarely seen, and one that hints at the truth of his nature." The older man plucked the brush from Wulfe's fingers, then shook it at him. "A man who hides his thoughts with ease but whose actions show him to be deserving of more respect than he has gained."

Wulfe reclaimed the brush with impatience. "I have no need of respect. There is a task to be done and I will see it completed."

Duncan's words were gentle. "What do you mean to do with the horse, lad?"

"I am no lad..."

"Nay, you are a man of principle." Duncan folded his arms across his chest and confronted Wulfe, barring him from leaving the stall when he might have walked away from the conversation. "You plan to sell your horse. I see it in your every gesture, as well as how the decision troubles you."

Wulfe heaved a sigh of defeat. "And so you have solved the mystery. Why ask me about it? Are you not content to leave me be now?"

"Nay, I am not. Tell me why."

Wulfe surveyed the stables, but knew the older man would not abandon his query. "The company has need of another steed and I have no coin with which to buy one."

"Christina comes with us then."

"She is a pilgrim, joining our party to return home."

Duncan grinned, a mischievous expression that put stars in his eyes. "You bought her freedom!"

"I but endeavor to help a pilgrim..."

Duncan interrupted him. "You could ask for assistance from the company, lad."

"I could," Wulfe acknowledged. "But experience has shown it to be an exercise in futility to appeal to my fellows for any aid. Matters are resolved when I see them so."

The older man ran a hand over Teufel's neck, smiling when the destrier tossed his head. "He is magnificent. You must know that you will be cheated of his value in this den of thieves called a city. And who can say what his future will be?"

Wulfe's throat tightened to have his own fear named with such accuracy. "I would endeavor to find him an owner who would take good care of him..."

"As much as you? I doubt that man can be found." Duncan shook his head.

"I thank you for your concern," Wulfe said stiffly. "But I know what must be done."

"Duncan?" Fergus called from beyond the stall, and Wulfe returned to his grooming as the older man stepped into his lord knight's view. "Would you take Laurent this day and see if you can find a decent palfrey to buy?"

Wulfe spun to look at the Scotsman as he came into view. This could not be a coincidence, though Fergus did not glance at him.

"I know that Isobel will have my liver if I tell her of the silks for sale in the market yet do not bring her some. The saddlebags are full to bursting as it is, so it will do little harm to buy another steed."

"Provided I am not cheated," Duncan countered. "And there is any decent mount to be had. They are more for ships and boats, here, that much is clear."

"There must be pilgrims selling horses before they sail east," Fergus replied.

Wulfe could not fight the sense that this conversation was for his view.

Duncan scoffed. "I imagine there are fewer embarking, but I will look."

"Take Laurent with you. He has a good eye for horses and has not left this abode. It will be good for him."

"Aye, my lord."

"You need not do this," Wulfe interjected and both men turned to look at him. To his relief, they did not pretend that he was wrong.

"Aye," Fergus said gently. "I must." He arched a brow. "I have great fondness for my liver, after all."

Duncan chortled at that and left the stables, leaving the two knights facing each other.

"This is no jest," Wulfe said. "And it is not your responsibility..."

"But it is a contribution I can make," Fergus said. He stepped closer. "Particularly if you will not use the coin of the order to ensure the defense of a pilgrim."

"I would," Wulfe admitted very quietly. "If I had not been robbed."

Fergus straightened. "Does he know?"

Wulfe shook his head at the reference to Gaston. "Not yet."

Fergus nodded, scanning the stables as he clearly considered this. He reached beneath his jerkin and withdrew a small sack of coins. He closed his hand over it and passed it to Wulfe, their gazes holding. "He need not know," Fergus said, mouthing the words.

Wulfe accepted the coin, relief flooding through his heart. "Keep a tally that you are repaid."

Fergus grinned. "You may be certain of that." He reached up and rubbed Teufel's nose. "Such a fine creature you are. It will not be too soon that we ride out and you can run, my friend."

Wulfe gripped the coin, stunned to have experienced such kindness. His chest was tight with his relief. "Thank you," he said when Fergus turned to leave, and his voice was hoarse.

That man nodded, then left the stall, and Wulfe brushed Teufel more gently.

Suddenly Duncan appeared again, ducking back around the horse. "Do you think Christina would favor a new gown?" He spread his hands. "I will be in the market this morn and a bargain might be found."

"I think she would welcome the opportunity to look more like the pilgrim she is," Wulfe admitted, thinking how the hue and cut of her kirtle so clearly revealed her occupation. Once he would have kept that observation to himself, intent upon taking responsibility for its resolution himself, but he began to see the merit of trusting others in this company. It was a strange feeling, to not battle the Fates alone, but Wulfe suspected he could readily become accustomed to it.

Was it possible that simply asking for a desire could see it fulfilled?

"I shall see what can be contrived," Duncan agreed, his assistance so readily won that Wulfe blinked. The older man nodded once, then ducked out of the stables with purpose, leaving Wulfe to his task.

He leaned his brow upon Teufel, feeling lighter than he had in years.

"Good morrow, Gaston," Duncan said suddenly, and Wulfe spun to look into the courtyard with surprise. To his pleasure, Gaston was indeed crossing the courtyard, purpose in his step. He did not look fully hale and was yet pale, but the fact that he had risen from his pallet this morn was good news.

That he raised a hand to Wulfe and turned toward him meant that he had come to consult upon their course, which was better news, to be sure.

Truly, the day was filled with far more promise than it had been but moments ago.

Christina fell asleep again, despite her expectations, and awakened to find the sun shining brightly through the window. There was a bustle of activity in the courtyard below. She could only reason that the wine had made her sleepy.

She said her prayers again, feeling in particular need of divine grace.

What should she do this day to aid Wulfe? She had not learned much from the boys the day before, but perhaps she had established some trust with them. She had not mentioned Laurent's secret to Wulfe and wondered again who knew.

Who could she trust in this house?

She had need of more knowledge to know for certain.

To her surprise, she found Ysmaine at the board. That woman glanced up at her and continued her meal.

"Good morning, my lady," Christina said and curtseyed. "Might I ask after your lord husband's health?"

Ysmaine smiled, and Christina saw the signs of a sleepless night. "It seems there was little reason to fear. He rose this morn, declared himself hale, and insisted upon visiting his destrier." Her lips tightened slightly. "They are nigh inseparable."

Christina refrained from comment, having noted that Gaston tended to sleep in the stables. "It must have been a shock to him to awaken in your bed," she dared to say, her tone mischievous.

The lady chuckled, as if she knew she should not. "I dare say he will recover from that, as well."

The two women shared a smile and Christina's opinion of Gaston's wife only improved. There was a step in the corridor then, and the older nobleman appeared in the common room.

"Good morning, Count," the lady said, but Christina hastily turned her back upon that man. He sniffed, as if in disapproval of her presence, and returned the greeting to Lady Ysmaine only. Christina had no desire to be recognized by him, if he was Helmut, so she took her bread and honey into the courtyard. The sun was lovely and warm, the bread fresh and the honey luscious. She savored her freedom and her recent sleep, taking her time over each bite.

It was Wulfe who had given her so much.

The portal to the street opened audibly, and Christina glanced toward it. It was the merchant, Joscelin, returned from his night revels and clearly he was in a merry mood. He waved to some comrade, then beamed at all the company. There was a bounce in his step as he crossed the courtyard, and a gleam lit his eye as he spied Lady Ysmaine.

"Lady Ysmaine!" Joscelin crowed. "It is so fortunate that I should see you first..."

Christina endeavored to be invisible. The merchant passed her with barely a glance. In the stables, men's voices rose slightly. Were Gaston and Wulfe arguing? It was unfortunate she could not discern their words.

She did, however, listen to the exchange in the common room, hoping to determine whether the nobleman Ysmaine addressed as a count might be the villain she recalled all too well.

"Did you see him?" Gaston asked once he stood in Teufel's stall, his voice low. Not far away, Fergus brushed his steed, but the boys were at the far end of the stables and beyond earshot.

"No more than a shadow," Wulfe admitted in an equally quiet tone.

"The ploy failed, then."

"We drew the villain out, that much is certain."

It seemed a small gain given the price to Gaston, and Wulfe again felt guilt that he had not warned the other man.

The portal to the street was opened, and the merchant Joscelin returned. Wulfe watched as the portly man waved farewell to his acquaintance. Though he had clearly been absent from the house, it was unlikely that he had been Gaston's attacker. He was too short.

Though he might have hired someone to do it for him. Wulfe wished he had caught a glimpse of the acquaintance.

And to be sure, Joscelin would have the connections to sell a prize such as the one Christina said they carried.

He watched the man proceed to the common room, noting how he immediately joined Ysmaine. Were they in league together? Did the lady wish to be rid of her new spouse? Indeed, *she* might have hired the man who had attacked them the night before.

"Has your wife not been widowed twice?" he asked Gaston.

That knight took umbrage at the question. "Of what import is that?"

If Gaston's nature was too trusting to discern this truth, Wulfe would make it clear to him. "We were not followed to Venice. The treasure is yet secure, according to Fergus." That man gave a minute nod, his head visible over the back of his destrier. "Perhaps there was another reason you were attacked."

"You cannot still suspect my lady wife."

He had to be told the truth. "She refused to summon an apothecary for you last night."

Gaston averted his gaze. Was he unsurprised? "She was merely optimistic."

"It was before we knew the extent of your injury." Wulfe leaned closer. "Then she cast every soul but her maid from the chamber." He shook his head, then Gaston's impassivity made him fear he spoke too harshly. Wulfe deliberately made a jest. "In truth, if I did not know you to be too cursed stubborn to die, I might have feared you would not survive the night."

Fergus snorted.

Gaston spared a glance across the courtyard, his gaze clinging to his wife, who chatted with Joscelin. Wulfe guessed that he was more troubled by his wife's choice than he would have liked to admit aloud. "Yet you did not intervene or protest?"

"What protest could I have made? I but watched and listened as well I could."

"She knows of healing," Gaston ventured, no real conviction in his tone. "Perhaps she perceived more than you did and more quickly."

Wulfe said naught.

They stood in silence before Gaston spoke again. "I fear she may have guessed more than I would prefer of our errand."

There was a fear Wulfe could put to rest. "I think not," he retorted. "Her assumption was faulty, though I saw no reason to correct it for it was useful."

Gaston clearly did not understand, but he had not heard his lady's charges. "How so?"

"She was quick to accuse me of enticing you to seek out whores."

The other knight was sufficiently dismayed that he failed to hide his reaction. "Ysmaine said as much?"

"Aye, she was heartily vexed with me. I did tell her that our errand had been your idea, but she did not believe me."

Gaston was clearly appalled. He looked again at his lady wife.

"I was so relieved that she concocted a plausible tale that I dared not argue with her." Wulfe grimaced. "To my own discomfort."

"How so?"

"Christina believed her."

"Well, you have naught to fear in that," Gaston said, his manner brusque. "You have told me repeatedly that Christina is not your courtesan or companion. Doubtless, she will be left behind on our departure and her conclusions will be of no relevance." He leaned closer to the other knight and dropped his voice to a whisper, his eyes flashing with resolve. "I would thank you, though, to refrain from tarnishing my repute with my lady wife. She and I are bound until death us do part."

Wulfe felt the need to state the obvious. Loyalty to his wife was all good, but there was peril before them and Gaston could not dismiss it so readily as that. "Given last night's incident, death may come sooner than you had planned. I suggest this tactic: that you and I both avoid our respective women. Let the villain believe that dissent has been sown between us."

And in this way, the women would be protected. The villain's eye had slid from Wulfe to Gaston, but Wulfe would not have it move to Christina. Gaston nodded welcome agreement.

"Agreed. But let us ride out as soon as may be." The knights exchanged a look, then Gaston's eyes began to sparkle. "Now let us argue loudly about our departure and our route. I will insist upon granting you advice you do not desire, as has happened before."

And the other knight's counsel would guide their path. Wulfe knew the routine but realized now that he had best follow Christina's advice and disguise the fact that Gaston truly was in command.

When Gaston chose to argue about the route, he left Wulfe no alternative but to argue against the path he would have taken himself, in order to encourage the view that they were at odds.

Curse the man!

CHAPTER ELEVEN

Christina made a feast of her dish of honey and piece of bread, trying to ensure that she did not have reason to move before the count completed his meal.

She was yet upon the steps when Wulfe and Gaston stepped out of the stables, their dispute becoming more audible. It appeared that they wished to feel the sunlight, for Wulfe tipped his face back and closed his eyes at its caress.

Or perhaps he prayed for strength. Christina knew that Gaston vexed him as few other men could.

Wulfe then fixed Gaston with a stern look, and his tone was so temperate that she knew it cost him mightily. "The tolls on the Saint Bernard Pass are well known to be expensive beyond belief, and there are thieves, to be sure," he said. "That is why I suggest the alternate route to the southwest that the merchants use, through the Mont Cenis Pass..."

Christina glanced up, intrigued. Why did he argue against the Saint Bernard Pass? It was used frequently, and that route made much sense.

Was it possible that he did not want to be parted from her so soon? The notion made her heart skip a beat, but Wulfe might have been oblivious to her presence as he debated their route with Gaston.

"Which will leave us much farther south than Paris," Gaston replied. "And is a longer journey from Venice. I thought you were the one who wished to reach Paris with all haste?"

Wulfe swore softly, and Christina dared to hope that he ignored her a little too completely to be unaware of her presence. Indeed, the back of his neck was ruddy, a flush that was clearly discernible in the sunlight.

As if he were discomfited.

As if he had not hidden his thoughts well.

She set her napkin aside and smiled at him, watching the pair openly.

Wulfe shot a glance in her direction, scowled, then frowned at the pavement. "The road may be longer but it is said to be in better repair. We shall make better time."

Gaston shook his head. "And what of Hamish? He had a convulsion yesterday by all accounts. We dare not move him so soon."

"I would not hasten overmuch, but I would reach Paris before the Yule," Wulfe countered, then dropped his voice low. "Perhaps you do not truly wish to claim your holding." His gaze flicked to Christina and this time she noted that his eyes were blue again. She doubted those in the common room could hear him. "I could relieve you of the burden."

Gaston smiled. "We are at odds," he murmured, as if in reminder.

Christina was intrigued.

Wulfe nodded slightly, then his voice rose. "And still you maintain that we should delay our departure but use the Saint Bernard Pass," he declared, shaking his head. "If we left promptly, we could take the longer route and use the better road, yet perhaps arrive sooner."

"Certainly the decision is yours," Gaston said, with newfound deference. "I merely share my impressions and the tidings I have gathered, both here and in Jerusalem."

Did the pair work together? She hoped as much.

Wulfe sighed mightily. "And again I must cede to your experience. Saint Bernard's pass it shall be, and we shall depart on Monday, with the apothecary's permission."

He met Christina's gaze then, and she could not look away. How long would the journey take? A fortnight? It would depend upon the weather and how long they rode each day.

Still, she could not deny that she already was troubled by the prospect of parting from Wulfe. Would she ever see him again? She imagined not, for their paths led in very different directions.

The prospect was troubling.

Christina heard the count rise to his feet in the common room, as if he meant to depart. She turned away from Wulfe, as if indifferent to his presence, to ensure she could spy upon the count. The knights returned to the stables, declaring their intent of making an inventory of the supplies for the horses. Christina stood with her face slightly averted as the count swept past her, his disdain clear, striding to the stables in his turn.

He walked like Helmut. He was more heavily set than Helmut had been, to be sure, but years had passed and they were both older.

The lady Ysmaine was alone at the board, the mercenary Duncan seated on the opposite side of the table.

It was an opportunity Christina dared not miss. She carried the empty dish from the honey into the common room and took the place beside the noblewoman. Ysmaine spared her a smile and continued her meal.

"Who is he?" Christina asked, ensuring her tone was idle. "He seems most pleased with himself."

"I suppose his pride is not undeserved," the lady replied. "He is Everard de Montmorency."

Christina could not fully hide her surprise at this. It *was* Helmut then, and he had been so base as to steal the name of the nobleman he had once served. What else had he stolen from Everard? What fate had befallen that gracious man?

Helmut must have killed him as well. How else could he have stolen the man's name? His signet ring? His garb? The realization was enough to make her ill.

"Truly?" she asked, nigh choking on the word.

"And the Count of Blanche Garde, besides," Duncan added, apparently impressed by this title. "A man whose piety is well known in Outremer."

Christina fought the urge to laugh aloud. Piety? That was the last attribute she would credit to Helmut!

Duncan stood and claimed a piece of bread, dipping it into the honey beside Christina. He winked at her. "I doubt he would savor your wares."

The implication was clear that Duncan would. She smiled politely at him, trying to strike the balance between being friendly and not encouraging his advances.

"Do you know him?" Ysmaine asked to Christina's surprise.

She shook her head and lied. "I have merely heard his name. As Duncan notes, his piety is well known." Christina smiled then, hoping to divert them both from the notion that she knew Helmut at all. It would not do for him to suspect the truth. "To even be in the same abode as such a man is most amusing," she said lightly. "Perhaps I should try to seduce him, to see whether his deeds are as lofty as his words."

Duncan chuckled at that.

But Christina's mood was not so playful as she would have had them believe. To suspect that her husband's killer was in the same abode as she, to fear that he had murdered not once, but twice, with no repercussions left her hands shaking. That he should feign to be a pious man was an outrage beyond compare. Her fingers fell to the girdle that was a mark of the change in her own fortunes after Gunther's untimely death and she could bear to wear it no longer.

Christina removed it and pooled it upon the table, her revulsion so vehement that she struggled to hide her feelings. She had to do as much, though, for the lady was watching her. She had also to keep her hands busy, to vent her fury on some item.

The girdle would be it. Christina grimaced and began to break it apart into its component links.

"You might try to seduce me," Duncan teased, then seated himself on her other side. He smiled at her. "Though you might find it more of an easy victory than you seem to prefer."

Christina endeavored to match his tone. "And what is that to mean?"

"Only that you seem to like a challenge. It is a rare courtesan who would seek an enduring alliance with a knight like Wulfe. I cannot imagine that you will succeed in that, though I enjoy watching your attempt."

Christina could not stop herself from glaring at him. He had judged Wulfe and clearly found him lacking, from her observations, though that knight had shown her more kindness than any other man in years. "I am gratified to know that someone finds amusement in my situation." she said, her tone dismissive, then turned her attention to the kirtle.

Duncan saluted her with his wine and drank deeply of it.

"What will you do with it?" Ysmaine asked moments later. Christina knew the other woman watched her, apparently fascinated. Was it possible that she did not know the import of the girdle?

Christina smiled in anticipation. "Destroy it." She met Ysmaine's gaze and found only incomprehension. "It marks me as chattel, and I would be chattel no longer."

"Has it any value?"

"Its destruction will bring satisfaction, which might be value enough."

"Will you discard them?"

"Not yet. I will keep them, in case there is a purpose to be wrung from them."

"Have you a sack for the pieces?"

"Nay. Why?"

"I will give you one," Ysmaine said, much to Christina's surprise. "There is one in my belongings for which I have no use." Christina could not help but stare at her, so astonished was she that a noblewoman would grant her a gift. Ysmaine seemed to be amused by this. "It is only a plain cloth bag."

"Yet more than any soul has given to me in a very long time." Christina blinked quickly. "I thank you for this courtesy, Lady Ysmaine. Your kindness is much appreciated."

The lady left the room to climb to her chamber and Christina found her throat tight. Two souls in this party she would count as innocent—Wulfe and Ysmaine—for she believed she had seen their true natures. Her instinct was to trust them.

The rest had yet to prove themselves, but one she knew for certain was a black-hearted villain.

She had to tell Wulfe the truth so he was warned.

Pious.

The quality, when linked to Helmut, made Christina want to scoff aloud. She stood in the darkened common room that night, watching Helmut and Joscelin play at dice. Evidently they did this most nights. Evidently Helmut usually won. She lounged in the corner, behind him and out of his view, waiting for Wulfe to leave the cursed stables.

When Gaston abandoned the common room for the stables, she dared to hope that the knights kept watch or some such. She feigned an interest in her nails, noting how Gaston spoke to Duncan, who was wrapped in his cloak in the courtyard and seemed to be their sentry.

To her delight, when Gaston disappeared into the darkness of the stables, Wulfe emerged shortly thereafter. As usual, he moved with purpose, coming directly to the common room. He poured himself a cup of wine, ignoring her pointedly, and watched the game.

Christina knew he could not be interested.

"Finally," she purred, rising to her feet in one smooth move. She caressed Wulfe's arm, stole the cup of wine from his hand, and granted him an alluring smile. "I cannot bear to wait any longer." Then she took the pitcher of wine as well and swept from the room, hoping he would follow.

"I would have another cup!" Joscelin protested.

"Control your whore," Helmut snarled, and Wulfe's silhouette appeared in the doorway.

"Take a cup but leave the rest," he suggested, but Christina fled up the stairs. She heard his footfalls behind her and raced into the chamber, halting before the window with pitcher and cup.

He paused in the doorway, granted her a look, then marched across the room. "What jest is this you play?" he demanded in a growl that made Christina smile.

"I would speak with you. Alone."

"I have told you..."

"I know which of the party is the villain," she said with quiet heat, interrupting him.

Wulfe blinked. He glanced from the pitcher to the doorway and back to Christina.

"I suggest that you pretend you cannot resist me," she murmured. "No one expects a true conversation when people meet abed." She raised her eyebrows, daring him. "They will never guess that we conspire."

While he considered that, she raised her voice and darted away from him. "I will not surrender the wine so readily as that," she declared, her tone mischievous. "My price is a kiss, sir." Christina laughed, ensuring that she sounded flirtatious. "If indeed you can halt at that."

She had a moment to fear that Wulfe would not take her challenge, but then his eyes flashed. He grinned and lunged for her. "I shall teach you to challenge me thus, wench," he cried, and she emitted a sound of delight that did not have to be feigned. She twisted out of his grip and put down the pitcher. When he claimed it, she ran to the far side of the chamber. Once there, she slammed the portal and turned the key in the lock.

Wulfe spun to face her, his surprise clear.

Christina then flung the key out the window to the courtyard, well aware that Duncan watched them with avid interest.

"Temptress," Wulfe murmured, but there was no real complaint in his tone. Indeed, he seemed unable to tear his gaze away from hers.

The room was much warmer than it had been just moments past. Christina felt alluring and powerful when Wulfe watched her thus, and she liked that his gaze remained upon her face, not the flesh she revealed to view. She strolled toward him, untying the lace of her chemise, then bent and swiftly blew out the flame on the lantern.

"Convince me, sir," she purred, loud enough that she could be overheard. "I await your instruction."

Duncan's laughter rose from the courtyard below but Christina cared only for the gleam of Wulfe's eyes. "You tempt me overmuch," he murmured. "Who is the villain?"

"The kiss is not the price of the wine," Christina replied softly. "But of my confession."

Wulfe smiled and put down the pitcher. Christina's heart skipped at the resolute gleam in his eye. He closed the distance between them with a single step and caught her close. She could feel his heartbeat against her own and loved being crushed against his lean strength. They were yet before the window and she was certain that Duncan, if not others, could see their embrace.

In truth, she did not care. She cared only for Wulfe, the smile on his lips and the intent in his eyes, and wished he would kiss her soon.

Indeed, she might not confess what she knew until he had granted her far more than a kiss.

"Everard," Christina finally had the opportunity to whisper, but Wulfe had forgotten what they meant to discuss. The lady's touch nigh overwhelmed him, and once he had claimed her lips, he had been able to think only of her charms.

He pulled back and considered her, even as she repeated the charge.

Everard the villain?

It was startling that Christina's assertion so closely allied with his own suspicions. That compelled him to argue the other side, the better to ensure that their conclusion was sound. Her ploy of feigning to make love was a good one, and his body responded with vigor to the feel of her in his embrace. Wulfe bent and nuzzled her neck, savoring the scent of her skin, and kissed beneath her ear.

"But he is the Count of Blanche Garde," he protested, his words barely uttered against her flesh.

"Perhaps so," she replied, her voice just as quiet. "But this man is not Everard de Montmorency."

Wulfe pulled back to look into her eyes. "How can you be certain?"

"They were both in our party of pilgrims," she admitted, and he saw nary a doubt cloud her expression. "Everard was a pious man, and he found an accord with my husband, Gunther. They talked long into the night upon matters of faith and did so many times on our journey." She sighed and slid her fingers into Wulfe's hair, arching her back. Her touch sent fire through his veins and her expression was more than enticing. When she parted her lips thus and gasped, it was all he could do to refrain from kissing her soundly.

He indulged himself with one sweet kiss, telling himself that it was for Duncan's benefit. "How many years ago was this?"

"Of what import is that?"

"He might have changed much, if it has been a long time."

Christina granted him a skeptical look. "So much that he resembles his man-at-arms more than himself?" She framed Wulfe's face in her hands and brushed her lips across his, then hooked her ankle around his. He fell, just as she had intended, tumbling to the pallet with her sprawled atop him. Christina braced her hands on his shoulders and smiled down at him, her legs straddling him, and Wulfe was certain there was no finer place in Christendom he might be.

"Tell me of him," he invited.

Christina unbound her hair, working out the braid as Wulfe watched, fascinated. "The mercenary I met as Helmut has taken the place of his employer, Everard," she said quietly. "And evidently has lived under his name these many years in Outremer."

Wulfe frowned as he considered this. "I suppose it could be done."

"Of course it could be done." The lady was dismissive. Indeed, she shook out her hair in that same moment, then leaned her weight upon him. Her eyes were bright with conviction but Wulfe found himself keenly aware of the press of her breasts against his chest. "Many of the noblemen and knights in Outremer have lived there for many decades. They might have heard of Everard's repute but not met the man himself—or had met him as a child."

She bit her lip. "Do you think he killed Everard?"

"I cannot imagine how he would replace the man otherwise."

Christina winced. "Nor can I." She sighed. "Everard was a lovely man," she murmured and her endorsement only made Wulfe wish to ensure the nobleman was avenged.

"And Everard's holding was Blanche Garde," he mused, barely aware that his hands had fitted around Christina's waist. He was more aware of a different reaction to Christina's proximity.

"Is that of import?"

"It might be. Few pilgrims halt there, and if any did arrive at his portal, he could declare himself too ill to entertain them, if need be." He shook his head. "Still it would be a troublesome situation to manage. Why do as much?"

Christina chuckled, bending to kiss his earlobe. Wulfe's eyes closed in pleasure at the sensation. When she whispered in his ear, he shivered but locked his hands more tightly around her waist lest she move and halt this divine torment. "Why take the name of a rich man when one could be a mercenary instead? Truly, Wulfe, you cannot be so innocent of vice as this."

Wulfe nigh lost the thread of the conversation when Christina touched the tip of her tongue to his earlobe. When she nipped at his ear, he rolled her abruptly to her back, knowing he could not endure much more. She smiled at him, her eyes sparkling, for she knew well what spell she cast. "Could the true Everard have simply fallen ill? Many do on the road to Outremer."

Christina bit her lip and Wulfe watched with hunger. "Everard was very hale when last I saw him and that was here in Venice. He might have been tricked on the ship to Outremer. Many slip from the decks of ships in the night and their bodies are never found." She made an alluring sight, the lace on her chemise was unfastened and her hair in disarray.

"Perhaps he had assistance in that."

"How so?"

Wulfe found his hand sliding from her waist to cup her breast. "I have heard tales of men convinced to drink themselves insensible, then robbed and killed."

Christina arched her back and made a little purr of satisfaction.

Wulfe caught her nipple between his finger and thumb and caressed it, ensuring that she was as tormented with pleasure as he. Even though the cloth, he could feel her nipple tighten to a peak. She gasped and writhed beside him, her cheeks flushed. "Or cast overboard," she said, her words wondrously breathless. "I suspect we will never know the truth of it, for only Helmut knows what he has done."

She bit her lip and closed her eyes, moaning his name.

Wulfe recalled another detail that allied with her tale and halted his caress. "And the true Everard must be dead, for his father lies on his deathbed. It is said that this man returns there now, having delayed overlong in returning to France."

Christina braced herself on her elbow to meet his gaze. "Aye, who better to recognize that he is not Everard than Everard's father?"

"Indeed."

She frowned. "Why would he go to France at all?"

Wulfe could only guess. "Outremer is besieged. Perhaps Blanche Garde has little chance of standing against the assault of the Saracens." He *had* thought it strange that Everard would abandon his holding rather than defend it. "Perhaps he has few allies."

"Perhaps some soul has guessed his truth."

Their gazes held for a moment, then Christina tipped her head back. "Wulfe!" she cried out suddenly, her voice high as if she were lost in pleasure.

He considered her in surprise, but she smiled at him and moaned with new vigor.

"Oh, *Wulfe*!"

"Temptress," he growled, then kissed her throat. She cried out with apparent pleasure, and he could not resist the feast she offered. He interlaced their hands and held her captive beneath him, savoring the heat of her kiss. When he lifted his head, her eyes were sparkling.

"Where is it?" she demanded, and Wulfe could not understand her meaning. She smiled. "His holding," she added in a whisper, and he knew himself to be distracted indeed.

He rolled away from her and sat with his back against the wall, out of Duncan's view and away from Christina's beguiling touch. "Between Jerusalem and the port of Ascalon. Fewer take that route than to Jaffa. Even riding from Gaza, I chose the road to the east of Blanche Garde and rode through Bethgibelin instead."

Christina moved to sit beside him and he could see from her expression that she considered this. "Perhaps he hopes to arrive too late at his father's deathbed and take that holding beneath his hand instead."

Wulfe could not believe it. "Surely some soul will recognize him there!"

Christina met his gaze. "It has been almost a decade, Wulfe, and I know full well how ruthless Helmut can be."

"How?"

Her lashes swept down and her voice grew husky. "He killed Gunther."

Wulfe was horrified. "Did you witness this crime?"

"Nay. I saw them argue."

"About what?"

"Gunther would not tell me." Christina's lips set. "He believed I had taken a dislike to Helmut, which he saw as uncharitable. I never liked him," she said with quiet ferocity. "And my instincts are always right."

"Indeed."

"I saw him follow Gunther when he went to ensure our passage to Outremer several days later. Something was amiss. He had no reason to follow Gunther, so I followed them both." She swallowed, her discomfiture clear. "But there was a crowd and I lost sight of them for a precious few moments. I only found Gunther because I knew his destination."

"And?"

She lifted her gaze to his, and Wulfe's heart clenched at her despair. "He was dead," she whispered, and her tears began to fall.

He gathered her into his arms, wanting to console her even as he realized that she still loved her lost husband. She clung to him like a child. "How?" he murmured into her hair.

"Stabbed with his own knife and left in a pool of his own

blood." There was bitterness in her tone. "His purse was gone, as if it had been the work of a frightened thief, but the wound was savage. There had been no attempt to simply injure him. The assailant's intent had been murder."

"And you believe Everard did it?" Wulfe could not call the man by the name Christina insisted was his own.

"I saw him in the crowd!" she declared, even as she pulled back to look at him. Wulfe looked to the window and dropped a finger to her lips to remind her. She flushed and lowered her voice. "And I saw the satisfaction in his expression before he pulled up his hood and disappeared."

"And what did you do?"

She trembled a little in his embrace, so painful was this memory. "Two monks came to my assistance and took Gunther to a chapel. They said a mass for him, even knowing that I could not pay with coin. I offered them the ring that sealed my wedding vows, but they declined to take it." She heaved a sigh. "I could not pay for a burial, either. I know not where he is laid."

Wulfe feared the man's corpse might have been cast into the sea, but did not wish to upset her with the suggestion. "Do you know their foundation?"

Christina shook her head. "I was so distraught. I sought it later, but this city is a veritable maze. All I know is that their robes were undyed wool, and they were kindly."

In that, she had described most of the monks in Christendom.

"And when I returned to the inn where we had been staying, the portal was barred against me. I was told that our goods had been seized for our failure to pay the fee for the room. I had naught but the clothing upon my back."

"And the ring," Wulfe reminded her.

"And the ring," she admitted.

"Surely you sold it to see yourself fed."

Christina was clearly affronted. "Surely I did not."

"Where is it?"

"Safe."

He frowned, dismayed to learn that she had refused to part with a piece of jewelry, which surely she did not need, when he had been prepared to lose his destrier to ensure her welfare. He knew he should leave the matter be, but he could not. "You would rather starve to keep a ring?"

"I would still have starved," she replied, her lack of regret clear. "For I would have been cheated of its value and there would not have been sufficient coin to return home. Indeed, there would be no point in returning home without the ring."

"Because it was a token from your lord husband?"

"Because it was my wedding ring."

There it was again, the evidence that she yet loved Gunther. Though Wulfe could offer Christina very little and knew he had no right to expect any sweet surrender from her, still the realization disappointed him. It was unfair. It was unreasonable. But it was honest all the same. He had hoped to win her heart.

For she had claimed his fully.

He sat there, stunned by his own realization, and knew he dared never tell her of it.

Wulfe compelled himself to speak of more practical matters instead. "So, you would accuse a man of murder, but you have no evidence of his deed."

"You sound like Gunther," she said, her tone dismissive. "I know he is wicked!"

"That is not the same as being a murderer."

"I nigh saw him!"

"But you did *not* see him," Wulfe felt obliged to counter. "It could have been a thief."

Christina's lips set. "I do not like him and my instincts are infallible."

"Christendom is replete with men I do not like," he noted. "God forbid that they should all be murderers."

She laughed, surprised, then frowned at him. "You would mock me."

"I remind you of good sense," he said gently. "Recall how your position has changed. Who will believe the word of a whore over that of a nobleman?"

"But he is an imposter."

"Even if you were believed in some court, opinion could be

swayed with coin, which neither of us possess but Everard holds in abundance." Wulfe touched a fingertip to her chin, compelling her to meet his gaze. "Do not make this claim aloud until you have proof, I beg of you."

Her expression was mutinous. "If I find proof, will you aid me in ensuring that justice comes to him?"

Here was the truth of Christina. She loved her husband still, and would avenge him. Although it was reasonable, Wulfe found himself wishing he could do more than aid her in that quest.

If even he could assist in it.

"Perhaps." Wulfe shook his head at the flash of anger in her eyes. "It is not a question of my resolve. I merely doubt that evidence can be found after so many years."

"I will find it," Christina vowed. "Upon that you can rely."

He nodded, liking her determination well, even if it was in the name of justice for her beloved spouse. He was too aware of her softness beside him and the allure of her scent, as well as the anticipation conjured that must be denied. "Do you not think it time that you found your pleasure?"

Christina smiled. "Because you are tempted by proximity?" She did not wait for a reply, to his relief, but emitted a moan that nigh shook the floor. Her eyes were sparkling with delight at his astonishment.

"Do not be surprised," she advised in an undertone. "I have learned to feign this pleasure well, for such pretense is oft required." Her lips twisted. "It is said to be good for the trade of the house."

Before he could reply, Christina arched her back and moaned again. "Wulfe!" she cried, her voice rising high. Indeed, she ended his name with a gasp that prompted a reaction within him. She parted her lips and closed her eyes, running her tongue over her lips.

Wulfe had to move away, the better to ensure that he was not tempted to partake of the feast before him. Christina's chemise was unlaced and he could see the ripe curve of her breast as she panted with evident pleasure.

"Wulfe!" she gasped. "By Saint Margaret! By Saint Ursula!" She began to pound her fist upon the floor, her voice rising higher and higher. Wulfe could not tear his gaze from the vision she created. His body responded with predictable enthusiasm, though he knew she was not his to claim.

"By Saint Christopher and Saint Rupert!" Her fist hit the floor with increasing speed, matching precisely the tempo he would have taken had they been locked in an intimate embrace. "By the archangel Michael," she moaned. "And all the heavenly chorus. Wulfe! I beg you for release! Wulfe!" She screamed then, fairly shaking the house to its foundations, her fist striking the floor rapidly as she seemingly found her satisfaction with an endless moan.

Then she opened her eyes and smiled at him, mischief dancing in her gaze. "Oh Wulfe," she purred and he had to put distance between them. He stood and stared at the wall, some steps away, endeavoring to control his desire.

She loved her husband yet. That should be sufficient realization to cool his ardor and remind him of his duty to defend orphans and widows.

The weight of Christina's hand landed upon his back. "You are welcome to claim what you have bought," she murmured, but her words only drove home the realization that to do so would be wrong.

Wulfe knew he had to adhere to the rules of the order to ensure his own future.

Christina was not his to touch.

He strode to the table and quaffed a cup of wine, fighting to still his reaction, and refused to look upon her. He claimed the pitcher of wine, unable to forget Christina's feigned pleasure. That did little to discourage his own arousal. He had never seen the like and truly, he wished to witness it again.

Nay, he wished to participate and make it genuine.

Wulfe scowled at his own folly and leaned out the window. "Duncan! Might you favor me with that key?"

The older man bowed. "It would be my pleasure, lad. Of course, you have had your pleasure already." He chuckled at his own jest, but retrieved the key.

Duncan cast it to Wulfe without further comment—though Wulfe suspected that happy state would not last, given Duncan's grin—and Wulfe snatched it out of the air. He made for the door, knowing that he would only loose Christina's hold over his thoughts when he was away from her. He was certain the lady could not surprise him more, but was to learn his mistake.

He had unlocked the portal and had his hand upon the latch when Christina spoke.

Her voice was lazy and soft enough to send fire through him anew.

But it was her words that startled him into spinning to face her.

"How many of you know that the squire Laurent is, in truth, a girl?"

Wulfe's shock might have been more satisfactory if Christina truly had been pleased by his touch. As it was, she felt cheated and more than a little irked. She had hoped to tempt him to possess her one last time, but he had held fast to his principles.

And she, curse her nature, had sufficient principles of her own to refuse to test him further.

What cursedly poor fortune it was to finally find a man whom she might love with all her heart, only to discover that he had no right to claim a bride?

Wulfe stared at her in dismay, slowly closing the door. "You jest," he said, but she knew he did not believe it.

Christina shook her head. "She might even be a Saracen."

He blinked at that, his astonishment clear.

She liked that he did not ask again, that he evidently believed her. She could not be glad that he was so shaken by this revelation. He, she was certain, had not known.

"They said he oft helped in the stables at the Temple," he said quietly. "I guessed there was some Saracen blood in his veins, but thought him a bastard, perhaps an orphan."

"Another for your collection?" she teased and moved to stand beside him. Wulfe appeared to be puzzled. "Stephen told me of his parents, and of Simon's history."

"Simon is not an orphan."

"He might as well be. An oblate has no known kin." She brushed a speck from his tabard. "And you are without kin, as I am without a spouse or defender in this city." She smiled at him. "I like that you protect widows and orphans, Wulfe."

Her words seemed to discomfit him and he stepped away from her. "But Laurent? Truly?"

"Are you shocked to learn his gender?" Christina leaned closer. "Or to discover that the treasure has been entrusted to a girl?"

If Wulfe had been shocked before, now he was doubly so. His eyes rounded in horror. "Do not speak thus aloud!" he said, his words forceful for all that they were almost mouthed.

"You knew!" she charged in a hot whisper.

"You knew!" he retorted in kind.

Christina laughed. She spared a glance to the window and moaned his name anew, panting a little as her eyes sparkled. "Why?" she mouthed and Wulfe shook his head.

"I was not told." His lips tightened and he spared a glance toward the window, though Christina suspected his thoughts were of Laurent and his saddlebag. "If you guessed, who else did so?"

"The one who has taken it into protective care."

He eyed her warily. "It is there no longer?"

Christina shook her head. "I witnessed the transfer."

He nodded, his eyes glittering as he considered this. "And you know its location?"

She nodded.

"And are convinced of its safety?"

Christina nodded again.

"Is there any deed I can do to defend it?"

"Not so long as we are in this house, I think. Its defender is most vigilant."

He eyed her, his gaze clear. "Yet you will not tell me who it is?" There was no question in his tone.

Christina put her hands on his shoulders, her heart leaping as she stepped closer to him. She touched her lips to his throat and felt him swallow. "Every woman has her price, Wulfe," she whispered.

"And every man has his limit," he muttered to her surprise.

Christina found her nape caught in one strong hand. She was drawn to her toes and had but a glimpse of the purpose lighting Wulfe's eyes before his lips closed over hers.

It was a demanding kiss and satisfying for all of that. Christina pulled him closer, opening her mouth to him, ensuring that he knew she wanted all he had to give and more. The kiss heated her blood to boiling, the grip of his hands upon her making her feel claimed in truth. He backed her into the wall and feasted upon her lips, fairly devouring her as he let his passion loose.

Christina was both thrilled and awed. She met him touch for touch, savoring his possessive kiss.

It ended all too soon. Wulfe released her and took a step back, his eyes flashing as he surveyed her. "And they say that all the sirens are in the sea," he whispered, before he pivoted, set the key upon the small table, and left the chamber.

Christina remained as she was, catching her breath and waiting for her pulse to slow. She heard Wulfe descend the stairs and heard Duncan call a teasing greeting. A horse neighed and she knew he was in the stables, but still she simmered for his touch.

And Wulfe, she could tell, was not as immune to her as he would have preferred her to believe.

Christina closed her eyes and dared to pray for the one solution that would make her every dream come true.

SATURDAY, JULY 25, 1187

Feast Day of Saint Christopher and the apostle, Saint James the Great

CHAPTER TWELVE

aurent, a girl?

Once Christina had drawn his attention to the matter, Wulfe could not believe he had not realized as much himself. The supposed boy was so small and delicately wrought. The truth seemed so obvious, at least in hindsight.

Wulfe sat sleepless in Teufel's stall that night, his thoughts spinning and his flesh aflame. He yearned for what he had not shared with Christina and consoled himself with an attempt to solve several riddles.

It was a poor substitute for the pleasure the lady could offer, but he meant to redeem himself before reaching Paris.

Laurent slept, as always, draped over that saddlebag. At some point, it had held the treasure, though Christina insisted the treasure had been moved to safer custody. Was Laurent's gender the reason why?

How could Wulfe not have noted the truth sooner? He supposed his assumption had been based upon the endorsement of the other knights in the party, those from the Jerusalem Temple.

Did Gaston know Laurent's secret?

How much of a secret was it?

Why had neither alerted the Temple to the presence of a young girl in the stables? It seemed he was not the sole one inclined to bend the rule, when it so suited him.

But why had the treasure been entrusted to a young girl? She could not have the strength to defend it. Wulfe supposed that her very appearance led to the conclusion that she could be trusted with naught of value. It was a risky ploy, if the one who had given her the prize knew the truth.

Did Fergus know? Wulfe had to believe that it had been that man's decision to allocate his baggage as he had. Though Fergus had been entrusted with the treasure, it must have been his choice to entrust it to the girl.

Events did seem to make that allocation appear wise. The oldest of Fergus' squires, Kerr, was not a soul in whom Wulfe would have entrusted the care of any secret. Truly, he would not have even granted the boy the responsibility for brushing his steed. Kerr was of that ilk who gathered tidings of others and did as much so overtly that none would trust him a whit.

And Hamish, the younger boy, well, he was not the keenest of wit. He was not a bad boy, but he was clumsy. He might well have dropped the treasure, and if it was fragile at all, seen it ruined before it reached its destination.

Perhaps the girl had been the best choice.

What of Duncan and Bartholomew? Was Wulfe the sole one who did not know that Laurent was a girl?

Wulfe rolled over, endeavoring to sleep. If Kerr gathered secrets, perhaps that boy had discovered some detail that could identify the villain. Wulfe resolved to ask Stephen about the other boy. Then he tossed and turned, unable to sleep for he could not forget the sweet heat of Christina's kiss.

How would he deny his desire for her, all the way to the Saint Bernard pass?

It was dawn when Wulfe had the idea.

All night he had burned with desire denied. All night he had been tormented by the conviction that Christina had loved her husband, Gunther. Why else would she have kept the ring he had put on her finger, even at considerable discomfort to herself? Nay, it was a sentimental choice, and one that said much of the lady's affections.

There was little point in wishing that his own prospects were different, and that he might have more to offer Christina, if her heart was claimed by another. It was for the best that they would part at the Saint Bernard pass, likely to never see each other again.

Wulfe told himself this repeatedly but could not believe it. The fact was that he would have liked to have had Christina in his life in some capacity, even if he could not be with her in that most intimate way. He would like to see her husband avenged, to give her peace, even if the deed did not win her affection for himself.

He loved her, and her happiness was of greatest import. Perhaps it was best that she loved Gunther still, for she would not feel their parting as keenly as he did. She would not pine for him, as Wulfe knew he would always yearn for her.

It was dawn when he realized that he might be able to ensure that the lady at least recalled him with fondness. Soon, they would leave this city, and he doubted that Christina would ever return here. Venice had to be a city of bad memories for her.

But he might be able to contribute a good one.

Wulfe dressed in haste, rousing Stephen to accompany him on this errand. They slipped into the quiet streets and Wulfe set a brisk pace.

"Do we fetch a present for Christina?" Stephen asked.

Wulfe spared the boy a glance. "Why would you ask as much?"

"Because I think you like her."

"Do you?"

"You never brought another woman home with us," Stephen continued, despite Wulfe's discouraging manner. "And she makes you smile."

Wulfe wondered how many others had discerned the lady's effect upon him.

"I like her very much," Stephen confided.

"And why is that?"

"Because she tells us stories in the afternoon. Two days ago, she told us of Saint Christina, and how she was trapped in a tower by her father. She would not worship false idols, though, and no matter what they did to her, her faith sustained her." The boy dropped his voice in confidence. "It was awful what they did to her."

"I can imagine."

"And yesterday, she told us about Saint Mark and how he came to be the patron of Venice." Stephen wrinkled his nose. "They stole his bones from the Saracens by hiding them beneath pig carcasses, then put them in that big church and Saint Mark has blessed the city ever since."

Wulfe refrained from commenting that not all in this city had been blessed, and that Christina knew the truth of it, but he let the boy chatter on. It was good to see Stephen so animated and cheerful, particularly since Wulfe knew that the boy had told Christina his own tale.

"What do you think of the others in the party?" he invited when Stephen fell silent.

"I like Bartholomew, for he protects Laurent."

Wulfe was intrigued by this morsel. "Does he?"

"Aye, they have been friends for years, Laurent says. Bartholomew ensures that he has a fair share when the food is brought to the stables. Bartholomew says that Laurent knows much about horses, though truly, I see him only sleeping with Fergus' baggage." Stephen wrinkled his nose. "Perhaps he is still tired, for he was very ill on the ship."

So Bartholomew likely knew Laurent's secret.

"He was indeed," Wulfe acknowledged. "Such illness can weaken even the strongest warrior."

"Do you know that he took that saddlebag with him, even when Fergus asked him to aid in choosing a new palfrey?"

"Did he?"

"He can scarce carry it, for it is so heavy, but he does not wish to disappoint Fergus. He even insists that it must carry naught of value, but Fergus entrusting it to him is a test he refuses to fail."

Wulfe could well imagine.

Stephen smiled. "Truly, Fergus brings many gifts home for his betrothed, Lady Isobel. I hope she loves him as much as he loves her."

"I hope she does as well."

"She is Kerr's aunt, you know."

Wulfe glanced at the boy. "I did not know that."

Stephen nodded sagely. "Duncan said they should never have had the wretch in their company, had it not been for the lady's insistence. Do you think that means he dislikes Kerr, as well?"

"As well? Do you dislike Kerr?"

The boy nodded again, grimacing. "He is always sneaking around, and he is not kind to Hamish at all." Stephen fell silent for a moment, then continued in a rush. "He said there is a Templar treasure entrusted to our company."

Wulfe struggled to hide his shock.

"And he says that he will find it."

Wulfe's heart clenched at that. If Kerr had claimed the treasure, he could not believe that Christina would think it safe in that boy's custody.

Nay, someone else had stolen it to keep it safe from Kerr.

But who?

Stephen continued. "Kerr was arguing with Hamish about it that night on the ship, the night that Hamish was hurt."

Wulfe stopped and confronted the boy, who was proving to be a fount of information. "Do you know whether Hamish was struck or fell?"

Stephen shook his head. "I did not see, but I believe Hamish."

"Then who struck him?"

The boy grimaced. "Probably Kerr, for he did not like that Hamish argued with him. He says he did not, but he might be lying."

He might indeed. Wulfe resolved in that moment that he would discover what the boy Kerr knew before they left Venice.

Stephen's eyes lit. "Perhaps it was someone else, for Hamish vowed he would find the treasure himself."

"He did?"

"Aye." Stephen frowned. "I think he did not believe Kerr and wished to prove there was no treasure. Perhaps Kerr struck him for that." He shrugged. "No one likes Kerr. He even said that Laurent was as weak as a girl, and Bartholomew struck him for his words."

Some matters began to make sense to Wulfe. He could understand why Christina had taken to telling stories to the boys in the stables each day and guessed where she had learned as much as she had in so short a time. "So that was how his eye was blackened."

"And Bartholomew said we should not tell, for he would ensure that Kerr kept his silence in future."

"Has he?"

Stephen pursed his lips. "Only when Bartholomew is around."

Had the villain learned something of the treasure they carried from Kerr? Wulfe was resolved to find out, and his pace quickened without him realizing as much.

"Where do we go?" Stephen asked, surveying their surroundings with curiosity.

"You will see. It is this way," Wulfe said, indicating a small street that wound to the right.

"Have you been here before?"

Wulfe smiled, thinking of Christina's comment about his protection of orphans. "Several days ago. There is a monastery just ahead that I visited." He scanned the route ahead, then smiled when he spied the portal he recalled. "Here." He tugged on the rope and heard a bell ring inside.

"It does not look like a monastery to me. It looks like a house."

"Not all is as it appears, Stephen."

The boy nodded. "Aye, Christina is not like other whores we have met. Duncan thinks she is a noblewoman in truth."

Wulfe lifted a finger for silence as a small window in the door was opened. He could see one eye in the shadowed space beyond, then a gasp of satisfaction.

"Brother Wulfe!" Brother Franco declared in a whisper as he opened the portal. "I did not think to see you again." His gaze dropped to Stephen, then he looked at Wulfe with a question in his eyes.

Wulfe dropped a hand to Stephen's shoulder. "This is one of

my squires, Stephen." It was only then that he realized the boy might be surprised to see the fate of other orphans. "I came to ask after your memory, Brother Franco."

"Not so fine as once it was," that man acknowledged, then stepped back and gestured in invitation. "But my brethren remember a great deal. They are at *matins*, but soon will break their fast. You are welcome to join us."

"I thank you for that." Wulfe inclined his head and waited in the courtyard with Stephen, well aware of how that boy surveyed his surroundings. Several faces appeared in the shadows, the children who lived in the establishment curious about the arrivals.

"It still does not look like a monastery," Stephen whispered, indicating the open door of the chapel. "Save for the monks praying."

"It is more like the priory, in that there is labor done here in God's name, by men who have taken their vows." Wulfe smiled at the boy. "The brothers feed and shelter orphans."

Stephen looked about himself with new interest. It was but moments before the bells of the chapel pealed and the brothers filed out of the shadowed space. They nodded at Wulfe and Stephen, curiosity in their eyes, and proceeded in silence into the refectory.

"Is it like the priory in that none should speak while at a meal?" Stephen whispered.

"I expect as much," Wulfe advised in an undertone. "Eat a little lest we insult their hospitality, but recall that there are many hungry mouths in this abode."

Stephen nodded as Brother Franco beckoned to them. They were seated between him and Brother Matteo and warm bread was placed before them. There was honey, as well, and some cold meat. Wulfe realized he should have seen Stephen fed before their departure if he had expected to boy to resist such temptation. The boy was of an age to eat heartily whenever opportunity presented itself.

"You have a question for us, Brother Wulfe," Brother Franco said. "And I would give permission for it to be shared at our meal." The brethren regarded Wulfe with interest. "Please, if you know of any reply, share it with Brother Wulfe."

"Indeed," Wulfe said. "When last I was here, I mentioned a widow in our party. I had thought she might seek to join a religious order."

Brother Franco nodded. "I recall as much."

"I did not realize that she had seen her husband murdered, much less that he had been assaulted in this very city."

The brethren looked up as one, their meal forgotten.

"He was stabbed most cruelly and died before she reached his side. He was also robbed."

"Such misfortunes are known to occur in all cities, Brother Wulfe," the older Brother Matteo said with quiet regret.

"Indeed, I recognize as much. The reason for my query is this. She says she does not know where he is laid to rest, and I doubt that she will ever return to this city again. It is clear that his loss is a great wound to her still and if she could visit his resting place, it might give her solace."

"But how should we know such a detail? Hundreds if not thousands of pilgrims die in this city each year."

"Aye, but it occurred nine years ago. She said that several monks were the sole ones to come to her aid, that they said a mass for him and ensured he was laid honorably to rest. She cannot recall who they were or where their chapel was located, so great was her grief."

Brother Franco shook his head with obvious regret.

Before he could speak, though, Brother Matteo tapped his finger on the board. "Nine years? And a pilgrim? From whence did he come?"

"I am not certain." Though Wulfe knew that Christina meant to leave their party at the pass, he did not know her destination, much less whether her goal was her family home or her husband's abode.

Brother Matteo nodded as he considered that. "Might I see her? It is possible that I will recognize her and thus the man in question."

Christina awakened late again, having lain awake long into the night with dissatisfaction. Wulfe's kiss had fed a desire that was not easily dismissed, and she felt that she had not slept well.

She dressed all the same and opened the portal, only to find a folded pile of cloth outside the door along with a pitcher of warm water. Clearly both had been left for her.

Christina shook the cloth and discovered it was a kirtle. She smiled at its modest lines. It was not new and it was not elaborate. The plain green wool was sturdy and unadorned. Tucked into the folds of cloth was a simple white chemise and a veil that was both plain and generously proportioned. The kirtle was of the right length for her, more or less, and would fit, more or less, but was neither luxurious nor provocative.

Christina adored it. She retreated into the room and shed the kirtle from Costanzia's establishment as quickly as she could. She washed with vigor, as if she would scrub away the shame of the life she had been compelled to live, then donned the chemise and the kirtle. She braided her hair and coiled it up on her head, as she had once worn it every day. The veil was arranged and pinned over it, and she wished she had a glass to see the transformation in her appearance.

She removed Gunther's ring from the pocket in the hem of her old kirtle and strung it on to one of the laces from that garment. She made a necklace of it and hid the ring between her breasts, liking the feel of the cold stone there. She would never again fear for its safety.

She truly would leave this place behind.

Christina rolled the old garments together and descended to the common room, much delighted with her appearance. She would have to thank Wulfe for his generosity.

She was breaking her fast when Duncan appeared, that man sparing her a smile. "Fits well enough, lass," he murmured. "Though it is a mark of your beauty that even garbed modestly, you might tempt a man."

"I thank you for the compliment."

Duncan grinned. "And not for the garb?"

Christina was startled. "This is a gift from you?"

"You need not be so surprised, lass. I thought you might prefer to abandon the mark of your former trade."

Only the mark of it? Christina lost her appetite at that, for she feared she understood his expectations. "But I cannot pay you," she protested, hoping he did not request that the debt be rendered in kind.

"One day you will," Duncan said amiably. He spared her a twinkling glance. "I would not expect a woman to sate more than one man per day as you pleasure Wulfe, and truly, I would not vex him willingly by attempting to claim what he defends as his own."

Christina had naught to say to that. Did Wulfe consider her to be his own? She doubted as much, particularly given that their coupling was a charade, but it would only be folly to correct Duncan.

"I apologize that I did not realize this was your generosity. I thank you."

"And you are welcome." They ate in silence then, even as Christina considered the merit of adding Duncan to her list of those she trusted.

It would have been an easy choice, had he not been so obviously appreciative of her charms. She knew well enough that desire could tempt men to deeds beyond expectation.

"Christina!" a boy cried and she turned to see Stephen racing across the courtyard. "You must come."

"Come where? And why?"

The boy dropped his voice to a conspiratorial whisper. "Wulfe has a surprise for you, and he bade me fetch you." He raised his voice then. "I thought you might like to see the arrival of the ships, my lady."

Christina hesitated, wondering why Wulfe had not come himself. Duncan seemed to share her wariness for he removed a knife from his belt and slid the scabbard across the table to Christina. "Take it," he advised quietly.

Christina knew enough of this city's perils that she did just that. She thanked Duncan again, then followed Stephen. To her relief, Wulfe waited around the first corner. He was tapping his toe with impatience and scanning the streets. At the sight of her, though, he stepped forward. His approval of her changed appearance was clear and he bowed before tucking her hand into his elbow. He set a brisk pace that she matched as Stephen ran beside them.

"Why do I think we are not going to see the ships arrive?" she asked and his smile flashed.

"We may have a better surprise for you than that." His gaze flicked over her. "I see that Duncan is as good as his word."

"You knew he meant to do this?"

"We agreed that you would prefer to look more like a pilgrim, though I had no coin to see it done. Duncan offered to see the matter addressed."

"He is most gallant, then."

"I think him smitten," Wulfe acknowledged, and Christina wished it might have troubled him more. "Let us make haste."

Christina's new garb was both blessing and curse.

Though it pleased Wulfe to see her dressed as a noblewoman, the simple kirtle was more than sufficient reminder that she was not his to touch. He should honor her, as an aristocrat and a pilgrim, and not desire to touch her anew.

The strange matter was that he found her more alluring in modest garb, not less so. She walked taller and held her head high. With her hair braided and her curves disguised from view, her eyes seemed more remarkable.

There was a coolness between them now, a formality that he should have welcomed, for it should have made it easier to recall that their fates could not be joined. Her posture made it clear that Duncan had been right about her lineage.

The change between them made Wulfe regret that he had so little to offer to a woman of her ilk.

Save this one gift.

He hoped that it would please her.

Christina was clearly curious about their destination, for she glanced his way repeatedly. "I did not know that the arrival of the ships could be seen from this quarter," she said finally.

Wulfe smiled. "That was but a ruse to draw you out."

"You persuaded Stephen to tell a falsehood?" she teased and the boy grinned.

"I agreed to do as much, my lady, for I wished you to be

surprised."

"Then you are in league together."

"Indeed we are," Wulfe said, halting before the monastery. He turned to Christina. "Do you have your husband's ring?"

Christina's smile faded and she paled. She did not reply, but pulled a cord from the front of her kirtle. It was fashioned into a necklace, and he saw the glimmer of gold as she pulled the ring strung upon it out of her chemise. At her enquiring glance, he nodded and she removed it from the string, placing it upon her left hand. It was a gold band with a large blue stone set in it. Wulfe blinked that she should have concealed a prize so rich. She considered the ring on her hand for a long moment, her face pale, and he wondered whether she had guessed the surprise.

He rang the bell and Brother Franco opened it promptly. He said naught but peered at Christina, then gestured. Brother Matteo appeared at his side, his eyes narrowed. He was much older than his fellows, his face lined and the remainder of his hair white. His eyes were dark but bright. He scanned Christina's features, then his gaze dropped to her left hand. The monk bent to peer at the ring on her finger, then he smiled.

"It *is* you," he said quietly. "I shall never forget this ring, or the lady who offered it in compense. I wondered that you did not return."

"I did not know where I had been."

Brother Matteo smiled. He turned to gesture to the courtyard and the chapel beyond. "Come, my lady. Come and see where your beloved husband lies at rest."

It was a humble chapel, simply ornamented and not overly large. Gunther would have liked it, Christina knew, for it seemed to resonate with the faith of the brothers who worshipped within it.

He could have found no finer place to rest.

There was a single beeswax candle on the altar, which was a simple wooden table, wrought strong. There was only a square of linen adorning the altar, a pottery chalice and plain wooden plate atop the linen for the communion. The floor was tiled and the space was cool, the sole source of sunlight coming through a crevice in the wall above the altar. It was like an arrow slit, but formed in the shape of a cross between the gaps in the bricks.

Gunther had been laid to rest in the wall to one side of the altar. Christina knew that they could not entomb any bodies beneath the floor, as was the custom elsewhere, because of the *aqua alta*. Those high tides washed through the city each winter, turning plazas into lakes and the lower floors of houses into pools.

She knelt before the altar and prayed for Gunther's soul and his immortal rest. She felt her heart fill with tranquility and a measure of joy to know that Gunther had been in such good care. She heard the sounds of the children who lived with the monks in this place and smiled as they argued about the distribution of bread in the adjacent rectory. They ran and shouted, despite the admonitions of the monks, and Christina was gladdened by the sounds of their vitality.

Aye, Gunther must be pleased to be in such company.

She wept quietly for his untimely demise, his lost dreams, and his goodness. And by the time she rose to her feet, she was doubly determined to see Helmut pay for his crime.

Christina straightened and crossed herself, genuflected, and surveyed the simple chapel with pleasure once again. Wulfe had given her this, the opportunity to say farewell, and tears pricked at her eyes again that she should know such generosity.

She left the chapel to find Wulfe waiting for her in the courtyard. He showed none of the impatience she had witnessed in him before. Several of the boys had gathered around him, examining the hilt of his sword and fingering the hem of his chain mail hauberk. He was patient with them, his manner kindly, and she saw adoration in the way that Stephen looked at him.

"They are a rare breed," Brother Franco said from behind her, evidently having followed her gaze. "It is no small thing to wage war for God and justice."

Christina smiled in agreement with that. "I am so grateful for this opportunity." She turned to face the monk. "I would thank you all for your charity to my husband. I know he would think well of this place."

"Indeed?"

"Indeed. He loved children. We went on pilgrimage because we had none. He wished to atone for our sins in the hope that our match might no longer be barren."

The monk nodded with understanding. "But God saw his goodness and gathered him close instead."

Christina found her tears rising anew. "Thank you, Brother Franco. Thank you for those words. Gunther was a very good man." She pulled the ring from her finger, knowing what she must do. "And he was a man who understood not only that debts must be paid, but that alms should be given where they can grant the most difference. Nine years ago, your brethren declined this ring as payment. Today, I give it to you as alms. In Gunther's name, I ask that you see children fed and housed."

"And masses sung for his immortal soul." To her relief, the brother took the ring. "It is a rare prize, sister. Are you certain?"

"I am. I know that Gunther would wish it to be so."

Brother Franco turned the ring, letting the gem catch the sunlight. "A sapphire?"

Christina nodded. "Cut in the east, by what I was told. Do not be cheated. It is an old stone, for there is a blessing carved into it in Arabic. My husband's forebear brought it home from crusade. He was among those knights who took Sidon in 1110."

"A family piece?"

"But Gunther has only a widow," Christina said softly, knowing her husband's older brother had claimed every other token in the family treasury. This piece had been Gunther's sole legacy and she would grant it as he would have wished. She closed the monk's fingers over the gem. "And she gives this willingly."

"Bless you, sister," he said. "I will ensure that your gift casts a long shadow. Gunther and his forebears, and his widow, will be remembered well in this place." He blessed her and Christina felt a tremendous relief flood through her.

She squared her shoulders and strode toward Wulfe, who had been watching her. Her past was laid to rest, because this man turned her footsteps toward her future.

Christina wept.

Wulfe had hoped that he had been right about her husband's resting place, and he had anticipated that she might be emotional if he was proven to be so. He had not expected that she would return to him with her face wet from her tears.

Nor had he prepared for his own reaction to the sight.

He wanted to console her. He wanted her never to weep again. But she mourned her husband, dead these nine years and still holding fast to her heart. He could not summon a word of consolation to his lips, but took his parting of the monks and escorted her back to the house.

They were halfway there when he thought about the ring. He glanced downward, verifying that she had surrendered it to Brother Franco, but did not dare to ask.

Christina noted his look, though. "I gave it as alms," she said. "They will know where to sell it to see the best price, and they will make the coin last. Gunther would have wished for this."

"I thought they declined to accept it before."

"They did. Perhaps they thought it might be taking advantage of my grief. I surely was not thinking with clarity on that day."

"And now you are?"

"Aye," she acknowledged with welcome conviction. "It is not rational, and I know it well, but all these years, I knew I had to defend that ring. I knew I could not sell it. I knew it had a purpose and a place, though I could not discern it. I thought it was because I had vowed to him to keep it always, but on this day, I saw the truth." Christina tugged Wulfe to a halt. "It belongs there, where children will be fed and defended because of it." She bit her lip and he saw her tears fall anew. "He loved children," she whispered, her words hoarse. "Yet I gave him none. Now he is surrounded by them." She nodded and her tears fell like gems. "It is right."

Wulfe's throat was tight. He dared to touch her elbow, no more, and guide her down the busy streets. "You should not blame yourself for this. You loved him, and that is no small thing."

"How would you know as much?" she asked, not in challenge but in curiosity.

"You weep, though it has been many years since his passing."

Christina smiled sadly. "I weep, Wulfe, because I did not love him enough. I was young and he was much older. He was a good man, but I saw only the age between us. I resented being compelled to wed a man so many years my senior, and in truth, I did not regret at the time that my womb was barren. I was dutiful and I honored him, but he ought to have had more." She swallowed. "I weep because I did not love Gunther as he deserved."

At that, Wulfe took her hand in his and gave her fingers a squeeze. He did not believe her words, for it was clear that she held her husband yet in high esteem. He would not argue the matter with her, though. "You honored him then and you honor him now. Perhaps no man deserves more."

She smiled at him through her tears, then heaved a ragged sigh. "Pledge that you will come to me this night, Wulfe."

He made to protest but she placed her fingertips over his lips to silence him.

"This is all I will ask of you. You gave me a great gift this day and I would show my gratitude."

How Wulfe wished she might ask for more from him than physical pleasure and solace, even though he knew he could not offer her more.

"There is no need," he managed to say but Christina shook her head.

"There is every need. I understand your resolve and I would not have tempted you, not if you had not done this goodness for me." Her eyes were bright in her appeal and she looked so vulnerable that Wulfe knew he would not be able to deny her any request. "One last night, Wulfe. I beg of you."

He bent and kissed her fingers, wanting to step away but knowing he could not. "One last night," he agreed and heard her catch her breath with relief.

"I will ensure you do not regret it," she whispered, but Wulfe was not certain that was within the lady's power.

He was weak but he was greedy. He would take what the lady offered, knowing it would be the final tryst between them.

The rain began when they sat at the evening meal and ate fish stew yet again. Christina was not the only one whose appetite was less than it might have been, nor was she the only one to be quiet. The sound of the rain in the courtyard seemed to echo the tranquility that had filled her.

All came aright.

All came aright because of Wulfe.

There was naught more right than following him to his chamber after the meal, naught more right than undressing him in silence. They said naught, for there was naught to say.

This was the last time.

This embrace would have to suffice.

They loved with quiet ferocity, granting each other a pleasure that left them both trembling. Their mating was potent and powerful, enough to spoil her for the touch of any other. She felt a communion with him, as if their thoughts and feelings were as one, and it was enough to make her yearn to seize this moment and keep it forever.

Though that was not to be.

Christina clung to Wulfe in the aftermath, savoring the heat of his embrace and the beat of his heart beneath her cheek. She listened to the rain, at peace as seldom she had been. She felt replete, as if their souls had been joined, and the feel of his fingers in her hair made her close her eyes against her tears.

What would she give to spend every night this way?

Christina never meant to utter the words aloud, despite the way they filled her thoughts. But in this moment, when all seemed so right, she thought it would be a travesty to keep the confession to herself. "I love you, Wulfe."

For a heartbeat, she felt the sudden tension in him. Christina had time to hope that he might reply in kind, but when he did not, she hoped he might not have heard her confession. When he eased her aside and left the pallet, she knew he had. When he dressed in haste and left the chamber, she knew her feelings were not returned.

The realization was devastating.

Once Wulfe's footsteps faded from the stairs, there was only the sound of the rain falling on the stones in the courtyard far below. Christina closed her eyes and wept silent tears. She knew a thousand tales of lovers destined to never be together and such stories had always rent her heart.

That was naught, it turned out, in comparison to living such heartbreak herself.

MONDAY, JULY 27, 1187

Feast Day of Saint Pantaleon
and of the
Seven Sleepers of Ephesus

CHAPTER THIRTEEN

love you, Wulfe.

Four words Wulfe had never expected to hear from any soul and, marvel of marvels, they had been uttered by Christina. He had been astonished, pleased, then skeptical.

He did not believe for a moment that Christina tried to deceive him. Nay, in the moment that she had uttered the words, she had believed them. The difficulty was that he did not believe it possible for her to have surrendered her heart again.

Not so soon after she had wept those tears for Gunther.

She felt indebted to him, perhaps, or grateful that he had found Gunther's grave, but love? Wulfe could put no credence in the claim—as much as he might have liked to do so. He reminded himself that he could not offer her a future of any merit. He dared not make a similar confession to her, for his pledge would be true.

Still, Wulfe recognized the lady's power over him. If she entreated him to love her, he would lose hold of his principles. He would err, and they would both pay the price of that.

Wulfe avoided Christina deliberately after that, for it was the only sensible choice. No one need know how he savored her sweet confession, over and over again, nor how he wished his life might have been different.

By the time they rode out on Monday morn, he felt drawn as taut as a bow string. It was raining just as heavily as it had rained the day before, but they could not delay in the hope of better weather. They rode through the twisted streets of the city at a snail's pace, slowed by the number of people.

Wulfe wanted to put his spurs to Teufel and bolt into the countryside. Indeed, he felt a strange desperation to put Venice quickly behind them, and knew it was not solely because he feared for Christina's safe passage through the city gates. He also dreaded the solitude of the road ahead, the quiet corners, and the villain hidden in their ranks. Was it Everard? He could not say for certain. The sense that he must wait on the villain's move only made him more impatient, more restless and more agitated.

And that was before he spied the dark-haired whore.

They were riding through a small plaza, nigh at the gates, when he heard a woman's laughter. Wulfe immediately recognized the beauty who had been presented to him first at Costanzia's house. She was ripely curved and beautiful, her lips red and her hair gleaming black. She laughed at the words of some merchant and threw back the hood of her cloak, parading across the plaza like a queen. She was oblivious to the rain and by her manner, it might not have fallen upon her. She looked richer and more vital than those who gazed upon her, and she knew her power well.

Indeed, she savored it.

He spotted two of the protectors who had relieved him of the order's coin, loitering not far behind the woman. They spoke to each other, the gaze of one lazily following the ebony-haired whore. She surveyed the crowd with a smile, seeking opportunity. Wary, Wulfe touched his heels to Teufel's sides. His party rode across this end of the plaza, destined for the wider road that led to the city gates on the west, and all increased their pace at his behest. Still, the whore made a slow path in their direction, one that might well intersect their course.

What if she saw Christina?

Would she call out to the men?

Wulfe ducked his head and rode on, turning his face the other way to encourage his fellows. Christina was near the back of the party, riding one of his palfreys, and had pulled up the hood of her cloak. Stephen rode the palfrey newly acquired by Fergus, at that knight's invitation. Christina's face was yet visible, but there was no way he might warn her without directing the attention of the whore to her.

He swallowed, gauging the distance to the point where the wide road left the square. He glanced back at the whore only to find her looking at him. She stared, the way her lips parted in surprise revealing that she recognized him.

Her gaze roved over his party and Wulfe's heart clenched when he realized she had spied Christina.

She glanced back at the men and he scarce dared to breathe.

Then she treated Wulfe to a winning smile. What did she mean to do? Would she reveal them? Would Christina and all the coin be lost? He had a moment to fear the worst, then the whore raised one hand to her lips.

She blew him a kiss, her eyes shining.

He saluted her, and they shared a smile, then she spun to continue her stroll in the opposite direction. Costanzia's men followed her, oblivious to what she had seen, and Wulfe was relieved beyond belief that she deliberately led them away.

It seemed that he was not the sole one who wanted a different future for Christina, and that was good news indeed.

It was a wretched ride, though Christina wondered whether any other member of their party was so very glad to be leaving Venice. She did not care about the weather or how much discomfort she had to bear. The sooner this city's gates were behind them, the better.

Wulfe seemed to share her sense of urgency, for he urged Teufel to a gallop as soon as they had passed through the city gates. The mud flew from the hooves of the horses and they were all drenched to the bone, but Wulfe did not slow their pace. Christina would have ridden through the night to be farther from Venice, but she knew the horses deserved more kindness than that.

Still she was disappointed when Gaston insisted that they halt that evening. It was dark and they were all cold, but still it seemed to Christina that Venice was too close. Wulfe protested, but Gaston made no better show of heeding the Templar's command than he had previously. The place they halted appeared to be a tavern, for there was much raucous shouting from the well-lit building, and Christina did not care for the sound of drunken revels.

She would not sleep this night, to be sure. She bit her tongue and resolved the make the best of the matter.

They were granted use of a barn for their accommodations, and one that was more dirty than any Christina had seen in many years. There were no animals resident in it, so the manure was well-rotted and ripe indeed. Judging by Wulfe's displeasure, the price of the pit had been overly high.

Joscelin and Everard took one look at the barn and declared their mutual desire for a cup of ale and a game of dice. They left their steeds to be tended by the knights' squires and departed for the tavern, arm in arm.

Christina exchanged a dismayed glance with the lady Ysmaine, then she and the maid set to work. The lady would have assisted, but she seemed both quiet and cold and the maid was quick to pluck the broom from her mistress' hands. Christina let the maid fuss over Ysmaine as she helped to put matters to rights. Cloaks were hung over beams and the floor swept out. The boys tended to the horses and the knights carried the dung outside. Christina could not imagine that they could sleep in such a place, and it seemed of small advantage to have a roof overhead.

Once the floor was cleared, several of the boys went to the tavern with Fergus and Gaston to fetch their meal. Duncan bade Hamish and Simon aid him with some loose boards found in the back of the barn, and they created benches at the clean end of the hall. Wulfe hung a pair of lanterns there. Laurent huddled shivering, still wrapped around the saddlebag.

"Would that we had a fire," Duncan murmured, with a glance at Ysmaine. "The ladies would welcome the warmth."

Wulfe shook his head. "Even if we found dry tinder, this entire barn might burn. Better to have the lanterns only, for we may quickly fall asleep."

Though his decision was wise, Christina was chilled to her marrow. Ysmaine had a change of clothes and so did her maid, but Christina could only wring out her hem. Laurent, she noted, huddled shivering, still wrapped around his saddlebag, and Stephen sat alongside him. The pair seemed to have become friends. By the time the stew was brought from the tavern, Christina could not have been the only one damp with perspiration from their efforts.

She supposed she had survived worse.

"We shall all have chills in the morning," Ysmaine's maid predicted, her voice low and her tone dark. Christina could not dispute that. The scent of the stew was not particularly appetizing, but she supposed it would be better than naught at all. Bartholomew returned then, his expression disgruntled, and complained about the price they had been charged for fodder for the horses.

Christina sought the latrines then and found them by scent alone.

Indeed, naught in her life had prepared her for such filth. She could not endure it. She spared a glance to the tavern, then continued into the forest, where the pine trees gave the air a better scent. Surely one person could relieve herself in this forest without defiling it overmuch? She found a thicket that would hide all sight of her from both tavern and barn and crouched as she lifted her skirts.

She had only just sighed with relief when she heard voices. Christina could not have said why she did not reveal her presence—perhaps it was those instincts upon which she relied—but she crouched lower and fairly held her breath.

It was a man from the tavern who strode to the latrines with a young boy. They spoke quietly together and she could not be certain of their identities. Was the boy's hair fair? It was difficult to be certain from a distance and in the rain. How tall and broad was the man? They were both wrapped in dark cloaks, and that made Christina think of the villain at the brothel.

She bent lower so as not to be detected and waited. Surely they would not be long. She heard Fergus shout from within the barn, urging his squires to come and eat. Wulfe called to Stephen and Simon, the sound of his voice making Christina's heart thump. She did not even dare to hope that he might offer to keep her warm this night, for he had scarce acknowledged her presence all the day long.

It was clear that her confession had offended him, but she was glad it had been uttered aloud all the same.

As she watched, the man from the tavern left the latrines, but did not stride back to the tavern. Where was the boy? Christina peeked over the shrubbery, peering through the rain. She heard the man's footfalls but could not see where he had gone.

"Kerr!" Fergus shouted from the barn. Christina could see him in the portal, silhouetted by the light and peering into the night. "Come eat before you must go without!"

There was no response, save the patter of the rain. Fergus said something to the others in the barn, then Christina saw him don his cloak and march out in search of his squire. He appeared to consider the tavern, but strode to the latrines first.

Christina wondered who the other man had been and where he had gone, fighting a sense that it was folly to reveal herself as yet.

Then Fergus shouted and she knew she had chosen aright.

"Zounds!" he bellowed. "Help me!"

What was amiss?

Christina saw the company spill out of the barn in response to Fergus' cry. Even the men in the tavern spilled out to look, their curiosity kindled, and she saw lights swinging in the darkness as several strode down the hill to explore.

Was that the silhouette of a man entering the barn, after the others had left?

Christina picked up her skirts and moved quietly through the forest, intent upon finding out.

The boy, Kerr, was dead.

Poisoned, even.

Wulfe had seen much in his days, but he would have been happy to have not witnessed this. Poison was an unkind way for any person to end his life and could not have been by choice. By the time the men reached Fergus, the boy's color was wrong and his face twisted with pain.

Wulfe knew the matter could not end well.

Gaston and Fergus tried to aid the boy, and Gaston shouted for his lady wife, who knew aught of healing, to assist. The lady, to her credit, strode through the mud and rain in what had to be her only clean and dry kirtle, and did not shirk the task.

It was too late though. Kerr was convulsing when the men poured out of the tavern, shouting drunkenly. Wulfe surveyed the company gathered there, hoping to spy some clue as to who had done this foul deed.

All appeared to be concerned and fearful.

But all were not there. Fergus, Duncan, and Gaston tried to aid the boy, Bartholomew watching worriedly. Stephen and Simon had followed Wulfe and watched with undisguised horror. Hamish was paler than was his wont as he watched his fellow squire suffer. Though Kerr was not popular, no one wished such a fate upon another.

Nay, someone had wished this fate upon Kerr.

Christina was missing, as was the count, Everard, whom she so disliked. It was impossible that they might be together. Joscelin was not present, but then, he and Everard had gone to the tavern to play at dice.

That habit of Everard's troubled Wulfe, for it gave credence to Christina's assertion that the count was not who he declared himself to be. Surely, no pious man would play at dice with such enthusiasm?

And where was Everard? Wulfe was certain he could identify Joscelin's portly figure among the silhouettes of those approaching from the tavern.

Where was Christina?

Wulfe thought at first that the squire Laurent was missing, then spied the squire in the shadows behind Bartholomew. When Wulfe saw that Laurent did not carry the saddlebag, he feared that Kerr's state was providing a timely distraction.

Had Christina tried to intervene?

Wulfe left the group and hastened back to the barn, fearing what he would find.

The saddlebag was gone.

There was no sign of Christina. She could not have taken the saddlebag into her own care, for she knew it no longer contained the treasure. Or had she striven to deceive another? Had she drawn the villain's attention to herself to protect another? Fear welled within him.

Wulfe realized that the barn was darker than it had been and saw that one of the lanterns was gone. He pivoted and found Duncan fast behind him. The older man's gaze flew to the spot where Laurent had been hugging the saddlebag and he paled.

"Zounds," he whispered.

So, Christina had been right.

"We must find it before it is taken far," Wulfe said through his teeth, though in truth he was more concerned for Christina.

"Curse this rain," Duncan muttered. "We cannot discern a trail."

The pair strode into the night again, searching the darkness for some hint of the prize's location. Someone had carried it from the barn and could not have gotten far. The hue and cry from the vicinity of the latrines disguised much sound, but there was a sudden glimmer of light in the forest on the far side of the tavern.

Duncan must have seen it as well, for the two men strode into the rain as one. That distant light disappeared, but they crept close to the spot, endeavoring to make no sound at all. It was clear that Duncan had stalked prey as well, for his identification of the spot where the light had flared was nigh identical to Wulfe's own.

Where was Christina?

Wulfe thought he could discern the silhouette of a figure and put a hand out to halt Duncan. That man had already frozen in his steps. The figure was too tall and heavyset to be Christina, but cloaked so that his identity could not be discerned. Had Christina been injured? Or had she returned to the other group?

They eased closer in silence, Wulfe's thoughts filled with questions.

The figure bent over something, moving furiously. There was a sudden cry of fury, then a crack of some item striking the ground. The figure came crashing toward them so suddenly that Duncan was shoved aside and Wulfe scarce managed to step out of the way. He made to pursue the villain, but something was cast at him.

He ducked and something shattered against the tree by his side. It was only when the pieces glittered that Wulfe realized it was the lantern from the barn.

The villain's favored weapon.

Praise be that it rained with such vigor and there could be no fire. Wulfe would have chased the fleeing figure, but a woman spoke softly behind him.

"Wretch," Christina whispered.

Wulfe spun to find her bending over a lump on the ground, Duncan at her side.

She was hale!

When he drew closer, he could see that there was a round rock before her, partly unfurled from protective layers of cloth. The saddlebag itself could be discerned, discarded to one side.

"He knows it was a trick," Christina said with no surprise.

Duncan nudged the rock with his foot and exhaled. "I must say that I am relieved."

"Is the real treasure safe?" Wulfe asked her with quiet urgency.

Christina nodded without hesitation.

The men exchanged a glance.

"What did you see?" Duncan asked. "Do you know who it was?"

"I have no proof," Christina said. "For I did not see him clearly. When all ran to the latrines, I saw a silhouette return to the barn. By the time I drew near, that person left the barn again, carrying something. I followed, hoping to see his face, but when he lit the lantern I was behind him. I tried to move closer, but I was not quick enough."

The thought that she had been so close to the villain, the one who would kill to gain the treasure, struck fear into Wulfe's heart. That she knew the location of the prize and what it was only made him fear more for what could have happened.

"You should not have taken such a risk," Wulfe chided. "We

know this villain will kill to see his ends achieved. Do not put yourself between him and his prize!"

Christina lifted her chin. "My life is mine to risk as I so choose," she said softly. "And I will always choose the greater good."

"You could have been injured!" Wulfe protested, but her expression did not soften.

Duncan looked between them, his expression thoughtful, and Wulfe looked away.

"What happened at the latrines? Why the hue and cry?" Christina asked and Duncan shook his head.

"The boy was killed."

Christina gasped. "Not Laurent?"

The older warrior grimaced. "Nay, it was Kerr, and there will be hell to pay for that, you can be certain." Wulfe looked at the Scotsman without comprehension. "The adored nephew of the lady Isobel, the betrothed of Fergus. She will never let him forget this, of that you can be certain."

"You do not like her much, do you?" Christina asked softly, but Duncan only gave her a hard look as a reply.

"My view is of no import in this matter," he said gruffly.

"What else did you see?" Wulfe asked Christina.

"Only a man and a boy came from the tavern to the latrine. The man left and the boy did not. While I sought a glimpse of him, I lost sight of the man."

Wulfe nodded, wishing some soul had seen the man clearly and witnessed the poisoning of the squire. He did not doubt that the villain had planned the matter to be exactly thus.

"Poison?" she asked. "Truly?"

"Truly," Duncan verified and she grimaced.

"No soul deserves such a fate as that," Christina said quietly.

"Mark my words," Duncan said grimly. "The lady Ysmaine will be blamed for it, for she was the one who bought poison in Outremer."

But someone had either stolen poison from her, or bought more. Frustration roiled in Wulfe that this villain should be so fortunate so consistently.

Or perhaps he was merely experienced in his vice, and knew how to ensure his deeds were not detected. He recalled Christina's conviction that the man she called Helmut had killed at least twice.

He should be brought to justice.

Duncan bent then and rolled the rock into its cloth, then placed it in the saddlebag again. The others could be heard returning to the barn. "I say we keep the feint," he said, his tone practical. "For it may prove to be of use later. I will tell Fergus, and undoubtedly Laurent will learn the truth, but I would ask that the others not be told."

Perhaps the fiend would reveal his knowledge.

They nodded agreement and returned to the barn individually, ensuring that they blended into the company unnoted. All were present by the time the company gathered in the barn again, and Wulfe wondered where the treasure might truly be hidden.

He knew that he was not the sole one in the company who wondered as much.

Surely Christina would not take such a risk again?

The company was restless, even once they were settled for the night in the barn. The foul deed committed upon Kerr might have been an unwelcome guest at the board. Lady Ysmaine was pale and sat wrapped in her cloak by her maid. Evidently she was estranged from her husband on this night, doubt about the origin of the poison having done its work.

Laurent was pale, that squire's gaze flicking from one knight to the next, as if in fearful anticipation of some recrimination. Everard and Joscelin had returned to the tavern to play at dice.

Hamish wept quietly for his fellow squire, or perhaps out of shock, and Fergus looked grim. Duncan patted the weeping boy's shoulder, but clearly was not accustomed to granting comfort. Stephen and Simon sat together, near Wulfe, and looked very young. Wulfe leaned against a pillar, booted ankles crossed, and his features lost in shadow. The lantern flickered and Christina wondered whether they would sit in silence until the light was gutted.

She could not bear it.

"Perhaps we have need of a tale to distract ourselves from the night's events," she said brightly, not truly surprised when many turned to her with relief.

"Do you know whose feast day it is today, my lady?" Stephen asked, and she smiled at the boy for encouraging her effort.

"Indeed. Today is the feast day of the Seven Sleepers of Ephesus." She spread her skirts with her hands, recalling the details of the story. "They were seven men of good families who were of an age with each other and good friends, as well. They lived in the days when Decius was the emperor and were all Christians. Decius sent word to Ephesus that temples should be built for the Roman gods and that all were to worship them. Any who refused to do so would be executed. So great was the fear amongst the people of Ephesus that friends betrayed friends, fathers betrayed sons and sons betrayed fathers."

"They did not betray each other?" Stephen demanded, his incredulity clear.

"They did not," Christina said. "But they confessed to their faith and were chastised by the emperor himself. Because of the affluence of their families, he granted them a reprieve and bade them reconsider their choice. Instead, these seven friends gave all their wealth away to the poor, then retreated to a cave in the hills to take refuge from the emperor. There they fasted and prayed."

"They must have become hungry," Stephen guessed.

Christina saw that Simon was listening intently and that Laurent's eyes were wide. Perhaps Laurent recognized the alternate version of the story of the companions of the cave. Christina smiled at the girl to reassure her and "Laurent" tentatively smiled back. "They did, and one of their number, Malchus, dressed himself as a beggar to go into the city and try to get them some food. While there, he heard that Decius had decreed the seven friends should be hunted and brought to their execution. He returned to the cave to warn his fellows, and though they consulted, it seemed their martyrdom was inevitable. They prayed for strength to face the coming trials. By the grace of God, they fell into a deep sleep and were discovered thus by the emperor's men."

The boys leaned forward.

"The emperor himself came to look upon them, for they could not be roused. Indeed, they might have been struck to stone. So, the cave was walled up, lest it was a trick to allow them to escape. Two of their fellow Christians, Theodorus and Ruffinus, wondered whether they might be witnessing a miracle. They had the tale of the seven friends written down and tucked the scroll into a chink between the rocks that secured the entrance to the cave. And so the martyrs were nigh forgotten."

Christina lifted a finger. "Until, some three hundred years later, heresy abounded in the city and the Christian emperor feared for the souls of his citizens. God knew that a miracle was needed and so he urged a shepherd to build a shelter on the side of the same mountain where the seven companions had taken refuge in their cave. To build the shelter, the shepherd removed the rocks that had blocked the entrance to the cave. With a breath of will from God, the seven friends awakened. They believed they had slept but a night and were hungry indeed. Malchus offered to again go into the city for bread and also to learn how the hunt for them was to proceed. Once again, he dressed as a beggar, and once again, he left the cave, fearing he might not return."

"But the city was not as Malchus recalled. Instead of the new temples built by Decius, there were churches everywhere. The people openly professed their faith in Jesus and he could make no sense of it. He wondered whether he had gone to another city in error, for this one bore so little resemblance to the one he knew. He thought his wits addled by hunger and tried to buy bread, but the baker would not take his coin."

Laurent sat up. "A hue and cry was raised, and a crowd gathered, for the coin was ancient and valuable," the squire said. "The baker thought this man must have stolen it, while others thought he had found a treasure and should share its location. As you might imagine, he was most confused by all of this."

Christina smiled. "The crowd demanded that the man they believed to be a stranger prove his origins. The man gave his name and that of his parents, but no one knew of any of them."

The boys looked between Christina and Laurent, who smiled at each other even as Laurent continued. "He cried out in vexation, for still they called him a liar, and demanded to be taken to a magistrate of the emperor. When he named the emperor who he knew ruled the territory containing the city, the crowd fell back in awe. He could make no sense of their reaction and asked what was amiss."

Christina dropped her voice. "The baker told him that emperor had been dead for centuries. But the Christian emperor who now ruled the city came to see Malchus. He believed he saw the hand of God in these events and begged to be taken to the cave. There he embraced all seven of the men who had slept so long, saluting them as saints. The hidden scroll was found in the chink and read aloud, and the people rejoiced, for their true faith was restored by this evidence of the truth of the resurrection. The seven friends laid down to sleep then, and this time they did not awaken. They were laid to rest in golden coffins and the cave was embellished with gold and other riches. It became a shrine, a great holy place that was testament to the power of God and the promise of life beyond death that he offers us all."

There was silence when Christina finished her tale, but it was not so melancholy as it had been. The rain still pounded on the roof and the barn still smelled, but something had changed.

She felt the weight of Wulfe's hand land upon her shoulder. "I thank you for this reminder on this night," he said quietly. "Let us all pray for Kerr's immortal soul and hope that each of us has the chance to awaken to new promise."

New promise.

As Christina prayed, she began to think of home, of old promises and legacies. For the first time, she dared not just to wonder but to hope that there might truly be a new beginning for her.

It was no surprise that she wished for it to be with Wulfe.

WEDNESDAY, AUGUST 12, 1187

Feast Day of the martyrs
Saint Andeolus and Saint Tiburtius,
and of
the virgin Saint Waldetrudis

CHAPTER FOURTEEN

hristina was appalled to realize over the ensuing weeks that she had been utterly mistaken about the knight Gaston's regard for his lady wife.

It was enough to shake her conviction that the greater good must prevail.

She had believed that Gaston and Ysmaine had found love in their marriage, despite their match being recently made. But it had been clear on the night of Kerr's death that Gaston thought his wife responsible for the squire's demise. She had hoped his mood would pass, but it had only grown more vehement. Indeed, Christina began to fear that Gaston might put his wife aside.

Over his unfounded suspicions.

She was outraged by this lack of gallantry.

Ysmaine, apparently, was shaken by it. She seemed even more ill than she had previously and spoke only to her maid. The maid cast furious glances in the direction of Gaston when she believed herself to not be noted, and Christina could not blame her.

It was clear the man did not know the risk his lady wife took for his benefit. Aye, it was apparent that Ysmaine knew something of herbs, and evidently, given what Bartholomew said, she had both carried a measure of aconite from Jerusalem and had identified the poison that had killed Kerr as that same herb. Still, Christine knew that Ysmaine could not have killed the boy so viciously, and surely her husband understood his lady wife's nature as well as Christina did.

Or were all men cursed to be blind when it came to women? She found herself irked anew that Wulfe had never responded to her own sweet confession, though it had been made unwillingly. It was clear to Christina that he wished for there to be no bond between them.

Perhaps he thought of her as just another whore.

That the lady Ysmaine had taken the treasure into her own custody at some risk only annoyed Christina more. She believed, given Ysmaine's character, that the noblewoman tried to protect the prize her husband was charged to defend. But he spurned her, and as far as Christina could discern, had never even asked her about his suspicions.

Of course, they had spent long days in the saddle after Kerr was buried, as if Wulfe would hasten to the pass and be rid of her with all haste. In truth, Christina suspected he simply wished to reach Paris, so he could return to Outremer. She was sore and tired each night when they halted, but that ensured that she slept dreamlessly. Each day brought them closer to the Saint Bernard pass, which was mere days from her home.

As that abode became closer, Christina found herself thinking of her sisters and her mother and hoping all were well. She recalled days in the herb garden and the orchard, helping with the labor to be done there or simply playing with her sisters. She could nigh see the carved pillars of the church in the village and hear again the resonant voice of the priest as he blessed them all. Was he still there? What of the cook and the alewife, the seneschal and the armorer? Christina could see every corner of her father's demesne in her memory, though she doubted it was exactly as it had been nine years before.

She had not dared to think of it while in Costanzia's house, for she feared never to see her home again. There was no point in tormenting herself with the memory. Each day, though, brought her closer.

What would she tell her family of these years? As little as possible to be sure, for her mother would be shocked by what Christina had been compelled to do to survive. Indeed, her mother would wish to see her wed again, a prospect that did not fill Christina with anticipation. She would be glad to be a widow, to have a roof over her head, and a daily meal in her belly.

Would they suggest she retire to a convent?

It would depend upon the gender of her sisters' children, to be sure. Christina again considered the possibility that she might not have been the sole one to be barren. She was the eldest, after all. Although Miriam's wedding had prompted Gunther to embark on crusade, her youngest sister, Anna, might not be wedded as yet.

What if neither Miriam nor Anna had a son?

It was late when the party reached the inn at the summit of the Saint Bernard pass, and the air was crisp. The stars were already emerging and the light from the inn was most welcome. Wulfe was keenly aware of the silence between himself and Christina, but though he yearned to speak with her again, he dared not do so.

He was sickened by the prospect of her leaving their party on the morrow. He had already resolved to give her the palfrey she had been riding, for it would ensure that she arrived home more quickly. That could only increase her safety.

He would have preferred to escort her to her family home himself, the better to see that she arrived, but the treasure and missive had to be delivered to Paris first.

Would she grant him a farewell kiss?

Would he have some token to remember her by? He had no right to ask for one, but he wished for a lock of her hair.

Wulfe had no doubt that if he asked, she would grant him one, but he did not wish to give her expectations he could not fulfill.

So it was that he was covertly watching Christina when the party dismounted. He had dismounted and was holding Teufel while the boys slid tiredly from their saddles. "Take Christina's palfrey first," he bade Stephen, knowing that she must be tired.

She smiled at the boy when he reached for the palfrey's reins, then flicked a glance at Wulfe that made his heart clench.

All too soon, she averted her gaze.

Meanwhile, Ysmaine walked toward the portal, her exhaustion clear.

"I shall see to your steed, my lady," Bartholomew said and the lady turned to thank him, as gracious as ever she was. Wulfe saw her cloak flare but thought naught of it, until he saw Bartholomew's surprise. Behind the squire, Gaston's features set to stone.

Ysmaine spun and closed her cloak with one hand, apparently alarmed as she hastened anew for the portal. Gaston strode behind her and caught her elbow in his grip, his expression more forbidding than Wulfe had ever seen it.

It appeared that Gaston's serenity could be disturbed.

What was amiss?

"My lady," Gaston said grimly. "I would have a word, if you please."

Wulfe watched the lady square her shoulders, then glance up at Gaston as if unconcerned. He knew otherwise. "Aye, sir?" Her hand dropped to her belly and rested there, as if she were round.

With child.

Wulfe blinked. So soon as this?

"You bear a child," Gaston charged, and Wulfe understood that their conclusion was the same. It could not be Gaston's child, if Ysmaine were so ripe already.

The other knight's mood suddenly made perfect sense.

"Indeed, sir," Ysmaine replied, her chin high. "I understood you desired a son."

The other knight's eyes flashed fire. Though Wulfe was glad to see that some matter could infuriate Gaston, he would not have wished these tidings upon any man. To be cuckolded and deceived was most foul. To learn of it before a company of his fellows was yet worse.

Though he had not been certain of Ysmaine's plans, this was an unwelcome shock.

Had the old man been right that *all* women were

untrustworthy?

Gaston was clearly dismayed. "It seems of robust size to have been conceived in Venice less than a month ago."

"Perhaps I erred and he was conceived in Samaria," the lady said, bold in her lie.

"Still, to be so round in but a month." Gaston's tone faltered, as if he were uncertain.

Ysmaine was undeterred. "Perhaps he is tall, like his father."

Christina, who had followed the pair, made a dismissive sound. Gaston looked back at her, but she shrugged. "That babe was conceived three months ago, at least." Gaston glared at Ysmaine who blushed. "You must have bound it down to disguise it thus far."

"Aye," Ysmaine agreed hastily. "But I could bear it no longer, and I feared for the child."

This was reprehensible! She risked the welfare of the child in order to better deceive her new husband! Wulfe was appalled.

"As indeed you should," he muttered, unable to hide his disgust.

"Three months?" Gaston demanded of his wife. "*Three* months!"

"It cannot be so long as that," Ysmaine protested. "Not quite."

"I should say not nearly. We have been wedded only *one* month." Gaston glowered at his wife, then fell silent in his fury.

Wulfe could not believe his fellow knight had made such a blunder. "Did you never see her nude?" he asked in an undertone, unable to keep from glancing at Ysmaine.

Her lips tightened, but she was unrepentant.

"She kept herself covered, always," Gaston confessed, then added with scorn. "I thought her modest."

"Manipulative, perhaps, is a better choice of word," Wulfe felt compelled to say. To his surprise, his words drew Christina's ire.

Aye, she spoke to him for the first time since Kerr's demise, but the exchange was not one he might have hoped to have had.

"And what other opportunity to ensure her own salvation would she have had?" she demanded of him. "You behave as if women have all the choices that men do in this world, and I assure you, that is not the case."

"She could have told him!" Wulfe insisted.

"And lost the aid of the sole person who had offered to assist her? Aye, there is a good way to starve." Christina's lips tightened. "Or to end up in my trade."

Wulfe was chastened, for he knew that Christina saw much parallel between her own experience and that of Ysmaine—save that Ysmaine had found a champion in time. Or so he had thought until this day.

Perhaps their situations had more in common than he had believed.

"Did you sell yourself like a whore?" Everard asked Ysmaine, his lip curled.

Gaston glowered at his wife, his anger so evident that Wulfe was somewhat surprised. It seemed that when Gaston ceased to be impassive, his emotions were more readily discerned than those of any other man. It was strange. Wulfe would have expected the other knight's composure to slip in increments, not to abandon him entirely in an instant.

Perhaps it particularly troubled him to be cuckolded.

"I prayed," Ysmaine asserted to the count. "But it is said that God helps those who help themselves."

Everard shook his head and continued into the inn. "I am glad indeed that I have never seen reason to wed. It is true that women are the source of all perfidy."

"You said neither of your husbands had consummated the match," Gaston said, his words thrumming with anger.

"They did not." Ysmaine dropped her gaze, then swallowed. "I am sorry, my lord," she said. "We had to eat."

"There are alms for the poor," Gaston snapped.

"Not so many as one might hope. The sisters gave us shelter, but little more."

Gaston raised his voice with anger, clearly determined to shame his wife before all within earshot. Truly, the entire company might have been rooted to the spot, for they stared and listened, apparently unable to do aught else. "Confess the truth now, with all this company as witnesses. Did you lie to me, Ysmaine of

Valeroy?"

Ysmaine nodded. "I knew not what else I might do, sir. I entreat you..."

"I shall hear none of your entreaties!" Gaston shouted, then shook a finger before her. "I demanded but one thing of you."

"Honesty," Ysmaine agreed, her voice much smaller, then lifted her chin. Her lack of guilt was astonishing, truly, and made it hard to feel compassion for her. "But I can explain, sir, if you but grant me the opportunity..."

"But one request I made of you and that one thing you could not supply!" Gaston roared. "There is but one explanation I would have from you in this moment, and it requires only a single word in reply to my query." He turned his glare upon his wife but she did not flinch. Did she think her choice had merit? Wulfe was shocked.

"Do not be so fool as to lie this time," Gaston growled.

"I would not, sir."

Gaston pointed a shaking finger at her belly and ground out the words. "Do you bear *my* child?"

Ysmaine bit her lip. Her tears rose, but Wulfe did not trust them to be genuine. She appealed to Gaston. "I fear I do not, sir."

The other knight did not linger to hear more. He marched toward the stables, like a man whose world had been shaken.

"Gaston!" Ysmaine shouted after him, but if anything, he walked more quickly. "Gaston, I can explain!" She fled after her spouse and grasped at his arm. "If you would but grant me a moment of privacy..."

"Madame." Gaston spoke so coldly that Wulfe found his manner too harsh. Then he flung away his lady's hand, as if he could not bear her touch. "There is not a single word you could utter to me that I would care to hear."

Ysmaine stood where he left her, weeping bitterly. Her maid went to console her and the others shifted their weight, feeling awkward at what they had witnessed. Wulfe found his attention turning to Christina, whose fingers had risen to her lips in apparent surprise.

Then she glared at Gaston.

Why did she suddenly take Ysmaine's side? What had she realized?

He sensed that he missed a key detail.

And that Christina knew it.

Yet again, he yearned to speak with her.

But Christina spun and strode into the inn, her gaze fixed on the ground.

There was no doubt about it. Wulfe had to speak to her before they parted ways in the morning.

If naught else, he would not have the last words between them be such harsh ones.

Christina had to leave the company once she realized the location of the treasure.

It was beyond clever for the lady Ysmaine to have disguised the reliquary as her own pregnant belly. No one would investigate that part of her person, and she would always be certain of its location. It could be in no safer place.

She sighed in disapproval of Gaston's reaction. Could he not give his lady some credit? Could he not ask her what had happened instead of spurning her in front of the entire company? It was beyond a lack of chivalry. It was churlish.

And worse, the lady had only her maid to aid her in defending the treasure now. At least before, her husband had gone to her bed some nights. Now, Christina imagined that Ysmaine would scarce dare to sleep.

That would not leave her sufficiently well rested to be alert and defend the prize.

Curse the man for refusing to even listen to her explanation! Ysmaine might have explained the truth in private and had his protection, but it seemed that Gaston's pride had been sorely pricked. She would not have thought him so intemperate in his reactions, but that solely proved that a man's true nature could not be readily anticipated.

She had only concluded as much when Wulfe came to sit beside her. She spared him a cool glance, disliking how he had taken Gaston's side.

"You may take the palfrey on the morrow," he said, putting a cup of wine before her on the board. "I would not have you walk."

Christina spared him a glance. "I thank you for that."

He smiled crookedly at her. "You need not sound so surprised. Have I been so foul as that?"

"You were unkind to Ysmaine this day."

He frowned. "I was surprised. I did not think her deceptive."

"Or unchaste?"

His gaze met hers. "I understand that choices must be made," he said quietly. "I do not blame you for your choice, nor do I blame her for hers. One must do what is necessary to survive." He sipped his wine. "I think it a poor decision to deceive Gaston, though. He will not soon forget that, and they are wedded until death does them part."

Christina was intrigued. "You think then that she should have simply told him?"

Wulfe nodded.

"He might have struck her."

"Nay, not Gaston."

"But he was livid on this day!"

"He was shamed before the entire company. He would not be alone in being a man who responded with greater fury in such circumstance."

"He ensured that she was shamed, as well," Christina could not help but note.

Wulfe smiled again. "Aye, there is that."

She had an idea then. "Will you talk to him?"

He glanced up with evident surprise.

"Encourage him to make amends with her," Christina urged.

Wulfe shook his head. "We have much evidence that Gaston does not heed my counsel. I fear it will make no difference, save to vex him further."

"I believe she has good reason for her choice and has need of his protection."

The Templar frowned and sipped his wine. "He should forgive her, because she has need of him? It would be better if the matter were more balanced."

Christina dropped her voice to a whisper. "Who says it is not?"

Their gazes locked and she saw understanding dawn in Wulfe's eyes. He straightened and turned to survey the room, sipping his wine, but she could fairly feel excitement thrumming through him.

He spoke louder when he continued. "As I said, the palfrey is yours to take on the morrow. How far is it to your family's holding?"

"I thank you for the offer, but I will ride all the way to Paris with you, after all."

"Indeed?"

"Indeed. I would take the opportunity to visit my cousins before returning home," Christina lied.

Wulfe was not fooled and she knew it. "What is it?" he asked in an undertone and she knew he referred to the treasure.

But he had said he was likely to be tested on his compliance with the order to not look, and she would not imperil his place in the order any more than she already had.

To remain a Templar was his sole desire, after all.

Christina pretended she had not heard him. "Indeed, they always ride to my father's holding for the harvest, so I will be able to ride there with them." She smiled at Wulfe. "Even better, you need not surrender a horse in this gallantry."

"I would pay the price willingly."

"I would not ask it of you."

"I would grant it to you."

"I will ride to Paris." Christina watched as Wulfe nodded thoughtfully. It was clear that he might have continued their conversation, but Gaston entered the common room and glanced Wulfe's way.

Summoning him.

Wulfe rose and bowed once to Christina, then followed the other knight. He clapped Gaston's shoulder, as if consoling him, and the pair left the common room together.

Christina shivered, feeling suddenly cold, and rose from the board herself. She would speak to Ysmaine and if her sympathy was welcomed, perhaps defend both lady and treasure in the night.

"My lady wife hides the treasure," Gaston confided to Wulfe, his voice the barest murmur as they left the hall behind.

Wulfe was not surprised by this, given his conversation with Christina, but he was surprised that Gaston knew the truth.

Gaston continued. "I took her maidenhead but a month ago, and her belly was flat. She hides the treasure there to ensure its safety."

"Clever," Wulfe said, not wanting to say more.

"Dangerous," Gaston corrected, as grim as ever Wulfe had seen him. "My learning of it before the company meant that I had to spurn her. The villain must see us as divided, for I must appear to believe in her deception to defend her safety."

"Yet you cannot protect her."

Gaston was clearly dismayed by this. He shoved a hand through his hair with rare agitation. "I do not like the risk she takes. Yet I cannot reveal the ruse to be what it is. I fear I will not even have the opportunity to defend her!"

"You might have taken the opportunity to let her explain."

"I should have," Gaston growled. "But I erred in the moment of my surprise and now my course is set."

Wulfe put a hand on the other knight's shoulder to reassure him. "Fergus and I are two to defend her, and we make four with Bartholomew and Duncan. We shall see your lady defended."

Gaston inhaled sharply and scanned the sky above. "I do not like it."

Wulfe could not help but smile. "It seems the gift of women who claim our hearts to know best how to vex us," he said, earning a sidelong glance from Gaston.

"Do you truly have no prospects beyond the order?"

Wulfe shook his head, wondering at this query. "None."

Gaston frowned. "Perhaps you might command the knights sworn to a baron you knew well." He held Wulfe's gaze. "I return to claim a holding and would have men sworn to me I can trust fully."

Wulfe caught his breath. "You cannot truly mean this."

Gaston nodded. "The task is yours, if you desire it."

"I thank you." Wulfe was stunned by the generosity of this

offer. He did trust Gaston, and had he been convinced of Christina's affection, the offered position might be the perfect solution. But he suspected that her return home would only rekindle her ardor for her lost spouse. He might leave the order and lose the opportunity to fight for Jerusalem, only to find himself alone in Gaston's barony.

"I have surprised you, and see as much," the other knight said quietly. "Think upon it until we reach Paris."

Wulfe nodded and expressed his gratitude for the opportunity. He was surprised to realize that the prospect of dying in defense of Jerusalem had lost some of its luster, but still he was sworn to the order, and still he would see this quest fulfilled.

The lady Ysmaine and the prize she carried must be defended to the best of Wulfe's abilities, without any other soul realizing that he knew the truth of her burden.

Surely that was challenge enough to occupy him.

MONDAY, AUGUST 24, 1187

Feast Day of Saint Ouen and Saint Bartholomew

CHAPTER FIFTEEN

hey reached Paris in the last week of August, on the feast of both Saint Bartholomew the apostle and Saint Ouen, Bishop of Rouen. The weather was foul again, but the streets thronged with people celebrating the feast day.

Christina deliberately let her palfrey ease to the back of the party. It was easily accomplished, given their slow progress. Wulfe, too, looked back less frequently once they were surrounded by pedestrians, for he strove to keep the party together and to ensure that they moved steadily forward. The task was sufficiently challenging that he did not keep such a vigilant eye upon her.

Ysmaine also fell back in the group, her maid by her side. Christina did not know whether this was by accident or design, but she saw both Duncan and Fergus ease their steeds closer to guard her sides.

There could be no doubt that they knew the truth of Ysmaine's burden.

Christina was certain that Helmut knew the truth as well. If he had not realized it before, Ysmaine had been sure to inform him of it several nights before.

They had paused in Provins and shared a meal together, the last such before Joscelin left them for his own home. The little merchant had been determined to fete them, as thanks to the knights for ensuring his safe return. Christina did not doubt that he intended to win the favor of Ysmaine as a client, as well, for he had hastened to his warehouse to bring her several gifts.

Ysmaine, however, had professed exhaustion and retired early, shortly after that man's return. Christina had watched Helmut when Ysmaine had paused before climbing the stairs to the chamber above the common room. Ysmaine's maid had hastened ahead of her mistress to prepare the lady's bed, and Ysmaine had halted, as if winded. Christina wondered if she had intended to draw every eye. Ysmaine had placed a hand on her lower back, seemingly oblivious to Helmut's gaze upon her.

Then she had knocked her supposed belly with her fist, apparently by accident. The metallic clang had made Helmut straighten for a heartbeat before he hid his response in the act of sipping his ale.

There was no disguising the glint of avarice in his eye, though.

Christina was dismayed. The lady had made herself prey, and she was resolved that Ysmaine should not pay the price of Helmut's greed.

He had purportedly left the party when they had ridden onward to Paris, declaring he would take another road home the better to reach his father in time. Christina did not believe it. Nay, he would not let Ysmaine from his sight. He meant to follow them.

And Ysmaine relied upon it.

As they rode, Christina realized that Ysmaine's choice could only mean that she did not carry the reliquary any longer. Ysmaine drew the villain's eye to ensure the treasure was safely delivered to the Temple, which meant that she could not possess it. Ysmaine must have made another exchange. Christina did not doubt that Helmut would kill her whether she surrendered the location of the reliquary to him or not.

Where was the treasure?

Christina's gaze fell upon the maid and the bundle she clutched. It was supposedly Ysmaine's old and discarded garb, which the maid would keep for her own, but it had been a means of moving the reliquary before. Christina was convinced that Radegunde had been entrusted with the treasure, and suspected that Ysmaine would draw Helmut away from the party to ensure its safe delivery.

She could not let Ysmaine be injured.

She would use Helmut's feint herself.

Christina relied upon Wulfe taking the path to the Temple that Gaston had advised. Once through the city gates, the party was assailed on all sides by beggars and merchants. The horses lost their pacing for a moment, until Wulfe shouted and compelled the party to form a tight group. He reached back and seized the reins of the steed closest behind him and the others did the same, ensuring that none might straggle behind. As soon as Duncan had seized the reins of her palfrey, Christina slipped from the saddle, hoping that none would note her departure.

If Duncan saw, he gave no sign of it.

She ducked into the crowd and made for the shadow against one wall, her gaze clinging to Wulfe's figure. She might have imagined that he sensed what she had done, for he glanced back with a frown. Her heart leapt that he might halt the company and foil her plan, so she hid behind several large casks. To her satisfaction and disappointment, Wulfe turned his attention to the road ahead once more.

Could he truly forget her so readily as that?

Or had he discerned the same scheme?

It was only when Christina was on her feet that she realized it might not be so simple to follow the party. The horses cleaved a path through the crowds, but one that quickly disappeared again. Christina thought of a river flowing around a rock, but continuing beyond it with no sign of the interruption. She made slow passage through the busy streets and was glad not only of the size of Teufel but Wulfe's armor. The bright glint of sunlight upon steel was like a guiding star.

When would the lady Ysmaine leave the party? She had to have a scheme to draw out Helmut, or she would never have switched the relic with the bundle. And where was Helmut? Christina did not imagine for a moment that he had truly abandoned the prize, and repeatedly looked back, hoping to catch a glimpse of him.

The bridge to the isle was so congested that the horses had to ride in single file. Doubtless few steeds were ridden across it on a feast day like this one, for it was thick with jugglers, merchants, and merrymakers. The large plaza before Notre Dame was even more packed with celebrants than the streets had been and Christina despaired of catching up with the party. She could see them far ahead.

They had halted.

And Gaston had turned back.

This had to be the moment! Christina shoved her way through the crowd, needing to be close enough to see what transpired. She leapt to the top of a merchant's table, earning a curse for disturbing his wares, and saw Ysmaine disappear from her palfrey's saddle. Gaston roared, his bellow fit to be heard even at a distance.

Christina kept her gaze fixed on the lady's fair hair. That her maid remained resolutely with the party meant that Christina was right about the maid's custody of the reliquary.

But Helmut would not know that. Nay, a man of his ilk would assume that the lady meant to steal the prize for herself, for that was what he would have done.

Christina caught a glimpse of Ysmaine, and then another. That was enough for her to guess that the lady made for the cathedral itself. Where else would a former pilgrim seek sanctuary? Christina suspected, though, that Ysmaine would not find a safe haven there. She raced around the perimeter of the square, knowing it would be faster to take the longer path.

Christina reached the porch only to discover that there was no sign of the lady. She scanned the crowd, terrified that she had erred and that Ysmaine was endangered, only to note a familiar man striding toward the church.

Helmut.

Mercifully, the cathedral was graced with a number of portals and he made for the farthest one. Christina drew up her hood and ducked inside, blinking rapidly when she was engulfed by the darkness.

Far ahead and to the left, Ysmaine lit a candle at an altar and bowed her head in prayer. A lump rose in Christina's throat as Helmut moved to stand behind her. The lady stiffened, and Christina wished she knew whether it was surprise or the point of a dagger that prompted her reaction.

Helmut urged Ysmaine away from her prayers so readily that she guessed it was the latter. Christina barely had time to step back into the shadows and let her hood fall over her face before the pair swept by. They were so close as they left the church that she could have touched either of them. Instead, she murmured to herself and twitched, as if she were one of the unfortunates who oft sought assistance through prayer.

Helmut spared her the barest glance of revulsion and pushed Ysmaine back into the sunlight. Christina guessed that he intended to take the lady to a private location, divest her of the reliquary and then take her life. He would not be pleased to find himself deceived, and Ysmaine might pay dearly for her choice.

Christina also guessed that Gaston would not abandon his lady wife so readily as that. She lifted the small bag from her belt and smiled, knowing that Costanzia's belt would finally have a fitting purpose.

She gave chase to Helmut, dropping one of the glittering links of the jeweled belt at regular intervals on the path he took.

Christina only hoped she had enough to mark the entire trail.

What madness was this?

Wulfe found no consolation that his doubts about including women in the party were proven to be justified in the end. Ysmaine abandoned her steed on the Île de la Cité, just as Christina had abandoned her steed inside the Porte Saint Victor, and once again a ripple of confusion passed through the company. Wulfe wanted only to proceed calmly and as planned to the Temple, but it seemed the women would see his scheme abandoned.

Why did Ysmaine depart with the reliquary? Wulfe might have ridden after her himself, at least until he caught the gaze of the maid Radegunde. She clutched the bundle of clothing she had carried since Venice, but it seemed to Wulfe that she held it more tightly than before.

Ysmaine had entrusted the treasure to her.

They must ride on, as if all were as planned. Gaston might have followed his lady wife, but to Wulfe's relief, that man recovered himself. At his terse command, the others moved forward with more conviction. Wulfe granted Fergus a glance and that man began to usher the party onward from the rear.

They were so close to the Temple. Naught could go awry now!

They crossed the bridge to the north bank and the crowds thinned ahead. The road was sufficiently open that Wulfe took a breath of relief. He might have spurred Teufel to greater speed, but Gaston suddenly appeared at his side.

That man was more agitated than Wulfe had ever seen him, but he had no chance to ask what was amiss. Gaston shoved the reins of the palfrey that his wife's maid rode into his hand

"Ride!" Gaston commanded. "Ride for the Temple and let none stand in your path! Ensure that she is with you to the last."

Gaston knew the girl had the treasure, and worse, his cry had ensured that all others knew it as well. There could be no subtlety now.

Wulfe would have given Teufel his spurs, but Gaston slapped the destrier's flank hard first. The horse neighed, then broke into a gallop of his own volition. The palfrey bearing Radegunde galloped fast beside him. Wulfe held that beast's reins and murmured to Teufel, hoping the girl would not fall. People took one look and fell back in fear.

Far behind him, Wulfe heard Fergus shout and the sound of hoof beats on the stones. For his part, he made for the gates of the Temple with all speed. The familiar tower loomed high over the walls ahead.

"Sir! Is it far?" the maid demanded.

"Hold fast," Wulfe commanded. "There is the gate ahead."

"Aye, sir. I will not drop it."

There was a determination in her tone that reassured Wulfe. The horses thundered down the road and Wulfe roared when any dared to step into the street ahead of them. Merchants and men fell back, a woman spilled her bucket of water and cursed them with a raised fist. Chickens loosed from a garden squawked as they fled back to their haven.

"Open the gates!" Wulfe bellowed when they drew near enough that he might be heard. The porter revealed himself, stepping out to look down the street. "We ride on a matter of urgency for the Temple!"

The porter took one look at Wulfe's tabard, then saluted and disappeared again. Wulfe heard the creak of the portcullis and marveled that it had been closed during the day. He slowed Teufel to make the turn, looking up and down the street for any sign of pursuit.

There was none that he could discern, but still he did not halt.

"Bend low," he advised the maid, though truly he was the sole one in danger when they rode beneath the partly raised portcullis. She exhaled shakily when the horses stopped on the far side of the bailey, Teufel snorting and stamping after his run. The others cantered into the bailey behind them. Wulfe dismounted and offered his hand to the maid, who hugged the parcel close.

"I assume there is cause for this disruption," a man said coolly, and Wulfe spun to find the Grand Master surveying him.

He put the maid upon her feet and dropped to one knee in a low bow. "Sir, we have ridden from the Temple in Jerusalem, entrusted with a message for you."

The Grand Master arched a brow. "And you bring a woman into the Temple. What is your name, brother? It seems that the rule's burden upon you is a light one." The remainder of the company rode into the bailey then, and the Grand Master surveyed them. His lips pursed and he looked at Wulfe again. "I assume there is an explanation for this."

"Of course, sir. I am Brother Wulfe, most recently of the Gaza Priory, sir. I rode to Jerusalem to take tidings from my master, only to be dispatched upon this quest by Brother Terricus..."

"Terricus? Excellent. I have been awaiting his tidings." The Grand Master put out his hand.

"I do not carry the missive, sir."

"You have lost it?"

"It was entrusted to another knight in our party, a knight

leaving the order to claim his family holding."

The Grand Master surveyed the company with obvious expectation.

"He does not arrive with us, sir," Wulfe admitted.

The older man frowned. "You have a most curious way of delivering a missive, Brother Wulfe."

"He pursues his lady wife, sir, for he fears for her safety."

The Grand Master's silver brows rose even higher. "Then we are to expect more women to arrive within the walls of the Temple?"

"I believe so, sir."

"At least his whore is no longer with us," Bartholomew muttered, and the Grand Master inhaled sharply.

He turned a piercing gaze upon Wulfe. "Have you a whore, Brother Wulfe?"

"Nay, sir," Wulfe said, glad this was now true. "We did, however, escort another pilgrim from Venice who had need of our assistance."

"That is a novel way to explain such a situation, Brother Wulfe." The Grand Master's lips thinned. "If you do not have the missive, then why the ruckus of your arrival?"

"Because of this, sir," the maid said and dropped to her knees before the Grand Master. That man took a step back, perhaps thinking that she desired some deed of him, but Radegunde pushed back the cloth that protected her burden. Though she was before Wulfe, he could see that she was still trembling after their ride.

Then he saw the Grand Master's eyes widen and his face pale.

Wulfe took a step forward and was stunned himself. A golden reliquary was cocooned by the rough cloth. It was studded with gems, surely worth a king's ransom, and shone so brilliantly in the sunlight that it was difficult to look directly upon it.

The Grand Master fell to one knee and reached out a hand, as if he did not dare to touch it. "The reliquary of Saint Euphemia," he whispered in awe, then dispatched a man with a curt gesture.

He looked up to meet Wulfe's gaze. "This is missive enough, Brother Wulfe," he said, his voice hoarse. "Indeed it is more of a message than I would choose to receive. If Brother Terricus saw fit to remove it from the treasury, then Jerusalem will fall." He stood and swallowed, looking older than he had just moments before. "If it has not already," he added in a whisper. "These are foul tidings indeed."

Wulfe heard the Grand Master's words, but could not tear his gaze from the majesty of the reliquary. Christina had been right. A villain would readily kill for such a prize as this. Christina had been certain that the villain was Everard, and he had left the party two nights before.

Unless it had been a feint and he followed them, to have the element of surprise upon his side.

He understood that the lady Ysmaine had left the party to ensure that the villain did not steal the treasure on the last part of its journey.

And Christina had gone to Ysmaine's aid.

Though Gaston had given chase, that might not be sufficient to ensure the welfare of both women. If the knight was compelled to choose, it only made sense that he would save his wife first.

Wulfe spun away from the Grand Master and seized Teufel's reins. He flung himself into the saddle and turned the horse toward the gates, which were just closing. "Hold the gates!" he cried.

"Brother Wulfe!" the Grand Master shouted in outrage. "You do not have permission to depart."

"I must finish what has begun, sir."

"You must provide a report of all that has transpired...."

"Not in this moment, sir." Wulfe bowed his head and urged Teufel onward.

The Grand Master raised his voice imperiously. "I order you to dismount, Brother Wulfe! I command you to render a full accounting of your journey immediately..."

Wulfe winced, for this was the first time that he defied a direct order from a superior.

But he did not halt and he did not glance back.

The Grand Master sputtered.

"Has he no shame?" Bartholomew whispered as Wulfe rode past him.

"The tower falls," Fergus said inexplicably.

"Perhaps the foundation was undermined," Duncan said, and the Scotsmen nodded at each other. It was evidently a private joke.

The Grand Master did not share their amusement. "Brother Wulfe!" he roared. "The gates will be barred against you and you will be reprimanded for this disobedience..."

But Teufel slipped beneath the lowering gate like a shadow chased by the dawn.

And Wulfe felt free.

He would willing surrender all that was his to ensure Christina's safety.

Indeed, he just had.

Once in the street, he gave Teufel his spurs, hoping they were not too late. The destrier galloped with fearsome speed, as if he sensed Wulfe's urgency. He heard hoof beats behind and looked back to see Stephen and Simon fast behind him, Stephen grinning with delight. It was clear the boy guessed his intent.

People fled from their path with terror, and Wulfe wondered whether the horse looked like a demon loosed from Hell. Teufel's hooves clattered on the bridge, and he snorted at the greater crowds on the island. They parted before the beast, though, as if Fortune was finally on Wulfe's side.

He made the porch of Notre Dame with greater speed than he might have hoped. Ysmaine had fled in this direction, as if making a path for sanctuary. Surely no villain would assault her there. He turned Teufel in place, the horse tossing his head and snorting with impatience to run, and then he spied it.

A faux gem of familiar orange hue glittered between the cobblestones.

Some distance away, he spied another.

Wulfe smiled, glad beyond all that Christina had anticipated pursuit. He urged Teufel onward, bending from the saddle as he followed the trail, and hoped all the while that he would arrive in time.

Christina followed Helmut and Ysmaine stealthily, fearing that she would be caught. She knew full well how savage he could be and had no desire to corner him. Nor did she wish to abandon Ysmaine to his scheme, whatever it was.

She dropped the gems at intervals, her spirit quailing as their number diminished. Would he ever halt? Finally, he ducked into a narrow alley with only a single gate at the far end. He glanced back so suddenly that Christina barely had time to hide herself, then she heard a latch drop.

She peeked to find the alley deserted.

What was behind the gate?

How could she enter without being observed?

Christina crept closer, her grip tight upon her sack of remaining stones. She hastened down the alley and listened. Heart pounding, she lifted the latch and peeked through the crack, only to find Helmut with the lady in a small courtyard. His horse was tethered under a shelter at the far end of the space, and it was the same one he had ridden from Venice. She had feared that he might have accomplices, but there were none.

Of course, then he would have been required to share the spoils.

He turned on Ysmaine, and Christina knew she had to stall for time, lest he kill the noblewoman before assistance arrived. This was the moment to be bold.

If not to goad him to anger, and the making of an error.

She had only to think of Gunther to be filled with a thirst for justice.

Christina opened the gate wide and spoke clearly, hiding her fear of what Helmut might do. "At least some soul is gratified by your presence," she said, keeping her tone languid.

Helmut jumped in a most satisfactory manner, then spun to face her. Coward that he was, he held Ysmaine before himself, his knife at her throat. "What are you doing here?"

Christina leaned against the gate. She smiled at him, knowing she appeared more confident than she felt. She liked how her manner and her presence troubled him. "Let us say that I wished to ensure the welfare of another woman."

He snorted. "Whores care only for their own advantage."

"You might be surprised to learn what whores care about."

Christina eyed the blade he held against Ysmaine. "Is it the mark of a pious man to abduct another man's wife?"

She was not surprised that he did not reply.

"Doubtless you want a reward of your own," he sneered. "Is it not all about the coin for your kind?"

Christina surveyed the courtyard, which was barren indeed. "I fail to see any chance of reward in this place." She met his gaze anew. "Unless your desire is for the lady's charms."

"In which case you would offer your own instead?"

She smiled, ensuring her expression was seductive. He was agitated, though whether it was due to her presence, the situation itself or his reaction to her, she did not know. Christina did not much care. She wanted to provoke him to err, no more and no less.

"You might find me more to your liking as a partner." She strolled toward him, letting her hips sway in invitation. His eyes flashed and she saw him catch his breath.

But then, she knew he was not as virtuous as he would have the others believe.

"Do you think I failed to note how you watched me when you thought yourself unobserved?" It was a falsehood, but the claim might unsettle him. He might fear his truth had been revealed. She halted a step before him and reached for the tie of her chemise. "For a pious man, you showed a very earthy interest in my wares."

Helmut pretended to be disdainful, but he was watching that tie.

Or the flesh revealed when it was loosed.

"I merely disapprove of you and your trade."

"Because you are a man above reproach," Ysmaine interjected. "Abduction and assault are fair play."

"And murder," Christina added with a smile. "Do not forget murder, my lady."

"I do not know what you mean..." Helmut protested, but she saw a wariness dawn in his eyes.

This was the moment that had filled Christina's dreams.

She reached out a finger and collected blood from Ysmaine's flesh, then displayed it to him. "Your manners are lacking, sir. This lady is nobly born and wed to a knight. What cause have you to threaten her life?"

"This is a private matter," he huffed. "She holds property of mine."

Christina arched a brow. "One you own or one you would claim?"

"How dare you speak thus to me?"

"I have seen you look," Christina murmured. She drew the laces from one side of her kirtle slowly and he watched hungrily. She turned so that the shadow of her breast would be visible to him through the garment's sides, and he stared. Slowly, she lifted the wool so that he would be able to see her nipple. He did not so much as blink. "Would you like a closer look?" she asked in her most sultry tone. "Perhaps in exchange for the lady's freedom?"

"Whore," he muttered, tearing his gaze away. "I will not barter with you..."

"Vermin," Ysmaine said and tried to escape his grasp. Helmut swore and gripped her more tightly again.

Christina unlaced the other side of her kirtle, ensuring that his view was improved.

"I am Everard de Montmorency," he declared, his words falling in haste and fury. "Count of Blanche Garde and heir to Château Montmorency and I will not tolerate..."

"*Are* you?" Christina demanded, interrupting him.

He was shocked. Not surprised, though, not truly. "What do you insinuate?"

She smiled, knowing it would vex him. "Only that I know you are not Everard de Montmorency."

Helmut was at a loss for words. The lady Ysmaine looked between the two of them, perhaps choosing who to believe.

"How exactly do you plan to convince them at Château Montmorency that you are Everard in truth?" Christina asked. "It was simple to take his place in Outremer, where he was known only by repute, but it will be more difficult to trick his own kin."

Helmut inhaled sharply.

Christina pretended not to notice his discomfiture but held his gaze and eased closer. She had to get that knife away from

Ysmaine's throat. A flick of the wrist could see the lady killed, whether it was an intentional gesture or not.

"Is that why it took so very long for the duke's faithful and pious son to embark on the journey home to say a final farewell to his father?" she demanded, watching the anger spark in his eyes. She provoked him further, knowing he was close to losing his temper. "Did you hope the father might die before you arrived? As a dead man himself, Everard could not have managed the journey at all, but it would have been folly for the imposter who had stolen his name and his purse to reveal his own lie."

"You lying whore!" Helmut flung Ysmaine aside and snatched for Christina, but she had been warned by his eyes. She kicked him hard in the crotch before he took two steps. He paled and fell to his knees, and Christina found her own anger rising. She kicked him in the head without hesitation, knowing she would not be sated until he lay dead in a pool of his own blood.

Just as he had left Gunther.

"No one truly looks at a whore," she charged, hearing her own anger. "We are breasts, at best. But I invite you to look again, to look at my face this time." She took a shaking breath as he looked up, his fingertips falling from his own temple. "*I* was in the party of noble pilgrims who traveled east with you and Everard. *I* was with my husband then, but perhaps you never look at noblewomen, either. The fact is that I *know* that you are not Everard."

Helmut snarled and lunged after her, hands extended like claws. Christina let him catch her. It was the sole way Ysmaine might escape.

She reached into her garter and seized Duncan's dagger, which she had hidden there, when he could not see her move.

"You lie!" he bellowed as he seized her by the hair. Christina gave Ysmaine a warning look and the lady seemed to understand. Helmut then slammed Christina back into the wall of the house and did so with such force that the breath was driven from her.

She slumped, hoping to evade more violence, but he raised his hand to strike her again.

Scoundrel! Christina jabbed with the knife, knowing that

surprise would be on her side only the first time. The wretched man saw it in time and leapt to one side so that she missed. He seized her and flung her to the ground, using the force of her own blow against her.

Christina laughed, knowing it would startle him. "I do not lie!" she declared and smiled at him with confidence. "We meet again, Helmut," she murmured and inclined her head.

He blanched at the sound of this name.

Ysmaine's eyes were round.

Christina advanced upon Helmut with the blade before herself, as intent upon having the lady know the truth as ensuring that Helmut knew himself caught. She might not leave this courtyard alive, after all, and she would ensure he did not hide his crime again.

"You were the mercenary assigned to defend your lord and employer, and I remember you well. My husband noted then that you were lying and lustful, and you are still vermin, if better garbed." She sneered at him and he leapt toward her, trying to seize the knife. They struggled over it, even as Ysmaine watched.

"Run, my lady!" Christina cried.

The lady was spurred to action, although her feet betrayed her. She stumbled as Helmut nigh wrenched the blade from Christina's grip and she feared the day to be lost.

Helmut, it seemed, would have his say, as well. He grasped Christina's hair, pulling it back with vigor so that she was compelled to look at him. She could not see Ysmaine and only hoped the lady gained her freedom.

"You!" Helmut whispered, his gaze roving over her features. "You are Juliana, the wife of Gunther..."

"Who was slaughtered for the seven pennies in his purse, after he had discerned your true nature." Christina reminded him savagely. "Did you take his purse, as well as his life? I would not put it past a man of your ilk."

"I am no thief."

She laughed, knowing it would irk him. Let him beat her. Let him silence her. The feat would not be readily done, and it would be worth the price to see Ysmaine safely beyond this villain's grasp.

Helmut struck Christina hard across the face, and she did not have to pretend to fall to the ground. She was dizzy from the force of his blow and feared she might not be able to occupy him long enough. Indeed, she could scarcely keep her eyes open.

There was a crack in that moment, and she glanced up to see that Ysmaine had struck Helmut in the back of the head with a rock. He turned on the other woman like a mad beast, and Christina dared not close her eyes.

"Run, Christina!" Ysmaine urged, though there was little chance of that. She could not even get to her feet.

She watched in horror as Helmut struck Ysmaine so viciously that she lost her balance and stumbled backward. He did not waste a moment in grabbing the bundle that was disguised as her belly. He tore it away with a savage gesture, revealing that he knew it was not a child. He then flung Ysmaine aside so that she fell heavily against the stone wall.

Ysmaine put out her hand to halt her fall, but tumbled to the ground all the same. Even in her current state, though, Christina could enjoy that Helmut cradled some false replacement for the reliquary and not the true prize. Surely he would flee. Surely she could close her eyes for a moment before aiding Ysmaine.

But she heard the sound of straw being moved and felt it fall over her. She opened her eyes in time to see Helmut strike his flint and set strands of straw alight. He cast them into the scattered dry stalks and the fire spread quickly. The courtyard filled with smoke with terrifying speed and she could barely discern him as he seized the reins of his horse.

"Farewell, ladies," he sneered. "Is it not said that witches should be burned alive?" He flung open the gate and the wind fanned the flames to burn faster.

Ysmaine coughed as she dragged herself to Christina's side. Christina wanted to reach for her hand, to urge her to be still until Helmut was gone, but the horse suddenly stamped and whinnied.

"Gaston," Ysmaine whispered.

"I believe we have unfinished business, sir," that knight said.

Relief surged through Christina.

Someone had followed her trail.

The lady Ysmaine would be safe, and Gunther would be avenged.

Though it was what Christina had believed she desired above all, it seemed less than satisfactory now that the goal was achieved.

Still, it was to be her due. She heaved a sigh and let her eyes close.

CHAPTER SIXTEEN

nly vermin assaulted women.

Only a fool touched Gaston's lady wife. One look at Ysmaine, pale with blood on her hands, was enough to set his blood aflame. That this fiend had intended for her to be burned alive, that he would abandon her in such circumstance, made Gaston want to kill him slowly. He had never been filled with such a desire for vengeance.

But the lady he loved had never been so threatened before.

He assessed the flames and saw that Ysmaine bent over Christina. She might have fled and saved herself, but that was not her nature. Rather than his wife perishing in this fire, he would see Everard left to die in flames.

Gaston stepped back and lifted his sword to Everard's chest. "*En garde*," he murmured, and the words had barely crossed his lips before the villain lunged at him. Their swords clashed hard and Gaston felt his cheek nicked. He parried hard, driving Everard back against the wall with a flurry of blows. He forced that man away from the gate and was aware that Ysmaine tried to rouse Christina. He wished the women were safe, but he knew enough of his lady to guess that she would not abandon her companion.

He sliced down hard, compelling Everard to drop the reins, then slapped the horse. The beast fled the fire, darting through the gate to the street.

One life was saved. He had three yet to ensure.

"You attack the wrong person!" Everard protested. "The whore means to injure your wife."

"I heard only you strike my lady wife," Gaston growled and moved quickly, his blade slicing Everard's shoulder. "Wulfe was right to doubt your intent from the outset. What man of merit abandons a holding when it is about to be besieged?"

"You know naught of my intent..."

They battled, moving back and forth, almost evenly matched. When Gaston landed a blow, it was because Everard did not relinquish his grip on his burden.

"You speak aright," he replied, wanting to provoke his opponent. If the man who called himself Everard was angered, he might make a mistake. "All these years I have believed you to be Everard de Montmorency, for I had no reason to doubt the tale you told. Now I learn that this is a lie."

"The whore lies!"

"You lie," Gaston countered and saw his opponent's eyes flash. "Why did you not return to France to visit your ailing father sooner?"

"I had a holding to defend."

"But you left it unprotected in the end."

"I saw that it was doomed."

Gaston scoffed. "Your tale makes little sense, unless you are a coward. Why did you leave Outremer by coming to Jerusalem first?"

"I sought the aid of the Templars! It is your sworn task to accompany pilgrims on the road..."

"You were nigh at the port of Jaffa in Blanche Garde. Had it been your desire to leave Outremer in haste, you could have been a-sail before we even left Jerusalem." Gaston shook his head. "Nay, the reason is in your grasp. You came seeking a prize to steal."

A partial roof on the opposite side of the courtyard fell in then, tumbling to the ground in a flurry of sparks. The flames burned higher as the wood caught and more dark smoke filled the air. Christina coughed and Gaston saw Ysmaine coax the other woman to her feet. There was something amiss with Ysmaine's hand, but he would see to that later. He willed them to move more quickly.

"I am not on trial!" Everard retorted. "I need not explain my choices to any man..."

"Nay, you are condemned, by the burden in your own grasp."

"But..."

"All you must do to prove your innocence is surrender it to me," Gaston invited. He lowered his sword and stretched out his left hand, knowing full well what his opponent would do. The women were passing through the gate, and the fire had nearly turned the courtyard into an inferno.

The man who called himself Everard attacked. "I owe naught to you!" he roared even as their blades clashed hard. "I will not answer to a monk who breaks his vows by taking a wife!" He battled hard against Gaston and jabbed suddenly. Gaston stepped back and only then saw the peril he had not realized.

Ysmaine had returned to the portal, doubtless seeking him. He could not warn her to retreat, not without calling his opponent's attention to her presence. He felt his lips thin to a grim line when she pulled her eating knife and sidled along the wall behind the villain.

The woman had too much valor, to be sure.

"You will die here, and the tale with you," Everard sneered. "I will sell this prize to see my own future secured."

"Someone else will recognize you."

"Silence can be bought, and I will have the funds."

"You did not silence Christina."

"Not yet," Everard replied grimly. "I shall see to that." He kicked a barrel toward Gaston with savage force. "And you will not survive this day to share the tale." Ysmaine eased toward the villain, though Gaston did not reveal her presence. He jumped over the barrel and attacked Everard, hoping to distract him from any sign of the lady's presence behind.

But Everard leapt aside so that Gaston's blow missed. He seized Ysmaine, spun her and flung her toward the brightest blaze of the fire. She stumbled and cried out, but Gaston did not wait to see his lady fall into the flames. He lunged after her and caught her against his chest. Unable to keep from tumbling after her, he cradled her from the force of their landing, then rolled her beneath himself to shelter her from the flames.

By the time he rolled to his feet, Everard was through the gate. Gaston heard the other man slam and lock it from the other side. He hauled Ysmaine to her feet beside him and they raced to the gate as one. He fought against the latch, but to no avail.

He spared a glance to the flames, then caught her around the waist. He fairly flung her to the top of the courtyard wall. "Jump, lady mine!" he commanded when she hesitated atop the wall.

"Aye, jump," Everard purred from the other side of the wall, the sound of his voice sending a chill through Gaston. "Grant me another pretty prize."

Ysmaine hesitated. Gaston heard a cry that he thought might have come from Christina. Ysmaine danced backward as the other man evidently lunged at her. Gaston heard the imposter laugh, then the clatter of hoof beats.

Ysmaine leapt down from the top of the wall on to the other side.

Gaston watched the flames come closer. The summit of the wall was too high for him to heft his own weight there. Indeed, he could not even brush the summit with his fingertips. There was naught in the courtyard to climb upon, for all was aflame. He shouted but there seemed no one to hear his cries. The smoke was thick, and he began to cough, fearing that Everard had called his fate aright.

At least Ysmaine was safe.

Gaston heard her swear, then the latch rattled. "It is so hot!" she complained, and he heard her kick the gate. To his relief, she unfastened the latch from the other side, and fresh air billowed into the courtyard.

"He has seized Christina and ridden that way," Ysmaine declared as Gaston stumbled into the alley. He grabbed her hand

and led her away from the foul place, coughing to clear his lungs. To his relief, Wulfe was in the square before the cathedral, astride his black destrier.

Gaston knew then that all would be well.

Christina awakened to the smell of hay and rotted manure.

Surely she could not be back in that foul barn again?

One eye was swollen shut and her hands were bound at her waist. She was lying in the hay of an unfamiliar stable and her head pounded.

The last thing she recalled was Helmut seizing her and striking her across the face.

It was dark, which was no reassurance. It had been only midday when she and Ysmaine had battled Helmut. If it was night and she was yet in his captivity, then no one had followed to assist her.

Was Gaston dead?

Had the lady Ysmaine braved the inferno of the courtyard to try to save her spouse?

Had they died together?

Christina did not want to think about it. Despite her misgivings, it was clear that they had loved each other, and their match had held promise for the future. She wanted to think of them happily together, in Gaston's holding, their home filled with sons.

Some souls should win their hearts' desires, even if she was not to be one such.

"Awake yet?" Helmut demanded and kicked at Christina's legs to make her so. "I do not have all night, wench." He kicked her again and she emitted a grunt of pain, unable to stop herself. He crouched down before her and smiled.

Christina spat at him. The angle was wrong, and her spittle landed on his tabard, but it was sufficient to earn her a slap of his leather glove. She closed her eyes but he seized her chin, hauling her to a sitting position.

They were in a villein's cottage, she realized, not a barn. Judging by the sounds beyond its walls, it must have been far from any abode. The walls were stone and she did not doubt that the roof was thatch. The floor was dirt and it looked to be a simple hut, in which the family lived at one end and their livestock, at least in winter, at the other. There was a blackened hole in the roof, where undoubtedly smoke from a fire had risen, though it did not seem that any fire had been lit on the hearth recently. The thatch was worn overhead and she could see patches of the night sky beyond.

Helmut grabbed her chin and Christina closed her eye, the better to avoid the sight of him.

"Where is it?" he demanded, and she could feel his hot breath upon her face.

"What?"

He struck her again for her impertinence, but she did not care. Christina opened her good eye and saw a bundle of clothing spread on the floor of the stable.

She smiled that he had been vexed in pursuit of the reliquary again. "Do you even know what it was?" she asked and he glared at her.

"A prize, a prize from the Templar hoard and the sole one they saw fit to save. What else did I need to know?"

"That it was beautiful," Christina said softly. "The most beautiful reliquary I have ever seen."

"You saw it! *You!*" The notion infuriated him. "How rich was it?"

"A prize beyond compare." She sighed. "Wrought of gold and lavishly inlaid with gems. Large, as well. It was truly a marvel."

The confession did little to please Helmut to be sure, and Christina was glad the treasure had evaded his grasp. She continued, intent upon tormenting him with her words, if naught else.

"Saint Euphemia was tested in the time of Diocletian, in the year 303, for she would not sacrifice to false idols. No matter how she was tormented or violated, she came to no harm. It was said that the angels defended her, because of her faith."

"I care naught for such detail," he snarled. "Was the reliquary truly so rich? Describe it to me."

"I saw rubies and emeralds, as big as my thumb," Christina lied. "Amethysts and sapphires, and gold so heavy." She shook her head. "It had been fashioned to honor as the lady saint whose relics were contained within."

"Where is it?"

"I do not know," Christina admitted, and he struck her again, harder than he had before.

Indeed, he split her lip, and she tasted blood.

She supposed she could have gotten to her feet and run, but she was not certain she could have managed to get far given her current state. She would save that tactic and perhaps take him unawares, when her head cleared a little more.

Helmut, though, anticipated her. He seized the end of the rope that bound her wrists and cast it over a beam, hauling her to her toes, then knotting it so that she could do little more than swing before him.

She would kick him when she could surprise him.

Christina would die here, and she knew it, but she would vex him mightily first.

"Where?" he demanded again.

She looked down at the ground and avoided the question. "Many miracles are attributed to Euphemia's relics," she continued mildly. "Indeed, at the Council of Chalcedon in 451, she defended the humanity of Jesus."

"She was dead!"

"Yet two scrolls were put in the casket with her saintly remains, one arguing that God alone is divine, and one that Jesus was both man and divine. In the morn, the casket was opened and the scroll defending the divinity of Jesus was in her right hand, the other scroll cast at her feet."

"A trick, no more and no less."

"A miracle, no more and no less," Christina corrected. "Just as when the golden sarcophagus that served as her reliquary was stolen and cast into the sea. It should have been lost forever, but was recovered by two brothers who were fishermen. Her relics were hidden for many years, then scattered, evidently this great prize coming into the possession of the Templars."

Helmut folded his arms across his chest. "I ask you again. Where is it?"

"If it is truly night, I suppose it is safely in the Templar treasury at Paris by now."

"I do not believe it! You have stolen it!"

"Because you would have done so?" Christina let her scorn show. "Trust me that I have no desire to have even an inclination in common with you."

"Whore!" He struck her again, making her spin like a fish on a line. "You will die here for your deception and none will mourn your demise."

"Who will mourn yours, Helmut?" she asked, but he ignored her question.

His eyes flashed. "Do not call me that! That man is dead."

She scoffed. "Nay, it is Everard de Montmorency who is dead. Do you not think his father will know the difference?"

"I will arrive too late for the old man to see me."

"And you think they will simply grant you suzerainty of his holding?" Christina shook her head and laughed, ignoring the blood that dropped from her lips. "Truly, Helmut, you have not planned this scheme with your usual care."

"I had to leave Outremer sooner than expected. I had thought to claim the treasure, the better to barter for the support of the Templars in providing evidence of my identity."

"I had thought they could not be bought."

"All men can be bought." Helmut leaned closer, his eyes narrowed. "*All* men have a price. Losing the greatest prize of their treasury, the one they sought to save above all others, might well have been the price of the Templars." He stepped back and surveyed her with disgust. "But you, a woman and a whore, cheated me of my due."

"Just as you cheated me of mine," Christina retorted. "Why did you kill Gunther?"

"Because he knew, of course. He saw me steal Everard's signet ring." Helmut threw out a hand and the ring of Montmorency glinted on his finger. "A minor baron under his father's thumb, but still a man who had more to his name than I could ever hope to hold." His lip curled. "He could not even defend himself. How was it right that he held more than me?"

"You had formed the scheme to steal his name even then."

"I formed the scheme of replacing Everard as soon as I was hired to defend him. He would have taken a pilgrimage to some closer point. It was I who encouraged him to journey all the way to Outremer. That was the sole way I could take his name, his reputation, and all the wealth that would come to his hand." He smiled a little. "For such a pious man, a mere mention of the Holy City was sufficient to make his heart burn to see that place himself. It was easily done."

Christina thought she heard a footfall outside the barn and dared to hope that some person listened. "And how did he die, dear Everard?"

"Dear?"

"I was fond of him. He was a kindly man."

"He was a fool!" Helmut said with disgust. "He trusted with no cause to do so."

"I suppose his fate was decided once you had his ring."

"He thought it lost. Gunther knew better, but I could not let him confide the truth in his comrade. Nay, they could not linger at the board long into the evening ever again. When Gunther left the inn alone, I knew I had to seize opportunity." He smiled a little in reminiscence. "I looked him in the eye, you know, as the knife sank home, just so he would know who had claimed his life."

"You are fortunate he did not tell anyone."

"I made sure he could not. I took his purse to make it look like a theft." Helmut walked around her, and Christina feared what he would do when he was behind her. She twisted to watch him, cursed by her one swollen eye. "I knew his wife had his confidence. I thought you might know what Gunther knew, so I ensured that you had no chance to warn Everard." He sneered. "I should have guessed that you would survive by parting your thighs."

Christina kicked hard and fast, landing one boot on his groin. Helmut fell back with a moan and paled. He straightened suddenly, pulling his dagger from its sheath and dove toward Christina. "Burning is too good for you!" he muttered, but the door to the barn was kicked open just then.

"I would not do that," Stephen advised. The boy stood

silhouetted in the portal, his own knife drawn.

He was alone.

How could that be?

Helmut scoffed at the sight of the boy. "Who are you to stop me?" he demanded.

Christina heard a faint rustle overhead. Had someone climbed through the roof? If so, she knew who she wished it to be.

Indeed, her heart thundered with new hope that she might leave this hut after all.

"Is your affection for this whore so great, boy, that you would die for her?" Helmut continued. "What would your knight say of such misplaced loyalty?"

"He would call it well deserved," Wulfe replied from above them

Christina looked up to find Wulfe crouched on the beam overhead. He cut the rope that held her captive with one strike then leapt at Helmut. Stephen charged the supposed count from the portal, driving his shoulder into the back of his knees. Helmet lost his balance and fell, just as Wulfe landed atop him. The pair rolled across the floor, battling for supremacy. Wulfe landed a pair of solid blows and Helmut's nose began to bleed. Wulfe cracked the other man's wrist when he would not relinquish his knife, then rolled him to his belly and sat atop him.

"The rope, if you will, Stephen," he said, his gaze sweeping over Christina with concern. That his thoughts were so visible and his eyes so blue made Christina's heart soar.

Did he do what was right, or was her love returned?

Stephen sawed the rope that bound Christina's wrists, then took it to Wulfe.

"How dare you do this?" Helmut fumed. "I am Everard de Montmorency, Count of Blanche Garde, and you have no right to submit me to such an indignity..."

"But I heard from your own lips that you are one Helmut, who killed Everard," Wulfe countered amiably. "And even if that is not so, you have sorely abused a woman."

"She deserved it, the whore..."

"No woman deserves such treatment. You, however, should be

so fortunate as to be condemned to suffer no more than a blow to the face." Wulfe tugged Helmut roughly to his feet and pushed him out of the barn.

"You cannot kill me," Helmut fumed.

Wulfe smiled. "Of course not. I have no suzerainty in these lands and you have committed no crime against my own person. As much as I should like to leave your fate to the lady's discretion, I fear there is another court better suited to judge your crimes."

"What do you mean?"

"I mean we ride for Montmorency. I will send Stephen ahead, to take word to the old baron, in the hope that he rallies in order to see his beloved son one last time."

Helmut paled. "You would not do as much!"

"Stephen," Wulfe said and the boy stepped forward to bow low. "Do you know the location of Montmorency?"

"Aye, sir, for you told me just this day how to get there."

Wulfe smiled. "And you are blessed with an excellent memory. Ride ahead of us, Stephen. Take the faster palfrey. We shall be fast behind."

"Aye, sir." Stephen ran out of the barn, and Wulfe gestured that Christina should precede him. She stepped out into a starlit night filled with greater promise than she might have expected.

Simon stood a distance away with the horses. She untied the tethered reins of Helmut's steed and led it to the others, not wanting Wulfe to be distracted from his task. Stephen rode off with enthusiasm, and Wulfe bound the other end of the rope to his saddle.

"I will ride," Helmut insisted but Wulfe only shook his head.

"You will walk, for I will grant you no opportunity to escape. It will only take a few days to reach Montmorency, and truly, you can use the time to pray for your immortal soul. I do not doubt that you have a great deal to confess in your prayers."

While Helmut fumed, Wulfe returned to Christina's side. He considered her injuries and touched her cheek with a careful fingertip. "I should like to kill him myself," he murmured.

Christina claimed his hand and leaned her cheek against it, ashamed that she shed tears of relief. "I thank you."

He did not kiss her, but fetched a cloth and sent Simon to soak it in the cool water of a nearby stream. He bathed her face, a frown between his brows, then bade her hold the cloth against her swollen eye. Then he lifted her to the saddle of Helmut's steed, and as the moon drew clear of the clouds, they rode in pursuit of Stephen.

To Montmorency and justice long overdue.

FRIDAY, AUGUST 28, 1187

Feast Day of Saint Augustine of Hippo

CHAPTER SEVENTEEN

ulfe hoped that he could give Christina one gift that encouraged her to remember him with kindness, in ensuring justice for her lost husband. They spoke little as they traveled to Montmorency, and their passage was not quick with Helmut walking. Wulfe used the time to consider how best to prove Helmut's guilt.

The simplest plan would be to ride through the gates, with Helmut's hands bound, and accuse him of his crimes before the duke and his court. Had there not been such a lapse of time since Everard's departure, Wulfe would have preferred that scheme. That it had been a decade since Everard's departure from his father's home meant that many in the keep would be too young to recall him. The memory of others would have faded. Helmut had Everard's signet ring, but was unshaven and dirty.

If Wulfe escorted a man who claimed to be the duke's son into the bailey, bound like a prisoner, outrage at his treatment might ensure that none looked too closely at the man himself. Christina's testimony might be dismissed, for she was a stranger and not garbed as an aristocrat, and he was similarly unknown in these parts. He would hope that his Templar surplice would give him credibility but that could not be guaranteed. If Everard had been as well loved as Wulfe suspected, people might find it preferable to welcome him home and ignore a stranger's charges.

A bolder ploy might be the better choice. What if he let Helmut arrive as Everard? Surely people would look more at the man? Surely Helmut would err and reveal that he was not Everard?

Wulfe could not forget that his own father had recognized him at a glance, more than a decade after having but one glimpse of him as an infant. Everard's father—and much of the household—had seen the duke's son at full manhood.

Surely the truth would be discerned?

In the end, Wulfe resolved to trust that it would.

They had halted close to the duke's keep that last night, for he wished to arrive at the court in the morning. It seemed to him most likely that the father might be awake earlier in the day rather than later, or that a sickened man might be more alert then. Helmut fumed at being restrained, but his shock was clear when Wulfe unbound his hands.

"Simon, you will ride with me on this morning," Wulfe said. "And the lady will ride your palfrey."

Helmut eyed him with suspicion.

"To allow that you ride your own steed." Wulfe grimaced at a realization. "Or Everard's steed. I have no idea whether you stole that from him as well."

"What is this?" Helmut demanded.

Wulfe spoke mildly, knowing he took a risk but certain it would bear fruit. "We reach our destination. Here is the keep of Montmorency. Surely you recognize it?" He smiled. "I welcome you to prove your identity to those within and claim the legacy of Everard. Here is your opportunity to show the lady's charges wrong. If you succeed, I will depart and leave you to your ill-gotten gains." He held Helmut's gaze, even as that man's eyes lit. "Be aware that if you flee, or if you injure the lady again, I will hunt you down. I will ensure that your demise is not an easy one, and no court will raise a hand against me."

Helmut shivered at the menace in Wulfe's tone but he spared a glance at the distant keep, his hope clear. He squared his shoulders and licked his lips with some trepidation. "I will prove the truth to be so," he declared with a bravado Wulfe thought undeserved. He fingered the stubble upon his chin and messed his own hair, surveying the dirt on his tabard with satisfaction. "They will never discern the difference," he murmured, but Wulfe was not so certain of that.

Indeed, he relied upon the opposite.

Christina said naught, but merely looked between the men. That she did not challenge Wulfe encouraged him that his course made sense to her.

They mounted and set out on the fine road that led to the village. With a gesture, Wulfe ensured that Christina was far to his left, on the opposite side from Helmut, and that his hand was clear to seize his sword. Simon had the wits to leap from Teufel's back if need be, and Wulfe was glad that both boys had learned so readily.

"I will declare that you escort me, and you will not challenge it," Helmut said, his anticipation evident.

"You have no lack of confidence," Wulfe noted.

"The missive said he had gone blind," Helmut sneered. "You are a fool to grant me this opportunity, for you will see that I will triumph."

Christina sniffed, her doubt of that most clear and they rode on in silence.

At the gates, Helmut cantered ahead and raised his voice. "Open the gate!" he shouted. "It is Everard returned home! I pray my father yet breathes!"

There was a cry of delight from the porter and Wulfe glimpsed Stephen inside the bailey. It was clear that preparations had been made for the return of the duke's son, and many were gathered to witness his return.

Helmut rode with confidence beneath the gates, pausing to greet members of the court by name. "Eustache! How well you look! How does Margaret fare?"

"Very well, my lord," responded that man and bowed low. "I thank you for recalling her."

"How could I forget? I pray that son of yours who was so reluctant to enter the world is hale?"

Eustache beamed. "He is tall and strong, my lord, just as you declared he would be."

Helmut gave a great booming laugh, obviously a mimicry of Everard. The sound seemed to reassure many.

"Of course, he knows them all," Christina murmured. "Surely some soul with recognize him."

But it seemed those in the bailey saw what they wished to see: their lord's son returned home in time.

"What excellent tidings!" Helmut dismounted, then turned to the man who took his steed's reins. "Yvan? Is that you?"

"Aye, sir!" The ostler bowed, then ruffled his own hair. "There is more silver than once there was, my lord, but I am yet here."

"And good it is to see you. I am certain the steeds in my father's stable are glad of your fine care."

"This is a handsome beast, sir."

"Do you think? I had to choose another in Outremer without your wise counsel, and could only do my best."

"I think him most fine, sir. Some oats and a good brush, and he will be ready to run anew."

"Excellent. Excellent!" Helmut loosed that laugh again and this time, more in the company smiled. He raised a hand, ensuring that his signet ring flashed in the sunlight.

"He lies well," Christina said softly.

Wulfe nodded but once, watching the other man with care. The greatest test was yet before him.

Helmut gestured to Wulfe. "And I have been so fortunate as to be escorted on this journey by a knight sworn to the Templars. Pray make him welcome."

Gazes slid from Wulfe to Christina and he did not doubt they noted the bruises upon her face. He said naught, letting Helmut contrive an explanation.

"Another in need of the order's defense," that man said in a whisper. He granted a significant glance at Wulfe, as if to intimate that Wulfe was responsible for the bruises, and Wulfe caught his breath in outrage.

"He was so noble as to defend me from an assailant's attack," Christina said, touching her fingertips to Wulfe's arm. "Had he not happened upon us in that moment, I should have died."

The company nodded approval at this, a situation more in line with their expectations of knights of the order.

Helmut laughed again, and it struck Wulfe that the one trait of Everard's the other man could reliably mimic was quite inappropriate for visiting a beloved father's deathbed. "Oh, I have so many tales to share," Helmut said, shaking his head. "But first, I beg of you, show me to my beloved father."

"He awaits you, sir," said an older man who must be the castellan. "Though he is not well." That man's expression was inscrutable, but Wulfe noted how he could not seem to stop surveying Helmut.

The castellan had doubts.

The father would only have more.

Christina had no intention of leaving Helmut's success or failure to chance.

As soon as possible, she went to the kitchens, for all the world a maid seeking some morsel of bread.

"Is it true?" the cook asked her and she was not truly surprised that tidings journeyed so quickly as that. He was a man not much older than herself, and she wondered whether he had been in this abode ten years before. "Does the lord's son return?"

"Apparently so."

"And the Templar saved you from abuse?"

"Aye. He is an excellent man and a doughty fighter."

"So they are all said to be." The cook nodded. "I should like to have a look at this son of the duke's. He fairly took his time returning to see his father."

"You cannot make an accusation against my lord Everard," declared an older woman, clicking her tongue at the cook. She was forming loaves of bread and had flour upon her nose. "He is a man above chastisement, so pious and good that he fair had a halo as a boy." She smiled. "We thought him one of the angels come to earth."

"You might have been deceived," the cook said. "There is many a man whose heart is not as good as his countenance would suggest."

The woman shook her head. "Not this one. Ah, he was good from the cradle. He must have had good reason to delay his return, and I am certain his return will give strength to the duke, even now."

"He has need of every bit of it," muttered the cook, and Christina appreciated that there were no stars in his eyes.

She accepted a piece of bread at the woman's invitation and a cup of ale. "Your lord Everard must have been blessed with many friends, then," she dared to say.

"Aye, he did." The woman halted and faced Christina, one floured hand propped on her hip. "My lord Everard has never had any ability to discern wickedness in others. Even when he grew to manhood, he always believed the best of every soul."

"I will wager there were those who took advantage of that trait," the cook said, his manner dour. He tasted a sauce, the spoon held out by the saucemaker's boy, and shook his head. "A measure more salt, I think."

The woman raised her brows. "Aye, there was, to be sure. I remember a companion of his. God in Heaven, but the duke chose that warrior to accompany his son and defend him on his pilgrimage. I was glad to see the last of him, that is for certain, for there was aught in his manner I disliked." She pivoted to face Christina. "Tell me that the mercenary Helmut did not return with my lord Everard?"

Christina put down her cup, knowing she had found the ally she sought. "Perhaps you should come and greet the lord returned," she said quietly.

The cook and the woman exchanged a glance, then both wiped their hands and strode toward the hall with purpose. She could only admire how protective they were of their lord duke and hoped their testimony would be believed.

The cur would succeed.

Wulfe could not believe it.

The duke was carried to the hall to greet his returned son, and but one glimpse of the feeble invalid made Wulfe fear the outcome. Helmut was exultant, though he hid his reaction well. He feigned dismay at the first glimpse of his father, then straightened as if unwilling to trouble the older man with the truth of his reaction. Several in the hall nodded in sympathy, but the old duke clearly could not see far.

"Everard?" he demanded, his voice reedy and thin.

"Father!" Helmut declared, his voice booming so loudly that none could fail to hear it. Clearly this was a trait of the true Everard, for the old duke sat a little taller. Helmut then emitted that laugh and the duke gripped the arms of his chair. "I had tidings that you were unwell," he said. "But here you sit, as fit as ever!"

The duke chuckled to be so teased and Wulfe saw a tear glisten on his cheek. "My son," he whispered and reached out a hand.

Helmut crossed the room, flung out his cloak and dropped to his knee to kiss his father's ring. "I am mired from the road, Father, and unfit to be in your company in this state." He ensured that his voice broke. "But I had to see you as soon as possible."

"My son!" the duke declared and gripped Helmut's hand.

Surely, he could not be so readily fooled?

The duke's hands were thin and lined with blue veins. He looked feeble and thin, and clutched at Helmut as his tears flowed. "How does my son look, Rupert?" he asked the seneschal who stood protectively behind him.

"Like a changed man," Rupert said tightly. "Indeed, I would scarce have recognized him, save for the ring on his finger."

Helmut uttered that laugh yet again, and truly Wulfe tired of its sound. "Ah, Rupert, you have always been the most vigorous in my father's defense." He dropped his voice low. "I prayed at the Holy Sepulchre that you would find relief from the ache in your left knee. Has it improved?"

The seneschal was visibly startled. "It has not, but I thank you for the prayer, sir." He peered at the new arrival, his doubts shaken.

Wulfe was horrified by Helmut's dexterity with falsehood. How could he convince them all to see the truth that stood before them?

It was clear they wished for this illusion to be truth so vehemently that they would disregard their own impressions, lest the duke be disappointed. He must be held in great fondness by his people, which made this travesty all the worse.

"I am glad to have seen you again, my son," the duke whispered, his voice hoarse. He did not relinquish his grip upon Helmut's hand and that man gave a fair impression of a devoted son kneeling at his father's feet.

"You!" a woman cried from the far side of the hall and Helmut looked up.

An older woman in an apron, flour all over her kirtle, marched across the floor in fury. "How dare you return to this place, and without my lord Everard? What have you done to him, fiend?"

The duke looked bewildered. Anger flashed in Helmut's eyes for a heartbeat before he, too, managed to appear confused.

The seneschal straightened, eyes glittering as he watched.

Wulfe saw that a dark-haired man with his sleeves rolled up had accompanied the woman. He watched with obvious curiosity. Beside him was Christina, her expression so filled with satisfaction that Wulfe knew she had ensured the woman arrived in the hall in this moment.

"Marthe, is it?" Helmut said, as if uncertain of his memory. He snapped his fingers as the woman bore down upon him. "Aye, Marthe! I remember your baking well, to be sure, for there has not been another in all these years to make a loaf so fine and light..."

"It should be more than my baking you recall, you cur!" Marthe declared and struck him across the face.

The entire company gasped.

"Marthe! You forget your place," the seneschal said, but with no real heat.

"I am not the one who forgets. Look this man in the face! He is not Everard! He is that black-hearted villain Helmut, that mercenary hired to defend my lord Everard." She looked him up and down. "From my stance, it appears that he tries to trick us all, to feign that he is Everard!"

Whispering began but Helmut stood tall before her. His tone became imperious. "You have no right to make such an accusation..." he began but got no further before the duke lifted his head.

"You do sound like Helmut," he said quietly, his hands shaking as he folded them in his lap.

"Father!" Helmut appealed, changing his tone. "Surely you cannot take the word of a woman from the kitchens against that of your own son?"

"If you are his own son," Marthe said, challenge in her tone.

"I am!" Helmut laughed again. "It is evident to all."

The seneschal's lips tightened. "The truth can be readily proven," he said softly but with resolve. "My lord Everard has a pattern of moles upon his back." He snapped his fingers and four men of the guard fell upon Helmut.

"This is an outrage! Father, you cannot allow this indignity to be served upon me..."

But the duke waited for his seneschal's verdict.

Wulfe bit back his smile as Helmut was easily divested of his tabard. That man struggled but he was no match for the determined knights. Only when they removed his chemise, leaving him bare chested, did the fight abandon him. He bowed his head as Rupert walked around him and the hall was silent in anticipation.

"No moles," Rupert decreed. "I am sorry, my lord, but this man is an imposter who would steal your son's legacy."

The duke dropped his head to his hands and wept. He looked even smaller and more fragile than he had before, and Wulfe regretted that the truth stole the one thing that could have given him solace.

The seneschal watched his lord, sympathy in his gaze, then took command. "Bind him." Helmut fought the knights but was no more successful than before. In moments, he was bound. "He will face the duke's justice when the duke sees fit to hear whatever case he can make in his own defense."

"Everard had everything!" Helmut roared with bitterness. "He was weak and unskilled with a blade. He granted mercy where it was not deserved. He could not keep his coin, but granted alms to beggars at every turn. He had no right to be wealthy, to be a knight, to gain a holding, when I, I who have fought for every trinket that has come to my hand, was so much better in every way."

"Save in your heart," Wulfe said and the seneschal nodded.

"Did you kill him?" the seneschal asked Helmut, his tone deceptively mild. His eyes were flashing with an outrage that Wulfe shared.

"I took from him what he held only in disdain," Helmut declared bitterly. "He gave away his coin but I savored it. He cared more for the life he thought he would have in heaven, so I dispatched him to it."

"Cur!" Marthe shouted.

"Vermin!" the company cried as the duke wept.

Wulfe found himself turning to Christina as Helmut was led to the dungeon, only to find that her face was streaked with tears. She was smiling though, and he could nigh sense the relief that filled her.

Gunther had been avenged.

He had given her this gift, and now their ways must part.

But first, he would escort her to whatever place she called home, even if the extra time in her company would only torment him. He told himself that he was not in a hurry to face any discipline from the Grand Master in Paris, but that was not why he would choose this path.

He wanted to know for certain that Christina was safe.

Christina could not bear to see the anguish of Everard's father. How tragic to end his days knowing that his most beloved son was lost. She thought of her own mother then, and wondered whether her own disappearance had distressed her mother.

It had never been her intention to do as much, but Christina had been so distressed by her own situation that she had not sent word. She had thought it more cruel to contact her family when she was unable to leave Venice, but now she wondered whether her pride had kept her from asking for help that might have been willingly offered.

What if her mother had died in her absence?

Christina left the hall and wandered the gardens behind the keep, sickened by the possibility.

Indeed, the bile rose without expectation, and she was sick. At least she managed to reach the pile of deadened leaves and clippings left to compost over the winter. With shaking hands, she buried the evidence of her illness, only to realize that an older woman watched her from a patch of kale. It was not Marthe, for this one had darker hair, but there was a welcome pragmatism in her manner.

"Is it the spawn of the villain or the Templar?" that woman asked, much to Christina's confusion. When she shook her head, the woman shrugged. "Either way, you will have a long road ahead of you, my dear."

"I do not understand."

"Do you not? To bring a child into the world without the support of its father is a challenge to be sure. Not so uncommon as that, but still not to be desired." The woman winced and returned to pulling weeds. "But if the villain is the father, the lord might be kind to you. Indeed, you would both have been cheated by the same man, and he might be generous for that. The duke has compassion, to be sure."

Christina smiled. "I am merely ill this day, which is most inconvenient, but I am not with child."

"Are you not?"

"I am never with child. I am barren."

The woman chuckled. "You shall see by the spring whether that remains the case or not."

"But I cannot be pregnant! It is impossible."

"By the way that Templar looks at you, I would say it is very possible indeed. Take my counsel and do not argue that 'tis a virgin birth. It is better to acknowledge the truth from the outset."

With child. Christina surveyed the garden without truly seeing it. Could it be so?

"You look most surprised. Did you truly not know?"

"I still do not know."

The woman worked a stubborn weed free. "And when did you last have your courses? Have you been intimate with a man since?

How many days have you lost your meal? You need not confess it all to me, but it might do you good to think upon it."

Christina had not bled since several weeks before meeting Wulfe in Venice. She counted on her fingers. He had arrived at Costanzia's house on the feast of the Magdalene, July 22. It was now the feast of Saint Augustine, well over a month later. They had been intimate, multiple times. And her belly had been in great turmoil since leaving Paris.

Could she carry Wulfe's child?

She stared at the woman in wonder.

"Your breasts then," the woman continued. "Do they seem larger? And tender?"

"They do," Christina acknowledged and sat down hard, for her world had been shaken. A new hope made her heart flutter. Was it possible that neither of her younger sisters had yet borne sons?

Was it possible that she could give Wulfe a future outside of the order?

"You truly did not know then," the woman said, and Christina realized that she had come to stand beside her. "I am sorry if I surprised you, for I thought you did know. It is better, though, to know sooner than later."

"Aye. I am glad to know. I thank you."

The woman smiled, her expression kind. "May you and the babe be blessed, my dear."

Christina smiled and impulsively embraced the woman. "Thank you," she said again, then hastened to find Wulfe. Somehow she had to tell him the news.

She could not make such an intimate confession in company. Nay, she had need of a moment of some privacy, the sooner the better. Christina hoped that Wulfe was yet determined to escort her home.

They camped in the forest that night, not so far from Montmorency keep but well beyond the village. It had been clear that they, as the bearers of ill tidings, had not been welcome to stay, though the baron and his family had offered the invitation. Wulfe had declined politely, insisting that they had far to travel, and Christina was just as happy to be far from Helmut.

As much as she disliked and distrusted him, she realized that she had no desire to witness justice being done. It was sufficient to know that he had been discovered and would pay for his crimes.

The stars were numerous that night, and they had provisions from the kitchens at Montmorency. They had been granted a skin full of good red wine, bread, and hard sausage, cheese, and apples. Wulfe and the boys had made a fire, the boys gathering wood at his dictate, and they sat around it after their meal. The horses were tethered nearby and a small stream splashed as it passed the spot they had chosen. The snap of winter was in the air, though they would not be overly cold that night. She kept her hand over her belly, aware that it was rounder and wondered what Wulfe would say if she told him of the babe.

Would he deny that it was his own? She watched him covertly, doubting he would be so churlish. He sat on the opposite side of the fire, with his legs stretched out and crossed at the ankle, his easy posture giving her a curious joy. He was less stern than when she had met him, more at ease, and she liked the change well.

Nay, he would not decline his role in the creation of their child. But the confession would trouble him, she could guess, for he believed he could not wed her honorably. It would make him aware again of his lack of fortune, and she did not wish to make him feel like less than he was.

All the same, she wondered what she would do, she and this child growing within her.

She dared to hope again that her sisters had not been more fortunate than she. What if she returned home to find that they had not borne a son yet?

What if Wulfe's child was a boy? The possibility of granting the son that every man must desire was enough to send a thrill through her, even without the possibility of her father's legacy to be won. She lowered her gaze, considering how the truth might be shared, sooner rather than later.

"Would you tell us a tale, my lady?" Stephen demanded.

"Surely you have had sufficient tales of saints to sate you?" she teased, wanting to keep silent on this night, the better to think of possibilities. "I say it is time for Wulfe to share a tale."

He flicked a glance her way and to her surprise, he ceded. "Perhaps it is so. I know only one tale, though I would share it with you."

The boys exchanged grins and leaned close to listen.

Wulfe stared into the fire. "Once, there was a young man. Indeed, he was not much older than either of you. He set out to seek his fortune." He paused and frowned. "It sounds thus as if he chose to seek his fortune, but in truth, the choice was made for him. He had grown up in the woods, in the care of a gamekeeper. When that man died, the young man was alone. He had naught to his hand, no advantage, no parent, no relations or even a home to call his own. He sought his fortune in order that he might survive."

Christina knew then that he told of his own life.

"He traveled far and saw much before one day, he was welcomed into the abode of a gamekeeper. That man had a scheme, unbeknownst to the young man, though it quickly came to fruition. The nobleman who held sway over that holding visited the gamekeeper, as was his custom, and the gamekeeper presented the young man as a candidate to train with the lord's own son. The nobleman was much pleased with this suggestion, for it seemed he had been seeking an opponent of suitable size and strength for his nephew."

"He wished for his son to win," Stephen suggested.

Wulfe smiled. "He wished that his nephew was not defeated every time. His own son was older and had earned his spurs, so the nephew had little chance against him. The nobleman told the young man that while more is learned in defeat than in victory, the nephew had need of a more fairly matched opponent. And here was the offer he made the young man: if he would agree to spend five years training in the nobleman's household alongside the nephew, the nobleman would dub him a knight as well."

"There is a fine offer!" Simon exclaimed.

"Indeed. The young man was quick to accept, and so began the most challenging five years he had ever known. He learned much in both victory and defeat, and became an accomplished swordsman. He learned of strategy and tactics, and even better, he and the nephew became good friends. They earned their spurs together and were dubbed on the same morning, and such was the generosity of the nobleman that he saw them both armed. The young man knew that the nephew's blade and armor was better than his, but that was only right. He was no kin and the nobleman had granted him more than could have been expected of any other."

Wulfe sipped his wine. "And so it was that the nephew returned home, and since the young man was again resolved to seek his fortune, they traveled together to that holding. It turned out that the nephew had a sister of remarkable beauty. He thought little of her charms, for she was younger and had always followed him when they were children, but when the young man saw her, he might have been struck to stone. By virtue of her beauty alone, he loved her, and he knew he would do any deed to win her hand in his own. It must be said that his good fortune thus far had given him high expectations, but I cannot fault him for such optimism. Indeed, it seemed the maiden favored him."

"Did he wed her?" Simon demanded.

"Did he win a keep and a holding, then wed her and have many sons?" Stephen asked.

Christina smiled at their enthusiasm and dropped her gaze to her hands, fearing that she knew how this tale would end.

"He pledged his love to her, and it was well received. It seemed that naught could go awry for this pair, and when she kissed him fully, he thought his heart would burst. And so it was that he hoped to gain a wife in marriage, but alas, such good fortune was not to be."

"Whyever not?" Stephen asked.

"Because the lady confessed her secret to her brother, who laughed at her. It seemed she had always vowed that she would wed a prince or a king, and her brother teased her that the knight who had gained her affections was not even of noble birth. He meant naught by it, for he thought her love was true, and indeed, I think he was pleased that his friend had earned his sister's affection, but the maiden claimed she had been deceived. She spurned the knight from that moment hence and refused to even speak to him again."

"Her love was meager, then," Christina dared to say.

"Indeed." Wulfe was taut with this admission and it seemed the rejection still stung. "Her affection had a high price, a price higher than he could pay."

"But what happened to him?" Simon demanded.

Wulfe shrugged. "He left that place and rode on, his heart bleeding that his lady's love had not been sufficient to accept him as he was. He knew then that he would never dare to love again, and he joined a military order, the better that he should not be tempted to err anew."

"And the sole women he knew were whores," Christina guessed.

Wulfe's gaze met hers across the fire. "Aye," he said, his voice husky. "Never the same one twice."

"Then he was always alone?" Stephen asked.

"Aye."

"That is no tale," Simon complained. "He should have met a princess, or found a treasure."

Wulfe smiled. "I do not doubt that he would agree with you."

There was silence between them, then, save for the crackling of the fire.

"Christina tells better tales," Stephen noted, his tone disgruntled.

"Then perhaps you should not have asked for one from me," Wulfe said gently.

The boys, undeterred, turned to her, their faces alight. "Will you tell us a tale, my lady?" Stephen asked.

Christina smiled. "I have heard the same tale," she said, well prepared for Wulfe to quickly look her way. "But the ending differed in the version I heard."

"Truly?" he said softly. "Then perhaps you will share it."

"Aye, share it!" Simon and Stephen said as one.

"The tale was the same to this point, but the young man continued to seek his fortune. He was a knight by now, as you know, and one who was certain of the place of women in his life. Then one night, he met a widow who was not so ready to let him escape her affections. She kept him by her side for a day and a night, and then when he left, she followed him."

"She cast a spell upon him, to be sure," Wulfe said.

Christina smiled. "Perhaps the magic was between them, for it seemed that neither could turn away from the other. And so they spoke often, and they laughed together, and they found their thoughts to often be as one. They lay together and confessed their secrets to each other, and they even solved troubles together. Then one day, the woman realized that she had conceived his child."

Wulfe nigh dropped his cup at that, and his eyes widened in astonishment.

"Were they wed?" Simon asked.

Christina smiled and shook her head. "Nay, for the knight believed he had naught to offer a bride. I gather that he was still wounded by that other maiden's inability to see his true merit. The truth was, though, that this lady had only sisters. Because the knight had not met her family, he did not know this, and she had not spoken to him about it. But her father had been much convinced that holdings should be passed down from father to son. Because he had no son, he decreed that the first of his daughters to bear a boy would see that son inherit the estate. And so it was that the lady asked the knight to escort her home, and she prayed every night and every morning that their child might be a son, so that the knight would believe he could wed her in honor." She fell silent then, her gaze clinging to Wulfe's.

"Another matter they might resolve together," Wulfe murmured.

"And what happened?" Stephen asked.

"Was it a boy or a girl?" Simon said.

"I do not know. That was all the tale that I heard. I knew only that they traveled together to her family home. I hope it was a boy and that the boy became heir, but I do not know for certain."

Stephen exhaled with dissatisfaction. "That tale is little better. A good tale deserves a good ending."

"And perhaps this one had such a happy resolution," Wulfe said firmly. "But the hour is late and we rise early to ride on." He rose and kicked the fire, scattering the coals, as the boys wrapped themselves in their cloaks. He turned to Christina, his gaze bright in the darkness. "It is damp this night," he said softly. "I would ensure your warmth, my lady."

Christina smiled and rose to her feet, only too happy to comply.

A child!

Wulfe was both shocked and delighted. He schooled his expression with care until the boys were bedded down and he had ensured that the horses were tethered. He returned to Christina then, snared anew by her luminous gaze. He spread his cloak on the ground and they lay down together, then he pulled her into his embrace and wrapped his cloak over them both. She nestled against him as she had that first night in Venice, her back against his chest, her legs curled before his own. The softness of her hair teased his nostrils, and her scent aroused him. He found his hand not only sliding around her waist but landing on her belly. His fingers spread protectively over her and Christina locked her hand over his own.

"A child?" he murmured into her ear.

"A child," she agreed softly.

"How can this be?"

She twisted a little so that he could see the sparkle of her eyes. "Tell me you have not forgotten our couplings already," she teased.

"Never," he said and meant it. "But you said your womb bore no fruit."

"And never has it, until now. I cannot fathom it myself." She sighed. "We undertook the pilgrimage because I was barren, but I never reached the shrine of Jerusalem. There can be no absolution for my sins, and truly they are greater now than they were then."

"You did not conceive, not even in Costanzia's abode?"

She shook her head and he believed her. "I knew I would not. They had potions and preparations and I used them, to be sure. There was no choice. But I knew I would never conceive a child."

"For you had not completed your pilgrimage," Wulfe concluded.

Christina nodded and nestled against his warmth.

He curled a tendril of her hair around his finger, thinking about her other confession. "Is the rest true?"

She nodded and rolled to face him then, her words soft between them. "My father was resolute that holdings should pass only to men, but I have only two sisters. I am the eldest, and all assumed I would be the first to bear a son."

"So it was more than a love of children that prompted Gunther's choice?" In truth, Wulfe was glad to hear that Christina's husband had not been so saintly as he had imagined.

"He was a younger son. Although he had a noble family and had been knighted, there was no holding to fall to his hand. My father liked him well and ensured our match was made before he died. All believed the future would be secured within a year."

"But it was not."

Christina shook her head. "My sister Miriam is three years younger than me, and she had a most devoted suitor, even then. Otto was the son of a distant cousin, another younger son with no legacy. He had played with us when we were small, and he had always favored Miriam. She favored him, as well. We had been wed almost four years when their betrothal was announced, and Gunther feared that opportunity would be lost."

"And you have had no word from home since?"

"I dared not send word of my situation," she admitted softly. "For I could not change it." Christina shook her head, then looked up at Wulfe.

He had to ask the question, though it was a churlish one. "Are you certain the child is mine?'

She smiled at him, and he was glad she did not resent the query. "A fair question, Wulfe, but there can be no doubt in the reply. I tried to avoid my responsibilities in Costanzia's house. I had bled two weeks before your arrival there, but had been lying about the persistence of my courses. On that day, Costanzia bade me find a patron for the entire night or she would cast me to the streets in the morning."

"Then my arrival was timely."

"As one would expect from a champion," she teased. "And there can be no doubt of the babe's father."

Wulfe nodded with relief and pulled Christina close. How he yearned to make a sweet pledge to her, but he had no right to do as much.

She clutched his tabard, and her tone became urgent. "Wulfe, what if Miriam and Anna have been as barren as me? What if they have borne only daughters?"

"It has been nine years," he said, scarce daring to hope.

"Nay it has been thirteen," she correctly quietly.

He nodded, his heart pounded at the possibility. "It could be so."

She smiled. "It could be."

"There is only one way to discover the truth," he said, watching as her eyes danced with anticipation. "We must ride for your home, with all haste."

"Aye," Christina said and curled against him with undisguised satisfaction. "Aye, Wulfe, we must." She sighed. "And I will pray, as seldom I have prayed before."

Wulfe would pray as well, though he doubted any entreaty of his would be received with as much consideration as that of the lady in his arms.

Was it possible that they might have a future together?

That was when he resolved his course: if one of Christina's sisters had claimed the legacy but the lady still desired him, he would remind Gaston of his promise.

WEDNESDAY, SEPTEMBER 16, 1187

Feast Day of Saint Euphemia

CHAPTER EIGHTEEN

Christina's heart was pounding when their small party crested the rise in the road and they looked upon her father's holding.

It was not large, but it was prosperous, and it looked still to be so. Her gaze swept over the vineyards, and she could tell by the activity in the fields that the harvest had been good. The roofs in the village were all thatched with care and the market was bustling. The river at the base of the valley sparkled and she could hear the great stones turning in the gristmill. The stone keep was perched on a mount above the village, its gates open for the day, and her father's insignia emblazoned the banner that snapped above its highest tower.

She found that there were tears in her eyes, for she had feared more than once that she would never see this place again. Wulfe was watching her, his expression guarded, and she smiled at him. "Come. The sentries will already have told my mother that there is a party on the high road. She will be curious."

When he hesitated, she eyed him anew. "So rich as this?" he murmured, his doubts clear.

Christina smiled and urged him onward. "No so rich as that," she chided, but Wulfe did not look to be persuaded.

Indeed, he appeared most thoughtful.

But she was home! She rode on at a canter, desperate to know the truth. The boys hooted and raced their steeds behind her, Wulfe and Teufel at the rear. Those in the marketplace turned with curiosity, then parted to let them pass. Christina heard the whispers of speculation, but she wanted to see her mother first herself.

If indeed, that woman still drew breath.

Before that fear could grow larger, the seneschal stepped out of the portal to the keep itself. It was yet Bertrand, though more grizzled than once he had been. Christina nigh called out in her relief. He assessed the party, then gestured to the bailey behind himself.

But a moment later, a tall woman stepped into view, ensuring that she did not halt until she was before him. Christina's mouth went dry in recognition. Her mother was dressed in her favored hue of blue, and there was silver embroidery on her cuffs and hems. Her veil was as white as snow, her circlet as silver as the hair beneath. Her gaze was as sharp as that of a falcon at hunt, and she peered at the faces of those in the party, her curiosity most clear.

Wulfe dismounted with a flourish and came to hand Christina down. He gave her fingers a minute squeeze just before she cast back her hood.

Her mother caught her breath and her hands rose to her mouth. "Juliana!"

"Good day, *Maman*," Christina said, finding her voice husky.

"It is a good day indeed that my child returns home," her mother said in a rush, then hurried forward to hug her tightly. They spun around together in a tight embrace and Christina saw Wulfe's confusion.

"Saint Christina was sustained by her faith," Stephen said quietly, and Wulfe smiled at that.

"Indeed, she was," he murmured, and she recalled how he had been certain that very first night that Christina had not been her name in truth. Right from the first, it had been impossible to hide her truth from this man, a sure a mark of the love that had grown between them as could be.

Juliana found herself blushing that she had lied to him at all, but Wulfe did not seem overly troubled. It was strange that she would have to become accustomed to her name again. Juliana realized that her mother was looking between her and Wulfe, assessment in her eyes.

"Escorted by a Templar knight," that woman said. "I would say that you have been fortunate indeed, Juliana, had it not been more than nine years since you left these gates."

"*Maman*, this is Brother Wulfe, most recently of the Gaza Priory." Wulfe bowed, and Juliana noted how keenly her mother watched him. "And his squires, Stephen and Simon."

"Is there a reason Gunther does not return with you?"

She knew her mother truly asked after the delay in her return. "He was killed, *Maman*, by a thief in Venice."

Her mother's lips parted and consideration dawned in her gaze. "You were alone in that city," she whispered. "My child!" Juliana's mother gathered her into an embrace that was even tighter than the first.

"I could not send word, *Maman*," Juliana whispered so that only her mother could hear. "I could not bear to tell you why I was forbidden to leave that city."

"And this man aided you to leave?" her mother asked softly. Juliana looked up to find that there was no censure in her mother's gaze. Her mother smiled. "Do not be surprised, my Juliana. I was the one who taught you to do what must be done for survival's sake. I would have sent aid."

"I am sorry, *Maman*."

Her mother kissed her brow and held her tightly, her voice rising. "What you must have borne! And you are far too thin." She pulled back and took a shaking breath, her eyes filling with familiar concern as she ran her fingertips down Juliana's cheek. "But home. So blessedly home." They embraced again, Juliana's vision blurred with tears.

Then her mother turned to Wulfe with her usual grace. "You must all come to the board," she invited, though she did not relinquish her grip upon Juliana's arm. "For I am certain there are tales aplenty to be shared. Bertrand!"

"Of course, my lady. The horses shall be well tended." Bertrand bowed to Wulfe. "Should you like to see our stables, sir? I know that many a knight does not rest easy without being certain of his companion's welfare. And what a fine destrier you ride! Was he bred in Outremer by chance?"

Wulfe and Juliana exchanged a glance of amusement as Bertrand chattered with his customary enthusiasm, even as he led Wulfe toward the keep's stables.

"You have affection for him," Juliana's mother whispered in her ear.

She could only nod.

"And has he good family?"

"He has none." She declined to tell her mother that Wulfe might be a nobleman's bastard, for she felt the tale was not hers to share.

Her mother looked thoughtful. "How gracious of him to escort you all the way home."

"Indeed." Juliana glanced up in time to see her mother shake her head.

"You should know that Miriam and Otto have three sons now," she said gently. "Otto is lord, Juliana, and he is a good one." She smiled, trailing her fingertips down Juliana's cheek, her gaze all too perceptive. "I hope you have not offered what is not yours to promise, my child."

Juliana swallowed and blinked back her tears. "Of course not, *Maman*," she said but her voice broke on the words. "It has been nine years, after all."

Her mother saw all that Juliana would have hidden and perhaps more, for she pulled her into another tight hug. Being home, seeing Gunther avenged, and embracing her mother was more than Juliana had hoped to experience, but her gaze trailed after Wulfe.

In her heart, she knew all of that was not near sufficient to sate her, though.

Christina had come from an advantage that astonished Wulfe. She believed her origins were not rich, but to him, this holding with its obvious prosperity might have been a king's palace. Though she had endured much in Venice, her upbringing had been so different from his that her expectations could not be as modest as his own.

She would not be content as the wife of a man-at-arms in service to Gaston. She deserved better than that, a titled knight who was at least the equal in wealth to her sister's husband, Otto, who had now claimed the family estate.

He was disappointed, to be sure, that Miriam had sons, but had not truly surprised. Wulfe was more shocked to realize that the sole opportunity he had of offering honorably for her hand would not suffice. Oh, she might accept him, but over time, she would tire of such status and limited opportunity. He could not bear to see her come to despise him for his lack.

Yet she would bear his child, all the same.

It chafed at him that he might leave a bastard in the world, even one who would likely be raised in comparative advantage. He had never desired to echo any feat of his father.

Wulfe knew full well that women oft died in the delivery of children, and though he prayed that would not be the case, he understood the ramifications. With no mother, his own child would be virtually an orphan.

His child, son or daughter, might share his own fate.

Christina would be tainted by the bearing of a child out of wedlock, though he knew she wished for a babe beyond all else. He had partaken of the feast she offered and it irked him mightily to leave her to face the consequences alone.

But what choice had he? He knew the realities of the world all too well.

That was one matter they had in common, he supposed. That would be why she had not argued with him when he had declared his resolve to leave, and had not entreated him to stay.

Christina—or he should say Juliana—knew. He saw the sadness in her eyes.

It was bittersweet to realize in this moment that her confession of love had not been a lie. She did love him, and he loved her, but he would not grant her a reason to yearn for what could not be. If he confessed his love, she might close her heart against all others. If she believed herself spurned, she might come to love whatever man her mother found to take her hand.

It was less, far less, than what Wulfe wished for the lady who would always reign in his heart.

What could he do?

He paused on the road, out of view of Christina's family abode, heartily disgruntled with his situation. To the west lay Paris, his sworn duty to the Templars, and certainly a reprimand for disobedience, if not more. Beyond that was Gaston's holding and an opportunity to labor for an honest baron.

But to the east lay Wulfe's past, in all its tangled shadows. He had vowed never to return, but he knew in this moment that he had to go back to have any hope of offering Christina a future.

To have any chance of claiming his heart's desire, he had to face his deepest fear.

His decision made, Wulfe gave Teufel his spurs and rode east, the boys fast behind him.

Wulfe had not expected to recognize the forest where he had grown up under the protection of the old man. Indeed, he had feared that one stretch of wilderness was much like another. As they rode, he feared he might ride for all his life, peering into forests, seeking some familiarity. He had feared he might never know his destination, even if he happened across it. He knew the forest had to have changed, and he doubted the reliability of his own memory.

As they rode, he began to doubt the merit of his quest.

Yet on the fifth day, they crested a rise to find a vast wood before them, and Wulfe's heart leapt in immediate recognition. He nigh cried out in joy. Aye, the hill curved the way he recalled, the river bent just so and he could have pointed to the spot where the banks narrowed and the water ran fast. In the deep pool below, a fish could always be caught for dinner. The berries grew abundantly in that distant clearing and there, where still there was a clearing, had been the location of the old man's cabin.

"Where are we, sir?" Stephen asked, evidently noting Wulfe's wonder.

"Home," he admitted quietly, feeling the tightness in his chest.

The boys looked with new curiosity, but Wulfe spurred Teufel on. He led the boys into the forest, the afternoon sun on their backs until they passed beneath the shadow of the trees. Every vista affirmed his suspicions, and more than one old tree was familiar. He felt as if the birds sang in welcome. It was cool in the forest, and to Wulfe's relief, he yet found it tranquil.

Just as he had as a boy.

He rode with confidence to the bank alongside that deep pool and instructed Simon to catch some fish and Stephen to make a fire. "You will find tinder and dry branches there," he directed, then took a deep breath of the scent of this forest. Its blend of pine and moss and undergrowth seemed specific to him, and he imagined he could feel the old man's ghost watching him.

"How can this be your home, sir?" Simon asked. "It is a forest."

"But I grew up near here."

"Like the young man in the tale," Stephen reminded his companion who stared at Wulfe in surprise. Evidently Simon had only just realized that there could be truth disguised in a tale.

It was in that moment that Wulfe knew what he had to do. He would pay his respects to the old man. They were long overdue. He left the boys and the horses, striding through the forest to the place he had dug that hole, so many years before. It was not far and he would not be gone long.

To his surprise, there was a second mound in the clearing, and it was a fresh one. The one he had created had settled and plants had grown over it, though the shape was yet distinctive. The new one was covered with fresh earth and there was a wooden cross marking one end of it.

Wulfe lingered in the shadows of the forest. Who had dug this grave?

Who lay within it?

He only realized moments later that there was an old man, leaning on his cane, at the other end of the grave. He was so still that he might have been wrought of stone. Wulfe retreated with the intent of returning later, not wanting to disturb the man's prayers. A stick cracked beneath his boot, though, and the old man straightened, looking over his shoulder.

"Who is there?" he demanded, his voice querulous and shaking. His hood fell back, revealing that his hair was as white as fresh snow. He winced and leaned heavily on his cane, pushing himself to his feet with no small effort, then straightened to look around himself.

Wulfe's heart clenched. Though the man was aged beyond expectation and clearly unwell, Wulfe would have known him anywhere.

In this place, there could be no doubt of his identity.

He stepped forward, revealing himself.

A servant stood abruptly, his hand upon the hilt of his knife, but Wulfe's father waved him off. Wulfe saw then that there were a pair of horses tethered on the far side of the clearing, and a hunting dog, which lay at their feet, its expression alert.

He and his father stared at each other for long moments in silence, then the older man walked toward him. It was painful to watch his progress, for clearly his injury troubled him greatly. He favored one leg and it seemed unable to support his weight. He had grown crooked since Wulfe had seen him last, and he seemed far smaller than once he had been.

Less terrifying.

Indeed, Wulfe felt an unexpected measure of pity for what his father had become.

Still, he did not move. He did not make it easier for this man, who had made naught easy for him. His father was breathing heavily when he halted before Wulfe and the hand upon the cane was shaking from the exertion of walking so far.

Still he was proud and stood as straight as he could manage, His gaze roved over Wulfe, and a glint of what might have been pride lit his eyes. Wulfe chose not to be softened by it. His father lifted a shaking hand to the scar on Wulfe's cheek, and his fingertip was surprisingly cold.

"Agneta's boy," he said softly, then nodded, needing no

confirmation from Wulfe. He turned slightly and gestured to the newer grave. "She would have liked to have seen you again."

If he meant to make an accusation, Wulfe would not apologize.

"I doubt that," he said crisply. "She abandoned me, after all."

Those pale blue eyes flicked to Wulfe again. "She chose, boy, chose between you and me, because I made her do as much."

"I was told that she was dead."

He nodded. "She might as well have been dead to her father, once she became my mistress. He did not approve of that or of me." He frowned. "I wondered always whether she regretted her decision."

Wulfe blinked. "The old man was my grandfather?"

"Agneta's father. Of course. That was why I could not marry her." He scoffed a little. "The lord of the manor wedding the daughter of the woodsman? Nay, it could not be so. It *would* not be so. My father forbade it and my father's word was law." He sighed, his eyes narrowing as he gazed at the fresh grave. "And so I wed a shrew of noble lineage, as instructed, and so cursed was our match that she never bore a live babe. She died, despising me."

"And Agneta?"

"She defied me in letting you live, in hiding you from me. I never knew she had any power for deceit until the day you and I met." He glanced again at Wulfe's scar. "And by the time my fury was passed, all had changed."

"How so?"

"Agneta learned of what I had done and returned to her father's abode. She never acknowledged me again." His brow furrowed again. "It is a strange thing that once a man's fortunes reverse, they cannot be set right again. All went awry when Agneta left me. We lost battles on our borders that we should have won. Our goods sold for less coin than expected at markets and fairs. Pestilence came upon our crops and illness rolled through our villages. Some said it was the wages of sin, and as time passed, it became harder to dismiss the notion." He gestured to his leg. "I was injured at war and the wound would not heal. Instead it festered, and even Agneta could not see the toxin driven from my flesh."

"She returned to you?"

"I implored her to do as much. She came only to look upon my injury, to relieve my suffering as much as she could. She bade me repent of my errors and rebuild my holding anew." He took a deep breath. "And then she left me again. Truly, the second parting was worse than the first, for I knew I should never see her again."

"Who buried her?"

"My men, at my dictate. I sent her gifts, foodstuffs mostly." He smiled. "She had an uncommon affection for angelica candied with honey, and it was one thing I could yet give her. My courier found her dead in her father's hut but a fortnight ago." The older man surveyed Wulfe again. "And here you are, too late for her to have seen the man you have become."

"You cannot deny your part in that."

The old man sighed. "I cannot," he acknowledged with what seemed like regret. His gaze trailed to the grave. "Perhaps it was Agneta's fate to always be cheated of her due." He leaned on his cane, wobbling a little. "Perhaps that was the price for loving me." His voice broke on those words and Wulfe felt compassion blossom within his heart.

"You should sit, sir," he said, speaking more gently than he had done thus far. There was a fallen log not three steps away, and it had been a doughty tree. He took his father's elbow and helped him to sit upon the log, noting how the older man sighed with relief.

He then impaled Wulfe with a look. "And so, against all expectation, my only son is returned. Why did you come?"

Only now did Wulfe see that his own tale echoed his father's, and having heard his father's confession, he believed he might gain what he sought.

He spoke bluntly, then, wanting to know the truth sooner. "I would wed the woman I love before she bears our child, and I have no right to ask for her hand." Wulfe frowned and swallowed, well aware of his father's avid gaze upon him. "I had thought you might affirm my lineage, that I could declare myself worthy of her."

"She is nobly born?"

Wulfe inclined his head.

"And she is with child?" At Wulfe's nod, he insisted. "Your child?"

"Aye, but even if it were not so, it is her child and I would see her future assured."

"How will you do as much?" His father flicked a fingertip at Wulfe's tabard. "No Templar takes a bride."

"I may take a position at a former companion's abode and serve in its defense." This was far less than Wulfe desired, but he did not have the audacity to ask his father outright for a legacy.

Indeed, he did not know whether there could be one. Did he have siblings? Had his father wed again and sired sons? Had the holding lost all of its value in these dark years after Agneta's departure?

His father shook his head. "It will not suffice. You must have more than noble blood in your veins. You must have a holding and fortune to your name. You must have a title to offer to her." He straightened. "I would not surrender a daughter of mine to less than that."

Wulfe turned away, fearing he had his reply.

The weight of his father's hand landed upon his arm. "I can grant you both, my son."

Wulfe glanced back, tempted but wary. "Indeed?"

"Indeed. I have no other sons. The holding is large and could be prosperous, especially if governed by a man other than myself."

Wulfe was still leery of his father's intent. "No doubt this gift would come at a price."

His father scoffed. "It is not a gift. It is a legacy." His gaze met Wulfe's, some amusement lurking deep within their pale depths. "But you are right. There is a price."

Wulfe arched a brow.

"Forgiveness," the older man said with force. "No more and no less than that." He offered his hand, his gaze searching, and Wulfe saw the hope in his father's eyes.

"A new beginning," Wulfe said quietly and at his father's nod, he gripped the older man's hand and shook it.

His heart leapt with the conviction that all would soon come aright.

WEDNESDAY, NOVEMBER 25, 1187

Feast Day of
Saint Catherine of Alexandra

CHAPTER NINETEEN

More than two months had passed since Wulfe's departure when the missive arrived.

Juliana had slept late again, having been restless the night before. Her belly was rounder and her breasts were fuller. She felt ripe and tired, and her mother's sidelong glances of concern did naught to improve her mood. Soon, it would be visible to all that she expected a child, and this without a ring upon her finger or a suitor in sight.

She dreaded her mother's questions about the father.

Her sister Miriam was as kind and generous as ever she had been, and her husband, Otto, was a good man. Juliana could not regret that he managed the holding, not when he was so tolerant of her mother and made her sister so very happy. Their sons were charming boys, and similarly, no person of merit could resent their good fortune. Her youngest sister, Anna, was not yet wedded but had nigh a dozen suitors. The delay came from her refusal to decide, not from lack of opportunity.

Juliana supposed she would be the scandalous sister, the one who bore a child out of wedlock and remained a burden upon the house's finances. It was not the life she had hoped to have, but she would not surrender Wulfe's child for any reason. If this was the price of raising a child wrought in love, she would pay it.

She dreamed of Wulfe, the one man who had desired her for herself alone, and suspected she would do so for every night of her life. She would have followed him willingly, even if he had taken his trade as a mercenary, and made the best of that wandering life. She knew he made a sensible choice in leaving her to return to the order, but she wished he might have chosen in passion, just once.

Though she knew it was not his nature to be so irresponsible. Indeed, that was part of why she loved him so.

She had hoped for a long time that he might halt to say farewell on his route back to Outremer, but after so many weeks, she knew he had to have completed his journey already. Her mother had received news that Jerusalem itself had been lost on the second of October and Juliana had prayed fervently for some sign that Wulfe had not been lost in that assault.

She had had none.

Yet she could not bear to think of him dead or even injured.

On this morn, Juliana was just descending from her chamber, the one she had shared with Miriam when they had been girls, when her mother hastened up the stairs toward her. That lady's eyes were sparkling with excitement. "What marvelous good fortune, Juliana!" she declared. "A suitor arrives for you!"

Juliana felt the surprise of the maid who followed her.

"For me?" she asked. "Surely there is a mistake."

"On the contrary, my dear, I am certain he has heard of your reputed beauty and sweet disposition." Her mother fussed a little with Juliana's kirtle. "Praise be you chose this one on this morn," she murmured with a little frown. "The deep green favors you very well and the cut, well, the fullness is flattering." Her mother forced a smile, and Juliana knew she feared the suitor would discern her state.

"I will tell him, *Maman*."

Her mother inhaled sharply but before she could speak, Juliana continued. "It is no good omen to begin a match with a lie, and no man is fool enough to believe his babe would come in but six months. I *will* tell him."

Her mother's lips tightened. "I suppose you are right, but Juliana, a suitor! Just when you have need of one. It seems to be God's grace at work, and I would not have any detail go awry. Perhaps you might not confide this truth to him at your first meeting."

"It might not be a good match."

"You are scarce in a position to be demanding," her mother said with a fierce look, then hastened Juliana down the stairs to the hall. A man stood in the midst of the hall, hands folded before himself as he waited. There was a dusting of snow on the shoulders of his cloak and he glanced up with interest at their approach.

"As I have told you, Juliana, here is the messenger sent to announce his lord master's arrival at our gates. This is Lady Juliana, my eldest daughter."

Juliana took a seat at the board and folded her hands in her lap. Her mother clapped for the fires to be tended and truly the hall did look inviting. Juliana watched the messenger survey the hall quickly and did not doubt he assessed the value of every trunk and rug before he bowed before her. His hair was dark and curled over his collar, and though he was yet a young man, Juliana did not doubt that the maids would be chattering about him. His livery was black and gold, and his boots were so fine that they might have been new. A young boy stood behind him, garbed in the same colors.

His lord was affluent then. Who might the man be?

"I do apologize for interrupting you so early," he said, though the hour was not early at all. "My lord would ensure that his arrival was anticipated."

"He does not like surprises, then?"

The messenger smiled. "He thinks it unseemly to cause trouble for a potential host."

"He is most thoughtful, then." Juliana's mother smiled in approval at that and she could fairly see her mother planning a wedding this very day and a lavish meal to follow. Doubtless her mother reviewed the inventory in the kitchen. "And who is your lord?"

"Sir Ulric von Altesburg," the messenger said with pride.

Juliana kept her expression polite. She had never heard of this man.

Her mother, however, had. "Would he be the son of Konrad von Altesburg?" she asked, her avid expression telling Juliana much.

"Indeed, he is, my lady. The only son of that man. They ride together and will arrive here shortly, to be sure."

Anticipation filled Juliana's mother's expression. She flicked a glance to Miriam, who had appeared in the portal. That woman nodded but once and hastened away, doubtless to dispatch some soul to kill some creature for the feast.

The messenger snapped his fingers and the young boy stepped forward with a trunk. He bowed and offered it to Juliana. "A token of my lord's esteem," he said once she had accepted the burden, then stepped back and unfurled a missive.

Juliana eyed the trunk with some trepidation. If it were a very rich gift, she would be hard-pressed to decline this offer. Miriam was back at the portal, her eyes shining with delight at Juliana's evident good fortune.

Knowing it could not be evaded, Juliana opened the trunk. She could not have said what she expected to be within it, but her lips parted in wonder at the silken fur that filled it to bursting.

"My lord knight would have you know that this autumn, he was the first to kill a wolf in the forests of his family holding at Altesburg. It is considered a portent in his family that when a son comes of age and kills the first wolf of the season, he should take a bride. My lord Ulric sends you this pelt as a token of his esteem and begs you keep it, whether or not you accept his suit."

Juliana glanced up in surprise that the knight in question did not assume his proposal would be accepted.

The messenger smiled. "I have been instructed to tell you that he believes a man learns more in defeat than in victory, though I do not understand why he would order as much in a moment such as this."

Juliana gripped the pelt, her heart hammering.

It could not be.

"Juliana?" her mother asked, evidently noting her shock.

"Surely you are not unwell?"

"Nay, *Maman*. I am fine." Juliana gestured to the messenger, even as her heart thundered. "Pray continue."

The messenger cleared his throat and did as much. "The true gift, he says, is wrapped in the pelt, the better to ensure its safe journey."

Juliana coaxed the pelt out of the trunk with care, ensuring that naught dropped to the floor. The fur was thick and of deep silver hue, and the pelt was large. Indeed, it was hard to believe that it had fit within the trunk at all. Her mother was directly beside her, fingering the fur and murmuring in appreciation. The small bundle sheltered within it fell readily to Juliana's lap. It was heavy for all its size and wrapped in a piece of silk.

She unfurled the fabric under her mother's watchful eye, only to find a small book.

"A devotional," her mother breathed in awe.

Indeed, her wonder was deserved. Such volumes were profoundly expensive, the trinkets of queens, not those of her family's ilk. Juliana turned the book in her hands in wonder. The covers were of red leather, so soft, and stitched with care. The vellum pages were thin and the script was tiny. There was a marker between the pages, and she made to remove it, for even this ribbon would leave an impression. Juliana's lips parted in wonder at the illustrations between the prayers, images so finely detailed that she feared they could not be real.

The marker was on a page with an illumination and Juliana could not help but examine it. A woman with long fair hair was being burned, and the rays of light around her head showed her saintly status. She appeared to be oblivious to the fire licking her flesh and the wounds where her breasts had been. Her gaze was fixed on a dove that descended from the sky, and her expression was rapturous.

It was an exquisitely beautiful image.

"My lord knight bids me tell you that he sought far and wide for this volume, for he wished his gift to you to include an image of Saint Christina."

Juliana looked up in shock.

The marker had been placed apurpose.

Saint Christina!

The messenger smiled. "He says he learned much from her tale, particularly how one might be sustained by one's faith when enduring a challenge."

Juliana rose to her feet, clutching the devotional in one hand and holding the pelt against her chest. "And what is your lord knight's name again?"

"Sir Ulric von Altesburg," the young man replied. "But I must confess that we oft call him Wulfe Stürmer, for he is fierce with a blade. He served as a Templar knight before returning to his father's abode."

Juliana gave a cry of delight and fled the chamber, scarce daring to believe her good fortune.

"You wear only slippers!" her mother cried from behind her. "You have no cloak!"

Juliana did not care about either. She fled across the hall and into the bailey. She burst through the portal and saw a large party approaching the gates, their insignia all black and gold. She ran across the bailey and through the gate, her heart singing when she saw the large destrier at the front of the party.

He was as black as midnight.

And the knight astride him had golden blond hair that shone in the sunlight.

"Wulfe!" she cried and he laughed aloud. He leapt from the saddle and Juliana could scarce see him for the tears in her eyes. He strode toward her and dropped to one knee, seizing her hand in his. Teufel followed him, though Wulfe had dropped the reins.

"Dare I hope my suit is well received?" he asked, his eyes sparkling.

"Aye, Wulfe. Aye!"

He laughed again and stood at her urging, catching her close and kissing her soundly. The devotional was pressed between their beating hearts, the fur crushed beneath her chin, and Wulfe's arms were tight around her. Juliana thought her heart might burst with joy.

"Are you well, then?" he asked when he broke their kiss, his gaze searching hers.

"Well enough but better now," she admitted. "My sister says I will feel better by the Yule, if our babe is like hers." She smiled, only now taking pleasure in her sister's words. "Indeed, she says it is boys who make a mother so ill so early."

"I care not if it is a boy or a girl," Wulfe admitted. "Only that you put your hand in mine."

"I do. I will. Surely we can be wed this very day."

Wulfe grinned. "Surely there can be no cause for delay. But you are not garbed for this wind!" He shed his own cloak and wrapped it around her, frowning at her slippers. Juliana laughed when he swept her into his arms and lifted her to Teufel's saddle. She saw then that Stephen and Simon rode with Wulfe, also adorned in his livery, and that there was an older man with white hair riding behind. That man inclined his head to her politely, but the boys would not be so restrained.

"I am glad indeed to see you again, my lady," Simon said.

"And I am glad indeed that you will be our lady," Stephen added.

"As am I." Juliana smiled at them both, holding her gifts with one hand while she gripped the pommel with the other.

"You should know that I have had an invitation from Gaston," Wulfe said. "I wrote to tell him that I had left the order and why, and he replied, wishing me well in my quest for your hand. He invited us both to Châmont-sur-Maine for the feast of Saint Nicholas, that we might witness Bartholomew gaining his spurs."

"That is less than a fortnight away."

"Aye." Wulfe spared her a glance. "If you feel well enough to make the journey, I would like to be there. He wrote that Fergus also lingered for the ceremony. We could be home by the Yule."

"I would wager that you will ensure my welfare," Juliana teased and Wulfe grinned at her.

"It would not be much of a wager," he replied, his eyes sparkling and she laughed aloud.

"I should love to go."

"Then it will be so."

Juliana watched Wulfe as he led Teufel toward the gates, and she knew she had never been so happy in all her days. Her mother and her sister stood at the portal to the hall itself, their hands clasped and their faces beaming. Otto joined them, nodding with satisfaction as the party approached.

Juliana kissed the devotional, knowing this was but the beginning of the joy that would come her way. She and Wulfe had taught each other to hope, and the future was theirs to claim.

He had proven to be her champion, indeed.

Continue the quest
of the Champions of St. Euphemia with...

THE CRUSADER'S KISS

Bartholomew burns to avenge the past—until Anna gives him a future...

Bartholomew returns to England to avenge his parents and reclaim his stolen legacy, only to be challenged by a band of thieves in the woods of the estate that was once his home. He captures the bold leader, only to discover that she is a maiden in disguise, with the wit and audacity that seizes his attention. He suggests a mock marriage to gain access to the keep, never guessing the union will tempt them both to desire more—but can Bartholomew trust a woman who survives by deception?

Anna wants only justice for the people of Haynesdale, no matter what the price, and does not welcome the interference of a foreign knight, however handsome he might be. Bartholomew could be a useful ally, if only she could be certain of his goals. Is this maddening and charming knight just using her to learn all she knows of the holding's history for some mysterious cause?

When Bartholomew's identity as the lost heir of Haynesdale is revealed, he becomes the prey of those who destroyed his family. Can he and Anna forget their distrust and work together for the future of Haynesdale—and their dawning love?

The Crusader's Kiss
Available Now!

ABOUT THE AUTHOR

Bestselling and award-winning author Deborah Cooke has published over fifty novels and novellas, including historical romances, fantasy romances, fantasy novels with romantic elements, paranormal romances, contemporary romances, urban fantasy romances, time travel romances and paranormal young adult novels. She writes as herself, Deborah Cooke, as Claire Delacroix, and has written as Claire Cross. Her Claire Delacroix medieval romance, *The Beauty*, was her first book to land on the New York Times List of Bestselling Books.

Deborah was the writer-in-residence at the Toronto Public Library in 2009, the first time TPL hosted a residency focused on the romance genre, and she was honored to receive the Romance Writers of America PRO Mentor of the Year Award in 2012. She's a member of Romance Writers of America, and is on the RWA Honor Roll. She lives in Canada with her family.

To learn more about Deborah's books, please visit her websites at:

http://deborahcooke.com

http://www.delacroix.net

CPSIA information can be obtained
at www.ICGtesting.com
Printed in the USA
LVHW091951250621
691029LV00021B/269/J